PAGAN SUMMER

BY

DAVID BEASLEY

-to cure the soul by means of the senses, and
the senses by means of the soul.--Oscar Wilde.

DAVUS PUBLISHING

SIMCOE   BUFFALO

Apollinaire said a coup d'oeil could catch the moment and Thorne Smith showed that the moment could be fun. This book is for the thousands who served in the Rockies for that moment in the century gone by.

Beasley, David, 1931-
      Pagan summer

ISBN   0-915317-07-9

    I. Title.

PS8553.E14P33 1997   C813'.54   C96-900672-1
PR9199.3.B3762P33 1997

DAVUS PUBLISHING

150 Norfolk St. S.   P. O. Box 1101,
Simcoe, ON N3Y 2W2   Buffalo, N.Y. 14213-7101
Canada   United States

DAVUS SUM, NON OEDIPUS

1

The end of June. The caddies were in their second week at Bampers. Mr. Runners had not expected them to strike. No one expected caddies to strike. Because the hotel paid their train fares from eastern Canada to the Rockies and gave them board and lodging for the summer months, a cry, 'Oh no they don't!' rang out bitterly from the manager's cabin on the edge of Lake Beautiful. Runners was dealing with a labour force whose members were all under twenty-one. The charge of 'exploitation' terrified him. Moreover, each caddie had been nominated by a very important person in the government, or railroad, or hotel business across Canada as had every porter, bell-hop, chauffeur, waitress, cabin-girl, bus-boy, and room-service carrier in Bampers. The dish-washers and launderers were the only employees he could tyrannize without fear of reprisal. They were on loan from city hotels in the east and had no pull higher than another manager. But the caddies *en masse* had indefinable power back home. Runners snapped his long thin fingers and looked hopelessly at his wife. She held open a newspaper in front of her, intimating that she, as the oracle, was not prepared to make a pronouncement.

Guests arrived and headed for the golf links. Rich and elderly, they would most certainly not carry their bags or consent to trailing a caddie-car. Bampers was renowned for the efficiency of its student staff. Its promotion as a millionaire's paradise depended on the presence of fresh faces and youthful figures issued from the loins of the best families across the country as well as on the exorbitant rates of its rooms. Naturally, new golfers were dismayed when faced with a sullen band of caddies who refused to budge from the steps of the caddie house. The strike, now in its third day, had not been entirely successful owing to a few scabs who carried double and were willing to work for thirty-six holes. Yet there was a record influx of guests due soon; most of the caddies would be needed. Runners bit his nails, quietly, so as to conceal the act from his wife. The caddies were having a meeting that night in order to bring pressure on the scabs. Many of them had written home about their 'exploitation'. Runners would be receiving complaints perhaps tomorrow or the following day. He ought to meet a delegation of caddies, at least to get a look at the ring leaders. It was too late in the season to think of importing replacements. (A few small boys recruited from the nearby town had broken down or run away after nine holes.) The other departments were struggling with inexperience and needed his attention. Runners held his forehead in his finger tips, covering his hard colorless eyes and thin red nose.

Runners was stymied.

Blair St. Clair looked the antithesis of Runners. Calm, self-reliant, he commanded the admiration of his fellow caddies who were almost all at Bampers for their first year whereas Blair had worked on the links the previous summer. Without demonstrating his dislike for the work, he referred slightingly to it and escaped it whenever he could. He made it perfectly clear that he had only submitted to carrying the golf bags of strangers during the day in order to enjoy the staff privilege of playing in the evenings free of charge. He forewent dinner at six to squeeze in as much play as possible before dark. Last year he won the Annual Staff Tournament, beating John O'Dreams on the seventeenth. O'Dreams broke his driver against a tree and swore that Blair would not win a second time. They practiced diligently: O'Dreams in the mornings if the orchestra was not rehearsing. The tournament, however, would not be held until the middle of the season. Even Blair considered the strike of more importance at the moment. Smoothing back his pompadour of light gold, he grinned. His red cheeks rounded out and his blue eyes twinkled for an instant.

'I'll come to your meeting, but I won't say anything.'

'That's all you have to do.' Dick Andrews glanced round at his three companions. 'Don'll do the gabbing.'

Blair, whose face had sullened to its habitual shy cast, broke into a big smile as the others laughed.

Don Clarking furrowed his brow and pulled at his peaked cap. 'Well, who the hell wants to work for nothing?' he complained looking at the faces of the taller boys. 'I'm not going to drag heavy bags up mountain sides under a hot sun for the price of an ice cream soda. Hell, we've got to put up the green fees or something. I haven't saved a cent yet.'

A wince of horror flickered over their faces.

'My old man said I had to make a thousand bucks,' Horsey Smith moaned. 'I'll be a thousand in debt.' He wrinkled his nose. 'He won't let me get a car next year.'

2

'Haven't you got a car yet?' Dick Andrews asked disdainfully. He held his straight handsome features aloft like a noble Roman.

Horsey's long, homely face came round to stare petulantly at Dick. 'If I can make some of my tuition, I get a car, see.'

Dick was about to make another haughty remark when he noticed Blair regarding him sardonically. He blushed. 'We're all in the same spot,' he said sympathetically. 'We can't go home; we'll be called failures. And is there anything worse than failing as a caddie?'

'Yeah,' Dixie Mitchell yawned.

The boys watched him stretch in his chair and peep through slit eyes in a humorous leer. His face had a tough, competitive look, although his whole attitude voiced the opinion that nothing was sillier than competition.

The boys began to smile expectantly.

Dixie drew himself up. 'Failing in love is worse.'

Don cackled and Blair looked on mildly amused.

'Who told you?' Dick asked amicably, afraid of Dixie's wit.

'Yeah, how do you know?' Horsey challenged boldly.

'You wouldn't understand if I told you, Horse Balls,' Dixie dismissed him and turned his tired smile on Dick. 'How are you going to make an effective strike if these Frenchies keep crossing the line?'

Dick smiled indulgently.

'You guys aren't tough enough!' Dixie snarled. 'You want to hold a gun to Runners' head. You want to show him unity. The way it is now, all he has to do is shout and the whole fuckin' lot of you piss in your pants. And it's lucky he doesn't know it,' Dixie grinned. 'Watch out or one of those Frenchies will tell him.'

'Jeez, yeah!" Don said. 'We've got to make them strike.'

'They'll ask us to pay them though,' Horsey said resentfully.

'Naw, they're just yellow,' Dixie cried. 'If you want 'em on your side you got to scare 'em more than Runners does.'

'They're okay,' Blair said. 'Everyone's got a right to his own opinion.'

'That's right,' Dick nodded seriously.

'You're screwed before you begin,' Dixie smirked. 'Well, get your meeting going, go on.'

3

'Let's rouse them down to the caddie house,' Horsey went to the door.

'Okay, let's go then,' Dick ordered.

The four of them left Blair dreaming of the dog leg hooking to the right from the fourth tee. They banged on doors and walls of the long hallway.

'Come out, you dirty Frenchies,' Dixie bellowed and reared back as Legourmand's huge hands reaching from a doorway encircled his neck. 'You're the cleanest Frenchman I ever saw, Ray, honest to God you are.'

Legourmand relaxed his grip. Since he was one of the instigators of the strike, he could afford to laugh. 'Just like one of those big chickens before Christmas.' He twisted round to chuckle with Gilles, but his room-mate turned away.

'You too, Gilles, damn you. We're gonna explain why we're striking,' Dixie rasped. He added a disparaging remark on French legitimacy, but it was lost in the bellowing of Don Clarking, who, slapping his hands against the wallboards descended upon them in full voice.

Sylvester was coming off duty, cutting across the lawn from the guest cabins to the staff area behind because he wanted to reach the staff dining room before it shut. Called a "patrolman" for lack of a better name, he wore a khaki uniform with brass buttons. Since noise from the caddie's cabin was not unusual, he intended to rush by, but the exodus of caddies from one end, as in a prison break, made him think of an uprising and his position as a patrolman in such an eventuality. One of his duties was to aid the policeman of the hotel, a retired mountie who wore a black police coat and who was known to everyone as Archie.

Archie had to keep surveillance over two hundred cabins and a great wooden lodge swarming with people wearing beautiful clothes and expensive jewelry. Archie also was responsible for the staff area after midnight, to see that the boys were not getting in the cabins with the girls and the girls in with the boys. What happened in the woods to any number of five hundred staff members was outside his jurisdiction.

Sylvester had no desire to police the grounds, but he felt bound to restrain any mass violence. If he did anything remarkable, his name might be brought before Mr. Runners and added to the list of hotel chauffeurs, which was the dream of

4

all patrolmen. As in Milton's poem, patrolmen bore their penurious existence standing and waiting for the day when they would be promoted to driving tourists to Banff or Lake Louise and receiving the rumoured twenty-five and thirty dollar tips. Occasionally, guests would ask them to take their photographs or to stand close to a bear while they took theirs for a measly quarter or a half-dollar. They barely made money to see the movie in town. Thus with a patrolman's instinct for promotion, Sylvester followed the mutinous horde of caddies to the wooden porch of their caddie house.

Dick Andrews brought a stick down on the railing and called for order. His voice drowned in storms of argument. Don Clarking jumped onto the table and screamed for attention.

'Ouch!' Horsey said backing away with hands over ears.

'All right,' Dick cried fiercely. He climbed beside Don. 'We want to know why some guys don't want to strike.'

There was silence. Twilight had crept over the ground accentuating the stretches of brown earth and darkening the lawns.

'If we stick together, we can get somewhere.'

'How about those town caddies?' someone called.

'There are only two left,' Horsey said. 'And they're bitchin' about the pay as much as we are.'

'That little one got stiffed today,' someone said. 'He went home bawling.'

A few of the boys laughed. 'Who was he working for?'

'Old man Weekes,' someone answered.

All the boys laughed.

'If we find anybody caddying tomorrow, we kick his ass,' Dixie called out. 'Did you hear that, Gilles?'

Gilles' face grew taut with determination. The boys stepped away. Embarrassed, Gilles stood with his back against the railing, and pushed with the muscles of his legs against the rungs. His strong square head strained forward from his shoulders, rounded in a student's hunch. 'I'm not striking.'

'Why not?' Dick shouted.

'Because I'm here on recommendation.'

'What is he talking about?' Dixie complained.

'If I get a black mark, it'll go against the man who recommended me,' Gilles snapped.

'Aw! Runners is just trying to scare us,' Legourmand tried to reason with him. 'He can't hurt us.'

But Gilles' words sent a chill of apprehension through them all.

'No, no,' Gilles shook his head as the others started to argue and gesticulate, and groups of boys formed about the recalcitrants who, like Gilles, shook their heads.

Horsey bit the stem of grass he held between his teeth. He spat at a spider web.

Aurmand Ruissillier shoved his thin hands into his pockets and shrugged his narrow shoulders clothed in the red jacket of Laval University. Sniffing his short brown mustache, he peered through steel-rimmed glasses at the scene. He didn't like these tall English bullies. Anyway, he had given up carrying bags of iron and wooden clubs over giant fairways. The golfers all seemed to be thick-headed financiers who resented the fact that an assistant lecturer in geography was caddying for them in order to learn English. Not only did they hardly speak to him, he was painfully exhausted after a day's work. Worried, he lost weight and couldn't sleep, until he found a job as a dishwasher in town. So the strike was of little concern to him.

Shadows deepened over the faces of the strikers. In a twinkling, darkness would be upon them.

'We gotta have a delegation for Runners,' Don Clarking screamed, hoping he would be chosen as a delegate.

'Dick Andrews,' Dixie rasped. 'What do you say? Eh?'

Andrews was selected by a chorus of acclamations.

'Blair,' Slim Johnson called, ripping a strip of bark off the porch post.

A louder chorus greeted the proposal. Blair's blond head appeared on the porch for an instant. The cries rose in a crescendo.

'Legourmand,' someone suggested.

'Yeah. Hey, Big Gourmand.'

The tall strapping French-Canadian grinned sheepishly.

'That's enough,' Bruce Bannister cried.

'How about me?' Don threw up his arms.

'Sit down, Clarking.' 'You'd sell us out, man.' 'Clarking, you're no dammed good.' A couple of fellows seized him by the arms and began to lead him back to the cabin.

The lamplights throughout the hotel area came on.

'Meet here tomorrow morning,' Dick shouted. His brown hair shone like copper. 'Give us a cheer for good luck.'

'Screw the luck; just get us more money.'

Dick laughed with those around him as the caddies streamed for the staff cabins.

Big Bruce Bannister bunted Aurmand into a post. His freckled face was impassive as he watched Aurmand resettle his glasses. 'Watch where you're going,' Bruce said.

Aurmand feared this rich boy the moment he saw the expensive leather shoes, size twelve, by the bed next to his. He glared at him with hatred.

A golf ball smashed the porch bulb, making everyone scramble, including the delegation who ran towards the main lodge with anxious thoughts about meeting Mr. Runners.

'I'll do the talking,' Dick said when they reached the lodge. 'You guys just support me.'

'Supposing he fires us?' Legourmand asked.

'He won't,' Blair said.

'All the caddies will quit,' Dick said excitedly. 'He'll have to ship all fifty-one of us back home, and my Dad will have something to say about that. He's in the railway business and he says they've lost too much money on special fares.'

'Bampers is the railroad and it's the government,' Blair said. 'Runners could send us home, but he won't.'

Dick and Legourmand knew that Blair was exaggerating to make his point in as few words as possible. They didn't understand, but they believed him.

'He better not,' Legourmand growled, brandishing his fist at the office corridor just then coming into sight beside the flagstoned patio.

'There's a light in Runners' office,' Dick pointed to the windows.

'Is he alone?' Legourmand asked apprehensively.

'Smiling Jack will be there,' Blair said.

Runners' assistant stiffly opened the office door at the sound of his name. Like a fish if it were standing on its tail fins, he seemed able to bend only at the ankles and at the neck. He bowed slightly from the ankles. 'Mr. Runners is waiting for you.' His sleek black hair, eyes, mustache, suit, shoes--all black--made him look like a professional detective incognito.

'Hello, Mr. Flowers,' Dick said.

7

Jack Flowers smiled darkly and led them into Mr. Runners' office. Runners stood up from his desk and, taking several paces to the side, gripped his hands behind his back in an alert at-ease position. His small eyes shifted from one to the other as the delegation ranged in front of him.

'What's the trouble, boys?'

Flowers quietly closed the door.

'We're not making any money,' Dick began importantly. 'We're poorer now than when we arrived.'

'Sir! That's how you address me, isn't it?'

'Yes, sir,' Dick admitted, peeved at being knocked off his professional stance.

'What's the good of striking in this rowdy way?' Runners asked mildly.

'We asked for a higher percentage of the green fees and they didn't give them to us,' Dick said.

Runners' left eye twitched. "They" referred to him, of course.

'Our golfers think the fees are high enough,' Runners said to Legourmand. 'What do you think?'

Legourmand nodded dumbly.

'What do you think?' Runners shouted, brows menacing.

'None of us thinks so or we wouldn't be here,' Blair drawled.

'You're in on this too, are you? Is this your idea?' Runners frowned.

Blair looked over his shoulder at Flowers and grinned.

'What is amusing you?'

Flowers spoke in a flat voice. 'We made a bet on that score, sir. That he would be blamed.'

'Oh,' Runners winced. His thin face seemed to drain of colour. 'So you lost to him, eh Jack?'

Flowers rested his dark head on one shoulder with a smirk. 'He has the blessing of the Gods. You can't beat Blair.'

Eyes twinkling, Blair regarded Runners as if waiting for a repartee.

'If you're so lucky, why do you need more money?' Runners' smile made a thin line under his big nose.

'They're not tipping this year,' Blair said.

Runners frowned. Blair's disarming manner gave everything he said an aspect of simple truth. 'Do you want me to tell our guests how much they should tip?' His mouth twisted sardonically.

'Raise the green fees,' Blair said.

Runners glared. 'The golf course is accessory to the hotel. It is not the other way around as you boys so unwisely think.'

'It seems to me,' Dick broke in, 'that people stay at the lodge just to be able to play on the course.'

Runners' face flushed, his body gave an involuntary quiver, and his head snapped round at Dick. His lips twitched as if several words were trying to escape them at once.

Startled, Dick gaped in fear. Legourmand clenched his fists to defend himself. Only Blair was unmoved.

Runners, conscious of Blair's steadfast look, spluttered and turned away. 'I am not going to have my hotel run by caddies, do you hear me?' he shouted.

Legourmand took courage. 'We want justice.' He glanced at Blair for approval.

Blair nodded slightly.

Runners spun round and snapped his finger at Legourmand. 'Are you threatening me? Justice comes from a judge, not from a band of rowdies and irresponsible ringleaders.' He shook his head sadly at Flowers. 'I don't know why I agreed to see them, Jack. They are just incapable of listening to reason.'

'What is your alternative?' Blair asked.

'Go back to work,' Runners said quietly, 'and we'll do our best to see that you get better tips.'

'We'll never agree to that!' Dick exclaimed. 'We've gone too far to back down.'

'Some of you have gone too far,' Runners warned him.

'The guests can afford higher fees,' Blair said evenly.

'No, they cannot!' Runners thundered. 'I know guests better than you do. I know the hotel business inside and out. I know what I can charge.'

The telephone rang. Flowers answered it. Runners took a turn impatiently. 'He's here,' Flowers said and held out the receiver.

Legourmand felt they were going to be fired.

With a swipe Runners clamped the receiver to his ear. "Yes.' The authority appeared to drop from his shoulders like husk. 'Yes, dear.' He glanced at Flowers and then down at the desk. 'All right.' He hung up and turned round to Blair.

'I am going to offer you a proposal,' he smiled weakly. 'The green fees will be raised to give you a dollar and twenty-five cents more per round. The golf course will make twenty-five cents more.' He took a deep breath. 'Does that satisfy you?' He thought he saw contempt in Blair's smile.

'That's great news, sir,' Dick said. 'The boys will work now.'

'On the condition,' Runners continued in the same tone, 'that I hear no more complaints.'

'Oh no, sir,' Dick said.

'Eh?' Runners cocked an eyebrow.

'No, sir,' Legourmand said.

Runners looked at Blair who was grinning at Flowers. He felt uneasy. 'All right.' He raised an arm to Flowers who jumped to open the door. He watched the delegation file out. When the hall door closed, he heard Dick's voice strike through the night. 'Hey Blair, you were right.'

2

Don Clarking stepped from behind the bushes by the tennis courts and accosted the delegates as they came from the lodge. When he heard the results he dashed to the caddie's cabin and called the caddies from their rooms to greet the delegation. Most were at the staff hall dancing and eating ice cream.

'Come on everybody. We've won! We've won!'

'The hell we've won,' Dixie hollered from his room. He swung his saxophone in front of him and set its reed in his mouth.

'What's the matter?' Don cried, staring in through the doorway.

Dixie took the reed from his mouth. 'It means we gotta go back to work. Do you call that winning?' He fixed his lips over the reed again.

Don waited for the sounds. Dixie would play the refrain of 'How High The Moon' because Dixie played nothing else. The sounds came: "Somewhere there's music, How high the moon"--stop. Don frowned. 'The least you can do is thank those guys. You nominated them,' he complained.

Dixie, rounding his eyes, blew, "Somewhere there's music..."

'Ah nuts!' Don waved him down and broke out the door in a fast run for the Staff Hall.

Deodora Adams stepped out of the waitresses' cabin, her long shapely legs gleaming through the dark. Don pivoted to a halt and screwed up the corner of his mouth. 'Hallo, Deo.' His eyes sought out the bust line.

'Hello,' she said distantly. Within a week of arriving, she had gone through a bellhop and a chauffeur. She had set her sights high above a caddie.

Don smelt the aroma of her slim, gorgeous form, or thought he did. He had asked the bellhop what her kiss tasted like, and he had said "tomato soup". Her mouth parted over her front teeth, slightly bucked, as she looked past him at the Staff Hall.

'Where are you going?' he asked.

'Have you seen Johnnie?' She hesitated to go over to the Hall.

'Who?' He felt a jab of jealousy.

'Johnnie O'Dreams,' she pouted, her large blue eyes fixing on him.

'Nope,' he shook his head as if the man were lost to her for the evening.

'Tell me if he's in the Hall, will you?'

'Sure.' He ran across the gravel and up the steps.

A deep voice called from the roadway fifty yards behind her. She saw Johnnie standing under a road lamp and signalling. 'Hi kid, come on.'

The worry of minutes before fled at the sound. Now she could tell the girls that she really had dated him, though he kept her waiting half an hour. She ran to him.

When Don came out of the Hall he saw that she had vanished. He went to the spot and peered about through the shadows but there was no Deo.

Johnnie looked down over his broken nose like a parrot over its beak. He put his arm around Deo's waist and drew her along a pathway.

'I thought you were taking me out,' Deo said.

'How far out do you want to go?' he chuckled.

She pushed away from him, her hands planted on his chest, feeling the strong flat muscles.

11

'Come on, come on,' he jeered. 'My car's just down the road.' His hair fell over one eye and he tossed it back. She liked the gesture. When he brought his lean face to hers, she let him kiss her.

'Come on, Baby,' he said finally, the scent of her neck and hair holding him to her for just another kiss and another. 'We're going to a party.' He licked under her chin. 'We don't want to be late because it's a small one, you know.'

'All right,' she said.

He embraced her hard and felt her breasts and then kissed them.

'Well, shouldn't we be going?' she smiled.

He started walking with her. A giddiness overcame them both and they stopped for just one more kiss--a long one.

'Okay!' he said. 'You're going to meet some very nice people. They've got their own cottage on a lake over there.'

They came to his convertible. Not very new, she noticed, but it looked warm and cosy--his personality. She was so enraptured with strong caresses and the romanticism of the night that she was sitting in the car and watching him climb behind the wheel before she thought of meeting strangers. 'Wait Johnnie! I mean, am I dressed properly?'

'Nothing's showing if that's what you mean,' he eyed her.

'Oh,' she pushed at him, 'for the party! Do I need a dress?'

'You're perfect,' he said, gunning the motor.

She looked down at her blue skirt and white blouse. A cool breeze tickled her arms and she clasped them above the elbows as they lurched forward.

'There's a sweater back there if you're cold,' Johnnie said, 'but I got a better idea. Come here.' He threw out his long arm and drew her against him. 'Tell me if you're cold.'

'No, I'm fine.' She snuggled her head against his shoulder and watched the blur of trees through the windshield. She put her arm along his leg in a careless way as if to signify that she was in accord with this sudden feeling of intimacy. The night air whipped at her hair. They sped into turns and rocketed into level stretches, the pine boughs reaching overhead and the stars twinkling through them. Johnnie jerked back. The car paused in flight; an animal flashed by the headlights. Deo fell back against the seat as the vehicle snapped forward again, a whine from the wheels remaining the only exclamation.

'Almost had venison for a midnight snack, Baby.' Johnnie brought his arm about her. He gripped the wheel harder and frowned as he thought of an accident in the past.

'How far is this place?' she pouted, enjoying the warmth from his body.

'Not far.' He chuckled down at her. 'Scared?'

'Why do deer have to jump out like that?'

'Compulsion,' he said thoughtfully. 'They're like people. You can't explain why they do things.'

She found this serious cast of his face attractive. She could run her hands over it like marble which stayed unchanging throughout the ages. 'Johnnie, is O'Dreams your real name?'

Laughing, he looked up at the trees. 'It is now.' He coasted into a turn. 'Anyway, it's not the name that counts; it's the person, isn't it?'

She nodded doubtfully. 'I guess so.' He made her feel that they were on a flying carpet, that the ground was miles below. She crept closer to him and pressed her lips on his neck. The line of his jaw brushed over her nose and she thought this was going to be one of the greatest nights she had ever had.

They went right at a fork in the road and swept by a sandy beach where black shapes huddled near the water, then went left along a bend to another lake, up a narrow driveway to the bright lights of a cottage.

'Some of these people have been around for years,' Johnnie said confidentially. 'I play golf with them. You're also gonna meet a few jerks from the golf house.' He parked his car alongside a handsome sedan. Other automobiles were parked here and there in the dark. A woman came to the back window and went away.

Deo sensed John's tenseness. He fumbled about with the keys and put his head down as if he were trying to calm himself. Deo laughed at him. 'If they're your friends, why are you nervous?'

'Me?' His dark head reared up in surprise. 'I'm not nervous. Come on, Baby. He took her arm and made her climb out his side of the car. 'Look.' He held out his face in the light from the window. 'Have I got any red stuff?'

'You're okay.' She pushed his face away.

Brushing his hair and straightening his coat, he led her to the front of the house which overlooked the lake. The door flew open, and a woman in a sweater and skirt, her hair straggling over her shoulders, threw up her arms. 'Hail, Johnnie boy!'

He grinned, his white teeth catching the light. 'Bett kid!' He ran up to her and she threw her arms about his torso, burying her head in his chest, but he had no time to clasp her because he was shaking hands with two men who came up behind smiling and laughing. 'Deo's come with me!' he laughed gesturing back to her as she stepped onto the porch. 'She's a kid, but she's dynamite, aren't you, sweetie?' He pulled her to him and she smiled nervously. 'This is Bett, Harry, Ed.' She barely had time to touch their hands when he whisked her inside. 'And Kate over there and that big dope who gets in my way anywhere from the tenth to the fourteenth.'

The big dope came over to her with hands outstretched and a gentle smile over his wide tanned face. He took her hands in his. 'Julien Kowalski. What can I get you to drink?'

As she answered, a pretty girl of eighteen walked in from another room.

'And Maureen,' Kate announced. 'Now you know us all.'

Johnnie wet his lips. 'Say, I don't know her.' He went to her as the others crowded about Deo.

Bett and Kate were in their thirties. Both must be married, Deo thought. They flirted with an assurance that no single girl could match.

'We used to stay at the lodge,' Bett said, 'until we found this place a few years ago. Do you golf, dear?'

'No,' Deo shook her head, 'I've never wanted to.'

'How sad!' We could have taken you golfing. We go all the time. Kate and I have been in practically every woman's tournament up here, haven't we dear?'

Kate pretended to be shocked. 'Not every tournament! But speak for yourself. You're older than I am.' Her pretty face resumed its sweet expression as she came over to them.

'You won it, didn't you, Kate?' Julien said returning with a Scotch for Deo.

'Runner-up,' she corrected him.

Julien looked blankly at her. 'I thought you won it.'

'Maybe there won't be a tournament this year,' Harry said. He was a fee collector who sat in a small round cabin by the first tee.

They looked at him in surprise, but Bett guffawed and pushed her fingers through his crew-cut. 'The caddie strike he means.'

'Oh these poor caddies,' Kate said. 'I think they get a raw deal.'

'Well,' Bett cried, 'do you tip them, my dear. I mean, they're only human. Some of us don't think so,' she grinned at Harry whose wooden face creased into a smile, 'but they do go to university or hope to go, gracious me, I mean they're striking for higher education. I think it's a very noble thing.'

'Not when you have seven hundred guests to consider,' Eddie admonished her. Assistant Pro, tall and dapper in slacks and black sports shirt, he could pose for an advertisement. His dandyism was misleading, however; he was the longest driver to play the Bampers course.

'Do they tip?' Bett asked him. 'No! They do not, and they deserve to drop dead carrying their own bags.'

'I hope you have a caddie,' Julien nodded.

'And do I!' She stepped back and, squaring her shoulders, marched in a circle like a mechanical soldier. 'I'd have him as a steady if he didn't give me the feeling I was being drafted.'

They laughed except for Kate who said, 'My caddie is my steady now. He's always on call.'

'You look as if you're boasting, dear. Who is it? Tell us?'

Bett put her tongue in her cheek.

'Slim Johnson,' she admitted.

'Oh, he's cute! He came with me once. Do you know him, Deo?' Bett asked introducing her into the conversation.

'Some of the girls pointed him out to me.' She looked across at Johnnie talking animatedly with Maureen. They were sitting on the red couch and Johnnie was leaning across her to snap up handfuls of peanuts from the magazine table.

Bett's eyes followed her look. 'Johnnie boy,' she called, 'we want to hear your views on the caddie strike.'

Johnnie looked round with a slap-happy expression. 'I've got news for you,' he said. 'It's over.'

'What?' Harry cried.

'I heard the caddies talking about it. The green fees have been raised a dollar fifty. It was like pandemonium in their cabin.'

'That no good Runners!' Bett shouted. 'That coward!'

Harry and Eddie squirmed with laughter.

15

'Take it easy,' Julien said. 'Your man is rich.'

'But he doesn't pay my green fees,' she cried. 'I'm not going to tip another caddie. My God! we'll have to start sneaking on at the fourth tee.'

'Don't try that!' Eddie warned. 'We'll be watching for you.'

'You would,' she growled. Dapper Eddie was too slick-looking, she thought, too nifty. He was counterfeit.

'I've gotta say,' Harry wagged his head sagaciously, 'we didn't expect this.'

'Nothing to it but find another oil well,' Kate shrugged.

'Damn Edmonton is getting so overcrowded,' Bett raved, 'every time you sink a drill, somebody screams.'

Johnnie roared and came stumbling towards them with his arms out, a whisky in one hand and peanuts in the other. 'Wait till you hear this. It's a pip.'

'About the banker and the oil well?' Hank asked. Johnnie's face fell. 'Yeah, Julien told us that before you got here.'

Johnnie gaped in disbelief. They laughed. Deo saw her opportunity and moved beside him.

'Is there anything else I can't tell you, eh? I mean like the night is dark,' he looked down at Deo, 'and you're so beautiful.'

'Give us a song, John,' Julien suggested.

'No,' he smiled. 'I can't sing without my orchestra.'

'Anyway, it's too early in the evening,' Harry groaned.

Johnnie shot him a long look.

'Do you want to hear my new record?' Bett asked. 'It's calypso and has it rhythm!' She slunk over to a record player. Her body was sturdy and well-proportioned. She wore clothes sloppily to soften the sexual allure, to make a man what she called "comfortable" with her. The vamp in Bett seized any opportunity to break loose as now when she whirled, hands on hips, to the first notes of the music, threw out her arms and hooked her fingers toward the men. 'Come on, honey, let's dance.'

Except for Julien, whose arm was linked with Kate's, the men took a step forward, and suddenly conscious they were three, stopped, flustered, to let Harry continue because he was Bett's present lover. She put her arms about his neck. In order to drive the envy from their minds, Eddie went to Maureen, and Johnnie, laughing guiltily, began to dance with Deo.

'You haven't noticed me all evening,' Deo said accusingly.

'The evening's just begun, Baby. You wait. I'll give you plenty of notice.'

She bent back from the waist. 'Is that supposed to be funny?'

'No, no,' he coaxed her to him, smoothing his hand along her back. 'I really mean it. You see, at parties I like to mix. Sort of savour the side delicacies before I hit the main dish.' He chuckled.

Deo glanced at the dark window pane. A branch was scraping at it in a sudden gust, as if wishing to attract her attention. Pine needles disappeared to one side clearing the dark pane for the full reflection of herself--bright-eyed and flushed. She tossed her head. 'You're not rocking with it,' she said. 'Get back and swing.'

Kate took Julien Kowalski to an easy chair and perched on the arm while he sat back in fatherly complacency. A square-jawed fifty-five, Julien had listened to Kate's troubles for a good many years. Her choirboy features, rosy in the artificial light, turned to him with the soulfulness he knew well. Of course, he wanted to make love to her, which was one reason why he advised upon her amours, but he battled on the stock exchange and drank to his dreams in the evenings. Her husband was his friend, which encouraged him to hide his wish, yet at times he wondered if Kate hadn't guessed and was enjoying his captivity.

'I'm glad you could be with me this evening, Julien.'

He stuck out his underlip. 'When you called, I left the house immediately. I'd drive two hundred and fifty miles for my Katie-bird any day.'

'You're my only real friend,' Kate said shyly. 'You've stayed with me.'

'Mac's your friend, isn't he?' he joked trying to offset the tender whisper in his heart.

'He's more often my enemy than my friend. I can't say if that goes for most husbands.'

'Maybe it goes for lovers,' he said, eyes twinkling.

'Maybe,' she smiled. 'Which brings me to the subject.'

'Which brings me to the subject,' he repeated softly.

She regarded him with mild amusement. 'I can save it, if you want.'

'Let's hear it.' He put his graying head back and watched her from the side of his eyes.

'I'm in love with a very young man,' she began. 'He's six feet tall, fair-haired and green-eyed.'

Julien laughed. 'Is this a joke?'

She bit her lip. 'I wish it were.'

He took her hand affectionately.

'He's going into second year at university. He's from the Maritimes.' She paused to think of further descriptions.

'It's not your caddie?' Julien guessed, alarmed.

'No, but he's a bellhop.' She raised her eyebrows as if to say "ipso facto".

Julien frowned. 'It's a little surprising, and annoying to think that a mere lad could...'

'He's not "mere",' she interrupted, 'I can tell you.'

'Well,' he squirmed to face her, 'how did you meet him?'

'I won't tell you that,' she smiled, the dimples catching at Julien's heart enticing him to enjoy her naughtiness. 'But I'll tell you it's been on for a week. I can't bear to spend a night away from him.' She glanced at the dancers. 'If it weren't for you, I wouldn't be here tonight.'

'Uh-huh,' he sighed. 'What do you want me to do?'

'Mac is coming up next week. I don't want him.'

'Katie, now.'

'I can't help it. Julien, let me work my way out of this. Time is all I need.' She gripped his hand.

'I could ask him to help the company out.' He looked in her eyes. 'But it would only take him a few days.'

She patted his hand. 'You're a dear.'

'He may not do it,' he warned.

'He will for you,' she smiled winsomely.

Pained, Julien looked away.

'They've put on a Fox Trot,' Kate nodded to the record player. 'You can do this with me.'

He stood up and took her in his arms. Her skin was soft and fresh to his cheek. A strand of hair caught on his nose and tickled but he wouldn't brush it away. The sensation was like a hurt which he bore to the end of the dance.

'I've got to go,' she whispered and spun away with an arm out to Bett. 'I'm leaving you, darling. Got to be on my way.'

'Not gone yet?' Bett said sarcastically. 'Won't you take your drink with you--finish it on the way to wherever you're going?'

Kate laughed.

'I mean, do, my dear,' Bett insisted. 'Perhaps you'd like to take the bottle. I mean, what have you been doing these nights?'

'Don't be hurt, Bett darling.' She held her arms out to her friend, concern wrinkling her brow. 'I've had a lovely time, but I made a promise.'

Taking her hands and kissing her cheek, Bett nodded glumly. 'I hope he's worth it, dear, that's all.'

'I've got to dash everyone,' Kate sang and waved.

Julien opened the door and accompanied Kate to her car. She smiled mischievously at him. 'Thanks for coming up.'

He clasped her arm and said with genuine warmth, 'Anything for you, Katie.'

She climbed into her car and started the engine. 'Heading back tomorrow?'

He nodded.

'Bett will give you a bed tonight. Bye dear.' She slammed the door, backed up the car, and sped away without waving or even looking at him.

As he stood scenting the pine and feeling the cool air upon his skin, he wanted to be a certain bellhop in Bampers Hotel.

3

D'Arcy Morgan had just buckled his arms behind his head and eyed the length of his body to his big toe sticking through his black bellhop sock when a horn sounded in the distance. He groaned and rolled onto his side. 'Nick!'

'What do you want?' Nick answered gruffly from across the hall.

'You're dressed, aren't you?'

'I'm lying down.'

'Tell her I'm coming will you?' D'Arcy knew that Nick would do anything to be noticed by a guest.

The horn blared again followed by the pad of Nick's feet along the corridor. Nick went under the porch light and waved, 'Coming!' The horn tooted twice. Nick went into D'Arcy's room and regarded him with admiration.

D'Arcy had told the hops all about Kate--what she said at particularly intimate moments and what she looked like--

never to her detriment, always in praise of her seductive beauty.

'Boy! you've got her panting.' Nick pawed his brush cut to the front with a lilting smile of wonder.

D'Arcy stretched his toes. 'Will you see if my white shirt's in the drawer.' He nodded at the bureau, the drawers of which were jarred open.

Usually Nick would not move at anyone's bidding but this was part of an act and he enjoyed acting. 'I don't see one,' he said gazing at the disarray of socks, pajamas, and underwear.

'Is there a dirty one then?' D'Arcy asked. 'Maybe she'll wash it.'

Nick crowed and rubbed his knob-nose. 'There ought to be half a dozen dirty ones,' he said.

'I'd better not push it that far this soon,' D'Arcy smirked.

'She'll send them to the laundry with her stuff.' Nick began pulling out dirty shirts.

'I don't want them.' D'Arcy laughing sat up and stripped off his khaki jacket .

Nick threw them at him. D'Arcy brushed them onto the floor.

'You dumb bear!"

Nick looked like a bear: his ears stuck out, his freckled cheeks bulged, his figure widening to the waist rounded in a large behind, and he stood lightly on his feet, often tap dancing along the hall when he felt happy. Moreover, he liked horseplay when he could shoulder close to an opponent and grapple him in his thick, muscled arms.

'Here's a clean collar.' Nick held out the rubber kind which the hops wore because they were easy to wash and quick to dry.

D'Arcy stood up and pulled off his trousers. He went to the bureau and setting a hand against it scrutinized the open drawers. His arm descended slowly to the third drawer and came back with a blue sports shirt. 'My trousers are on the back of the door,' he said.

Dropping the collar on the floor, Nick skipped to the trousers and took them down. He held them out for D'Arcy to step into.

'Just give them to me,' D'Arcy said, buttoning his shirt

Nick held the waist out like a hoop. 'Jump in.'

Once before Nick had called him a bad sport. D'Arcy didn't want to experience again Nick's disdainful mockery. He grinned bravely, prepared for a trick. 'I'm not a circus performer, you nut.'

'Mama's handsome boy is afraid that Nick will hurt him,' Nick lisped. He shook the trousers, the belt rattling. 'Come on, Fido.'

D'Arcy jumped on the instant. Nick with a cry of glee closed the trousers but not before D'Arcy's foot caught in one pocket and ripped it as he crashed to the floor.

Nick, screaming with laughter, slapped his knee and pointed at the ripped trousers. He didn't see the grimness in D'Arcy's eyes. D'Arcy leaped up catching Nick by the neck and shoulder. They fell against the wall, struggled, and sank to the floor. Nick slipped his arm about D'Arcy's throat and tightened it for all he was worth. D'Arcy tried to jerk loose. His chin was shelved on Nick's elbow. He gasped, seeing the room whirl, and dropped his arms. Nick quickly released him, and gave him a savage push in the face, sending him sprawling onto his back.

Two bellhops, just off duty, ran into the room. They went to D'Arcy who propped himself on one arm.

Nick chortled. 'That'll teach you to mix with men. You'd better stick to women, D'Arce, my boy.' He turned to the bellhops. 'I got some beer in my room. You guys want some?' There was a truculence in his manner that demanded acquiescence.

'Sure.' They glanced back at D'Arcy as they left.

Angry at himself for losing, D'Arcy threw the trousers onto the bed and took another pair from his closet. He put them on and brushed his shirt, all the while dreaming of how he would take his revenge. Nick was one number ahead of him on his shift. Their close rivalry built up a tension which was unexpectedly revealed in their off-hours.

'The next time I'm going to box,' he whispered ruefully.

He intended to change his socks but thought better of it. The blare from Kate's horn seemed to have sounded long ago. He panicked. Pulling on sandals he ran into the corridor and smoothed his hair as he stepped toward the door. Nick's voice pursued him; its relentless tone subtly turned against him.

Kate's car waited on the roadside. A man was leaning by the driver's window, hands in pockets and head down. D'Arcy sauntered silently across the grass. He hoped to overhear them. The slow dry chuckle of Mort, the clarinetist, created a cosy ambiance. D'Arcy reached the door handle on the other side before Mort noticed him. The pudgy good looks strained with curiosity when D'Arcy opened the door. Nodding curtly, D'Arcy sat in. He leaned over, took Kate in his arms, and kissed her. As he pulled away, he glanced up at Mort. The musician looked incredulous.

'Let's go,' D'Arcy said. 'Hi ya, Mort.'

Dazed, Kate pushed the ignition.

'You will be coming to our party, Mrs. Carr?' Mort blurted.

She reddened. 'We will be delighted, Mort. Sounds delightful.' She inched the wheels into a slow roll. 'Nice chatting to you.' She drove by the garage over which the musicians had rooms. 'Why did you do that?' She tossed her head angrily.

'I didn't want him to get wrong ideas about you.'

'You don't think he has the right ideas now!'

'He asked you to a party, didn't he?'

'He asked us to a party.'

'Like bull!'

She glared at him. 'Anyway, if you hadn't taken so long, he wouldn't have stayed talking.'

D'Arcy sucked in his lips and nodded thoughtfully. They were driving out of the lodge grounds. He glimpsed the shiny wooden shack where the patrolmen kept count of the hotel cars leaving and entering in the day.

'Where are we going?'

'Where would you like to go?' she asked banteringly.

'Stop here.'

'Why?'

'Stop here,' he barked.

Kate brought the car up sharply.

'Park at the side of the road,' he said patiently. 'We are getting out.'

With a snort she drove to the side. He stepped out and going round to her door, held it open.

'Where are we going?' she demanded.

He leaned inside, slipped his arms under her and lifted her out and onto her feet. He slammed the door and took her hand. They crossed the road and looked down on a river that looked black in the starlight. The rushing water sighed from its bed. A high lamp by the patrolman's shack gave them enough light to make their way down to the next level and to a wide trail on the lip of the bank. Leading Kate to the brink, D'Arcy sat and dangled his legs over the side.

Kate stared at the swirling black. She felt her life changing from one of complication to one of simplicity. D'Arcy gently pulled her down beside him.

His tough leanness provided her with more of a mental support than a physical luxury. She thought that man belonged to this over-size nature where the mind discovered its image. Woman was a phantom; she might haunt the valleys and ledges but not realise herself. She put her arms about D'Arcy and hugged him. She needed him to make her feel real.

'Why did you bring me here?' she asked.

D'Arcy pried her arms away and taking her hands folded them upon her lap. 'Just listen,' he said.

Behind them evergreens like dark giants moved in the breeze. The noise of the rushing river receded. A colossal stillness of sound replaced it in her consciousness. She sensed that D'Arcy was fascinated by it and somehow involved with it. Rocking against him, she made him look down.

D'Arcy cleansed of the pettiness of argument wanted to enjoy Kate's body in the fineness of the open air. He pushed her back on the grass and stroked her hair and cheek. Slipping his hand under her blouse, he caressed her breasts.

'What are we going to do tonight?' he mocked.

'Oh D'Arcy!' She threw her arms about his neck and held him fast.

He kissed her shoulder. 'Love should be made in the open air with the birds and the bees.' He unbuttoned her blouse.

'Don't, people might come.' She sat up, and he slipped the blouse off her arms.

'So what? Let them make love too,' he said. 'Why should we hide away in stuffy rooms when we have this majesty to frolic in?'

She laughed. 'You'd do well in a nudist colony.'

He frowned. 'If we all spent weeks in the nude every year we'd be healthier, and I don't mean because of the sun tan.'

'Ha, ha,' she said, 'well, my mental health is all right. It's yours that worries me.'

He kissed her breasts. 'No brassiere,' he said. 'I like that about you.' He admired them for their refinement of line. So

23

many breasts he had seen were just fleshy protuberances. He took off his shirt.

'You're not serious about this?' Kate regarded him with amused concern.

'I'm never serious about anything,' D'Arcy smiled. He dragged off the rest of her clothes, Kate being cooperatively permissive, and threw them in a pile.

Kate kneeled in the nude. 'It's too cold for this sort of game.'

'No, no,' he insisted, kicking the rest of his clothes into the pile and stretching mightily as if he were Tarzan. 'Back to nature.' He kneeled in front of her, kissed her lips, and, gazing at her, sat back on his heels.

She looked round uneasily. 'I don't like this, D'Arcy.'

'Relax! It's too dark for anyone to see.'

He sat beside her and put his arms about her. Succumbing to his warmth she lifted her lips to be kissed. The motor of a car droned to a stop on the road above. D'Arcy embraced her. She pushed her cheek against his and dreamily looked up. A human figure was outlined against the road light from the patrolman's shack. She stared until a second figure stood beside it. She started. A man and woman were preparing to climb down. D'Arcy, sensing her fear, looked up at them.

'D'Arcy darling,' she whispered, 'aren't you going to invite them to join us?'

He seized the pile of clothes and bundled it in both arms against his chest. 'Take your shoes. Quick,' he said and ran toward the evergreens.

Picking up a pair in each hand, she fled after him. She dropped D'Arcy's heavy pair and spent a few seconds trying to find them on the ground. Stubbing her toe on one shoe, she put her hand on the other, and holding them to her, turned in time to see D'Arcy disappear behind foliage a short way up the hill. She ran for the spot but when she arrived she hesitated to enter for fear she had mistaken it. Frightened, she peered frantically for any sign of D'Arcy. She thought of wolves and bears lurking behind the evergreens, and how she would defend herself with two pairs of shoes. The strangers had plunged into the darkness and might be very close by. 'D'Arcy,' she called softly. She ran to the side. 'D'Arcy.' His naked form appeared directly before her. He took her wrist and pulled her after him. Before she ducked behind the trees, she saw the woman step into the light by the roadside. She was about to tell D'Arcy that the strangers were going when she was struck by the familiarity of the woman's straggly hair. D'Arcy pulled her down on the soft pine needles and brought her tight against him. A woman's voice shouted over the sound of the river. 'Julien! What the deuce are you doing?' It was Bett. 'I thought I saw something,' Julien answered. 'I'm coming.'

Kate heard no more. She gave herself to D'Arcy.

4

'She may just have left her car and gone driving with friends,' Bett said, sitting exactly behind the wheel and steering carefully. 'You know, friends like to be together.'

'Women do strange things,' Julien said tiredly.

'My dear, you don't say you're worried about her.' She laughed gutturally. 'When I tell Kate about this, she'll think it's terribly funny. I bet she's having a whale of a time right now.'

Julien's mind harked back to the slope on the riverside. Was it his imagination that he heard a woman's cry for D'Arcy? He had looked about him on the trail and for an instant believed it rose from the river.

'We'll have to find a wife for you, Julien dear. I know, I've said it before, and I haven't done much. But I'll really look under every... banyan tree. I almost said rock, isn't that amusing?' Bett was saying. 'You're getting to be an old crock-- just too prudish to sleep in the same house with Harry and me.'

'Cabin,' Julien corrected her with a smile.

Bett laughed.

'Besides, if your husband happened by, he'd shoot me as an accomplice in all probability,' Julien said.

Bett laughed again. 'You know he loves you, dear.'

The satirical overtone made Julien think of Allan Steel's femininity. Strange how it appeared after his and Bett's child was killed. Allan had developed into a likable homosexual, seemingly well-adjusted to his mode of life.

'I haven't seen him for over a year. How is he?'

'You'll see him this summer,' Bett said sardonically.

As they drove by the garage, they noticed the lights on the upper floor.

'Looks like a party. Want to join them?' Bett suggested.

'No,' Julien clamped his lips tightly.

Bett stopped at the patio. Wooden lanterns hung on dark brown posts to light the way. The flowers bowed in sleep.

'They have a lot of reservations for tomorrow,' she warned. 'Might not get a room.'

'You know that's not true,' he winked in reference to their rendez-vous. 'There's always a room.'

'Very well, dear. I'll wait and drive you,' Bett said nicely as Julien got out.

'No need to.' He shut the door. 'You get back to Harry.' He walked quickly over the flagstones and turned round at the screen door.

Bett was staring sorrowfully after him. He waved her away and stepped into the lobby. Rich Persian carpets emblazoned the floor. The great nave with its hundred tables and lamps, Aladdin-like after dinner, was dark. The stone of the giant fireplace reflected a cold, ghostly presence. The lights at the front desk fell on the varnished cream wood. Julien could not see a night clerk. The night-hop who was supposed to watch the switchboard was probably making black market money selling booze to late drinkers. He waited until he heard Bett's car drive away before approaching the desk. A woman moved in the cashier's cage and a machine began clicking out the mathematics created by the flux of human whims and passions in the day. The black bangs and marble-hewn features of Lou were visible through the bars. She spun her large, well-formed body about when she saw him. 'Julien Kowalski!' She charged out of the cage and up to the counter with a large smile.

Julien leaned across the counter and kissed her lightly. Lou's sorrows had wrinkled the once smooth skin.

'Are you staying for a while?' Her dark eyes glowed.

He shook his head with a kind smile. 'Back to Edmonton tomorrow. How are your kids?'

'Fine,' she smiled with a nod of thanks.

He smiled and searched for something to say. 'Just one room.' He filled out the registration card.

Lou handed him the key.

'It's not the bachelor's cabin?' he asked.

Lou shook her head laughingly.

'Oh.' He regarded the number on the tab. 'I'll find it easy enough.' He patted her hand and pushing away from the desk walked over the verandah, down the steps and along the lane fronting Lake Beautiful. A sense of embarrassment at meeting Lou flushed his cheeks and forehead so that they burned. The excesses of youth were excessively humiliating.

After leaving Julien, Bett drove by the garage and parked. She watched the lighted windows to see who came into view. If the party looked interesting she might drop in.

Bett loved parties. Nothing was closer to Bett's idea of heaven than a chance to chatter, swig the old hard stuff, and make eyes at the boys, unless, of course, it was a new "Experience". She was not promiscuous, however; she had argued that moral point out with herself. She would only make love with her "type" which varied but was always "good-looking".

Tired of straining her neck and seeing nothing, she gazed out the other side across the lawn into the blackness. The eighteenth fairway hooked downhill and ended there. The club house looked like a pagoda in the dark. One lamp hung from a corner to light the path to the bachelor's cabin. Huh! she thought. What a name for a cabin! Ah, the memories!

Archie, the lodge policeman, stepped from behind a tree and crossed in front of the car. He peered at the windshield suspiciously. In the centre of the road, he stopped and looked up at the lighted rooms. The strains of a phonograph record drifted faintly down. Satisfied, Archie scratched his leg and then his neck. He took off his cap and brushed down his white hair. His face shone red and weather-beaten from many northern winters as he stared at the car once more. Then suddenly seeing Bett, he nodded, resettled his cap, and came over to chat.

'Nice night, Mrs. Steel.'

'I was admiring it, Archie, and regretting that I have to go home.' She started the motor.

Archie laid a hand on the door. 'I was inquiring about you of Mr. Runners the other day. Got you a cabin on Edge-In Lake, have you'se?'

'I'm afraid so and I'm late for a party. Bye-bye.' She glided the car away, and glanced in the rear-view mirror to see

27

Archie walking away head down. 'Well, I mean, it can't be helped,' she said.

The headlights flashed over a couple coming from the woods. She recognized Slim Johnson with a blanket over his shoulder. The girl was buxom. "Out bushing". Her mind leafed over the faces and figures of the caddies she had seen this season. There were two or three who might inspire her game.

Speed, speed; there was no traffic on the road. Harry was waiting; the party was still in process, though maybe they'd all be in bed by the time she got home. She laughed: wouldn't that be wonderful if they were all in bed by the time she got home.

Bett Steel would have guessed that Slim Johnson was virginal if she spoke with him, but Slim would not have known what was on Bett's mind. Although nineteen, Slim lived in the great world of first innocence. He took girls into the woods and petted them under cover. He was romantic and attentive to them. He wasn't shy. At times he had urges to express his desire, but he didn't know how, and tried not to think about it. Bruce Bannister recognized Slim's state. Bruce occupied the bunk over him from which he began discussions on sex before going to sleep at nights. Slim's astonishing ignorance became apparent; he began asking questions with obvious answers. One evening Bruce handed down a well-thumbed book written by a medical doctor. 'Don't read the forward,' he advised; 'it's dull.' Slim planned to start chapter one soon, although he didn't think he would find medical facts interesting. He left his girl with a big kiss at the entrance to her cabin and crept stealthily back to his own because it was past twelve and he did not want "Big Archie" to catch him.

There was a light in the corner room. Through the window Slim saw Dixie Mitchell drinking beer. He paused at Dixie's door wondering if he would be welcome. Then giving way to his fascination for Dixie's worldliness, he entered.

'Whoops!' Dixie had grabbed his beer and was holding it under the table. He put it back with a blithesome smile of welcome. 'The minute I saw that door move....' he snapped his fingers.

'Better close your curtains.' Slim looked at the window.

'You close them. We're concentrating,' Dixie said seriously.

Gregory Marchilly had not moved a muscle. His most engaging feature was a protruding upper lip which gave him the appearance of starting a pucker. Bushy eyebrows and a reflective expression helped him pretend to be an aesthete. He sat on a hard-backed chair facing Dixie across a square wooden table. His glass and bottle stood before him. The steadiness of his gaze would have found praise with Whistler whom Gregory admired.

'Begin again,' Gregory drawled musically.

Intensely serious, Dixie snapped out his forefinger at Gregory. He quoted Marlowe sententiously. 'You have committed fornication.' He paused and narrowed his eyes. 'But that was in another land, and besides, the wench is dead.' He raised his brows. 'The Jew of Malta.'

The two communicants sipped their beers. Gregory cleared his throat and assumed a glowering look. He thrust his forefinger at Dixie. 'You have committed fornication.' He lowered his tone, wheedling the words. 'But that was in another land, and besides the wench is dead. The Jew of Malta.'

They roared with laughter and slapped the table top. Slim, who had drawn the curtains, laughed with them. He planned to look up "fornication" in a dictionary.

'Want a beer?' Dixie asked him.

'Yeah, okay.' Slim took the proffered bottle.

'If we had money, we could play poker,' Gregory said, 'and take Johnson's away from him.'

Dixie chortled. 'Slim's good at poker.' He looked at Slim. 'And he's going to be a good worker and make lots of moolah this summer.'

Slim disliked the taste of beer but tried not to show it. 'Yeah, I am.'

'And, I trust, you will play us poker,' Gregory said.

'Maybe.' Slim pictured them playing all day instead of going to work. The wooden rooms and the simple bare furniture had the effect on him of imprisonment.

'Runners buckled under, goddamn him,' Dixie said, holding up his glass, 'but we'll face reality and drink to higher pay.'

'Here's to Anthony Runners in the House of Xanadu.' Gregory took a long drink.

'May he abdicate and be replaced by a more benevolent heir.' Dixie took a long drink.

'Amen!' Slim said and swigged from the bottle.

A gruff shout of command issued just outside the window.

'Big Archie,' Slim whispered, paling.

Dixie was on his feet and opening his cupboard. 'On the top shelf.' As they ran to set down their beers, he held up his hand. 'Listen.'

Archie was questioning someone who had difficulty answering.

'Relax,' Gregory said. 'We are needlessly alert.' He carried his beer to the table.

Dixie crept to the window and lifting a corner of the curtain, peeked out. 'He's got that little Frenchie!'

'Which one?' Gregory's eyes glistened.

'Aurmand Roosleberries.'

'Ruissillier,' Gregory said in affected French.

'What's going on?' Slim asked, concerned. He liked Aurmand.

'Arch has a grip on his shoulder and the little Frenchie's got one foot outside the door.' They heard Aurmand's mild voice chatter in protest. 'Arch can't understand him.' Dixie came away with a dazed smile.

'That's rather crude,' Gregory said, 'to catch a man on his own doorstep. We should see that justice is done.'

'That's right,' Slim cried angrily. He started for the door.

'Leave your beer, you nut!' Dixie said.

Slim stashed his bottle on a shelf by the door and dashed into the corridor. Dixie, clutching his stomach with laughter, followed him. But Gregory waited, listening for the opportune moment to make his appearance.

'What's wrong?' Slim cried.

Archie stared him down. 'That's my business, young fellow.'

Aurmand had resigned himself to Archie's grip. He looked pathetically through his rimless glasses at Slim. 'No bus,' he said.

'He missed the last bus from town and had to walk,' Slim explained with a sigh of impatience.

Archie looked doubtful.

'Take your hands off him,' Dixie said. 'He's a caddie.'

'Do you boys want to be reported to Mr. Runners?' Archie threatened.

'Why the hands, Archie?' Dixie insisted. 'He's not going to run away.'

'What's his name?' Archie demanded, maintaining his hold on Aurmand's jacket.

'Roosleberry,' Dixie said. 'The same as yours, Arch.' He and Slim laughed. Aurmand smiled faintly.

'None of your sauce. I'll have you before Mr. Runners in the morning,' Archie threatened.

'Let him go, eh?' Slim said. 'He won't do it again.'

Archie took away his hand and folded his arms like a stevedore in front of him. 'I seen him scuttle out between them maids' cabins.'

Slim looked at Aurmand who shook his head sadly, helplessly.

'He was just taking a short cut by the river,' Slim said. 'What the heck! He's a university lecturer. He doesn't have anything to do with maids.'

Archie's heavy jowls sank. He seemed confused.

'You'll have to be sure of your facts,' Dixie warned, 'because it's going to be a big scandal in French Canada.'

'Don't you fellows try to bulldoze me into anything,' Archie said suspiciously. 'I want to know the truth.'

'I woz in town,' Aurmand insisted, strongly accenting the "was".

Archie scratched his neck. He looked uncertainly at Aurmand.

'Well, I...'

Gregory appeared and raised his arm in salute like a king's messenger. 'Aurmand!'

The group spun round.

'Telephone,' he said. 'Long distance. Your mother.'

'My mother!' Aurmand gasped, his thin face wrenched in apprehension.

'Go on, man,' Gregory thumbed him in.

Aurmand scampered down the corridor.

Dixie turned on Archie with a look that despised him. 'Still going to arrest him?'

'I wasn't going to arrest him,' Archie said indignantly. 'I was questioning him.'

Dixie smiled at the others. 'Arch knows when he's licked. He's a good man.'

31

'You boys,' Archie grinned, a metal tooth glinting, 'go to bed or I'll report you'se all.' He turned stiffly and walked round the corner of the cabin.

His hand over his mouth, Dixie ran into his room bent at the waist. Gregory was lying on the bed, his head thrown back in screams of laughter. Dixie, seeing him, wheezed uncontrollably.

Slim met Aurmand dashing back from the telephone. Aurmand's fine features were churned up in worry. 'What telephone?' he asked in exasperation.

'No telephone,' Slim said. 'It was a joke.'

'I don't understand,' Aurmand replied. "English joke.'

'It's not English,' Slim said. He was sensitive to any racial antagonism. 'They think it's funny, that's all.' He walked along the corridor with Aurmand. 'Were you really in town?'

Aurmand stopped and stared coldly at Slim. 'You are my best friend, Slim,' he whispered. 'I tell you my secret.' He explained that he washed dishes from half past eight to half past eleven.

Slim nodded in astonishment.

'I eat better than here,' Aurmand said proudly. 'And the work is lighter.' He put his finger to his lips. 'Don't tell.'

'I won't,' Slim said. 'Let's turn in. I've got to caddie for that silly Mrs. Carr tomorrow.'

They tip-toed into their room and made their way through the dark until they could see with the light from the window. Bruce Bannister snored deeply. As Aurmand passed him, he made as if to spit in his face. Slim was shocked. It upset him to see one man being rude to another.

5

D'Arcy came on duty with the noon shift. At thirty seconds to twelve six bellhops in khaki uniforms with red lapels marched in single file from behind the hedge by the tennis courts, down the flagstoned steps, across the patio and into the lobby. The morning shift scattered into the sunlight as soon as it saw the approaching file. Nelles Lynes, the head bell man, displayed his customary shark smile as he watched the boys settle on the bench and fold their arms while the shift captain roosted on the stool at the desk behind them. Two pillars, great trunks from British Columbia forests, stood on either side of this desk. The bench stretched between them. As there was no room for the last boy to sit, he was ordered to empty the ashtrays throughout the lobby. Nelles paced in front of the bench. D'Arcy sneezed and pulled out his handkerchief.

'Catch a cold, D'Arce?' Nelles asked.

'Nope,' D'Arcy said.

'Some people have them,' Nelles said. 'Mrs. Carr was sniffling this morning.'

Nick giggled. The other hops smiled.

Nelles was several years older and studying for his Ph.D. Already he had the professorial wit. 'Carry on, Captain.' He sealed his lips in a half-smile and snorted a laugh at the captain.

D'Arcy watched him go with a pout of disdain.

'Careful,' Captain O'Flaherty warned.

Nick, as number one boy, said, 'Better send him to clean out the closet, don't you think, Cap?'

'We won't do that just yet,' O'Flaherty said. He was afraid of Nick. 'Catch the arrival list, D'Arcy.'

With a slow lurch, D'Arcy stepped to the Front Desk. He took the list from the blotter and scanned it as he brought it to O'Flaherty. He made out three good roomings before he handed it over.

O'Flaherty cocked his eye. 'Ah, here's one for me--cabin 98. Must be a big party.' He passed the list down to Nick.

'One's your limit today,' Nick said wrinkling his nose.

'I don't know,' O'Flaherty demurred. 'I could squeeze in a couple more.'

'If you do, the last boy won't get peanuts,' Nick countered.

The hops on the bench looked worried. Nick passed the list to D'Arcy who passed it down the line. D'Arcy had to maneuver with his two superiors to get one of the three good roomings. If Nelles came back on duty, D'Arcy would have to take a fifty or twenty-five cent grab-bag rooming. The interesting point about the grab-bags was their surprises; a hop might pick up a dollar with them.

O'Flaherty sent the hops running on messages which involved no tips. In this case the order of sequence began at the last boy. In his turn, D'Arcy had to take an envelope from Runners' office to his home. He went with his heart in his mouth. He had a social reason to fear Runners. The manager had been chasing Kate for two years without success. If Runners knew that D'Arcy was Kate's lover, he would find some reason to dismiss him, or demote him to caddie or patrolman. A secretary's slim finger tipped with blood-red nail varnish designated the envelope. As D'Arcy crossed the lawn with it, he wondered if this were a ruse of Runners to bring Kate's lover before him. He sidled onto the path in case Runners got angry at him for walking on the grass. Runners' cabin was set a distance apart from the others. D'Arcy knocked softly on the screen door.

'Who is it?' Mrs. Runners loomed behind the screen. She reminded D'Arcy of prim Puritan women who burnt other women for witchery.

He held up the envelope. 'For Mr. Runners.'

'Give it here,' she said shortly, slipping her ungainly-looking hand out the screen door.

The smell of liquor streamed through the screen.

'What's your name?' she asked considerately.

'Morgan.'

She nodded. 'That will be all.' She retreated.

'That won't be all!' Runners' voice thundered.

D'Arcy poised in the act of turning. He was terror-stricken.

'Come in here!'

'Tony,' Mrs. Runners started to dissuade him.

'No!' Runners insisted.

D'Arcy waited, hoping that Mrs. Runners would refuse him entrance, but she held open the door. He stepped in and smiled at Runners who sat stiffly in a rocking chair. Runners was drunk.

'Morgan,' he snapped. 'What's the meaning of these complaints?'

D'Arcy pictured jealous staff members scribbling anonymous notes to Runners about Mrs. Carr and the bellhop.

'I don't know, sir.'

'You wrote home, didn't you, eh? Admit it, admit it, admit it!' He ended in a high shriek.

'I don't know what you mean, sir,' D'Arcy stammered. He was beginning to despise Runners in spite of his fears.

Mrs. Runners broke in with a dry chuckle. 'He's not a caddie. Look at him. He's a bellhop!'

Runners turned a cold glare upon him. His eyes glimmered with recognition of the uniform. 'What are you doing here?'

'At your service, sir,' D'Arcy said smartly.

Runners smiled slightly. 'That's very good.' His tone was mild. 'Go along now.'

Mrs. Runners held open the door. She was smiling graciously. D'Arcy walked away. Perspiration ran down his sides. His neck felt hot. He sneezed and was blowing his nose when he saw the lodge bus draw up at the patio. It was full of incoming guests from the train.

Sprinting, he leaped a flower bed, ducked into the office corridor and moved swiftly down the lobby. He stepped into his place in the bellhop line-up just as the first guests came through the door.

O'Flaherty stood near the clerk. His round eyes searched out his victims amongst the arrivals. A curly black forelock hung over his forehead. It had earned him the sobriquet, 'Piggy', which had fallen into disuse as he rose from last boy to bell captain.

The hops looked over the first couple. Elderly, the man had a miserly aspect. He fussed with the pen when signing the register and looked in annoyance at those about him. D'Arcy laughed inwardly at Nick's discomfort, for O'Flaherty was bound to pass the old goat onto Nick.

O'Flaherty eyed the card handed him by the clerk and said quietly, 'Front Boy'.

As the boys watched Nick hang the couple's coats over his arm and lead them to the front verandah, they sighed almost audibly with relief.

O'Flaherty's eyes lit up at the next card. A family of three, looking, even smelling rich to a bellhop, confronted him. 'Come with me, sir,' O'Flaherty grinned. 'Have a nice trip? Your cabin is in a most lovely spot.' They moved onto the verandah.

D'Arcy stepped to the desk. He glanced at the next card, a poor number, and called 'Front Boy'. The following card was another bad risk. As he handed it to the front hop, he worried lest Nick arrive back and displace him before a good rooming came up. He scrutinized the line-up of guests. Some were definitely too dowdy to be worth much. The second group alone gave promise: a middle-aged couple with a grown-up daughter. He waited impatiently for the clerk to give him the card for a trio of old ladies. He called 'Front Boy' the instant it was in his hand, glancing at it nevertheless to make sure it was not a top rooming. As he surveyed his selection from the crop, he remarked the sexiness of the daughter. He might be in for double luck. The clerk's hand moved cautiously across the card. D'Arcy strained to make out the location--on the water! He looked through the screen doors, over the patio at the corner of the building around which Nick would be appearing any second. If he didn't get this card before Nick returned Nick would take his rooming. The guy was good for a dollar at least. His pockets bulged as if with American bills. He was leaning forward asking the clerk questions in some bizarre mid-west accent. D'Arcy winced at the clerk who noticed his pain. 'I'm sure your bellhop could tell you, sir. I don't know,' said the clerk. D'Arcy looked over at the corner. Nick was streaking across the patio. He was moving as fast as decorum would allow him. He burst through the screen doors. D'Arcy's fingers jumped for the card, plucking it from the clerk. 'Your coat, sir.' He slipped it off the man's arm. 'This way.' He stepped aside to let him pass. Nick, gasping for breath, came up to D'Arcy. 'I'll take it,' he murmured. D'Arcy grinned and said softly between his teeth, 'Too late.' Still wearing his smile, he took coats from the wife and daughter. 'Are you staying long?' he asked the daughter. He glanced back at Nick when they reached the verandah. Nick was standing patiently by the desk with his back turned, but the hairs on his neck bristled.

'We'll be here for a few days, I guess,' the girl answered. She bent lithesomely back to smile.

D'Arcy liked her carriage and her open personality. The question was: would she or wouldn't she? His experience warned him that this type wouldn't. He moved forward to open the screen door for her parents. 'To the right.' Guests on the verandah looked up from books and newspapers to size up the newcomers as they passed. Guests basking on the front lawn watched them wander along the walk to the cabins. 'It's called Beautiful,' D'Arcy nodded towards the lake, 'because it changes to several beautiful colours--blue, green. I've seen it white early in the morning.' Nick would have had a joke to tell at this point, but D'Arcy never attempted "stored" humour. He depended upon impromptu remarks. 'A bear was along here this morning, frightening some of the guests,' he said.

'Really!' the man said.

'We saw one when we were coming in from the train,' added his wife.

'He looked friendly,' said the girl.

'Well,' D'Arcy continued, 'they won't hurt you if you pay no attention to them.' He shifted their coats to his other arm and quickened the pace now that they were in front of the cabins. The guests, eager to listen, pursued him. 'Though some bears have homicidal urges, just like humans. That's why you shouldn't feed them.' They were moving at a fast clip, leaning forward like long-distance runners. D'Arcy hoped to get back in time for two or three more roomings.

'What's that again?' asked the woman, alarmed.

'One woman was peaceably feeding a bear when he clobbered her all of a sudden. He would have mauled her if some people hadn't chased him off.' He glanced at the number on the card--another few cabins.

'There, Sal,' the man nodded tersely at his daughter. 'And you wanted to stop the bus!'

'Oh!' his wife gasped, 'where is this cabin?'

D'Arcy, maintaining the pace, dumbly pointed ahead.

'It's too far out,' she complained, giving signs of sinking onto the doorstep of one of the cabins en route.

'The Governor-General stays right out at the point when he comes,' D'Arcy said.

'Oh, does he?' she said, putting new spring into her step.

'He gets a car to drive him out, I bet,' said the man rather hastily.

His wife stopped short with resentment.

'Here we are,' D'Arcy called. He raced ahead to the next cabin. Swinging open the door, he stood aside. The guests straggled in, the daughter first because she had weathered the course best. D'Arcy hung their coats in the closet and threw open the window in one bedroom. He rattled off information on meal times, all the while gesturing here and there to the bathroom, the telephone, the outlet for an electric razor. 'And how many bags, sir?' He poised his pencil ready to scribble on the back of the card.

'Aren't the porters bringing them?' the man asked.

D'Arcy could tell by his expression that he had tipped the porters very well. 'No. They just bring them to the back of the lodge and we bring them to the cabins.' D'Arcy pronounced the "we" distinctly. He scribbled down the number. He thought of being nice to the girl--it might be worth an extra quarter. 'I hope you enjoy your stay here.' She would be lonely unless she knew someone.

She responded willingly, 'I hope I will.'

He looked at her father who had finally pulled out his wallet.

'How long will those bags take to get here?' the man demanded.

D'Arcy adopted a determined stare. 'I'll bring them as soon as I have time.' There was an edge of double-meaning to his tone.

The man added fifty cents to the dollar in his hand.

D'Arcy took the sum with a bright smile. 'Thank you, sir. I'll bring them very soon.' He scribbled "daughter" on the back of the card when he was in the lane. He ran in long loping strides to the lodge. One advantage he had over Nick was that he could run faster.

He was in time for three roomings more and spent the rest of the afternoon sorting out bags and carting them to the cabins. The "daughter" and her parents were out when he dropped off their bags. He had made four dollars--which was a bad afternoon. However, he seemed to have sweated out his cold.

'D'Arcy!'

Jane hailed him from the path. Dressed in her polka-dot uniform, she was hurrying to the dining room. He used to bush with her last summer. Strange how the passage of one year could alter a former passion to an indifferent shout.

Sylvester used to take Jane out until the Rabbinowitzes arrived. They were an extremely rich and handsome family. They stayed at the lodge every summer. Horace Rabbinowitz owned canneries throughout the States. Always deeply tanned, his strikingly handsome features must have tweaked many a heart. Jaimie was a slimmer edition of his father, just as darkly handsome. He was twenty-one. He wore sportsman clothes. He drove a new convertible. He had so much money that he could go anywhere at anytime. Moreover, the family was linked with European Jewry, spending as much of its time in European society as in America, so that Jaimie had all the sparkling charm of a rich continental. Weighed against these facts was Sylvester's patrolman status. Sylvester made seventy-two dollars a month, all of which went towards his university fees. When Jane waited on the Rabbinowitz table,

Jaimie asked her for a date. Thus Sylvester's days of bliss with Jane terminated sharply, as if severed by the hand of Mammon himself.

At any rate, Sylvester rather envied D'Arcy's detachment. D'Arcy could see his old flame, tall, fair, daisy-bright Jane swish by him with Jaimie at the wheel and yet not have a jealous thought. Perhaps this was because D'Arcy was swishing in the other direction with Kate at the wheel.

D'Arcy went to his room, tiredly surveyed the clothes-strewn beds of his room-mates on the opposite shift, and took off his uniform. He hung it neatly. After dressing for the evening, he left his part of the room looking tidy. His bed had not been slept in for three nights and wouldn't be used tonight. It was easy to keep a room clean when you hardly lived in it, he concluded.

On his way to the mess hall he fell into stride with Slim Johnson.

'Caddie, aren't you?' he said.

Slim nodded.

D'Arcy introduced himself and learned Slim's name. He saw Blair heading for the course with his clubs.

'Come here,' he called.

Blair grimaced and, hiking his clubs higher, ambled over.

'Look, Buddy boy, tell Slim how good a caddie I was, ' D'Arcy ordered.

'As he says,' Blair said. 'I never saw him though.'

'That's right,' D'Arcy buffeted him on the shoulder. 'I was a caddie the year before you came. So you see,' he turned to Slim, 'how experienced I am in the ways of Bampers' life.'

Blair smirked. 'I'm going.'

'Blair boy,' D'Arcy said holding his arm, 'if you'd go a little later, I'd go with you.'

'We'd never do nine holes,' Blair said. 'You'd be in the woods half the time.'

D'Arcy blushed. 'Well, as they say, the best caddies make the worst golfers.'

Blair tossed his golden head in a laugh. 'Say,' he murmured, 'Slim can tell you about Mrs. Carr.' He turned and struck out for the links.

'What about her?' D'Arcy asked suspiciously.

'Nothing,' Slim said innocently. 'I just caddie for her.'

'Oh,' D'Arcy nodded. 'Pretty good golfer, eh? That is, for a woman.'

'She's okay,' Slim shrugged. 'She's just sort of silly, that's all.'

'Really.' D'Arcy bit his lip to keep from smiling. He could hardly wait to see Kate's reaction to this news. 'How is she silly?'

'She's flighty and always making eyes at the men. I think she uses golf as an excuse.'

D'Arcy frowned. 'Who was she with this morning?'

Slim noticed the hardening of tone. He was puzzled by D'Arcy. 'Johnnie O'Dreams, Jaimie Rabbinowitz and a woman.'

'Not Bett Steel?'

'No, not her.' Slim frowned. 'Why do you want to know?'

D'Arcy slipped his tongue over his teeth. 'I go around with Kate Carr.'

Slim blanched. He opened the mess hall door for D'Arcy who had taken on the mysterious quality of a magician in his eyes. He expected D'Arcy to leave him in order to sit with the other bellhops.

'Come on and we'll talk,' D'Arcy said leading Slim to a vacant table.

The waitress gave them soup as they climbed onto the bench. The long wooden hall was well-serviced by these buxom, sloe-eyed girls. D'Arcy saw Davey, the staff chef, scratching his ear and watching the eaters from the kitchen. He waved and sprightly old Davey jerked his hand up in salute.

'He's a great guy,' D'Arcy said. 'He'll tell you all about communism.'

'Yeah,' Slim said, astonished. He had reached the third chapter in the medical book and felt as if the scales of ignorance were falling from his eyes: everywhere there was novelty.

'But back to Kate Carr. You think she flirts,' D'Arcy said, privately amused.

'Don't tell her I said so,' Slim gasped in alarm. He wondered if D'Arcy made love to Mrs. Carr--as in Chapter Two. 'You see her a lot?'

'I'm seeing her tonight.' D'Arcy smiled at Slim's surprise. 'You can do me a favour by keeping an eye on her. I don't like my woman getting over friendly with other men, especially on the golf course.'

Slim nodded in agreement, although he didn't relish his new role.

'Did anything strange happen today?' D'Arcy asked.

'Strange?' Slim thought hard. 'Well, she and Jaimie Rabbinowitz hit their balls into the same woods.'

'You were with them, weren't you?' D'Arcy said angrily.

'Not at first. Johnnie O'Dreams wanted us to look for his ball on the other side.'

'Meanwhile Jaimie and Kate looked for their own. How long was it?'

'About ten minutes,' Slim said, fascinated.

D'Arcy gave a snort of relief, 'Nothing could have happened in ten minutes.'

Slim looked alarmed.

'No flirting, I mean,' D'Arcy said. 'Anyway, I know Rabbinowitz is too busy at the moment.'

'What's he doing?' Slim asked.

'Screwing my old girl,' D'Arcy said.

Slim sat back. He was shocked. 'Are you sure?'

'Oh, I know her,' D'Arcy smiled. 'Don't you worry.'

Slim ate slowly. He marvelled how D'Arcy could have known and boldly revealed the private affairs of others without the slightest sense of embarrassment. He began to doubt D'Arcy's integrity: he suspected him of being a liar, a braggart who would do anything to impress; maybe D'Arcy was just making fun of him. 'You know a lot,' he said soberly.

D'Arcy was too busy watching Nick's back-slapping at the far end of the room to notice the change in Slim's manner. 'I'm skipping dessert.' He stood up. 'I'll see you around, Slim, eh?'

Slim mumbled with his mouth full. D'Arcy appeared sincere then. As Slim watched him go, he pictured Mrs. Carr swinging her behind and walking out the door with him. Maybe D'Arcy wasn't bragging.

The sun hovered just above the mountain peaks as D'Arcy quit the staff dining room and sauntered by the caddie's cabin. D'Arcy never entered that cabin just as no caddie trespassed in the hops' cabin. Each group of employees had its private sanctuary regardless of status. Someone was playing the refrain to 'How High the Moon' on a sax. This was the lonely period of the evening, minutes before the brief twilight and the sudden fall of night. Thoughts of his uselessness to others and himself crept over him: fighting over quarters, toying with women, to be God-knew-what, maybe a salesman, since it was becoming one of the few jobs left to an Arts man, that is, if there were no technical sides to the product, and frittering away the moments of his life in casual conversation with souls as lost as himself. He looked at the mountains. The sun burnished the Pyramid and streamlined the snowy Edith Cavell. They seemed unapproachable in their majesty and yet akin to his spirit. He wanted to climb them; maybe he could make a sortie on his day off. He stopped short. Through the trees he saw Mama Bear with two baby bears. They were taking the path to the dump for a bedtime snack.

He walked along the road and cut across the lawn before he came to the garage. Toots Ainsworth was strolling towards him. D'Arcy was startled. As band leader, Toots seemed to appear only on the bandstand. The rest of his life was invisible.

'Hello,' Toots grinned sedately. His shoulders back, his expression serene, Toots was an impresario with a baton. He had conducted in hotels all his life with an even-paced rhythm that never offended. He wasn't meant to be popular, a "rave"; he was just meant to be there.

'No dinner concert tonight?' D'Arcy asked for something to say.

'Give us a break,' Toots chided him. 'We've finished that.'

'Hey Toots,' D'Arcy called after him. 'Play me that bungalow song as a favour tomorrow night?'

'We'll see,' Toots said without turning round.

The telephone was ringing. D'Arcy could see along the corridor. A hop was answering the call. D'Arcy speeded up on intuition. He heard his name called and loped into the cabin to the telephone.

'D'Arcy darling,' Kate said. 'What are we going to do tonight?'

'You should know by now,' he said dryly.

She laughed. 'No, but I mean seriously, darling.'

'I don't know.' Outside of sex and partying there was nothing to do. 'Have an ice cream soda in town,' he suggested.

'Don't be silly. I have an idea.' She paused. 'Jaimie Rabbinowitz asked us to his cabin for a drink tonight.'

'Asked you, you mean,' D'Arcy said. 'He hardly knows me.'

'Well, I am asking you,' she said sweetly. 'Want to go?'

'With his family and so on?' D'Arcy asked apprehensively.

'I suppose so.'

'They might recognize me.' D'Arcy quailed. 'I'd be embarrassing for you.'

'Not in the least, ' she laughed. 'This isn't a faculty tea, darling.'

He smacked his lips at the moot point. 'Okay.'

'Good. I'll honk at nine.' She sounded very happy. 'Bye, darling.'

D'Arcy hung up and turned round to face Nick.

'Lover boy's at it again,' Nick mocked. 'What's it tonight?'

D'Arcy curbed the impulse to ignore him. 'Rabbinowitzes have asked me round,' he said.

Nick's eyes flew open. 'You're full of it.' He followed D'Arcy into his room. 'I roomed them and they almost stiffed me--only two bucks for fifteen bags.'

'That's for jumping in out of turn,' D'Arcy yawned. 'If I remember rightly, I was supposed to room them.' And he added, 'Though I'm glad I didn't.' He stretched out on his bed.

Nick scratched his nose and chuckled. 'It's great to be in with a rich doll, D'Arce. What are you going to do when her hubby comes back?' He wore a satisfied smile.

'I'll leave that up to him,' D'Arcy said turning on his side. 'Will you get me a glass of water.'

Because Nick was interested in this particular point, he took a glass from the sink and spun on the tap. 'I suppose you know Runners likes Kate Carr.'

'Does he?' D'Arcy said.

'Better be careful, eh?' Nick handed him the glass. 'The manager on one side and the hubby on the other. Things don't look too promising, I'd say.' He giggled.

D'Arcy drank and handed back the glass.

'Have it all,' Nick insisted, throwing the rest at him and sprinkling his pillow.

'You fool!' D'Arcy shouted. 'Beat it.'

This time Nick noticed the grim look in D'Arcy's eye. He danced a little jig to the door and stuck out his rear before stepping into the corridor. 'Sweet dreams, D'Arce,' he called.

D'Arcy closed his eyes. He wanted to catch up on the sleep he had been missing lately.

6

Jaimie Rabbinowitz had hired a room-service boy as bartender. He rubbed his hands and darted about the room arranging chairs and straightening plates of hors d'oeuvres while telling the boy what labels to have on show. His mother and father watched him with amusement.

'Tell me, Jaimie,' said his mother, a young beauty, 'you haven't asked any staff tonight, have you?' She was whimsically referring to Jane.

'Yes, mother,' said Jaimie subtly preparing to turn the joke upon his mother, 'I've asked Johnnie O'Dreams.'

Mother and father sat up startled.

'You didn't!' said mother.

'Of course, he didn't, ' Horace Rabbinowitz demurred. 'O'Dreams sings with the orchestra every night.' He smiled at his wife's gullibility.

'He's taking an hour off to drop by,' Jaimie affirmed.

'Good God!' barked Horace, his handsome face rigid with scorn. 'With the Van Wallaces, the Vaughn-Smiths...'

'And the Prime Minister,' Jaimie chimed in.

The room service boy sniggered. Horace winced, the unfavourableness of his position looming before him.

'It's not that we object to staff who come from good families for the most part,' said Mrs. Rabbinowitz, swelling her bosom in matronly protest. 'It's just that O'Dreams is so obviously déclassé.'

'Oh mother,' Jaimie said irritatedly. 'I golfed with Kate Carr this morning and Johnnie was with us. I couldn't very well leave him out of the invitation. Besides, I like the man.'

Horace lifted his shoulders and threw out one hand. 'We'll make it work.'

'Here come the Nixbys,' Mrs. Rabbinowitz warned, quickly getting to her feet and taking a twirl to loosen out any folds.

Jaimie, looking natty in a blue Italian suit, welcomed the jolly Nixbys. His mother and father chatted with them while he fetched drinks. The Vaughn-Smiths joined the party. Others arrived. Five couples and some single girls were either standing in groups or sitting on the wicker furniture of the sitting room when Kate and D'Arcy entered.

'Kate!' Jaimie glistened. 'I am glad you came, really so awfully glad.' He guided her into the room, D'Arcy trailing. 'Mother. Kate's here.'

'Hello Sarah,' Kate beamed.

Jaimie stepped away to talk to people, but as he did he looked at D'Arcy and held out his hand. 'Nice to see you.' They shook hands and Jaimie disappeared behind a couple.

D'Arcy liked the welcome. He heard Kate say his name and turned to grasp Mrs. Rabbinowitz's hand. The peculiar attraction from the first time he caddied for her three years ago, acted upon him again. She suffered in the same way.

'I know you,' she flickered a smile.

'How are you this year?' D'Arcy was measuring her physical change.

She felt his eyes and squirmed slightly.

'Oh, so you know D'Arcy,' Kate said.

'He helps us out sometimes,' Mrs. Rabbinowitz smiled genially.

'He's quite the handy man,' Kate agreed, sensing their attraction. 'I think I'll introduce him to some of the others.' She took his hand.

D'Arcy smiled cavalierly and ran into a cold stare from Horace who raised his brows questioningly. Kate introduced D'Arcy to the Van Wallaces, a young couple who laughed easily.

D'Arcy was enjoying himself. Then Jane arrived. She moved about as if she were the hostess--gay and vivacious. 'D'Arcy, I didn't know you'd be here but isn't it nice?' He suddenly had nothing to say. His party talk seemed ridiculously inane--about animals in Bampers Park, as if he knew anything on the subject. Jane made him self-conscious, perhaps because she was so confident and rather lovely. D'Arcy edged over to Kate, but she was in the mood to expand, glass in hand. The lively atmosphere began to close in about him, transforming him into an observer.

Johnnie O'Dreams came in. He bowed here and there. He said a vulgar word inadvertently to the Vaughn-Smiths, interrupted Mr. Nixby, and made the Rabbinowitzes nervous. He found himself standing alone. D'Arcy joined him.

'Hi!' Johnnie cried.

'They've got the best Scotch back there,' D'Arcy winked. He found Johnnie was as eager to escape. He led the way to the kitchen.

As if by order there were two bottles of Scotch on the table. Johnnie opened one. 'How's Kate kid treating you?'

'Okay,' D'Arcy said.

Johnnie's eyes sparkled. 'She's damned good and don't I know it, ha-ha.'

'Lay off that,' D'Arcy said.

'This?' Johnnie held up the bottle.

'Kate and your memories and all that stuff.'

'Sure, D'Arcy kid.' Johnnie succeeded in unscrewing the top. 'Give me your glass. There's a snuff for you. Kills the pain.'

'Jeez!' D'Arcy said, eyeing the full measure that Johnnie poured, 'they must really give you a pain.'

'They do. Hotel life, D'Arcy kid. You gotta live it down, drink with it.'

'Money, money, money, money,' D'Arcy said bitterly.

'It's not that, it's what comes with it--all the guff,' Johnnie said. 'That bastard Runners eats my ass.' He looked viciously back at the party. 'He wouldn't have let me come tonight if he'd known.'

D'Arcy laughed. 'Me neither.'

'Ah, he's just an accountant clerk with a big title,' Johnnie said. 'You see, I gotta live under these guys all my life.' He took a long swig. 'I sing for my bread and butter and there's no way out. I'll never get any better. I'll just get laryngitis and die in a poor house, if they've got one for band singers,' he grinned.

'Trapped!' D'Arcy cried dramatically. 'We just have to have time to think. I'm climbing the mountains next week. Coming?'

'Never, D'Arcy kid, never.' Johnnie rocked on his heels and shook his head wildly.

Kate burst into the kitchen. 'Here you are, darling!'

'Darlings!' Johnnie enunciated settling his arm about her shoulders and laughing happily at the ceiling.

'I bet you were drinking before you came here,' Kate challenged him. 'Weren't you?'

'Yes, yes,' Johnnie admitted highly amused.

'We were discussing mountaineering next week,' D'Arcy said. 'Coming?'

'You're high enough as it is,' Kate punned.

Johnnie fell on one knee in laughter.

Jaimie strode casually in. He made a wry face. 'Rather noisy, people. Can't we return to the sitting room, if you don't mind.'

'Kiddo! Jaimie boy! we're coming back to meet your friends.' Johnnie stood up and swayed. 'I don't think I said hello to everyone.'

Jaimie opened the back door. 'Glad you were able to come, John.'

The cold dismissal sobered Johnnie somewhat. He half-smiled and shook hands with Jaimie. 'Swell time, really thought it was great,' and stepped into the night.

'I'm going this way too,' D'Arcy said.

'You don't have to,' Jaimie wanted to dissuade him.

'Meet me at the side of the hotel in a few minutes, Kate,' D'Arcy brushed by Jaimie and glared at him. 'All staff use the back door, don't you know?'

Jaimie frowned, hurt. He shut the door and, seeing Kate's look of sympathy, nodded for her to precede him into the sitting room.

Kate had been searching for some way to make a breach with D'Arcy. She wanted to be in the mood to receive Mac Carr. Her mind had to be free of thoughts of D'Arcy, her body free of his caresses. Maybe, she thought, his rude behaviour to his host could act as a starting point.

'Leaving so soon?' Mrs. Rabbinowitz asked, disappointed. 'Where's your young escort?'

'He went that a' way,' Kate thumbed.

'D'Arcy's left, has he?' Jane said, overhearing them. 'Oh dear, I wanted to talk to him.'

Kate resented the prerogative of Jane's tone. 'Well, he's not leaving the lodge. Perhaps you can stop him someday when he's paging through the dining room.'

Jane fixed her with a stare of puzzled amusement. Blushing, Kate stepped away, alarmed that she was provoked to make the remark which disclosed her feelings more frankly than she was willing to admit.

'You leaving also?' Horace took her wrist. 'And how is Mac?'

'He's very well.' She looked down guiltily.

'Uh huh,' Horace said. 'You keep him like that.'

'I'm trying to.' She pulled away. She felt Horace's eyes watching her go.

Keep Mac well? Since age sixteen she had been keeping Mac satisfied, but only his work could keep him well. Mac was a tycoon who was in love with stocks and bonds. Kate gave him two children, both packed off to summer camp. Mac was fond of his family and expected Kate to be around when he wanted her, but other than this animal proprietorship Mac showed no interest.

Kate cut to the back lane. Johnnie sat under a lamppost with his head ducked between his legs. D'Arcy was watering the back of his neck with a lawn hose.

'Okay, okay,' Johnnie was saying, 'now pat my face a bit.'

D'Arcy slapped him with the back of his hand.

Alarmed, Kate ran to them. 'Did he blackout?' she cried.

'Christ no!" Johnnie said. 'I'm not a deadbeat.'

'He just got a little wavy on his feet,' D'Arcy explained.

'You could say I was seasick,' Johnnie added.

Kate laughed.

'Kate, this isn't a joke. If Runners saw me, I'd be through.' Johnnie looked up, his hair plastered over his face. 'I should be in there singing.'

'Do you think you can walk now?' D'Arcy asked, throwing away the hose.

'Help me up, children.' Johnnie reached out his arms and Kate and D'Arcy lent him support until he was on his feet. 'By Jesus! is my collar wet! I'll have to change. I can't sing like this.'

'Be thankful it's dark,' Kate giggled. 'Don't get under the lampposts and no one will recognize you.'

They were approaching the lodge. A short figure dashed out of Room Service. It was Mort.

'Hey,' he waved them back furiously. They retreated by a cabin wall where he joined them. 'Runners has been looking all over for you,' he said to Johnnie threateningly. 'We told him you went to lie down for a few minutes.'

'What's that idiot got to do mixing in our band?' Johnnie demanded.

'He was just behind me a minute ago,' Mort whispered. 'He's got a nose like a bloodhound.'

Kate bent double giggling. 'Oh Mort, that's so funny and so true.'

They caught their breaths. The screen door on Room Service slammed. Runners was standing under the porch light. He posed in a dark summer suit, one hand in his suit coat pocket, the other laid against his nose. He seemed to be thinking or guessing. He took a few steps toward them. They pressed against the log wall. Runners returned to his post and resumed his stance.

Kate thought of decoying him away but was afraid his attention would be directed to the others if she moved. If D'Arcy were seen, he would be reprimanded, perhaps fired for being among guest cabins when off duty. Runners slowly walked to the front of the hotel, his nose up as if scenting the air.

Mort crept after him. The others crept after Mort. When Mort signalled that the way was clear, Johnnie led the other two in a sprint to Room Service.

'This is ridiculous,' he puffed, 'for a grown man to have to hide.'

At a mirror in the kitchen, he stopped to comb his hair.

Mort rushed in. 'Hurry up. He might come back any minute.'

'But my collar, my back is soaking, for Christ's sake!' Johnnie protested.

'Get up with the band and you'll be all right. We'll cover for you, but by God you look a mess.'

They went through the hallway and into the snack bar by a back door. Ten yards from the bar was the bandstand. Johnnie strode up to the microphone on the first bars of a song. Toots closed his eyes and then looked to the ceiling in thankfulness.

'I wasn't pushed, I didn't slip, I fell,' Johnnie sang in mushy baritone. 'Oh yes! Right into the middle of a warm caress.'

Kate and D'Arcy watched from the snack bar. They sniggered when Johnnie clutched the microphone to keep his balance. His eyes heavy-lidded, Johnnie appeared more lascivious than usual. Otherwise, he reacted by routine, he sang by rote.

'Isn't there something about that song?' Kate asked, wide-eyed in humour.

'I fell,' Johnnie sang. 'You bet! And if she hadn't caught me in her arms, I'd be falling yet!'

D'Arcy and Kate roared. Runners appeared in the entrance to the lobby. He looked on grimly. D'Arcy pointed him out to Kate.

'If he comes this way, I'm trapped,' he said.

'I'll save you, darling,' Kate smiled sweetly, 'like Pocahantas with John Smith.'

Runners turned abruptly and walked away. Flowers stepped from the shadows to accompany him. They disappeared.

'Let's beat it,' D'Arcy said.

They walked swiftly into the lobby and onto the patio, D'Arcy waving to the hops on the other shift, and up the hill behind the bushes by the tennis courts. D'Arcy took Kate in his arms and kissed her. When he released her, she put her head down thoughtfully

'What's the matter?' he frowned.

'My husband will be coming, darling.'

'So what?'

'You don't seem to understand my position or perhaps you don't care. Perhaps you're not able to consider others, as for instance your rudeness to Jaimie tonight.'

D'Arcy stared at her. 'Okay, Kate, if that's how you want it.' He walked away.

Kate felt a catch in her heart. 'D'Arcy.' He didn't stop. 'D'Arcy, wait.' She ran after him and caught onto his arm. He stopped and looked down in annoyance. 'I don't understand you,' she said. 'I don't want anyone but you.'

He smirked. 'Okay then. Let's go to your cabin. I'm dog-tired.'

7

On the fourteenth tee Kate decided to quit. 'It's useless. I've been hitting all over the fairway. You girls go on without me.'

'Kate dear, you're being foolish.'

'My score must be over a hundred.' She glanced at Slim who held the card. 'Besides, I'm spoiling your fun.' She swung her driver and plopped the head on the turf in a gesture of striking out for the wilderness. 'We'll make it another time, dears.' In spite of protests she took the path through the woods, her golf skirt swinging with an energetic rhythm expressing her vexation.

Slim followed in her wake. Her frustration had carried over into him. He hiked her golf bag onto his back and grimaced at the roots and scrubs.

Kate stopped abruptly so that he almost bumped into her. 'Did I bring my three wood today?'

'Yes, Mrs. Carr.' He took off the mitten and gave the three wood to her in exchange for the driver.

She liked to swing the light three wood. It weighed like a sword to do battle with her troubles.

'I'm not in top form, Slim,' she said. 'I'm lousy.'

'You might have pulled up your socks if you'd gone on,' Slim said.

She looked back curiously. 'I believe you're disappointed.'

He ducked his head and she smiled.

'Perhaps I'm not supposed to notice these things,' she said coquettishly.

Slim blushed. 'I was just thinking of the others having to play on alone,' he lied.

Kate sobered. 'They'll do all right.'

The sun sparkled off the leaves and smattered the ground in open spots. The pine scent of fine, pure air infused every living thing with a crisp spirit. Small birds winged swiftly through light and shade into thickets of saplings.

'We won't golf for a few days,' Kate said. 'I think I'm getting stale.'

'Okay, Mrs. Carr.'

'Do you think I'm stale?'

Slim puckered his lips in doubt. 'Just an off-day maybe.'

They came onto the third fairway. Kate fell back beside Slim as they skirted the trees. She scanned his straight slim form.

'You won't replace me with another steady golfer, will you?' she asked. 'I'll pay you for the days I won't be playing.'

'You don't need to do that,' Slim said, surprised. 'I'll be ready when you are.'

Kate gave him a pleased smile.

They passed behind the third tee where Legourmand and Bruce Bannister were waiting for their men to tee off. Bruce Bannister watched them with interest as if wishing to catch

Slim's eye. Slim felt embarrassed walking with Kate in front of Bruce. He had just finished the chapter on five ways of copulating. Bruce's freckled face had poked over his shoulder periodically to inquire how he was getting on, glee breaking into his features when he saw Slim's shy look.

'Had enough, Mrs. Carr?' one of the golfers hailed her.

'Plenty, thank you,' Kate smiled, her eyes glistening, happy to have attracted the men's attention. She handed Slim the three wood.

They took the lane to the clubhouse. Caddies slouched in the sun on the steps of the caddie house.

'What do caddies do when they're not working?' Kate asked as a lead into Slim's activities. 'Or shouldn't I ask?' she smiled winsomely.

'We don't do very much,' Slim said shyly. 'Most of us get a girl and a blanket and we build a little fire in the woods.'

Kate's eyes lit up. 'Oh,' she thrilled, 'that sounds like fun.'

'It's all right,' Slim said, slipping the bag into his hand as they neared the clubhouse.

'Is that all they do?' She rounded her eyes flirtatiously.

'Just about.' He didn't like to mention they drank beer.

Harry greeted them as they passed the fee master's box. He stuck his head out the window. 'Bett's been waiting for you.'

'Thanks, darling.' Kate started up the steps and abruptly turned to Slim with a five note. 'Just to keep you out of mischief until next time.'

'Thanks!' Slim gasped.

Kate ran ahead. Slim returned to the fees box to cash in his ticket.

'How ya doin', Slim?' Harry asked spilling out the pay in change. 'You making enough dough?'

'Sure.'

'I can get you a steady for the afternoon if you want,' Harry said benevolently.

Slim shook his head. He didn't want his whole day taken up. He wanted to loaf sometime. Dixie and Gregory hardly ever went to work. The fee masters had to rout them out of the cabin; there was even talk of fining lazy caddies.

With his pay in his pocket, Slim could hardly wait to store it in his bedroom. He liked seeing his money mount up. The privacy of his room in mid-day, the cabin empty, the sun hot on the roof causing a dry warmth in the furniture and mattresses, all these were accessory pleasures to the counting of his tips. He went to the back room to clean and shelve the clubs.

Kate rushed into Bett's arms.

'My dear, where have you been?' Bett cried. 'Three days!'

'I've been waiting for you to call.' Kate embraced her.

'But I did,' Bett pulled away regarding her accusingly, 'and you were never at home.'

'You just didn't call at the right time,' Kate said.

'Well,' Bett settled a hand on her hip and cocked one knee, 'just when is the right time, honey.'

Kate posed with a hand to the back of her head. 'Anytime you're in town,' she breathed.

They broke up in laughter and rested upon the furniture for support.

'Thank God no one else is in this room so we can have some fun!' Bett threw her arms to the ceiling.

'Let's order,' Kate said, calming down and going to the door. She looked up and down the verandah. 'Oh hello.' She signalled. 'Two whisky sours.' She turned to regard Bett with bright mischievous eyes.

'Quick, quick, quick,' Bett squealed rubbing her hands and running with Kate to perch on the sofa. 'Tell me about Mac. Is he staying in Edmonton? '

'In Vancouver till Monday,' Kate smiled.

'Ah ha,' Bett wagged her finger. 'I'll bet that's Julien's doing. What have you done about you know who?'

'I can't,' Kate sighed. 'I can't pull myself away.'

The boy entered speedily with two whisky sours. Bett regarded Kate with rebuke. The boy handed Kate a bill which she initialed. The boy retired.

'But you must,' Bett cried.

'I can't, I can't,' Kate put her hand to her head.

'How can you carry on faithfully with two men?' Bett said. 'I mean you can with five or ten, but never with two.' She jumped up and paced. 'You'll end up in the divorce courts.'

'Something's always worked out in the past,' Kate said. 'Of course, I've never known anything quite this strong.'

Bett giggled. 'No, never quite.'

Kate took a swallow of whisky sour. 'What about you?'

Bett looked coy.

'No more Harry?' Kate asked, surprised.

'We'll see about that,' Bett said. 'But for the moment it's not as much Harry.'

'I can't wait to meet him,' Kate thrilled.

'You will,' Bett said mysteriously, 'soon.'

Eddie looked in. His long strong jaw slid to the side. 'Uh huh! Want me to stay out?'

'Yes,' Bett said. 'Scram.'

Eddie reared back.

'Just girls' talk,' Kate said.

'Conspiracy,' Eddie mumbled and walked on.

'Well,' Bett arched her brows, 'to continue. He's coming for a few days next week, then flying to New York, and coming back late in the summer. Rather nice, isn't it?'

'Is he rich or is it on company money?' Kate marvelled.

'What's the diff?' Bett said. 'He's mine!'

They heard men's voices on the verandah. Bett peeked out the door.

'It's Tony Runners on a visit,' she whispered. 'My dear, he's actually sober.'

'He's quite a nice person when he's sober,' Kate said. 'But he never comes here.' Kate went to the door.

Runners stood regarding the railing upon which was a box of geraniums. Around him stood the club professional, his assistant Eddie, and the joking host of the golf house with his assistant. The joking host had just told a bad joke. The men were trying to laugh.

Runners snapped his head to the left and caught sight of the women. He dismissed the men with kind words. 'It looks fine.' He glided along the railing towards the women.

Kate and Bett were engaged in a discussion on dressmakers. They regarded the guests in deck chairs on the lawn and watched Runners from the corners of their eyes.

Runners cleared his throat and tweaked the knot in his tie. 'Hello.' He grinned like a fox.

'Well!' Bett hiccoughed. 'Tony Runners, what brings you here?'

He took a long step over to them. 'I heard two charming ladies were here so I came to see if I knew them. Luckily, I do.' He was speaking to Bett but his eyes were on Kate.

'Who are they?' Bett asked looking round.

Runners blinked and spoke directly to Kate. 'How are you? I haven't seen you this season.'

'I've been busy.' She looked full-eyed at him.

He touched her arm. 'Why don't we sit down?' He nodded into the room and the girls resumed their seats. 'Ah!' He observed the whisky sours. 'May I join you?' At the hint of a nod, he stepped smartly onto the verandah and snapped his fingers for the steward. He wiggled in his suit coat and pulled at his cufflinks.

'I'll leave you two alone,' Bett whispered licking up her drink.

'If you go,' Kate said between her teeth, 'I'll never speak to you again.'

Runners murmured in modulated undertones to the steward. He whirled about and glided into the room. Kate was holding onto Bett's wrist. Runners' eyes flickered over the scene. Glancing out the window, he took a chair near Kate.

'We'll have a record crowd this year it seems,' he said. 'The reservations are mounting up.'

'You must have a difficult time keeping count,' Kate said.

Runners smiled and buried a chuckle in his shirt front. 'That's Alick Sandhurst's job, not mine.'

'Who's he?' Bett asked.

'The accountant,' Kate said. 'No one ever sees him.'

'We keep him locked up with the books,' Runners grinned. 'But he happens to be out for a run with me today.'

'You dogs, you!' Bett slurred softly.

'I beg your pardon.' Runners, with an anticipatory smile, leaned forward, ear turned to catch Bett's words.

'Aren't we going to meet him? I mean, where the hell is he?' she said.

Runners pointed at the door. 'On the first tee.' He slid smoothly back into his chair.

'Waiting to be teed off, I suppose.' Bett went to the verandah as if to see the event.

The boy brought Runners a gin Collins.

'I was hoping I'd see you before this,' Runners regarded Kate appealingly.

'You've had so much to keep you busy,' she smiled, 'your wife and children.'

'Only thoughts of meeting you kept me busy,' he said seriously. 'You're the only one who counts, Kate.'

'Uh, uh,' she warned. 'Remember what I said last year? No mooning in public.'

He took her hand. 'It's you who decides.' He squeezed.

Kate clenched her teeth to keep from laughing. 'I know.' Oh Bett, please come back.

'I was thinking of giving a small party this weekend,' Runners said, testing for response.

Kate shook her head. 'I'll be awfully busy. Mac is coming.'

Runners frowned. He sat straight, pensive.

Bett strode in pulling Alick Sandhurst by the hand. 'I've found him!'

Alick, slightly stooped, bald on top, sandy at the sides, showed white and yellow teeth in a humble smile. Runners snapped out one leg and curved it over the other in a return to good spirits. 'Watch out, Alick, you're in dangerous hands.' He gulped his drink.

'At least they're not reeking with the blood of employees,' Bett retorted.

Runners faked a laugh.

'I'm afraid I do the executions,' Alick, chin down, smiled at Bett.

'How do you do that?' She reared back with hand on hip in a pose she knew attracted inhibited men as this Alick appeared to be--the shy little fool, she thought.

'I'm the one who runs the pen through their names,' he said.

'But that's on his orders,' Bett argued, pointing at Runners.

'But I commit the act, Mrs. Steel.'

'Alick's pen marks the end of the matter,' Runners said breezily. 'But no one is ever released from this lodge for capricious reasons.'

'Never,' Bett said, bitterly remembering staff friends who had experienced the wrath of Runners. 'There are rules to cover everything.'

Runners winced disapprovingly.

'There's a bit of work for me to do,' Alick said, edging to the door.

Runners leaped nimbly to his feet. He held his hand out to Kate. 'Will we see a lot of you this summer?'

'Oh, you will,' she laughed. 'I'm here for all of it.'

'Good,' he smiled, nodded at Bett. 'Enjoy your golf,' and flipped his hand out for Alick to proceed.

'Alick dear,' Bett called, 'take it easy on my bills, hmm, darling?'

Blushing, Alick backed onto the verandah. 'I'll do my very, very best, Mrs. Steel.'

Runners grinned and waved to Kate as he stepped out of sight.

'Is there anything more disgusting,' Bett said, 'than to see the manager and the accountant walking together? Why, it's like sending out the morality squad.'

'Tony's mind is on immorality,' Kate snorted.

'Exactly what I meant,' Bett said.

Kate shivered. 'I wish he'd get religion and put his conscience at rest.'

Bett laughed, brushing back her dark brown hair. 'Do you really wish that? Come on, Kate dear.' She eyed Kate mischievously. 'We all have to have our victims, don't we?'

'Don't say victims,' Kate said worriedly. 'I think of Mac coming on Monday.'

'Look! Let's clear out for a zip in the hills. Come on.' Bett led the way across the verandah to her sports car behind the clubhouse.

Kate caught sight of Slim through the back window. He was diligently cleaning her irons.

'There's my caddie,' she pointed.

Bett took a long sharp look. 'I can remember him without any difficulty.'

They sat in Bett's car and roared away to wherever the road might lead them.

The wind tore at Kate's hair. She opened her mouth to let it sweep through her insides and in her head. It was the image of D'Arcy's love-making which she hoped would be blown away. She filled her nostrils until her lungs ached.

They swung down long bends across the bridge spanning a green river and into an upgrade. On this side of the valley and towering mightily into the sky, a mountain dominated the scene. Kate felt like a moving speck. She watched the sun sparkle upon the flinty rock of Pyramid. Titans might have built this gigantic piece of nature as a prototype of those minuscule versions in Egypt.

'D'Arcy wants me to climb it with him next week,' Kate shouted.

'That!' Bett gawked. 'He's crazy. You won't make it up the foothills.'

'I was wondering what to tell Mac.'

'Leave it to your obituary,' Bett cried.

Rounding a grove of firs they shot into Bampers Town. A mountie stood in his red coat and wide-brimmed hat in the tree-bare park in front of the post office. He was waiting for the train to come in. Bett slowed down.

'There's O'Dreams and his new girl,' Kate said, 'going into the drug store.'

Bett swooped to a stop. 'No one can be more distracting than those two love-birds. Did you know Johnnie was married twice?'

'No!'

'His second wife is somewhere in Quebec--still married to him of course.'

They entered the drug store. Johnnie immediately threw up his long arm in greeting. Deo looked dreamily at them. She had been loved before, but never in the mountains by a glamorous singer. Bett and Kate joined them.

'Were you girls trailing us?' Johnnie winked.

'I wanted to show Kate a sample of true romance,' Bett said. 'They don't write about it anymore--not the real thing.'

Johnnie guffawed, embarrassed. Deo looked pleased.

'What's the secret?' Kate smiled at her.

'You have to be friends before anything else,' Deo said.

'Yeah, you give her a friendly smack when you get mad,' Johnnie said.

They laughed and Bett ordered milkshakes.

'Haven't had one for years,' Bett said. 'See how healthy romance is? We're not even afraid of extra calories.'

'I am,' Johnnie barked. 'I'm watching it. Too much booze, I guess, eh? What do you say, Kate?'

Kate giggled. 'How's the back of your collar?'

'My collar is dry, kid, but my neck's still wet.'

Bett seized Kate's arm. 'Don't look now, my dear girl, but your *bête noire* just walked in.'

Kate peeped over her shoulder. Mac was buying a chocolate bar.

Johnnie saw him at the same moment. 'Mackie kid!"

Mac Carr in rumpled trousers, open shirt, unshaven, casually turned to see across the store. He put his hands up, the finger tips caressing the fringe of short dark hair that circled his head. 'Oh no!'

Other customers watched them in good humour.

'Oh no!' Mac roared. 'The first person I see in this haven, in this paradise, has to be you! You son of a gun! How are you?' He strode to Johnnie, his pugilistic face beaming, his arm straight out.

'Mac!' Kate cried frowning. 'What are you doing here?'

'I'm buying a chocolate bar,' he said, pumping Johnnie's hand.

'Don't you remember? I like chocolate.' He bent across Bett and kissed Kate hard on the mouth. On straightening up he placed a kiss on Bett's forehead. 'When you're mature,' he gave Bett his old line, 'I'll kiss you properly.'

'You were not expected until Monday,' Bett said accusingly.

Mac threw up his hands. 'Circumstances change.' He regarded Deo. 'Ah now, Johnnie, she's pretty!'

'What circumstances?' Kate asked still frowning. D'Arcy would be waiting for her tonight. And the weekend! Oh God, what about the weekend?

'Well,' Mac looked at the ceiling and settled his pudgy hands in his pockets, 'there's some trouble with bellhops.' He looked down at Kate. 'Runners wants me to look into it.'

Kate swallowed.

'Another strike?' Deo asked, her big blue eyes searching out Mac's attention.

'Third strike,' Bett said grimly. 'And he's out.'

Kate clenched her teeth, eyes flashing. 'I'm busy tonight,' she said. 'I'll see you tomorrow morning.'

'That's all right with me,' Mac twisted a smile. 'I just hope it's going to be all right with you.'

'Let's leave, Bett,' Kate said.

'Till tomorrow, darling.' Mac's eyes smarted.

As Kate walked away with Bett she heard Johnnie. 'You need a drink, Mackie kid, like us.'

'Promise to drive me home and I'm game,' Mac said, 'cause once I start, I'm not quitting till I'm stinking.'

'You didn't do that very well, darling,' Bett said when they were in the street.

'I know,' Kate admitted glumly.

She saw their station wagon parked behind Bett's car. She looked in the back. Mac had brought the blankets and cooking utensils she wanted.

'I bet he recognized your car and guessed we were in the store,' Kate said. 'Maybe he saw us go in.'

'Does he really eat chocolate?' Bett asked.

'I've never known him to.'

They giggled. They got into Bett's car.

'He's sweet,' Kate said. 'I'll make it up tonight. I'll only see D'Arcy for half an hour.'

Bett put her tongue in her cheek and pressed the starter.

8

When D'Arcy left work at ten past six he met Kate by the tennis courts.

'Hello lover,' he said. 'You're early.'

'Guess what,' she said grimly.

He smiled. 'Your husband's back.'

'How did you know?'

'He's on the arrival list. We've been waiting for him to show up.'

'Well then, you know. I can't stay with you tonight.'

'Why did you come to see me?' He put his arm about her.

She rested her head on his shoulder and sighed tiredly.

'Take me to your cabin for dinner,' he suggested.

She stepped away in alarm. 'What if Mac comes?'

'Keep the door locked.'

'Darling, I can't do that. Anyway, he would break it down.'

'Leave it unlocked then,' he shrugged. 'I just thought it would be a good way to introduce me into the family.'

She laughed. 'I suppose it would be sort of fun.'

'Where'd you leave him?' D'Arcy asked.

'With Johnnie O'Dreams.'

'He'll be home drunk in that case.'

'Why, that's just what he said he was going to do. D'Arcy, you're awfully clever.'

'We've got that party anyway,' D'Arcy said. 'We'll be gone from your cabin by the time he gets there.' He looked at her.

'All right,' she smiled.

'Wait for me while I change.' He jumped the stoop to the threshold of the hops' cabin and disappeared into the corridor.

Kate looked at the thick criss-cross of the tennis fence. Such was her life, she thought--a repetition of tangles. The dark red guest courts lay smooth and vacant as usual. Eddie's girl, Maureen, was playing on a staff court against a man. She covered the court well and stroked long and hard. She seemed to be beating him. Maureen saw her and waved.

'Will we be seeing you tonight?' Kate called.

'You bet!' Maureen smiled. Demure and pretty, she displayed a calm determination in her movements. Good sort, Kate thought. Wish she would play golf.

D'Arcy leaped off the stoop and threw his arm about her. 'Let's go. I'm hungry.'

They walked along the back row of guest cabins. Bruce Bannister broke from the sitting room of a cabin. D'Arcy recognized him as a caddie.

'Hey you!' he cried.

Bruce halted in the middle of the lawn. He seemed undecided to flee or approach.

'Come here,' D'Arcy ordered.

'What is it?' Kate whispered.

'This guy thinks I'm a guest,' he said.

Bruce gawkily lumbered towards them in fear. 'Yes, sir.' He stopped three feet away.

'Come right up here,' D'Arcy demanded.

Timidly, Bruce stepped forward, towering a half-head over him.

D'Arcy clutched Bruce's windbreaker and jerked it outwards. Sheaves of note paper marked with the hotel insignia slid from Bruce's waist on to the lawn.

'Got the envelopes in your pocket have you?' D'Arcy asked severely.

'Yes sir,' Bruce admitted, his face and neck a violent red.

'Pick them up,' D'Arcy ordered.

Bruce fell on his knees and snatched at the paper beginning to roll away in the breeze. Kate turned away and clamped both hands to her mouth to muffle her laughter.

'Now see here,' D'Arcy said considerately. 'You don't need to steal. If you want note paper, come to me.'

'Thank you sir,' Bruce said with surprise. He stood with the paper clutched to his chest.

'Stuff that away,' D'Arcy warned, 'or a patrolman will catch you. Now run.'

Bruce ran, his long legs driving at the ground, and sliced through bushes behind the cabins.

Kate burst out laughing. 'The poor boy! D'Arcy, why did you do it?'

D'Arcy smirked. 'I used to steal guest note paper. I wanted to know what it was like to get caught.'

'That boy will never do it again,' Kate said.

D'Arcy shrugged. 'Caddies do it. I don't know why. They don't write that many letters.'

They went into the cabin. The Carrs rented the left side. D'Arcy resented the richness of the furniture. So rustic on the outside, so sumptuous on the inside. The whole set-up was a fake, he thought: people pretending to live like pioneers yet softening the life with a millionaire's comforts .

'I've got some pork chops,' Kate said switching on the stove.

'Give me some chops and we'll have pork later,' D'Arcy grinned.

'You!' Kate giggled.

He watched Kate from the doorway. Her hips and legs made him hungrier than the thought of food. With a pained expression he turned back to the living room, sank with a Calgary newspaper into a great easy chair and read by the light of the waning sun. A cowboy was being bucked by a bronco on the front page reminding him of the horse as a sex symbol. The cowboy reminded him rather strongly of Kate. What the hell am I in Arts for? he thought. He smelt the pork chops. He read on.

'Okay,' Kate said after half an hour.

She had fixed a full meal with tossed salad and lemonade. They ate in the kitchen.

'What I like about you,' D'Arcy said, 'is that with all your dough you're not spoilt.'

'I didn't always have it,' Kate smiled. 'When Mac married me I was sixteen from a poor family. For the first three years Mac didn't earn much. He was a garage mechanic. He had a little land. That was all. Then we hit oil.'

'And lived happily ever after,' D'Arcy said.

'We just began to live,' Kate said. 'If it hadn't happened, I would have had a pretty dead existence, and I wouldn't have known it.'

'You would have known it,' D'Arcy said. 'This is the twentieth century.'

'Maybe,' she admitted, 'but at sixteen I was too dumb to learn from books.'

'The hell!' D'Arcy said. 'Most people get their views from the funny papers.'

'You're so sarcastic, D'Arcy.' Kate poured them lemonade.

'Satiric is the word,' he said with his mouth full. 'Anyway, who says you don't look sixteen now.'

'I do.'

'Well, you're not as dumb as you might be,' he conceded. 'Luxury stops most people from thinking. That's what I like about you, besides other things: you can think.'

'Thank you. That's very nice of you.'

'You can make love pretty good.'

'Go on,' she smiled. 'I'm listening.'

'You can cook and I guess you can make a man happy.' He concentrated on finishing the first course.

Kate looked sadly out the window. 'I can't make a man happy,' she said. 'I can only satisfy him.'

'You make me happy,' D'Arcy said.

'Oh, tell the truth.' She frowned with impatience. 'Real happiness comes from within. I knew it for the last time before we struck oil.'

D'Arcy laughed. 'You're giving me the old story of riches bringing unhappiness.'

'No.' Kate pursed her lips. 'I said I started to live when we got rich. It's living that makes you unhappy.'

D'Arcy put down his fork. He looked deeply into Kate's eyes. 'I think I know what you mean. Excess--having too much materially is the same as having too little spiritually. But it doesn't have to be like that. There's a way out for all of us. We just have to find it, and I don't mean through the pursuit of the American ideal.'

'Oh D'Arcy, I love to hear you talk like that. Will you help me?'

'Will you climb Pyramid on Wednesday?'

Her face fell. 'What will I tell Mac?'

'That you're going up to find what's at the top.' He regarded her steadfastly.

She grinned. 'All right.'

He stood up.

'Wait,' she said. 'There's ice cream.'

'Save it,' he said seizing and kissing her. He took her into the bedroom and they made love.

D'Arcy awoke with Kate's body beside him. He fingered the nipples and ran his hand along the side and up the back. She opened her eyes.

'It's ten,' he said. 'I wonder if your husband came home.'

'Heavens!' She sat up.

D'Arcy seized her by the waist and brought her over top of him. 'It's okay,' he said. 'I'm hidden now.'

'Darling, let me go,' Kate whispered. She struggled and broke free. She tip-toed to the hall and peeked into the living room. 'He's not home yet.'

'Bring me a beer,' D'Arcy called. 'Then we'll go to the party.'

He heard the refrigerator door close, then Kate's bare feet.

Her beautiful form moved towards the bed. She held a bottle of beer with both hands in front of her.

'You look like that ad for sparkling water,' he said, taking the bottle. 'You know, the girl with the flea wings.'

'D'Arcy, we should get dressed,' she said worriedly. 'I don't know what has happened to Mac.'

D'Arcy laughed. 'It's simple. If he's with O'Dreams, he's drunk. O'Dreams had to sing, so he left him in the beer parlor with someone until he can go back and pick him up.'

'That means he's with Deodora,' she said sharply.

'What's wrong with her?--a healthy young creature.'

'I don't trust her name,' she said.

'That's about all you women go by--outward signs.' D'Arcy guzzled half the bottle and burped.

Kate was getting dressed for the party. She took out a red dress that swept low in the back.

'D'Arcy drank as he watched her. 'Jeez! That's what I like about you: no brassieres.'

'Aren't you getting dressed?' she said crossly.

He stood up. 'You're supposed to be happy after making love.' He put his arms about her from behind. 'But you're bitchy.' He kissed her neck.

'I'm sorry.' She faced him and pushed her forehead against his chin. 'But let's hurry. I want you out of here before Mac comes.'

D'Arcy shrugged. 'Okay.' Kate had her special circle of life, he thought; he was merely clipping it at a tangent.

He dressed and waited while she made up her face. He inhaled the sweet scents of the boudoir. They conjured up a fascination with the present, an hedonic impulse. He lit a cigarette and looked from the dark living room at the lamp-lit night. Raffles, the gentleman thief, pearl necklaces and the long slim arms of beautiful women. Kate stood beside him.

'I'm sorry if I sounded abrupt, darling,' she said. 'I'm treating Mac badly; although it's his fault because he didn't tell me when he was coming.'

'Sure,' D'Arcy said. They walked outside.

'I suppose I should have made the bed,' she said, 'but I don't care.'

'Why should you?' D'Arcy said. They walked quickly along the lane.

'I often wonder what would happen if Runners saw us leaving the cabin together,' she said. 'I think he told Mac about us, but I don't know what.'

D'Arcy felt a thrill of fear.

'Mac came back early for that reason.' She shook her head. 'The poor sap! You see, D'Arcy, Mac and I love each other very, very much.'

'I know you do.'

She turned on him in delighted surprise. 'How?'

'I've seen you the other summers. I could tell.'

'Oh God! It's wonderful to have someone who understands.' She reached for his hand and clasped it as they walked.

'I don't understand,' D'Arcy smiled. 'If I did, I'd have the secret of the universe.'

'But there's such a thing as intuition,' Kate argued.

D'Arcy nodded. 'The characteristic of art. But that's as undefinable as life itself.'

She puzzled. She found D'Arcy's words vaguely disturbing. She dropped his hand. 'Let's keep in the shadows.'

Music in sharp, hoppy beats skipped out from the ballroom at the back of the lodge. The patio's yellow lanterns shone on the flagstones. Guests in evening clothes moved behind the screen door. Kate and D'Arcy quickly passed by and turned with the road away beside darkened cabins to the garage. Singing and horn playing interrupted by laughter carried down from the lighted windows upstairs.

On climbing the stairs, they met Mort descending. He greeted them with a big smile. 'Surprise, Mrs. Carr!' He glanced at D'Arcy. 'Your husband's here.'

Kate backed down a step. 'Of all the places,' she cried.

'I'm getting us some goods. Excuse me.' Mort ran out the door.

'Come on darling,' Kate said. 'I'm ready to surprise him.'

D'Arcy grimaced. 'I'm not but let's go.'

They climbed to the landing and entered the hallway. A large room with wicker chairs and high round tables opened before them. The orchestra boys with their wives or town girls stood in groups chatting, drinking, some were dancing to the music from a record player. Mac Carr was leaning against the wall. He balanced a tall whisky in one hand at chin level as he listened to Eddie discuss a minute point in the approach to the sixteenth green. As he didn't appear to see them enter, Kate went directly to him. D'Arcy fetched the drinks.

Kate grabbed one of Eddie's gesticulating hands and stilled him. She regarded Mac. 'Enjoying yourself?'

Mac grunted.

'You're stoned,' she said. She turned to Eddie. 'He was drinking beer all afternoon.'

'I had dinner, I had dinner,' Mac insisted. 'Besides, I had an imbitibal... inimitable companion.' He pointed at Deo who was sitting and listening rather absently to conversation.

'You've been mixing your drinks and you'll be awfully sick,' Kate said. 'You should go home.'

Mac flourished his hand in question. 'Do I have a home?'

'Don't be silly,' Kate blushed. She felt Eddie's eyes condemning her. 'You say terrible things when you're drunk.'

'Deo said I could have a home with her.' He smiled and patted his pate. 'So I'm not too old.'

'How old are you, Mac?' Eddie asked.

'I have yet to see my forty-sixth birthday,' Mac sucked in his underlip, 'and I'm as virile as a goddamn bull.'

D'Arcy, arriving with Kate's whisky, overheard him. He thought of the bull of Minos chasing Cretan maidens through the labyrinth. Kate took her drink.

'How's it going, D'Arce?' Eddie said moving away discreetly.

D'Arcy was unnerved face to face with Mac Carr. The man was drunk enough to lash out.

'Don't be afraid,' Mac said eyeing him. 'I know who you are and I don't give a goddamn.'

'If you have to be rude,' Kate flared, 'go home.'

Mac took a long drink. Kate laughing gaily took D'Arcy's arm and spun them away to a group. D'Arcy felt uncomfortable. The drunken Mac seemed his responsibility. Yet there seemed nothing that he could do for the sake of Kate and Mac Inc.

The rest of the band players joined the party. Secretaries and front desk clerks came with them. Toots moved about being amiable.

Johnnie came for Deo. She was tight and should have been taken home. But Johnnie wanted to enjoy himself.

'Our first chance to have a party,' he told Kate. 'There was no one in the ballroom so we left a skeleton band there. Runners didn't notice. He was tippling. His wifely frigidaire had to usher him out.'

Mac Carr sank into a chair. He was drowsy. He held Deo's hand. D'Arcy stood alone at the far end of the room and studied him. Like a man in a whirlpool, he thought, he's being dragged down and he's waiting to be coughed out of the centre, when he'll have to swim for his life. There's something tragic about him because I don't think he can save his life.

Kate and Maureen were talking. Eddie took Kate for a dance and Maureen stuck her tongue at him. Maureen wandered to a table for cheese-bits. D'Arcy turned to her.

'What's it like being a reservations clerk?' he asked. 'Whenever I pass the desk, I see you all alone and looking bothered.'

She laughed. 'The bother comes from behind the desk, not in front of it.'

'I don't get you.'

'You have to keep putting off hotel personnel,' she smiled. 'It's not fun.'

D'Arcy turned aside and laughed.

'I'm in the doghouse now,' Maureen added. 'If I make any slip, I'll be fired out of spite.'

'Some vindictive bastard, eh?' D'Arcy frowned.

'I suppose I shouldn't be at this party because girls aren't supposed to be in men's cabins, especially if it's after twelve. But Eddie said this was a special case, being a party and everything.'

'If we're quiet, Runners won't do anything,' D'Arcy said.

'I suppose I shouldn't worry,' Maureen frowned. 'But to be fired is a disgrace.'

D'Arcy laughed. 'Only to the wicked little hotelmen.'

A harsh shout came from the staircase. Archie appeared in the doorway.

'Turn off that there gramophone,' he cried fiercely and, striding to the machine, clicked it off.

Consternation rippled like sensory waves through the ladies.

'Go away, you bloody nuisance,' Johnnie called out. 'You weren't invited to this party.'

Runners stepped into the room. 'Who said that?' he cried sharply. He stood ramrod straight. His eyes darted at his victims. His mouth formed a hard line. 'I want to know who said that,' he shouted.

There was no answer. D'Arcy noticed that Mac Carr was watching Runners with an expression of incredulity.

Runners stepped stiffly forward. 'It's twelve-thirty; you boys know that parties disturb our guests.' He spoke cuttingly. 'You girls know you shouldn't be in men's cabins. You can't be trusted.'

The big black shape of Smiling Jack Flowers moved into the room. He was short of breath from running. Archie stood at the doorway to block escape.

'You!' Runners signalled out a pretty girl. 'What are you doing here?'

She wrinkled her nose at the stink of alcohol when he approached.

'Take her name,' Runners commanded.

'She's my wife,' one of the musicians said.

'Then she should be in town where she belongs,' he snapped. He moved onwards, his beetle eyes selecting victims. 'This girl, take her name, and this girl, take her name.' Flowers obediently went to them and scribbled down their names.

D'Arcy felt frozen in a state somewhere between fear and an impulse to slug Runners.

Runners came to Maureen. He noticed D'Arcy and twitched a smile. 'Take this girl's name.' He paused to enjoy the horror upon her face. He moved on, coming to Deo. 'And this girl.' His gaze fell along her arm to see that she was holding hands with Mac Carr. He blinked. Mac glared at him. 'Leave her,' Runners murmured. He spun round and caught sight of Kate. The disgust on her face seemed to wilt him. He stepped back, brushing against Flowers.

'You people whose names have been taken will be in my office tomorrow morning,' he snapped. 'Now break up this party. It's against hotel regulations.' He glided out the door, followed heavily by Flowers. Archie stayed for a moment. He stared disdainfully about until he noticed the anger mounting in the pairs of eyes confronting him. He fled.

A few men shouted that the party was not over and that they intended to dance and drink the night away. But the girls were badly shaken. Some were crying. Tears flowed from Maureen's eyes. Eddie tried to comfort her. 'He won't do anything. I'll do something. I'll put in a word. Don't worry,' he said smoothly.

The party-goers finished their drinks and left in groups. Some sang as they descended the stairs but the joy was gone. Johnnie took Deo with him. Mac insisted on walking without help. Kate quickly kissed D'Arcy and accompanied Mac down the stairs. D'Arcy stayed on awhile to hear the comments of the boys in the band.

'Tony has a bad inferiority complex,' Toots remarked. 'He has to fire those girls. His pride won't let him back out.'

'The drunken ass!' someone said.

9

D'Arcy worked the early shift in the morning. He passed Runners' office on errands several times and saw Maureen through the open door. She was sobbing. Runners kept her waiting long over an hour. D'Arcy's heart went out to her. He knew that no staff member could interfere. Maureen's fate was entirely in the hands of the big stick who ruled them all.

'It serves her right,' Nick said. 'If she'd give a bit of ass, she'd save herself a lot of trouble.'

O'Flaherty agreed. 'She's not our worry.'

'She hasn't any big shot to back her up,' D'Arcy said. 'That's why Runners isn't afraid to treat her like that.'

'You fellows are in big trouble.' Nelles, arms folded, came slowly round the desk to face the hops. 'A certain party is missing a suitcase.' He gave them a shark grin. 'From the sheet it appears that our lover-boy roomed them.' He narrowed his brows over D'Arcy.

D'Arcy remembered searching for four cases and finding only three. 'I thought they made a mistake in the number.'

'Why didn't you wait to find out?' O'Flaherty demanded.

'He wanted to be off with his woman,' Nick said, smirking.

'They didn't return to their rooms until late,' Nelles said, 'and didn't realize one bag was missing till this morning.'

D'Arcy shrugged. 'I thought they were mistaken.'

Nelles looked away at the verandah. The lobby was quiet, sedately empty. 'I've called on the other shift. They'll search every cabin this morning. You will resume the search this afternoon.'

The boys looked down.

'Don't bitch,' Nelles continued. 'This could cost somebody his job.' He walked away.

'And that somebody is old D'Arce,' Nick sniggered and gave D'Arcy an elbow.

D'Arcy shouldered him away.

'Cut it out,' O'Flaherty said. 'I'll fine you both.'

The thought of losing a quarter silenced them.

'I want to think about this,' D'Arcy said. 'Will you give me time off?'

'It's crawling,' O'Flaherty surveyed the lobby. 'I'll give you half an hour.'

'Think hard,' the last boy advised as D'Arcy went.

On the path to the Staff Hall, D'Arcy wondered if he had made the mistake. He pictured himself searching for the case several times. Surely he could not have done the old closet trick and forgotten it. The trick was used to squeeze tips out of stingy guests. If the guests were out when the hop arrived with the luggage, he hid one case in the hall closet. When the guests telephoned complaining about the missing bag, the hop retrieved and delivered it with the excuse that it had been lost but found through a combination of luck and hard work. It usually worked for fifty cents, sometimes a dollar, and they were obliged to tip for the other bags. But D'Arcy hadn't tried it since the cabin girls caught on and began locking the closets for fear they would be charged with stolen property. He might have hidden it, though, and had it swept from his mind. His relationship with Kate was worrying him in spite of his determination to be detached from any emotional complication. But surely the cabin girl would have found it.

Davey, the Staff Chef, was standing on the stoop at the side of the dining hall. He was dropping bits of food into the mouth of a tall black bear.

'I bet she eats better than we do,' D'Arcy called.

Davey beckoned to him. 'Go away, Charlie.' He made quick, womanish gestures as if to frighten the bear off. Charlie settled onto all fours, grunted disappointedly, and ambled away.

'I seen you driving a nice looking car the other night,' Davey said, his wry old face wrinkling to a smile. 'You ain't a millionaire, are ya?'

D'Arcy laughed. 'If I said I was, you'd poison my soup.'

The morning sun shone onto the flat brown ground dazzling their eyes.

Davey squinted. 'You fellas are all lookin' to be like them. You think you're going to do it, don't ya? I tell you just do your work and you'll be happy. Keep your mind off those rich things.'

'Is that what you do, Davey?' D'Arcy suggested.

'I love my work cause I like you kids. I wasn't going to come this year--rheumatism and I'm getting old. But when Mr. Runners sent me an SOS I came because I want to help you. I cook good. I been cooking here for twenty years. There's no reason at all why I should get complaints about the food I give ya.'

D'Arcy nodded sympathetically. 'It's not your fault, you old geezer.' So it all came down to self-justification, he thought.

Davey's voice grew shriller. D'Arcy cut him short. 'We're all in the same boat, Davey. Keep cooking.' He moved away.

'Remember what I said about them rich things,' Davey called. 'They lead you onto the paths of wickedness.'

'Where else is there to go?' D'Arcy laughed.

The Staff Hall was empty except for the girl behind the counter.

'One cone.' D'Arcy slid a nickel to her.

He thought of the women he had picked up here, all for a lie-down in the woods. Self-gratification. To justify and gratify: it all came down to that.

He took his cone and licked the ice cream. He wandered downhill on the path to the staff lake. The leaves brushed against his face. He ducked and looked through the trees. Girls were sunning themselves on the dock. A dark girl with tremendous proportions was preparing to dive. She flicked her long black braids over her shoulders. He remarked the lust in her black eyes and her handsome physique. Indian blood was in her and could be stirred up. But it would be frustrating to go on to the dock when he had to return to work right away. He walked the path to the road. A lodge bus rumbled into sight on its way to town.

Departing guests stared from the windows. He recognized the "daughter" he had roomed and meant to look up. She saw him and looked away. Opportunity missed. Frustrating. And no Kate over the weekend, maybe not for the next week, maybe never again. He threw the tip of his cone onto the pavement.

He tried to imagine possible places where the suitcase might be, but in vain. As he strode along the corridor back to the bellhops' desk, Flowers stepped from the manager's office and accompanied him.

'What happened to the suitcase, Morgan?'

'I can't figure it out, sir.'

'We think it's been stolen,' Flowers said grimly.

'Do you have any idea who did it?'

'You're the prime suspect.'

D'Arcy laughed. 'Why would I want a suitcase?'

Flowers leaned closer. 'There were two thousand dollars worth of gems in it.'

D'Arcy's heart knocked his ribs. The hotel atmosphere took on the personality of a mystery story. Flowers acted like a stock character, the detective, but only Raffles could solve the case. 'And you suspect me?'

Flowers raised his eyebrows and left him.

Nick was alone on the bench. When he saw D'Arcy coming, he went behind to sit on the captain's stool.

'You're lucky you weren't here,' Nick chuckled at the consternation on D'Arcy's face. 'The rest of the mob have been sent on the search, except for O'Flaherty. He's got a rooming.'

D'Arcy sank onto the bench.

Nick leaned over him speaking softly into his ear. 'You poor bastard. Can't you remember what you did with it?'

D'Arcy shook his head.

72

'Runners is going to eat you, D'Arce. The hotel will be blamed for it, and you'll get the ax,' Nick gloated.

'You're a great help,' D'Arcy said.

Nelles appeared. 'That party has left the lodge. If we don't find the case, the lodge has to pay.'

'For Christ's sake!' D'Arcy said, 'okay.'

Nick laughed outright.

'Runners is waiting to see you, Morgan,' Nelles said. He nodded at the corridor.

D'Arcy bit his lip and went down to Runners' office. He sat on the chair in which Maureen had been waiting. Runners came from the inner office. His secretary closed the corridor door and disappeared into the inner office. They were alone.

Runners put one black shiny shoe in front of the other, scrutinized the toe and looked at D'Arcy. 'Stand up!'

D'Arcy jumped to his feet.

Runners regarded him sternly. There was silence.

'Did you take these persons to their cabin?' Runners asked mildly.

D'Arcy nodded.

'You are going to put us in a spot,' Runners said.

'I'm sorry, sir.' D'Arcy sensed an atmosphere of reasonable good-fellowship jellying out of the sombre depths.

'You haven't been behaving yourself too well recently.' Runner's sharp glance intimated the garage party, Kate, and wrongs yet to be disclosed.

D'Arcy nodded bleakly.

'I have been looking through your background.' Runners paused and rubbed the tip of his nose. 'How did you come to know the Prime Minister?' he smiled.

D'Arcy squirmed. 'My father did political work for him.'

Runners rounded his mouth and made a quarter turn as if this connection were not nearly as close as he expected. He rubbed his hand over his chin. 'He speaks well of you. It would be sad to disappoint him, wouldn't it?'

'Yes, sir.' D'Arcy envisioned his family in disgrace.

'I hope you will change your ways,' Runners continued in the same kindly tone. 'This is my advice.'

'Thank you sir.'

'If the case is not found, you will have to accept the responsibility.'

'All right, sir.'

73

'But we must find it at all costs,' Runners frowned. 'And quickly.' He squirmed in his suit coat. 'You may go.' He turned away.

D'Arcy ducked from the office. Nelles was alone at the desk. He looked disgruntled.

'A rooming just drove in.'

D'Arcy saw a tall, broad-shouldered man signing the register at the Front Desk.

'Unfortunately I have to be on call.' Nelles glared and waved him to the Front Desk.

'How long will you be staying, Mr. Slade?' the clerk asked pleasantly.

'A few days.' The man turned his broad handsome face to D'Arcy. 'My car's just outside.'

D'Arcy followed him to a black Buick parked beside the patio.

'I'll have to carry your bags to your cabin, sir,' D'Arcy said. 'You're not allowed to drive.'

'Oh,' Mr. Slade shrugged and sat in his car. 'The lanes are paved, aren't they?'

'Yes, sir, but not for cars.'

They were right outside Runners' office windows.

'Get in the other side,' Mr. Slade said, 'and we'll put this away.'

D'Arcy sat in. 'Go to the right for the parking lot, sir.'

Mr. Slade drove straight ahead.

'You're going to the cabins, sir,' D'Arcy cried, hoping that Runners could not see them.

Mr. Slade gave him a lazy side grin. 'No one can say you didn't try. What number is it?'

D'Arcy put his hand over his face. 'Take it slow.'

A room service boy bicycling round a corner pulled onto the lawn to avoid a collision. His tray slipped from his hand. Breakfast clattered to the grass.

'A little excitement,' Mr. Slade said.

D'Arcy watched the cabins go by. He knew approximately where they were headed. 'It's on the next lane down and there's no cross lane. Don't drive over the grass.'

Mr. Slade braked to a stop and yawned. 'I'll save you from the horror of that.'

They got out and Mr. Slade opened the trunk. D'Arcy took out two light bags.

'I suppose there's a golf course around here someplace,' Mr. Slade said. He saw D'Arcy's indulgent smile. 'Then take those clubs over when you go back and put them under my name, will you? Jake Slade.'

D'Arcy led him across the lawn to the second lane and into his cabin.

'Don't go through any rigmarole,' Jake Slade said. 'I can open windows.' He handed D'Arcy a dollar and the keys to his car. 'Keep them until I want them.'

Any hop should have been elated at coming into possession of an automobile, especially when Jake Slade did not seem the type to check the mileage. D'Arcy, however, was burdened with worry.

'How do I get a hold of some aspirin?' Jake asked, sinking his athletic body onto the bed.

D'Arcy went to the bathroom cabinet.

'I flew from New York to Edmonton last night, then drove here,' Jake yawned.

D'Arcy handed him a box of aspirins.

'By the way,' Jake passed a hand over his tanned brow, 'do you know a Mrs. Bett Steel? She inhabits these regions, I believe.'

'Yes, I know her,' D'Arcy said, curious.

'How the hell do I find her?' Jake drawled.

'They've got telephones on her lake.'

'Ah yes. Use the communications system.' Jake closed his eyes, still holding the box of aspirins unopened.

D'Arcy left quietly. He had to drive the car around the end cabin and back. He had almost passed out of the area without being observed when Nick spotted him. Nick had a telegram in his hand, which would net him a quarter at the most. On seeing D'Arcy, his eyes popped open and his brush-cut seemed to bristle. D'Arcy looked straight ahead.

He left the car in the parking lot just as the noon whistle blasted from the laundry beside it. He lugged the golf clubs to the clubhouse. Kate was sitting with her husband and other guests on the club verandah. She didn't look at him when he passed. We're finished, he thought gloomily.

He returned to the lobby to report. The other shift was on duty. The boys looked downcast. Nelles paced in front of them.

'Had a nice trip?' Nelles asked, sarcasm ready to leap from his tongue.

75

'I had to....'

'Look, Morgan. Runners gave all the boys a dressing-down.' Nelles's mouth went back and down. 'You weren't here. And you are the only hop who has not had to search for that bag.'

'It's not my fault, Nelles,' D'Arcy said.

Nelles compressed his lips and twisted his mouth. His eyes were angry slits. He could have been a shark coming up for the kill. 'You have a half-hour for lunch. You will come back here, take the pass keys, and go through every empty cabin by the lake shore.'

'Will I have to work tonight too?'

'Yes.'

D'Arcy shrugged and walked away, muttering something about twenty-four hour duty.

10

Kate had no thought for D'Arcy over the weekend. Mac spent a day recuperating from the party. Then Kate spent a day making love with him. The nights were a mixture of problem talk and snatches of sleep.

On Monday morning, Kate inquired if there had been any telephone calls. The operator gave her a message from Bett--to meet her with Mac at five for drinks on the clubhouse lawn. Mac decided to take Kate out for a round of golf before that encounter. They hired Slim and Dixie as caddies,

Dixie was not feeling well. Something bad had got in his beer, he said. Mac fell into evil humor when he fanned twice on the drive from the first tee.

'First time out this season,' he said loudly for the benefit of those watching from the clubhouse.

Kate hit a long ball straight down the fairway. Her approach shot was on the green. She holed the ball in one putt. She turned to giggle when Mac missed a short putt. 'This is going to be a fiery round, Slim. I feel it in my bones.'

Mac picked up the ball. 'The damned greens are too fast.'

They went onto the second tee,

Mac hooked into the trees, and Dixie cursed. Mac heard the curse and frowned as Dixie set off in search of the ball.

'Even my caddie's against me,' Mac said.

Kate laughed. 'It's your front foot. It's too far back.'

'My front foot has nothing to do with it,' Mac said. 'The damned tee is not level.'

Dixie found the ball by walking over it. Mac put it back on the fairway with one stroke. Kate approached weakly.

'You could use a little more beef,' Mac called. He hit a long shot back into the woods. 'What in God's name? You'd think I was just learning this game.'

Dixie cleared his throat significantly. Mac cast him a warning look.

'He'll pull out of it, Slim,' Kate said hopefully.

Mac slashed into trees, through a bush, and into the fairway. 'Give me my number two wood,' Mac growled.

'There's no two wood in your bag,' Dixie said sarcastically.

Mac clutched his ear. 'Did they forget to put it in?' he demanded. His face was hot. He was sweating.

Dixie handed him a three wood. Mac cracked the ball onto the green. 'Oh, Brother! What a shot!' he cried gleefully. 'My wife looks over-confident,' he told Dixie. 'That'll scare her.'

'What will I use, Slim?' Kate asked hesitantly.

Slim gave her a five iron. She put the ball beside the cup.

'I'll be a gentleman and give you this bugger,' Mac said grimly.

For the third tee-off, the caddies gave the golfers their drivers and separating from them, climbed the hill over which the fairway rose in order to watch where the ball landed on the other side. The fairway was a dog leg to the right.

'This guy's a pain in the ass,' Dixie said.

'He's kind of erratic,' Slim admitted.

Dixie groaned. 'Carry my bag, will you Slim? I can't make it uphill.'

Slim shouldered Dixie's bag.

'This is strictly for the birds,' Dixie said. 'I came four days on the train for this? I ought to have my fuckin' head examined.'

'Her husband's a millionaire,' Slim said as if in consolation.

'Most likely a mingy bastard,' Dixie scowled. 'Why did a good-looking broad like her marry him?'

'Money,' Slim said.

'Yeah, but Christ! there's a limit.'

Dixie grabbed trees to help him ascend. Slim saw Kate taking practice swings on the tee.

'They're waiting for us,' he said, speeding up.

'Let them wait,' Dixie growled. 'They can't expect us to run up a mountain just to watch them swing. But hey, Slim, don't you get a thrill the way that Mrs. Carr swings her ass?'

'Nope,' Slim said.

'Aw, come on. You must get a bit of a thrill. Man! you've got ice in your fuckin' veins.'

'She's just another woman to me,' Slim said, pushing ahead.

'That's right! Just another bitch!' Dixie stopped. 'I think we've gone far enough.' He wiped his brow.

'We should get up on the next ridge,' Slim advised. 'If he puts another out, you won't see it.'

'I don't want to see it.' He peered at the tee. 'What's he doing? Goosing her?'

'No,' Slim frowned. 'He's telling her to hit.'

'I think you're right about the ridge,' Dixie said, continuing to climb. 'We're like sitting ducks here.'

They moved onto the ridge. Dixie stood behind a tree and peered round it. They heard the crack of Kate's swing.

'Where the hell is it?' Dixie cried. He straightened up behind the tree. 'Why should I worry? It's your ball.'

Slim watched the ball bounce in the centre of the fairway and roll to a stop at the top of the ridge. It glinted in the sun.

'It's right opposite us,' Slim said happily,

'You lucky bastard. Watch out, here comes blunderbuss!'

Mac took a practice swing.

'Did he hit the thing?' Dixie rasped.

Slim laughed.

'Don't! He might hear you,' Dixie said. 'He's a sensitive golfer.'

Mac swung. They heard the crack.

'Watch out!' Dixie called falling to his knees.

The ball whistled through the trees, whipping the leaves, then fell and rolled on the downslope.

'He made it,' Dixie sighed. 'He's better when he can't see where he's going.'

They watched Mac hike off the tee in long swinging strides.

'Look how fuckin' proud he is,' Dixie said. 'He'll probably slap her behind like a lusty sap. He's patting her on the shoulders. What a drip!'

'Here's your bag,' Slim said, handing it to him.

'Bless it,' Dixie said.

Slim went onto the fairway and stood by the ball. Kate came smiling to him. 'Now for the green.' She selected a club and knocked the ball along the fairway. She giggled. 'The hill helped some, Slim.'

They heard Dixie call pleasantly, 'Nice hit, sir!'

'I know this hill,' Mac said. 'I always go for the same spot.'

He took an iron and settled the ball on the green. 'That's more like it. Come on, Katie. You're dragging.'

Kate put the ball on the edge of the green. Mac won the hole.

'It's the man with the drive who gets the buck,' Mac punned.

'You're so right, darling.'

He put his arm about her as they walked to the next tee. 'You wouldn't trade me in for another guy, would you now,' he said confidently.

'No, darling.'

'You can play around all you want till Papa comes home.'

She smiled.

'A bellhop.' He shook his head in amusement. 'It beats me.'

'Now don't, darling. You promised.'

'Don't say it like that,' he barked. 'It irritates me.'

"Well, you irritate me sometimes.'

They fell silent. Mac teed off straight.

'It's a long fairway,' he said, 'so don't bugger around.'

'I'll do exactly what I want to do with no advice from you.' She dubbed the ball. 'That's your fault!'

Mac coughed a laugh. 'You're worn out from over-activity,' he said.

'If you make one more crack,' Kate blazed, 'I'm walking in.' She walloped the ball down the fairway.

They walked to their respective balls.

'I'm all jumpy,' Kate told Slim. 'You'll have to help me calm down.'

'Pretend you're out with the ladies,' Slim said.

She snorted. 'No lady talks like Mac.'

'My wife,' Mac said to Dixie, 'is feeling the pressure.' He grinned. 'What do you advise?'

Dixie scrutinized the distance. 'A number two iron.'

Mac selected a number four. He hit short of the green. 'A number two would have put me on the fifth tee, eh, don't you think?'

Dixie twisted his mouth in doubt and said impulsively, 'Sure as hell a number four wouldn't.'

Mac glowered and threw the club to Dixie. Kate was already on the green. Mac chipped on.

'Swing from the elbows, not from the hips,' he told her. 'You're not doing the hula-hula.'

'I putt the best way I know how,' Kate said. She sunk the ball. 'And you know that's the way I do it.'

'But your game would improve if you learned the right way, Kate dear,' he persisted. 'You want to improve, don't you?'

'You are deliberately provoking me.'

'I beg your pardon!' Mac snapped.

Kate turned away in a huff and took her driver from Slim. Mac sunk his ball. Dixie gave him his driver.

For the fifth tee, the golfers climbed back and up several tiers of turf to a level even with the green. Between tee and green lay the fairway like a deep and treacherous gully. The caddies watched from the side of the fairway.

'Think they'll fight?' Dixie asked. 'I'd like to see a duel-- with clubs, up there against the sky.'

'He's rough on her,' Slim said.

'He has to keep her in trim. But he is a prick.'

'I guess big businessmen are like that,' Slim said.

Dixie regarded him with curiosity. 'Do you have big businessmen in your family?'

Slim shook his head. He was mystified by Dixie's sudden hostility.

'You stupid ass. What do you know about them? Making goddamn generalizations.'

'Why do you think he treats her that way then?' Slim blushed.

'They treat each other that way. It's a way of life.'

'But she's always very nice,' Slim said.

80

'She's nice to every good-looking guy,' Dixie smiled. 'You can't go by that.'

'You think it's her fault as much as her husband's?' Slim asked,

'What are you going to do, Slim? Write a column for married couples? Quote: If you and your husband don't agree, you both should compromise by giving in on that which is most important to you individually. The result will lead to mutual satisfaction and lasting happiness.'

The sound of Mac topping the ball into the creek in the middle of the fairway stopped Dixie. He cupped his hand to his ear and smiled. Words of abuse drifted down to them. Kate's voice echoed shrilly. Mac answered like thunder.

'Like the native call in reverse,' Dixie said. 'They're coming together with clubs. Why? Because they are married.'

Kate looped the ball high on the side of the hill. It rolled to the bottom. 'The first time she hasn't made it,' Slim said worriedly.

As they went to find the balls, they heard snatches of argument. Slim felt uncomfortable. Private disputes should be discussed in strict privacy, he thought. Only vulgar people overlooked the discomfort of others. But he felt that Kate was not responsible for the argument, in spite of her affair with D'Arcy. There was an honest quality in Kate that he admired. Such quality flourished in the world, never degrading it.

On the sixth tee which overlooked the fifteenth fairway from a shelf on the mountainside, the Rabbinowitzes, father and son, were laughing at the spectacle of the struggling, quarreling Carrs.

'Come father. We can play ahead now.'

'No,' Horace wheezed. 'This is too good.'

Mac knocked the ball high on the hill but it rolled to the foot. The Rabbinowitzes bent double with laughter.

'Never, never had such a hell of a round,' Mac's voice carried off the rocks and over the pines.

'Kate looks as if she hated him,' Jaimie said.

'I'm sure it is only the presence of the caddies which has kept them from physical conflict,' Horace observed slapping his knee. 'Where are our caddies by the way?'

'Up the fairway,' Jaimie pointed.

'We shall only have to wait upon these crawling devils in front of us,' Horace said. 'What do you say? Shall we join the Carrs? Keep them from each other's throat?'

'Yes, shall we?' Jaimie said. 'I like playing with Kate.'

The Carrs had reached the green. Dixie reclined on the edge. Slim held the flag pin.

'I can't stand a caddie who lies down,' Mac said quietly. 'It defeats me just to look at him.'

'You've got some grudge against everyone today,' Kate glared at him.

'You look at me like that again and I wrap this putter around your head,' Mac growled.

Kate turned on her heel and strode toward the next tee. Mac putted his ball and then her ball, until he sunk them both. He held his putter out to Dixie who slowly got to his feet and plodded across the green to take it.

Meanwhile Kate looked up to see the Rabbinowitzes grinning down on her. Startled, she smiled uncertainly.

'Well played,' Jaimie said.

Kate laughed with embarrassment. 'You weren't watching, I hope.'

'We enjoyed every moment of it,' Horace beamed.

'Mac and I play about twice a year and it usually turns out like this.' She stepped onto the level.

'But you were a stroke ahead,' Jaimie expostulated. 'Why didn't you finish?'

'Jaimie,' Kate breathed in mock anger. 'Don't make me explain the obvious.' She looked at Horace. 'I know you think I'm a poor sport. I've picked up very few times.'

'Not at all,' Horace said. 'There are days when golf becomes something else, perhaps a croquet match, when picking-up is quite legitimate.'

Mac climbed on to the tee. 'Croquet is too mild a word for it,' Mac said. 'Hello. How are you this year?'

Slim waited for Dixie.

'Who's that?' Dixie squinted at the caddies they were moving toward

'Marchilly and Gilles,' Slim said.

'Man!' Dixie laughed. 'Gregory should have murdered that Frenchie by now.'

When they drew close, Dixie said, 'Haven't you hit Gilles yet?'

'I don't hit people,' Gregory replied. 'It is not in my nature to be criminal.'

'Are you looking for trouble?' Gilles had a deep voice. 'I'm not and don't want it.'

'Listen to him,' Dixie chortled. 'Bloody coward!'

'And I don't like to be called names,' Gilles said.

'It's good for you.' Dixie put down his bag. 'Makes you humble. How much money you saved, strike breaker?'

'I'm doing all right,' Gilles said. 'I don't need your approval.'

'Just curious, you secretive little bastard,' Dixie said,

'Don't call me one more name,' Gilles warned, levelling his finger at him.

'Frog,' Dixie said, enjoying the rise he was getting out of Gilles. 'Hop out of danger, you might get hurt.'

'That's enough,' Gilles, tense, came up to him. 'Shut-up!'

'Looking for a paste in the mouth?' Dixie sneered.

'No,' Gilles said. 'But I think you are.'

'Go ahead,' Dixie smiled. 'Hit me if you can.'

'Don't tempt me '

'Afraid of me, aren't you?'

'A worm isn't afraid of you.'

'That's what you are,' Dixie cried. 'A goddamn little worm. We christen thee, Worm Gilles.'

Gilles clenched his fists. His face was red. His jaw jutted, skin pulled taut over his skullbones. 'You child.'

Dixie's eyes narrowed. His bulbous face grew menacing.

'Come on, you guys,' Slim said. 'Break it up.'

'It's just not done to brawl on the golf links,' Gregory said.

'Worm wants to start it,' Dixie rasped.

Gilles seized Dixie's shirt and twisted it in his hand. 'Take it back.'

'We can't unchristen you, Worm,' Dixie said, grabbing Gilles' wrist. 'Worm you are and Worm you stay.'

Gilles shoved Dixie sprawling.

'Look! They've teed off.' Slim tried to divert their attention to Jaimie's drive.

'Let them,' Dixie said angrily, picking himself up.

'Finish it when we're back in,' Gregory said, picking up his bag.

Gilles went back for his bag.

'Just like a Frenchie,' Dixie rasped. 'Afraid to finish what he starts.'

'It is finished as far as I'm concerned.' Gilles said. 'You fall down easier than anyone I know.'

Kate drove near them.

'You'll talk different when we're back in,' Dixie said grimly. 'I'll teach you manners.'

'Why not now?' Gilles smiled. 'Maybe you're scared.'

'Carry my bag, Gilles,' Dixie said.

Horace hit a long drive.

'Carry it yourself, weakling,'

'Now I ask you, friend Gregory,' Dixie said, 'do I have to submit to this sort of talk from an inferior?'

'Submission is a state of mind and, I might add, so is inferiority.'

'And only acting can change a state of mind,' Dixie said. He strode up to Gilles, bag in hand. 'Take it.'

Gilles spat to the side.

Simultaneous with Mac's drive Dixie struck with the flat of his hand against Gilles' ear.

Gilles dropped his bag and leaped at Dixie who stopped him with a hard punch. Gilles came forward again. Dixie backed away. They circled warily.

'You'll get it in the mouth,' Dixie rasped.

'Your head is coming off,' Gilles breathed.

'Ha. Big joke!' Dixie was grinning.

Gilles leaped seizing Dixie's arm. They fell to the ground. Dixie punched at Gilles who was trying to force a hold around his neck. They rolled onto the fairway. Gilles was astride Dixie, then pushed over. Dixie gave up punching. He wrestled.

'You stupid idiots,' Slim cried.

The golfers looked on from various parts of the fairway. Gregory went ahead to Horace's ball. Kate approached looking alarmed.

Blood flowed from Gilles' nose but he had succeeded in getting a leg lock on Dixie.

'Stop it, stop it!' Kate cried, pressing her hands to her face. 'They're going to get hurt.'

Mac was laughing from twenty yards away. The Rabbinowitzes were not concerned.

'Give it to him,' Mac called. 'Come on, caddie.'

'Won't anyone stop them?' Kate cried. 'Oh!' she called at Gilles. 'You're going to kill him.'

'Yes, I am,' Gilles said.

'The hell you are,' Dixie's voice came muffled from under Gilles.

'Slim, can't you do something?' Kate pleaded.

Dixie lurched up and over, lying on top of Gilles who retained the leg hold. Slim stepped up to them. He rabbit-punched Gilles twice, loosening the hold, and dragged Dixie away. Immediately Dixie was on his feet and running at Gilles who was getting up slowly. Slim drove low, hitting Dixie below the knees snapping him over hard upon the ground. Dixie groaned as if the breath was knocked out of him. Slim grabbed his legs and pumped them. Gilles, holding a handkerchief to his nose, lay down at the side of the fairway. Dixie regained his breath but could not get up.

'Whatever started it?' Kate asked.

'High spirits,' Slim smiled

'Tell them to get moving,' Horace shouted. 'Or we'll report them and have them sacked.'

'They can't go on,' Kate cried.

'We have to,' Horace said. 'We're holding up play.'

'The other two caddies can carry double,' Mac ordered. 'Mine wasn't much good anyhow.'

Dixie propped himself on one elbow and glared at Mac. Kate quickly took her shot. The others followed. Slim shouldered Dixie's bag and brought Gilles' up to Gregory.

'First time I've seen that happen,' Jaimie said. 'Were they fighting over money?' he asked Slim.

'Over prejudice,' Slim said.

'Oh,' Jaimie frowned. 'Well then, I don't blame them.'

'What did he say?' Horace called.

'They were fighting over prejudice,' Jaimie shouted. His words echoed in the mountains.

The group played on silently. Mac wanted to finish at the ninth and walk in. Kate agreed. By that time Dixie and Gilles had caught up and resumed their tasks.

'Are you going to report us, sir?' Gilles asked uneasily.

'No, no,' Horace threw his hand out. 'We'll forget it. By the looks of you, I would say you would want to forget it also.'

Gilles nodded. Dixie shrugged.

The Carrs picked up and cut through the woods.

'You were wonderful, Slim,' Kate said.

'Oh no,' Slim blushed. 'It was easy.'

'No one else would do it. You were the only man brave enough.'

Slim smiled. 'I'm glad you think so.' He ducked. He didn't mean to accent the "you".

'Are you, Slim? That's nice.'

Mac, who was listening, laughed sarcastically.

Slim disliked him.

Dixie trailed behind, kicking at the grass.

'We'll just be on time to meet Bett after all,' Kate said.

'I am not going to meet your silly friend.' Mac said.

'She's not silly.'

'I am going back to the cabin.'

'You are not. We promised her.'

'That woman doesn't deserve a promise.'

'Be good for once and treat her nicely. She's my best friend here.'

Mac snorted. 'You make a pair.'

Kate said nothing. They finished the walk in silence. Kate tipped both caddies. Mac went into the clubhouse but Kate saw Bett wave from a lawn table. She crossed over to her. A very handsome man stood up. His hair was graying about the temples. His smiling eyes tripped Kate's heart.

'This is my friend from the big city,' Bett said. 'Jake darling, I want to introduce you to my dearest friend, Kate Carr.'

'How do you do?' He took her hand. His was warm, sensitive.

'Hello,' Kate grinned nervously. 'My husband will be right out.'

'Ah, so you are married,' Jake said, with an air of disappointment.

11

Runners called the hops into his office. He regarded the line-up. Pouches darkened under his eyes. His voice was sharp, penetrating.

'Someone missing?'

O'Flaherty piped, 'Nick, sir.'

'Where is he?' His eyes searched their faces for response.

The corridor door slammed. Sound of running feet. The office door burst open. Nick stood on the threshold, a suitcase in his hand.

'I think I have it, sir,' he said smartly. He stepped to the desk and placed the case upon it.

Runners frowned suspiciously. 'Do you think it's the one, Jack?'

Smiling, Jack hovered over it and felt it. 'Hmm,' he mumbled.

The hops were alert, hoping.

'Where did you find it?' Runners barked.

'Maid's cabin, sir. Standing all alone. No one claimed it.'

Runners eyed him. 'How did you know it was in the maid's cabin?'

'Inquired in the kitchen, sir. One of the chef's helpers told me.' Nick's eyes were round and innocent.

'It fits the description,' Flowers said. He strained his thumbs at the knobs. 'But it's locked.' He wanted to see the gems.

'We'll wire them.' Runners was relieved. 'And we'll look into this.' He looked at Nick. 'That'll be all.'

The hops marched back to the lobby. They congratulated Nick. D'Arcy sat alone, pondering.

'Break it up,' O'Flaherty said. He sent them on errands.

Nelles walked casually to the front of the bench. 'You were lucky, Morgan.'

'So were you, Nelles,' D'Arcy said.

Their eyes met. They smiled. Nick sat beside D'Arcy. 'You should be thanking me, my lad.'

'Yeah, Johnnie-on-the-spot,' D'Arcy said. 'Dramatic entrance.'

'I was lucky,' Nick admitted. 'But when my old pal D'Arce was in trouble, I left no stone unturned.'

'Well, thanks.'

'Aren't you going to do me a good turn?' Nick said slyly.

D'Arcy wondered what he meant.

'You've got a car, D'Arce. I want to take my girl into town tonight. That old lodge bus comes back early, and there's no privacy,' Nick complained. 'You know how nice a car is. Didn't I give you one of mine once?'

'Not that I remember.'

'What about it for tonight?'

'Haven't got the keys.'

'They're in your room, my lad. Don't play games with Nick.'

D'Arcy shook his head. 'I couldn't risk taking it in myself, let alone lending it.'

'Come on, what are you afraid of?'

'If anything happens, I'm finished. That's the end.'

Nick tossed his head. 'Nothing's going to happen, D'Arce. Be a sport.'

D'Arcy thought of the odds. So far as he knew, no bellhop had been caught taking cars.

'Just this once, D'Arce,' Nick pleaded. 'I've got to be alone with her.'

'Okay. Since you know where the keys are, take them. But just tonight.' He had a premonition of accident and Runners' contorted features. 'Drive with your eyes open.'

'Don't worry, D'Arce. I'll look after your interests,' Nick smirked.

A lodge bus was loading on the patio. D'Arcy glimpsed Maureen. He went out to her and picked up her suitcase. She was talking with the other girls who had been fired.

'Oh, D'Arcy, thank you.'

'What are you going to do back east?' he asked.

'I'll find work,' she laughed. 'I'll be all right.'

He kissed her cheek, partly because he knew that other staff members were afraid to say good-bye. His eye caught Runners watching him coldly from his office window. D'Arcy returned his stare for a moment then took the case to the back of the bus for the driver to load. He waved to Maureen.

The other shift was marching down the hill, their red lapels looking like bright, official badges. D'Arcy made for the mess hall. He was hungrier than he had been after those anxious days of the missing case and lost love. He saw Slim ahead and caught up to him.

'How's my spy?' he smiled.

'You don't want me to spy now, do you?' Slim was surprised.

D'Arcy made a grim face. 'So I'm out of the running for good.'

'Oh, I wouldn't say that,' Slim said consolingly. 'It's just that her husband....'

'Skip it,' D'Arcy smiled again. 'Her husband's a twirp. She's welcome to him.'

They went into the mess hall.

'She doesn't get on very well with him,' Slim said.

'That's what you think. The matrimonial bands get twisted into pretty peculiar webbing sometimes.'

Davey came to their table and leaned his red hand upon it. 'I've heard you fellas had trouble over a suit case.'

'A little bother,' D'Arcy said.

'Funny, I saw one of you boys put it in the cabin behind us. It was there for a couple of days. Then the same fella takes it away again, says it's found.'

D'Arcy gaped. 'Are you sure?'

'Sure, I saw him. What's the idea?'

'No idea,' D'Arcy frowned. 'Just a practical joke. Forget it.'

Davey stepped away. 'Sure, but thought I'd tell you, my boy.'

D'Arcy made an okay sign with finger and thumb. He could neither understand Nick nor people in general.

Gilles came to sit with them. He had washed the blood off his face and changed his shirt.

'Can any of you caddies get off work in three days time?' D'Arcy asked. 'I want company up Pyramid.'

'That's my day off,' Gilles said, leaning forward with interest. 'I want to climb it.'

'Wear your running shoes,' D'Arcy advised. 'Anyone else free?'

'I wish I was,' Slim said. 'Maybe Don Clarking will go. I'll ask him.'

When finished eating, D'Arcy went to the Staff Hall. He had the feeling of drifting aimlessly. Pyramid would give him an objective when the time came, but meanwhile he could see no reason for existing. There were waitresses and cabin girls talking in groups. Was his only purpose to get on top of one of them?

The lusty dark girl came away from a group to stand at the counter near him. She turned and smiled.

'Saw you swimming the other day,' he said.

'When?' Her eyes flashed.

'When the sun was shining.'

She showed her beautiful white teeth as she laughed. This was Princess Laughing-Brook, the well-developed sparkling daughter of a chief. 'My name's Miriam. What's yours?'

D'Arcy sensed a quick rapport fastening him to her. He surveyed her great, attractive breasts protruding under her red sweater. She was in perfect proportion. A smooth brow, large, intelligent brown eyes, thick, well-rounded calves. In what stream does this Indian maiden swim?

'Want a smoke?' D'Arcy took out cigarettes.

She shook her head, wiggling her black braids. 'The room is too smoky. I like fresh air.'

D'Arcy jumped to the hint. 'Want to take a walk?'

She nodded with a flirtatious smile.

They walked past the girls' cabins and took the path by the shore of the Staff Lake. Loons were laughing near the rushes as the sun descended behind the mountain peaks. Miriam raised her face for great intakes of air, her bosom swelling. The bank of the river bed was low. They followed the wide trail beside the white rock and flowing water, as twilight deepened into night. A full moon rolled above the pointed pines.

Miriam was a cabin girl. In the winters she taught English and History in the top form of High School.

'I love it out here in the open. I think my soul was born in the mountain.' She gazed at the ridges dark against the sky.

'This is a soul in itself,' D'Arcy said. 'Why do you prefer this to Montreal?'

'Because it's wild and beautiful. Montreal is not,' she wrinkled her nose.

'And you're wild and beautiful, so you belong here,' D'Arcy smiled.

'That's nice of you to say.' Her tone placed him in her fifth form.

'I didn't say it to be nice,' D'Arcy rallied. 'I really think it.'

Miriam turned her head away. D'Arcy surveyed the outline of the woman and calculated how soon he could caress it.

'Do you feel the stream surging beside us?' she asked.

'Yes,' D'Arcy tried to slip his arm innocently about her, but she took his hand. They walked hand in hand. D'Arcy looked up at the stars. An atmosphere of romance engulfed him. Nature had become a sentimental ally against fearful imaginings in the night. The Indian maiden had cast her spell.

'Tonight when I saw you, I knew I would like you,' she said.

'Must we stay at arm's distance then?'

'For the time being. I believe in getting to know a person slowly.'

D'Arcy sighed. 'It's a strain on the emotions.'

'But we should always control our emotions.' She held his hand more firmly. 'Just breathe this heavenly air.'

Again he watched the swell of her bosom.

'Don't you love it?' she sighed.

'Yes, I do, but I don't know where we're going.'

'What does it matter? I could walk to the ends of the earth.' She smiled romantically at him.

Their feet padded softly over the dust. They crossed a wooden culvert. D'Arcy wanted to take Miriam under the trees. But he was afraid of frightening and losing her. She was an animal, half tame, who had been ensnared in certain moral rules.

'Just let me bring you closer.'

'Not yet, please,' she said gently. 'I want to enjoy the night.'

D'Arcy gave up desiring and accepted her interpretation of enjoyment. He watched with amusement. Some strange naiveté emanated from her like an all-pervading spirit that infused him, the trees, and the round yellow moon. He felt the pressure of her hand. Tender words escaped her lips. She was engrossed in experiencing and absorbing all about her. D'Arcy cupped her cheek in his hand and brought his lips to hers, but she turned her face away. He kissed her cheek.

'You like nature more than me,' he admitted.

'No.' Her braids swung as she shook her head. 'It's because of you that I feel nature.'

91

D'Arcy frowned suspiciously. He wondered whether she was trying to secure a male companion yet frustrate him. Such a state of affairs was considered prestigious in some feminine circles. He tested her.

'You really love nature with me, eh? Can you get a day off in three days time?'

She thought for a moment and counted on her fingers. Her eyes sparkled. 'That is my day off.'

'Good. I'm climbing Pyramid. Want to come?'

'Up the mountain?' she asked, alarmed.

'Right up the mountain.'

'But I've never done any climbing.'

'There's not much to it. There's no ice, so we don't need ropes and that stuff. Just wear your running shoes.'

'I don't know if I should,' she said.

D'Arcy looked at the winking stars.

'Are there going to be others?' she asked.

'Two. You'll be the only woman.'

The idea seemed to appeal to her. 'Do you think I can do it?'

'If you really like nature you can.'

'All right,' she smiled brightly, 'but you must take care of me.'

A strong urge to wrap himself around her and hold her full body flat against his own spiralled up from his loins. Clouds passed over the moon.

'The world has a magic all its own,' she whispered. 'Can you sense it?'

'At times like this I can,' D'Arcy said. 'But you are the magician.'

'What do you mean?'

'You found something special out here and helped me experience it. As long as we keep walking the trail, we'll preserve it.'

'And when we go back to the lodge?'

'It will be sacrificed to the Great White God of Progress,' he said. 'We have no choice but to sacrifice if we want to survive.'

They fell silent. A soft rain patted the leaves and covered their faces and clothes with tiny beads. Miriam looked lovely. He reached over and brushed the wet from her sweater. She allowed him to feel the shape of her breasts, all the while gazing ahead with a soft lustre in her eyes. The trail bent around the end of the Lake Beautiful and took them back to the darkened cabins of the Lodge.

They passed a long time in silence, their hands joined in a sensation of comfortable intimacy. A green bench faced the lake. 'Let's sit here for a minute before going in,' she said.

She sat straight as a dark goddess gazing over the water. D'Arcy sat beside her, held her hand, and watched her serenely ecstatic expression. At such a moment of rapture she was untouchable. But her pose invited some action from him. He leaned forward and kissed her gently on one cheek. A faint smile of beatific delight lightened her features for a moment, but she did not move.

'Now let's go in,' she whispered.

When they were by the Staff Hall she left him. 'I'll find my way. Leave me the last few minutes alone, please.' She skipped, waved and was gone. D'Arcy remarked how smooth and low her voice had been, warming the marrow of his bones and gently rocking his heart.

He returned to his cabin. A light burned in his room. Nick was sitting on his bed. D'Arcy's two roommates were asleep. Quietly Nick took his arm and led him outside. He appeared worried.

'It's the car,' he said glumly.

D'Arcy grabbed his shoulder. 'What did you do?'

'Cracked it up.'

'Oh,' D'Arcy sank to the ground and buried his head in his hands.

'I'm sorry, D'Arce. Jeez, I'm really sorry.'

'I'm finished.'

'We'll do something,' Nick promised. 'I went into a ditch and wrinkled up the hood and fender. Maybe I knocked back the motor, I don't know. But I got it down by the garage.'

'The guys will never be able to fix it,' D'Arcy said, head bowed, frowning. 'I knew this would happen.'

Now that he regarded Nick under the porch light, he saw the fear whitening his face. His own must be as pallid. They stared at the ground, almost waiting for it to swallow them.

'I didn't see the old turn, D'Arce. I smackarooed it.'

'I'll just have to telephone the guy and tell him his car's a mess.' D'Arcy started for the lodge.

Nick seized his arm. 'Don't, for God's sake! I'll get the boot!'

'You won't be mentioned. Give me the keys.'

Nick stuck his bristly head forward with amazement. He handed him the keys. 'You're really going to do this for me, D'Arce?'

'I'd better hurry before I have time to think. I might change my mind.' He ran down the hill across the patio and into the lobby. He cursed his misfortune which seemed especially bitter when he had just met Miriam, but then he could have been fired for any number of lesser reasons.

The night hop on the switchboard put him through to Mr. Slade's cabin. There was no answer. Dispirited, he talked to the hop who said, 'That guy Slade is at the Carrs. I sold him bourbon about half an hour ago. Pretty liberal guy.'

D'Arcy fretted. 'I wonder if I should phone the Carrs.'

'You know the missus, why not?'

'Bad news, an ill wind that blows me no good,' D'Arcy admitted.

'He looked sort of happy in spite of himself,' the hop said. 'Slade, yeah, that's his name.'

D'Arcy snapped his fingers. 'You're right. This is the perfect time to tell him. You're sure he's happy?'

The hop nodded. 'It depends on the guy, you know. I wouldn't tell Runners anything if he was drunk.'

'Eeeee!' D'Arcy swooned. 'Don't mention that name.' He went back to the telephone booth and listened to the buzzing.

The receiver on the other end was lifted. Record music and sounds of drunken singing preceded a gruff male tone.

'May I speak to Mr. Slade, please,' D'Arcy asked. He conquered a temptation to hang up.

'Who?'

'Slade! Mr. Slade!' he shouted.

Pause. He hoped Mr. Slade wasn't there.

'This is Jake Slade,' said a deep drawl.

'This is the bellhop who roomed you, sir. I know it's a little late.'

'It's one o'clock,' Jake said. 'Who is this?'

'The bellhop who roomed you, sir.'

There was a long pause pregnant with rumination, then came Jake's voice with accurate conjecture. 'You smashed my car.'

'Yes, sir, I'm terribly sorry.'

'You need a drink, if you haven't had one,' he mumbled. 'You know where I am?'

'Yes, sir.'

'Come over here right away. P.D.Q., do you understand?'

'Right, sir,' D'Arcy said smartly and hung up. He was trembling, but this invitation was a rare chance to save himself, unless, of course, Jake Slade became pugilistic when drunk.

12

Bett arched her brows. 'Who's our visitor to be, darling?'

Jake smiled mysteriously. 'A bellhop.' His smile broadened at Bett's gasp.

'But we're absolutely stinko,' Bett cried. 'We can't let the service see us like this.'

Kate giggled. Bett's sense of decorum altered with each new man. She had an instinct for selecting the right qualities.

'I've never known you to give a damn about that before,' Mac said.

'You just don't know me,' Bett said sternly.

'Damn! I should have thought,' Jake said. 'I should have asked you.'

'What hop is he?' Kate asked.

'A tall fair-haired guy.'

Kate caught her breath sharply. Mac noticed her reaction.

'He cracked up the car I hired in Edmonton. So we're going to talk things over.'

'Oh no!' Bett said. 'My dear, not here!'

'Get it over with,' Jake said. 'I'm a man of action.'

Bett smiled, 'You are, darling, you are.'

'Besides, he will give us some amusement, I believe.' He looked round at them. 'I'm sort of interested in watching people worm out of trouble.'

Mac took a long drink.

'Do you know his name?' Kate asked apprehensively, catching Bett's eye.

Jake puzzled. 'Why should I?'

She reddened. 'It's just that we who've been coming here know many of the staff.'

'Ah!' Jake nodded, 'democratic. Well, I never treat them badly. I just want justice done.'

'If I were you, I'd report it to Runners,' Mac frowned. 'The hotel will fix it all up.'

Jake shrugged and slouched into a chair. 'A bellhop is human. Hotel management forgets that. Anyway, I like young people. I like observing them,' he said with satisfaction.

Kate bit a nail. She worried lest the hop was D'Arcy. Mac might cause trouble. Besides, she couldn't face D'Arcy. She had dismissed him from her system and needed time to forget him. Bett was watching her with amusement.

'Trouble comes to us all when we least expect it,' Bett said. 'The boy was probably doing the town with his girlfriend.'

Kate started. Her heart gave a wrench. Bett giggled.

'Remembering when I was paying my way through college,' Jake said. 'Trouble was round every corner.'

'College boys get things too easy,' Mac said caustically. 'If you make your way like I did, you're tougher.'

'I wouldn't say that,' Jake drawled. 'Things are tough everywhere.'

Bett sat beside him and took his arm in both hands. Her eyes said that she wanted to be with him. 'Shouldn't we call it off and go home, darling?'

'I'd like to see the fellow,' Jake said. 'That is if the rest of you don't mind.'

'Oh no, we don't,' Kate said brightly,

There was a knock. Kate clasped her hand to her chest and answered the door. D'Arcy stood worriedly looking down at her. She closed her eyes.

'I'm to see Mr. Slade,' D'Arcy said distantly.

'So you're the boy,' Kate opened the door wide. 'Come in.'

'You got here fast,' Jake said.

Mac glared at D'Arcy. 'You knew the way, didn't you, eh?'

'Yes, sir.' D'Arcy approached Jake who waved him to a chair. A tense expectancy seemed to have come in the door with him. Jake settled his elbows on his knees and clasped his hands.

'Well now, what's your name?' Jake smiled engagingly.

'Morgan.'

'How did it happen, Morgan?'

Mac gave Kate a nauseous look.

'Just went for a run.' D'Arcy glanced at Kate. 'And didn't see the turn.'

Mac noticed Kate's concern. He broke in. 'When you're given keys in trust, you don't betray that trust.'

'No,' D'Arcy admitted.

'Unless you lack a sense of responsibility,' Mac continued. 'In which case you can't be trusted.'

D'Arcy nodded. He saw that the four of them had been drinking steadily for hours. There were two empty bottles of Haig and Haig on the floor.

'Uh huh,' Jake said. 'What will you drink?'

'Nothing thanks, sir,' D'Arcy said.

Jake looked at Bett. 'Give him a Scotch and water. Like that?'

'Yes, sir.'

Bett poured a drink.

'The car is at the hotel garage,' D'Arcy volunteered.

'Ah, yes, a place of refuge,' Jake smiled.

'What were you doing that you didn't see the turn?' Mac asked. 'Getting interested in the girl friend?'

'Yes.'

Mac laughed. 'What's her name?'

'I can't tell you,' D'Arcy said.

'Leave the questioning to me if you don't mind,' Jake frowned.

'There's no point if you don't get the facts,' Mac barked.

'The facts are not important,' Jake said. He smiled at D'Arcy. 'There's a bit of poetry in this incident. You were watching a woman instead of the road. That's rather commendable.'

The women smiled.

'It was stupid of me,' D'Arcy said.

'She must have been pretty,' Kate put in

'Sort of,' D'Arcy twisted a smile. 'Though not as pretty as some.'

Kate's eyes twinkled at him.

'This is getting us nowhere,' Mac grumbled.

Bett handed D'Arcy his drink. 'But you're still in uniform! That's risky, isn't it?'

D'Arcy glanced down at his khaki. 'I didn't have time to change,' he grimaced.

'Oh ho,' Bett rounded her eyes. 'You must be keen on this girl.'

'Not very,' D'Arcy said.

Jake laughed. 'Not now, I bet. Drink up.' He watched D'Arcy drink with amusement. 'The same thing happened to me. Women are the root of all evil.'

'Some of them are exhilarating,' D'Arcy said.

'Right!' Jake agreed and held out his hand for Bett to clutch.

Bett sat beside him. She was enjoying this inquisition

'It can also be depressing without them,' D'Arcy added, feeling bolder.

'A man of experience,' Jake nodded.

'What makes you say that?' Kate smiled winsomely.

'I was jilted once,' D'Arcy grinned at her.

'She must have been crazy,' Bett said, 'I mean, to give up a handsome young man like you.'

D'Arcy shrugged. 'It was an accident, like going into a ditch.'

Mac squirmed. 'It's very late, folks. Time we went to bed.' He turned to Jake. 'I'll inform the manager about him in the morning. He'll look after him.'

'I'd rather you wouldn't do that,' Jake said. 'What do you say, Morgan?'

'If he wants to, he can,' D'Arcy looked at Mac.

'I don't think we should, Mac,' Kate said.

'Oh no, you wouldn't,' Mac said fiercely. 'This phony could do anything and you'd forgive him.'

Kate laughed. 'D'Arcy is anything but phony.'

'Do you believe this crap about his girl?' Mac raised his arm in exasperation. 'He stole a car to whiz around town. He probably has never driven a car in his life.'

'He's driven,' Kate smiled bitterly. 'In fact, he's a very good driver.'

Jake raised his brows at Bett. 'Well,' he drawled, 'it's insured. I'll just tell the company that I cracked it up.'

'You're a fool,' Mac said. 'He'll take advantage of you.'

'How?' D'Arcy demanded.

'You'll show us how,' Mac said. 'I'll see that Runners hears about this.'

'Don't you dare!' Kate cried.

'I do dare,' Mac said. 'Any stupid bugger who gets in my way, gets what he deserves.'

'You had better not!' Kate warned.

'My dears, it's been a simply lovely party,' Bett smiled coming to kiss Kate. 'We hate to leave.'

'Wait a minute,' Jake said. 'Whose car is this? It seems to me...'

'It seems to me,' Mac interrupted, 'that the party's over. Goodnight.' He went into the bedroom.

'Come along, Jake darling.' Bett led him to the door.

Jake, puzzled, went obediently. 'Thanks Kate. Coming Morgan?'

D'Arcy followed them into the sitting room, but Kate prevented him from going outside with them.

'Give me a kiss, D'Arcy,' she said.

He hesitated, glancing back at the apartment.

'Please,' she said earnestly.

He took her in his arms and tasted the passion of her mouth.

'Am I still invited on the mountain expedition?' she asked.

He bit his lip. 'I'm afraid not.'

She stepped back. 'Then there was someone in the car with you.'

'Not in the car, Kate. No one but you could distract me that much.'

She made a face. 'That does sound false, awfully false. Oh, D'Arcy! What have I gone and done?'

'Things will work out,' he said. 'Never regret. Always look to the future. Isn't that our philosophy?'

'Don't make fun of me, my darling. I'm sorry. I want you very much.'

D'Arcy shrugged hopelessly. 'I want you, too. Good-bye, Kate.'

She went to the screen door and watched him disappear into the night. She took the empty glasses and bottles into the kitchen. Her life seemed reflected in the labels of the liquor bottles. It was encompassed by the design, overwritten by Scotch Whiskey, Canadian Rye, Dry Vermouth. She left the dirty glasses for the morning.

Mac was sitting in bed, waiting for her. 'Come here,' he said.

She went to the far side of her own bed and undressed.

He watched her steadfastly. 'Come over here.'

'No.' She put on her nightgown and checked to see if the window was open.

'Come to me,' Mac insisted.

Kate started to get into her bed. Mac reached over and seized her wrist.

'Let me go,' she said. 'Or I'll leave.'

He yanked her to his bed and held her against him.

She struggled. He kissed her face and neck.

'No, no,' she screamed. 'I hate you, Mac! I hate you!'

He came over top of her and she gave up struggling. As they made love, she watched the circle of lamplight on the ceiling. 'What can I do?' she said. 'What can I ever do?'

13

At supper three days later, D'Arcy met with Gilles and Don Clarking.

'Do we have to take a woman with us?' Don Clarking screwed up his face.

'I'll be responsible for her,' D'Arcy said.

Gilles looked concerned. 'Will she slow us up?'

'Don't think so,' D'Arcy said. 'We're not in a race anyway.'

'We have to get back on time for work,' Gilles said. 'I can't afford to waste time.'

'We're only going ten thousand feet up,' D'Arcy said. 'It's not to the moon.'

'Stop worrying, Gilles,' Don groaned. 'No one cares if we come back or not.'

Gilles frowned. 'I care.'

'You're just peculiar,' Don said.

'Maybe you'd like to fall down an avalanche,' Gilles suggested.

'If we go carefully, we won't fall,' D'Arcy said.

Don wagged his head. 'Don't let me walk behind Miriam. On the sidewalk, yea, boy yea! but not up a mountain.'

'Yeah, you wouldn't watch your footing,' D'Arcy smiled. 'Anyway she's waiting for us. You guys get your food and we'll meet you on the road.'

He took the path to Miriam's cabin. She was standing outside, waiting. She wore a duffel coat.

'The cabin mistress lent it to me,' she smiled. 'She said it would be cold tonight.'

'Looks warm enough for both of us,' D'Arcy eyed her. 'Running shoes, I see. Good! Let's go.'

They walked to the main road, D'Arcy remarking how bulky she looked in heavy clothes and imagining how supple she was underneath. They encountered the others. Gilles had the knapsack of food. D'Arcy introduced her.

Miriam spoke a few words in French with Gilles until the lodge bus stopped.

'Hey! The forecast said fine weather for tomorrow,' Don Clarking said.

'I'm afraid of those clouds,' Gilles frowned at the sky.

They climbed aboard, D'Arcy giving Miriam a pat on the behind and winking at Don.

'I've changed my mind,' Don said, 'I'll take rearguard.'

The bus roared into the turns. The expedition was underway.

They walked the road from town to the base of Pyramid and climbed the trail leading to the forester's hut. Night fell. Gilles insisted they stay in the middle of the trail lest they step over the side in the darkness.

'Are you sure that the forecast was good?' Gilles asked. 'I felt a drop of rain.'

'Just a little precipitation,' D'Arcy said.

Short bushes seemed like squatting bears at the side of the trail. 'This is wonderful,' Miriam said. 'The air is different already.'

'Canada The Wild,' D'Arcy breathed. 'For wild people like us.'

'I wish to mackerel we'd get to the hut,' Don said. 'This is spooky.'

'It's pleasant,' Miriam said. 'I like the night.'

'You wouldn't if you were carrying the food,' Don said.

'I will,' she offered.

'No, no,' D'Arcy said. 'It's my turn.'

'Please, D'Arcy, I want to take my share. Otherwise, I'll feel like an outsider.'

'You're welcome to it,' Don gave her the knapsack. 'But we won't hear any more sighs of ecstasy.'

The night air pierced their flesh. They were aware of their four spirits moving separately. They could barely make out the lines of the trail. To one side was the absolute black of the chasm.

'I see a light,' Gilles cried.

Directly above them was the light from a shack. They climbed a turn in the trail and approached the forester's look-out post.

The forester, a young, curly-headed man with a pinched face stood arms akimbo watching them. 'That's the way it should be,' he laughed as soon as they could hear. 'The woman carries the equipment.'

D'Arcy tried to take the sack from Miriam, but she wouldn't relinquish it until they reached the shack.

'That's what happens to the woman who tries to be a man,' D'Arcy said. 'She ends up bearing the bulk of the burden.'

'Wisely said.' The forester took the sack and put it in one corner. 'I'm just making tea. Will you have some?' he asked Miriam. He couldn't take his eyes off her.

'How did you know we were coming?' she smiled.

'I heard your shout, "There's a light!"' he said and laughed with them. 'I've had several parties visiting me this season.'

D'Arcy looked at the short telescopes, binoculars, notebooks. 'Don't tell me you use calculus up here.'

'Just textbooks,' the forester said. 'I have to try a supplementary exam end of August.'

'What university?' Miriam asked.

'McGill.'

'I'm from Montreal too.'

'Maybe we'll see you when you get back,' the forester said. 'I'm Howard.'

He met them all. D'Arcy sensed Miriam being drawn away from him.

'Can we use that little building out there to sleep in?' he asked suddenly.

'That's for another purpose,' Howard smiled, looking at Miriam, prepared to laugh with her. 'You can sleep on the floor, I guess. I'd like to offer the young lady my bed.'

'Thank you, but I'm roughing it with the others.'

Pretty rough in that bed, D'Arcy thought. Poor fellow hasn't seen a woman for a month or two.

'We should get some sleep,' Gilles said, annoyed that Miriam was receiving all the attention. 'We have to make an early start.'

'Yeah,' Don Clarking agreed. His face seemed to say that this was to be an expedition and not an exercise in flirtation. 'Can we turn in now?'

'Don't you want your tea? The water's hot.' Howard went to the stove.

'Oh, okay,' Don said unwillingly.

Howard gave a cup to Miriam. 'Cream and sugar on the table.'

'Isn't it wonderful to have supplies!' she said.

'A jeep brings them to me once every two weeks.'

'It must be lonely for you,' she said.

Howard gave cups to Don and Gilles. 'I get along. I have my friends, the birds and chipmunks. They eat out of my hand.'

He took a cup of tea for himself and said to D'Arcy, 'I'm sorry I have no more cups. You'll have to wait until someone is finished.'

'Tea's not my cup,' D'Arcy said. He reached in the sack for an apple and champed on it.

'Have some of mine,' Miriam said.

He took her cup with a smile of satisfaction and sipped. He handed it back. 'No, I don't like the taste.'

Howard's pinched features grew sombre. 'Pyramid is dangerous for a girl. Last week three men were stranded on a ledge. It took us forty-eight hours to reach them. They're in hospital suffering from exposure.'

'We won't let Miriam out on any ledges,' D'Arcy said.

'I hope not!' Miriam gasped.

'She shouldn't climb it,' Howard warned,

'He may be right,' Gilles said. 'We don't want anything to happen.'

'Headlines!' Don Clarking shouted. '"Bampers' Girl Suspended on Pyramid." And under it: "Caddies Took Wrong Trail, Cause Mishap."'

'It could be quite serious,' Gilles said.

'She could stay with me,' Howard offered,

D'Arcy shrugged. 'She's got all her limbs but it's up to her.'

'I want to come.' Miriam looked worriedly from one to another. 'I promise I won't get you in any trouble.'

'That ought to answer you,' D'Arcy said to Howard. 'She's a strong girl.'

'Strong determination,' Howard said, clucking through his teeth. 'I'll have to see this tomorrow.'

'Let's pray for sun,' Don said. 'If it rains, so help me God.'

'It's going to rain,' Howard smiled. 'I smell it in the air.'

'We won't see anything!' Gilles grimaced. 'What's the use of climbing?'

'On a nice day you can see right out to the prairies,' Howard said.

'Boy!' Don said. 'It had better not rain.'

'Let's turn in,' D'Arcy threw a blanket on the floor. He laid out another beside him for Miriam.

Howard took off his shirt and put on his pajama top. He waited until they were settled on the floor before turning off the light. He undressed in the dark and climbed into bed near D'Arcy and Miriam.

'Listen! That's rain on the roof,' he said on a note of glee.

D'Arcy threw one arm over Miriam's back. If she got up in the night at Howard's invitation, he would know it. He sensed, though, that the others noticed this action and disliked it. The woman divided him from them. He withdrew his arm. Tomorrow he could possess the mountain, a worthier cause.

The rain on the roof drummed them to sleep. D'Arcy awoke in the gray light of early dawn, looked about at the humps of bodies on the floor, and put his face back to the boards and slept.

Howard's clock alarm jolted them into the morning. Howard shut it off with a chuckling smile. 'Well, how did you all sleep?' He looked at Miriam.

'Comfortably,' Miriam said. 'I didn't mind the floor at all.'

'There's no sun,' Don Clarking cried. 'Just look at those dark clouds. Maybe it's clearing over there in the east.'

'The wind's blowing the wrong way,' Howard said, throwing wood in the stove. 'It was raining all night.'

'It's not very warm,' Gilles shivered.

'The winds are cold when the sun isn't out,' Howard explained. 'This is a bad day for climbing.'

'What if it rains when we're on the rocks?' Don asked. He clamped on his floppy summer hat.

'You've got your light rain coat,' D'Arcy said impatiently.

'I don't care about getting wet and catching pneumonia,' Don looked round-eyed at him. 'It's slipping on the slate into a valley a mile below. Anyone who risks that is crazy.'

'Come on,' D'Arcy sighed. 'You can imagine worse things. How about grizzly bears behind the rocks? They are licking their mouths as they watch you climb unwittingly towards them.'

Miriam laughed, full throated. 'Don't! You'll frighten me.'

They took turns washing at the pump outside.

'We won't see anything today,' Gilles complained.

'It may clear up,' D'Arcy said.

'Wouldn't it be better on a sunny day?' Gilles suggested.

'It would be beautiful,' D'Arcy agreed. 'But it's not our luck.'

Howard boiled water which they mixed with instant coffee. They made toast and divided oranges.

'You've got a good view of the mountains,' D'Arcy told Howard.

'Better without the mist. I check all points of the compass. There's been only one fire in three years in my area and we stopped it quickly.' He gestured to a wall telephone. 'Direct contact with town.'

'I love this place,' Miriam's eyes flashed. 'You're so secluded from the world.'

'The sun makes a lot of difference,' Howard smiled. 'Summers are superb in spite of the winds. I've often wondered what the winters would be like.'

'Brr!' Don shook his shoulders. 'It's cold enough today without making us think of snow.'

'We've got to get started,' D'Arcy announced.

'Moses! Give me another coffee,' Don cried.

"We'll be warm when we're moving.' Gilles fastened the knapsack on his back.

'Just one coffee. That's all I ask.'

'There's no more hot water,' Howard said, 'but I'll heat some for you.'

'Come on, Don,' D'Arcy urged. 'We haven't all day.'

'Miriam, don't you think you should stay behind?' Howard asked considerately, his gentle eyes beseeching.

'I want to do what the others do,' she said. 'I'm not quitting.'

'It's no use saying we'll do it another day,' D'Arcy frowned. 'We'll never have another day. Damn that weatherman!'

'Bring her back safely,' Howard called, watching them depart.

'Not for your pleasure,' D'Arcy mumbled under his breath. He led the way.

The woods thickened. They pushed through undergrowth and over fallen trees, holding branches back for each other and brushing the wet off their faces. The path widened and rolled up and down and around. A fresh smell of the wet greenery brightened D'Arcy's spirits. He sensed the adventure ahead. A soft shower fell on them. They walked on heedlessly. D'Arcy liked the thought of pushing into the wilderness. As the underbrush cleared, they came upon the woodland of tall and slim trees, and copses and thicker trunks. D'Arcy awakened to the rediscovery of himself. He felt that he belonged to the trees, to the undergrowth, to the secret nature under the treetops and clouds. When he broke loose from the city in the springtime, his heart used to thrill to see the snow melting to a stream on the soggy floor of the woods. His mind feasted upon the majesty of the Canadian country. Mist moved over them. It showered again.

'This is silly,' Gilles announced and stopped. 'I'm going back.'

'Wait,' D'Arcy said, 'till we get above the timberline.'

'It will be worse on the rocks,' Gilles reasoned. 'We can't see very far. What's the use? It's not going to clear.'

'Yeah, let's call it quits,' Don said. 'I'm getting soaked.'

'But we've gone so far,' D'Arcy argued.

'Just a quarter of the way,' Gilles said. 'I'm returning another day.'

'So am I, D'Arcy,' Don said sadly. 'You two had better come back with us.'

'When I start something, I finish it,' D'Arcy said sharply. 'You can quit, I don't care. I'm going on.'

Don jeered. 'You'll never make it.'

Gilles looked askance. 'You're crazy if you go alone.'

'Miriam will come with me,' D'Arcy said, looking at her. 'Won't you?'

She hesitated. Her brown eyes went questioningly from one to the other. 'If they think we should go back, perhaps we should, D'Arcy.'

'I don't care what they say. I'm going on. Now are you coming or aren't you?'

'But are you sure we can do it? We're alone,' she said worriedly.

'Of course we can. It's just like a Sunday walk.' He went to Gilles. 'Give us some of the food.' He took bread, apples, coffee, oranges and sandwiches from the knapsack.

'You're going to regret it, D'Arcy,' Don said. 'What are you going to do if you're caught on a ledge?'

'Jump,' D'Arcy smiled.

'There's that bloody rain!' Gilles cursed, wiping the back of his neck. 'Sorry to use such language in front of a lady.' He looked darkly at Miriam.

'That's all right,' she grinned. 'I don't mind.'

'She's not a lady, she's a mountain climber,' D'Arcy said, 'which is more than I can say for you guys.'

'I'll read about you in the papers,' Gilles said, turning away.

'You won't go very far,' Don smirked. 'You'll quit in a few minutes. We'll wait half an hour for you at the ranger's cabin.'

'We're not coming back till we get to the top,' D'Arcy said.

'Take your last look, Gilles,' Don shouted. 'We won't see them again.'

'Come on,' Gilles barked over his shoulder as he disappeared along the path.

Don Clarking waved good-bye and hurried after him.

'Don't you think we should go with them?' Miriam asked.

'No.'

D'Arcy led her onto the next ridge. The woods were thinner, the trees shorter, the greenery was lighter, having a pale lustre.

'Just one more ridge to cross,' he sang.

'I've been thinking that with each new one,' Miriam gasped. 'D'Arcy, I'm a little frightened.'

'Are you? That's good. It will make you climb better.'

'Don't you think we should go back?' Miriam insisted.

'No.'

They continued in silence. They came onto the soft mossy ground of tundra. The rock of the mountain stood waiting in the distance. On coming over a rise they startled a young moose drinking from a spring. It galloped away soundlessly.

'This is what I imagine the bottom of the sea to look like,' D'Arcy said. 'All the pretty green lacework underfoot.'

'It's heavenly,' Miriam said. 'I've never felt so invigorated. But do you think we can find our way back to the path?'

'We're on it, 'D'Arcy laughed. 'You see, we're coming to the rock. The green is worn to the bare ground and small stones are peeking through.'

Miriam gazed up at the gray rock. 'It's terrifying. It just goes up and up and up. D'Arcy, I don't see how we can climb it.'

'We can,' he smiled grimly. 'Come on.'

They reached a very steep hill of short grass. In climbing they had to grip at the weeds at times to keep their balance. Miriam lagged. She was gasping for breath.

'Don't rest,' he said. 'Do it all at once.'

'I can't.'

'It's not far.'

'D'Arcy, I can't go any farther. My legs are tired. I'm out of breath. Please, let's go back.'

'I thought you were a girl of nature,' he said bitterly, 'but you can't even get up a steep hill. You're a goddamn fraud.'

'I'm not!' she cried, 'but I want to go back.'

'Get over this rise and you'll feel differently.'

'I can't. It's too steep,' she wailed.

'You lazy oaf,' he shouted. 'You boneless tripe, you stupid female, coming on a hike with men when all you're good for is keeping house. You fat lump, you gutless fish-eyed stock of flesh.'

'I'll wait for you,' she cried.

'If you're eaten by a bear, he'd spit you out. You've got no spirit, no courage, no fortitude, no stamina. You're one of the lowest creatures that ever crawled the earth. You're weak-willed; you start off and haven't the spirit to finish. Are you afraid of a little exercise? Might take off some of that weight,' he cried, eyes blazing, teeth clenched in fury. 'You sack! You're dragging me back. I thought you were different. I would never have asked you to come if I'd thought you'd give up at the first little hardship.'

Stung, she began to climb earnestly, resolutely. He said nothing until he reached the boulder. He looked down and laughed. 'Keep it up. You're doing fine.'

Grinning, she clambered the last bit quickly and fell into his arms. She breathed heavily. 'I'm ashamed of myself. It wasn't so hard. '

'It looks easier from now on.' D'Arcy surveyed the strand of rocks leading upwards. 'And it's stopped raining.'

'I didn't notice.' Miriam looked about in wonderment. 'The mist is clearing.'

'A bit,' D'Arcy smiled. 'But we'll be lucky to see the sun. Let's go.' He led the way up the rocks.

Dark gray, their veins of colour neutralized by the rain, the rocks posed precariously as they had for eons. Gripping the sides and selecting footholds, D'Arcy sought out the way. He glanced back to see that Miriam was following in his steps. They concentrated on climbing, seeing only the rock towering over them, each high ridge appearing to be the top until they reached it and faced another. They passed between great boulders and sidled along the sides and wormed over the surface of rounded dun. Miriam kicked loose rocks. They listened to the thump of their bounces, striking echoes upon the solitude. Often the air grew still, but, on surmounting a ridge, they met a stiff breeze and seized the rock with sudden fear.

'Look, look!' 'Miriam cried.

The mist cleared directly below them. They looked down on a small green puddle.

'I bet it's Lake Beautiful,' D'Arcy said.

Clinging to the mountain, they surveyed the world they knew. Black, blue, yellow-brown puddles dotted the green valley below.

'Oh,' Miriam thrilled. 'I can't look.'

'You could almost roll off right into it,' D'Arcy laughed.

They pushed on with an increasing sense of elation. He gave her a hand over rough spots and guided her slowly in the steepest places.

'How are we ever going to get down?' she asked.

'Just slide.'

'But I couldn't bear to look. It gives me a compulsive feeling, as if I had wings and could take flight.'

'Let's rest,' D'Arcy said. 'I think this rarefied air is getting to us.'

She laughed. 'I'm all right. I'm just making fun.'

'We'd better have an apple anyway.' He took two from the sack and handed her one.

They munched, smiling at each other, eyes dancing delightedly as they leaned against the mountain which had come to seem like a faithful friend.

'The Egyptians built pyramids to hallow the dead,' D'Arcy said. 'I wonder if the creator built this Pyramid as a memorial to creation.'

'But that would mean that creation was dead,' Miriam said. 'It isn't. It's still living.'

'Pyramids were made to house the corpse yet they signified that the spirit lived on. They were really built for the spirit. Couldn't this mountain represent God's affirmation of the invincibility of the creative spirit?'

'D'Arcy, you're right! I feel it. This mountain has a spiritual quality about it.'

'It's nature's tombstone, an everlasting memory of living things,' D'Arcy smiled. 'The source of inspiration, for it is the remembrance of the past that inspires the present.'

'But surely every high mountain has a spirit,' Miriam said, pointing at the snows of Mount Edith Cavell disappearing into the clouds.

'Every mountain is different. That one stands for nobility or purity. You'd have to climb it to know which. This stands for memory. For the human mind, the shape is the symbol; and the symbol is meaning, understanding. But one thing we can say, all great mountains are beautiful.'

A stone slipped from under Miriam's foot. She grabbed D'Arcy's shoulder.

'And dangerous!' she laughed.

'Like a woman,' D'Arcy said, kissing her.

'Oh don't, I feel like swooning.'

'Onwards!' he shouted, 'ever onwards!'

They climbed to new ridges, pausing for breath, and continuing. Small areas of snow began to appear. They skirted a large glacier. Miriam picked up snow and threw it at him.

'It's wet,' she shouted.

'Perfect for a fight,' he cried and withdrew to a distance.

Scooping up snow they took cover behind boulders and packed snowballs. D'Arcy charged, ducking her barrage, and raining her retreat. She fired her reserve, striking him in the chest and face. He went back for more snow, slipping and falling on the glacier, gripping the ice and regaining the rocks. Shouting like a banshee, he stormed her fort, grappled the maiden in his arms and scrubbed her cheeks.

'Surrender!' she cried.

They fell into the snow and rolled upon their backs. He came over her and kissed her.

'Love on a glacier,' he laughed. 'We couldn't do this on Mount Edith Cavell.'

'Why not?'

'Symbol of Purity,' he said.

Laughing, they shouted their happiness at the rocky ridges below and listened to the fluctuations of the human sound fading into the expanse of grey sky. The clouds closed off their view. The two of them on a stretch of rock represented the world as far as they could see.

'There is something original about this,' D'Arcy said.

Miriam threw her face up at the sky and let the full rich sound of her laughter penetrate the atmosphere. D'Arcy gazed at her longingly, as if she were the first Eve.

'Do you think the Garden of Eden was just rock?' she sighed.

'Sure,' he grinned. 'Fruition came after fertilization. Symbolically the rock was paradise--no tilling the soil, no milking the cows, no harvesting, just lolling about licking up the lichen like Darwin's iguana. Then the idea was born, proved enjoyable, and presto! we had vegetation.'

'I do feel far away from everything,' Miriam gazed at the wall of cloud. 'As if we were reduced to the bare essentials.'

D'Arcy stirred. 'If we lie here much longer we may not reach the top.' He stood. 'Ready to go?'

She nodded and followed him. Presently the mountain narrowed like the neck of a bottle. They climbed quickly, shouting to one another with excitement. D'Arcy stepped onto the top, a flat surface of several yards across. He raised his arms exultantly to Miriam. An ecstatic bliss beamed from her face as he helped her onto the mountain top.

'I've done it!' she cried. 'I've actually done it!'

'We're on top of the world,' he laughed. 'Alone against the clouds.'

'D'Arcy, it's wonderful!'

They discovered a tin weighted down with stones upon which were carved names and dates left by previous adventurers.

'Shall we leave ours?' Miriam asked. She was upon her knees, scanning the inscriptions.

'I won't,' D'Arcy said. 'The mountain itself is the mark of our achievement. Our names are accessory--unknown symbols.'

'I won't either,' she said.

They strolled about, gazing at the clouds, down the rock sides and at one another. Their elation subsided gradually. They linked arms and faced the cool breeze which had begun to pierce through their clothes. The rock was damp. They lay side by side, crooking their arms under their heads and looking up at the clouds which seemed almost reachable.

'I'm disappointed that we can't see anything,' Miriam said.

'So am I,' D'Arcy agreed. 'And if the sun were out, it would be good and hot here.'

'Strange being alone with you like this,' she said. 'It's romantic isn't it?'

Her body seemed to float with the clouds. There was no earthiness, no sense of fulfillment. She allowed him to run his hands over her outline like a blind man who wished to know if she really existed. A kiss, two kisses but that was all.

'In spite of the triteness of the idea,' D'Arcy said, 'the act of making love on a mountain top is unusual. It seems inevitable for a man and woman when they lie against the sky. But with you, it would be sacrilegious.'

'I wouldn't let you, anyway,' she smiled indulgently.

'It's damp and cold,' D'Arcy murmured. 'We should get started if we want to get back before dark.'

A feeling of depression began to weigh upon him as they started the descent. Miriam was in high spirits at first but she eventually fell silent. They progressed rapidly, rarely halting.

D'Arcy pondered the significance of the climb. He was glad to have persevered against dissuasion. The experience brought him close to his beloved nature, so close that he had almost become one with it. He felt, however, that Miriam had come between him and the realization of his joy. Instead of helping him fulfill it and taking part in it herself, she had used herself to prevent it. He could not understand his dejection completely, but he knew there had been a finality. He would never reclimb Pyramid regardless how beautiful the weather, how clear the visibility, and he would not continue seeing Miriam in spite of her attractiveness.

They passed over the tundra and across the timberline. At a fallen log, he stopped and dealt out the sandwiches. They were hungry and ate quickly. Miriam brightly asked him questions about the woods, which he answered shortly, then about himself, which he could not answer, so low had his spirit sunk. He allowed no trace of disappointment to appear on his features.

'You're awfully strange, D'Arcy. Why are you so silent?'

'I'm worried about getting back in time,' he said. He went to the stream and drank, then brought a cup of water to Miriam. 'We can eat the bananas as we walk.'

He pressed quickly along the path, pacing down one slope after another until the muscles of his thighs and stomach strained. Miriam followed closely behind. She wore an expression of resignation and self-righteousness. She had not the slightest doubt that whatever the cause of D'Arcy's behaviour, it was wholly D'Arcy's fault.

They reached the ranger's hut. Howard greeted them, extending his hands to Miriam.

'Won't you stay for tea? This poor girl needs a rest. You have really worked her.'

Miriam grinned. 'It was good exercise. I feel I've lost pounds.'

'I was watching for you with the instruments,' Howard said, 'but I couldn't see through the clouds.'

D'Arcy noticed a telescope directed at the mountain slope. Not even a mountain top is private, he thought He went to the outhouse. When he returned, he saw Miriam at the window. She was standing in front of the telescope as Howard adjusted it from behind her. An expression of naughty glee illumined her face.

'The apotheosis of clandestine love,' D'Arcy mused aloud. 'Let's get going,' he shouted and crooked his arm at her.

She frowned in disappointment. Howard came to the door. 'You haven't had your tea.'

'You know damned well it'll be dark soon. We're not spending another night here,' D'Arcy said. 'Thanks just the same.'

'Miriam wants to rest,' he said.

'She can stay if she likes,' D'Arcy smiled. 'And take the trail down tomorrow.'

Miriam heard him. She assumed a serious expression. 'I have to get back to work.' She buttoned her duffel coat.

'Not till the afternoon,' D'Arcy cried. 'You'll have plenty of time.'

'Yes!' Howard seconded eagerly.

'No.' She shook her head and smiled brightly. 'I can't take chances. Good-bye, Howard.'

The pain in Howard's eyes made D'Arcy laugh.

"What's funny?' Miriam asked crossly.

'Hermits,' D'Arcy said. 'But at least this one gets paid.'

She waved to Howard. 'I'll see you in town, maybe.'

'Will you? Is that a promise?' he shouted.

She smiled mysteriously and rounded the bend with D'Arcy. His depression was gone. He was back in the absurdity of everyday life with its absurd characters like Miriam. He could laugh.

The descending sun gleamed forth from under the clouds, sending rays of rose and pink aslant across the landscape. From a ledge they saw the tiny town of Bampers below. It seemed to be waiting in the sunshine for them.

14

On D'Arcy's order, Nick had driven the crippled car to a garage in town and fetched it after repairs were made. Jake was waiting in the lobby with Bett. Sunshine streamed through the verandah screen and the tall windows onto the lobby rugs. Jake flipped cigarette ash into a silver ash-stand.

'It's been such fun,' Bett caressed his fingers.

'I will admit,' Jake said, 'that I spent more time with you than I thought you would want me to.'

'Oh!' Bett thrilled, 'but I haven't had nearly enough of you, darling.'

'What I meant was,' Jake said, 'I thought I'd get more golf in. When is that tournament?'

'Don't you dare forget it!' Bett looked alarmed. 'I'll be counting the weeks till you're back with me.'

He stroked her hair. 'So will I, Bett. The end of August, isn't it?'

'The twenty-sixth or eighth or something. Now don't forget.' She raised her finger. 'My husband will have driven me to the brink of madness by then. If you don't show, I'll never be sane again.'

He shifted his broad shoulders to a more comfortable position. 'I'm harum-scarum.' He raised his brows in amusement. 'You don't want to trust a guy like me.'

'I know you,' Bett sent him a kiss. 'And I need every moment you can spend away from women's underwear and hosiery.'

Jake turned aside to smile.

'In both your working and non-working hours,' she added and rounded her eyes naughtily.

'I sell nail-polish and things like that,' he chuckled. 'Why make the underwear sound so important?'

'I have a feeling you'd have more success in that line,' she said seriously.

'You know, you're looking sexier every minute,' he said stirring restlessly and glancing at the bell captain's desk. 'If I don't get my keys soon, I'll be obliged to stay another night.'

'Oh please!' She grasped his hand.

He grinned handsomely. 'I'm a pushy guy. Someday I'd like to see a sign reading "President Slade". It may be President of Men's Galoshes Inc. but what do I care. I'm in the American rut, Bett honey. I can't get that name plate out of my head.'

'Don't I help?' she pouted.

'You help me forget it. I've enjoyed these days, Bett. Really, they've really been great.'

'Jake,' she smoothed her hand along his arm. 'Why don't you come back to Canada? You can get a job with less money. It's not so important.'

'You might as well ask me to commit suicide. You see, I'm a guy who likes to be on the offensive. Playing defence would make me unhappy. I couldn't do it. I'd have so many worries, I'd die of cancer.'

'You'd get used to it,' she insisted.

'For fifteen years I've been American,' he paused, studying her. 'That's a long time of good things.' He shrugged. 'My pioneer principles have been washed away in thousands of television commercials.' He laughed suddenly. 'I have been cleansed of conviction.' He saw D'Arcy approaching. 'You might say that I am the mechanical man.'

'The car is ready, Mr. Slade,' D'Arcy said handing over the keys.

'Thank you, D'Arcy. You're a good man.' He got up. 'Take care of Mrs. Steel until I come back in a few weeks.'

Bett stood beside him. 'I'm not at the lodge, darling. Did you forget?'

'No, but if you're around here,' he frowned, 'you want to keep in with a guy like Morgan. I have a hunch he didn't crack up any car.' Smiling, he punched D'Arcy lightly on the shoulder and strolled away arm in arm with Bett.

Nick was watching from the desk. He ran to open the door to the patio. 'Your car's right outside, sir,' he said cheerfully.

Jake looked at him curiously. 'Thank you.'

Nick came to sit beside D'Arcy on the bench. 'You've got your hooks in good rich bait, D'Arcy, my boy. Too bad he's going.'

'There are hundreds like him,' D'Arcy said guardedly.

'Oh no, there aren't! He paid that bill without batting an eyelash.'

'Insurance,' D'Arcy shrugged.

'Yeah but....' Nick shook his head. 'He said nothing to Runners. You're sure about that.'

'I don't know,' D'Arcy looked down the corridor. 'Here he comes. Maybe he's found out.'

Runners glided sombrely towards them. He skirted the Front Desk, stopped, rested an arm on the counter, and glared at the hops and over their heads at the lobby.

'Gives me the willies,' Nick whispered.

'O'Flaherty!' Runners said crisply.

'Yes, sir,' O'Flaherty jumped from his stool and dashed up to Runners.

'I want those boys kept busy.' Runners turned away. He smiled at Deo who had been elevated to Maureen's post as reservations clerk.

Deo smiled back. 'Morning, sir.'

Runners sidled round to her counter and, leaning upon it, watched the hops run about emptying ash trays, straightening verandah chairs, and darting out the screen door on errands. 'How are you today?'

'Well, thank you, Mr. Runners.' Deo was nervous. Her big blue eyes made her seem as innocent as a child.

'May I see the list for tomorrow,' he smiled nicely,

She handed him a typewritten sheet. He surveyed it, pursing his lips, frowning, scratching behind his collar.

'Miss Adams....' he began, then looked searchingly at her. 'May I call you Deo.'

'Yes, sir, please do.'

'That's your name, isn't it?'

'Yes, Mr. Runners,' she smiled charmingly.

He smiled warmly and handed back the list. 'Good work. Except for one or two items.' He grimaced. 'The Righthouses will not arrive until the day after tomorrow.'

Deo paled. 'I'm sorry.'

'You didn't know about it, of course,' he nodded understandingly. 'Bring your list to my office in fifteen minutes.' He walked away.

Frightened, Deo clutched her beautiful blond hair.

'It's nothing,' the male clerk smiled. 'Just act discreet and nothing can happen.'

'But what does he want from me?' she asked.

'A few kind words,' the clerk said. 'He wants a faithful staff.'

She took the list and looked at the clock. D'Arcy was dashing by the desk. She reached out to him.

'What's wrong?' he asked, alarmed at her expression.

'Runners asked me to his office in fifteen minutes,' she gasped. 'Hurry, tell Johnnie.'

'What makes Runners different from all the others?' D'Arcy laughed. 'You can flirt with him the same way. He can't touch you.'

'But he terrifies me.'

'Well, O'Dreams can't help you. Anyway, he's probably asleep. Just be nice to Runners. And keep him at a distance. We need someone like you to keep him happy.'

'D'Arcy!'

'I didn't say to satisfy him. I meant to keep him from showing his ugly side.'

'Promise me something?' she asked, pouting. 'Stay outside the door while I'm inside.'

'You want me to burst in at the first scream?'

'Just in case,' she pleaded.

'O.K., but don't scream.'

When D'Arcy returned from delivering the news sheet to the Golf House, Deo signalled that she was ready. She went to Runners' office. D'Arcy took a broom and dust-pan from the hop cloak room and brushed the rug outside Runners' door.

Runners was alone when Deo entered. She wore her boldest look.

'Sit down, Deo.' He pointed to the chair beside his desk. 'I have been wanting to chat with you for a long time.'

She sat down. 'That's nice, Mr. Runners.'

'Do you like your new post? I especially wanted a good looking young lady there. You are perfect for it.' His eyes dropped and rose.

Deo turned aside to cough.

'You have a cold?' he asked, concerned.

She nodded with hand up as if expecting another cough.

'The nights are cold,' he said. 'You must cover up. Did they give you enough blankets?'

'I think so.'

He reached across and felt her arm. 'You feel cold.' He smoothed his hand along it. 'You poor girl. I want my staff to be well looked after.'

'I'm fine,' she brightened.

He sat back. 'Are you happy at Bampers?'

'Very happy,' she sighed.

'You have made friends.'

'The girls are very nice,' she said. 'Lots of fun.'

'How do you find the men?'

She answered warily. 'They are very nice to me.'

'How long have you known Mr. Carr?' His look sharpened.

'Just this one week,' she smiled breezily. 'His wife is friendly.'

Runners hummed. 'It is not usual for staff to make friends with guests, but you are so pretty, I can't blame them for making your acquaintance.'

She lowered her eyelashes. 'Thank you, sir.'

'You strike me as the kind of girl who could get along with almost anyone.'

'You're very complimentary,' she said coyly.

'Occasionally I give a party for some of the guests. The next one is tomorrow night. I'd like you to be there.'

'Oh!' Deo blinked. She thought of rich and influential people and progress. 'That sounds like fun.'

'I will count on you at nine o'clock in my cabin.' His eyes gleamed.

'In your cabin?' she choked.

'Mrs. Runners will welcome you,' he added sharply. 'Let me see the list now.' He crossed out two names and pencilled in another. 'These are the changes, Deo.' He handed back the list with a smile and felt her arm. 'Not so cold. You will be a great asset to the lodge, Deo.'

'Thank you, sir. I'll do my very best for you.'

He regarded her with a gentle look as she stood.

'Is there anything special I should wear?' she asked.

'Just be yourself,' he said charmingly. 'That is enough.'

Deo stepped into the hall.

'Are you all right?' D'Arcy asked, starting up behind her.

She hushed him angrily, and walked quickly along the corridor.

'Did anything happen?' he insisted.

'Of course not!' she snapped. 'Mr. Runners is a very nice man.'

D'Arcy stopped short and watched her disappear into the lobby. He could scarcely believe her. He thought they were being watched and she was acting. He ducked into the cloak room and peered back into the corridor. Empty. He put down the broom and can. He took out an American cigarette, one of his tips, and lit it. Smoking was not allowed but all the hops smoked in this private sanctuary.

O'Flaherty entered. 'Where have you been, Morgan?'

'Working.'

'It looks like it. Give me a cigarette.'

D'Arcy gave him one and lit it.

A gleam came into O'Flaherty's eyes at his first puff. 'Mac Carr is checking out. You know that, of course.'

'I couldn't care less.' D'Arcy blew smoke at the ventilator.

'He won't be back for a week,' O'Flaherty said. 'You're in again, boy.'

'You can't tell about these things,' D'Arcy frowned. 'Anyway, I think I want to steer my own course. I'm getting sick of jumping for the chance.'

'If you don't want her,' O'Flaherty said. 'Just call me. I'd jump anywhere for that chance.'

'I guess I should too,' D'Arcy frowned. 'I wonder what's happening to me.'

'You're getting soft, Morgan. You won't snap up the extra buck acting like that.'

A ringing alarm blasted their ears.

'Ho Jeez!' O'Flaherty stepped on his cigarette. 'Fire alarm practice. Get out to the laundry. Quick!' He dashed away.

D'Arcy smoked his cigarette to the end. He noticed that O'Flaherty's butt was smouldering close to a pile of papers. The cloak room needed tidying. There were cartons with bottles of whiskey and ginger ale used for black-marketing at night. Empty boxes and papers were scattered about. O'Flaherty's butt fired a piece of paper. D'Arcy put his foot on it.

He laughed smugly. 'They'd all be practicing with their hose on the laundry while the Lodge burned down.' He stamped out his own cigarette. 'Last boy is going to have to clean this place.' He walked swiftly into the outdoors.

The fire truck rattled by him. Its ancient engine chugged. Its huge barrel of water rocked gently. Two men were hanging to its side and clasping the hose in their arms.

When D'Arcy arrived at the parking lot, the hose was attached to the barrel. Several bellhops and laundry men were pointing the nozzle at the wall of the laundry while the two last boys pumped at a see-saw machine. Runners and Flowers were watching, arms folded, smiling superiorly.

Nick caught sight of D'Arcy. He shifted an arm from the hose and beckoned to him. 'Come on, you loafer. O'Flaherty, look at him.'

D'Arcy ducked behind a group of spectators before O'Flaherty turned. He crept behind parked cars and came up a distance away where he could watch without being apprehended. So far the hose had spurted disappointingly. The last boys were pumping for all they were worth.

D'Arcy discovered that Kate stood in front of him. She turned round, as if on impulse, and saw him.

'There isn't a fire, is there!' she smiled.

'It's just entertainment for the guests,' he said.

'Oh! do you think they need entertainment that badly?'

'Something different,' D'Arcy smirked. 'Bored people are always looking for variety.'

Kate flinched. 'You, of course, are above being bored.'

'The difference is that I get bored with people, not with myself.'

'I see,' Kate smiled faintly.

'I don't think you do,' he said. 'For instance, this fire practice bores me because it's a farce. That engine couldn't put out a burning match box.'

'You said people bore you,' she reminded him sweetly.

'When people pretend, when there is no sincerity, I lose interest,' he said sternly.

'D'Arcy, don't say anymore. I know your little speech is meant for me. I could finish it myself. I shan't want to see you if that's how you feel.'

'You're jumping to conclusions,' he said. 'I still want you.'

She frowned puzzled. 'You're awfully strange. Something's happened to you.' She touched his arm. 'I must have hurt you. I'm terribly sorry.'

'You didn't hurt me,' he grinned. 'Don't get me wrong.'

The hose spurted. A long heavy stream of water struck the brick wall and cascaded over the wooden porch. A fireman directed the men holding the hose. They ran forward, backward, sideways, turning the hose on the eaves, at the pavement. The hops jogged tiredly about with bored expressions. Nick seemed disgusted.

'It looked effective,' Kate said. 'You see, it worked after all.'

'After a fashion,' D'Arcy shrugged.

She looked up winsomely. 'You have to have patience.'

'Okay,' he twisted a smile. 'I'm free this afternoon. Want to go for a swim?'

'I'm seeing Mac off at two,' she said.

'Pick me up at two-thirty.'

'Morgan!' O'Flaherty screamed. 'Get over here!'

D'Arcy, startled, ran to take a place at the hose. Kate laughed shrilly. She attracted Runners' attention. He was moving carefully towards her. She stepped casually away and broke into a fast walk behind the cars. On crossing the lawn, she glanced back to see Runners posed with a hand on a headlight as he gazed sadly after her.

'All right!' called the Chief Fireman.

The water was shut off. The men rolled up the hose.

'Fine him,' Nick suggested to O'Flaherty.

'That will cost you a quarter,' O'Flaherty said.

121

D'Arcy handed him a quarter.

'Someday you are going to get in trouble,' O'Flaherty warned. 'When I say go quick, you go quick.'

'Instead, he talks to his girlfriend,' Nick snorted.

'You guys looked funny,' D'Arcy laughed.

'Cut it!' O'Flaherty said. 'Or you'll pay another quarter.'

The hops walked sombrely back to the lodge. A fire engine rattled by. Nelles, standing on the patio, pointed to the other shift marching down the hill.

'Scram!' O'Flaherty ordered.

D'Arcy led his shift in a scramble up the hill. The noon sun was hot. He didn't relish soup, meat, and potatoes. His throat went thick and sticky at the thought. He lay in the shade beside the staff tennis court. Before closing his eyes, he saw Johnnie O'Dreams in the distance.

Johnnie walked up and nudged D'Arcy's foot. 'Hey! I want to talk to you,' Johnnie said worriedly.

'Not about Deo and Runners,' D'Arcy yawned.

'Yeah. How did you know? What's going on? She says she is going to his party.'

'Runners has a good eye for pulchritude. The rest depends on her, I guess.'

Johnnie thought for a moment. 'So it does.' He snapped his fingers. 'I was getting involved with that kid. This intermission came at just the right spot. I feel good. Thanks D'Arcy.' He strolled away and sprang over a bush onto the pathway.

Involvement! The word sickened D'Arcy. He wanted to float fancy free. Disturbed, he sat up. Blair St. Clair hiked by. He walked with one shoulder thrust forward as if carrying a golf bag.

'Won't be long,' D'Arcy called.

'Staff tournament? Next week,' Blair said. He approached D'Arcy. 'You coming in it?'

'Joke,' D'Arcy said.

'O'Dreams is on the course practically every morning,' Blair said thoughtfully. 'He wants revenge for last year.'

'He hasn't got the temperament,' D'Arcy said. 'You can beat him again.'

Blair smiled and brushed back his golden hair. 'Maybe. So long.' He hiked toward the mess hall.

D'Arcy saw Miriam in her cabin maid's uniform. She was walking gaily with other girls on the far side of the court. D'Arcy lay back in the sun and closed his eyes. He dreamed erotically of Kate.

15

Slim Johnson passed D'Arcy asleep on the lawn. He went silently lest he waken him. He had just banked another twenty dollars with the lodge cashier. He didn't want D'Arcy to ask why he was coming from the lodge. If anyone knew he was saving money, word would get around. Spendthrift caddies would harp at him.

Aurmand was speaking with another French-Canadian in his room when he entered. They switched to English for Slim's sake.

'Quebec women bad,' Aurmand sneered. 'Make love with clothes on.'

Slim was shocked.

'So they won't have babies,' Aurmand's friend explained significantly.

'Wretched people,' Aurmand said in disgust.

Slim thought guiltily of the girls he had pressed against. 'But they can use contraceptives.'

'No!' Aurmand shook his head severely.

Slim slipped his hand under his mattress. 'This book says you can.' He brought forth the medical book.

Aurmand's friend took it, glanced at the title, and threw it away. 'That's evil. You should not read this kind of thing. Making love is to produce babies.'

'Where did you get it, Slim?' Aurmand looked fiercely through his spectacles.

'The fellows have been reading it,' he countered. 'It's told me a lot.'

'You are Protestant?' Aurmand asked.

'Presbyterian,' Slim said.

Aurmand's friend smiled significantly. 'You are easily led astray.'

'Slim,' Aurmand sighed. 'I'm disappointed in you. Don't read about love until you marry.'

'And don't talk about contraceptives,' his friend added angrily. 'It is silly and morally wrong.'

'But why?'

'It's a long story,' the friend said.

'But if you can't prevent having babies, you can't make love,' Slim said. 'Everybody knows a big family costs too much.'

'That is right,' Aurmand nodded.

'Gosh,' Slim frowned. 'That must be why there's a lot of prostitution in Quebec?'

'That's the English influence,' Aurmand's friend said. 'English commercialism.'

'But they must be French prostitutes,' Slim argued.

Aurmand winced. 'You do not understand. Wait until you marry.'

'You are too young,' said his friend.

'I feel I'm stupid, I'm so innocent,' Slim cried angrily. 'No one told me anything. I had to read this book to find out. Why is love such a big secret?'

'Wait until you are in love,' Aurmand said.

'But I have been.'

'That was not love,' the friend smiled. 'When you marry, that is love.'

'It's so confusing.' Slim put the book back under his mattress. 'I wanted to make love lots of times, but I didn't because it's supposed to be wrong. Yet when I'm with a girl, everything works towards it. That book says contraceptives are the answer.'

'Forget the book,' the friend said. 'Listen to God. He knows the answer. He didn't create contraceptives.'

'There is another answer,' Aurmand said. 'Don't go with girls. They are bad.'

The door swung open. Bruce Bannister strode in. He ignored them and climbed into his bunk.

'But that makes us distrust girls,' Slim continued. 'And they will distrust us. I don't think that's right.'

'That is the only way to avoid desire,' Aurmand concluded.

Bruce looked over the side of his bunk. 'Are these mics trying to convert you, Slim?'

'No,' Slim smiled. 'We just decided we have to marry before we make love.'

Bruce exploded in guffaws.

'What is funny?' Aurmand snapped.

'You!' Bruce shouted. 'The whole pack of you.'

'Allons-y!' said the friend, darting up angrily.

'Moment!' Aurmand said.

'Non! Viens! On ne dispute pas avec les chiens.'

Aurmand followed him out the door. 'Soon, Slim,' he nodded amicably as he went.

'Soon what?' Bruce frowned,

'He means he'll see me again soon. Why the hell do you have to shout at them?' Slim frowned.

'That's the only way they understand. They think the whole world belongs to them. Their damned religion is the most important in the universe. Even their damned language is more important than the unity of the country. What did they tell you about sex?'

'They said I shouldn't read that book you gave me.'

Bruce clenched his teeth. 'Did they read it?'

'No.'

'Then how do you know?' He lay back. 'They want to tell the whole damned world what to do. Look!' He sat up. 'Why do you think that doctor wrote the book? To corrupt people? He wrote it for guys like you and me who won't find out anywhere else because those stupid mics don't want anyone to know.'

'Don't they know?'

'Of course they don't. All they know is what they're told or what they have to read. They've got their own books, their own authors, their own twisted mentality. Aw, they make me sick.'

'Well, I've finished the book anyway.' Slim handed it to him. 'Thanks.'

'Are you glad you read it?'

'Yeah,' Slim said. 'I think so.'

'You'll be really glad someday,' Bruce said.

Slim nodded. 'I hope so.' He didn't feel well. He changed into his swim trunks. 'I wish people could discuss without arguing.'

'You can't with that type,' Bruce said. 'They're too stupid.'

Slim swung a towel about his neck and strolled down the corridor. Cabin girls were sweeping the rooms and making the beds. He smelt the disinfectant from the wood. It was dank indoors. The staff cabin maids received no tips comparable to those earned by the guest-cabin maids. Some caddies, who understood the meanness of poverty, left them small sums, but the majority were either too rich or too keen on saving to think of the girls who cleaned their rooms.

The rallying thump of Dixieland resounded from the end room. Slim opened the door. Horns blared. Dixie Mitchell danced in short steps, flexing his knees, his hands up at shoulder level, a blissful expression. He strutted slowly up to Slim and back to Gregory who was beating at the tabletop with two dessert spoons.

'Man, man,' Gregory gurgled. 'Whoodelya, whoodelya, whoo, whoo, whoo.'

The music climbed to a crescendo with a shrill trumpet. Dixie spread his arms wide and rose on his toes. Gregory paused, hair over his face, jaw jutting with wild determination at the table top.

'Whirrreeeyahoo!' Dixie hollered. The ensemble, including Gregory, broke into an ear-splitting finale. Dixie jiggled round, snapping his fingers, eyes bright.

Backing out, Slim closed the door. He was afraid to let go like that. He faced life as if in subtle battle where he needed every impulse under his control. He took the trail to the Staff Lake. Outwardly calm, he felt his nerves dance excitedly from the effects of the music. There was a girl sprawled on the dock: Deodora Adams.

He stepped onto the boards and nodded when she looked up.

'Hi!' he said.

'Hi!' She put her head down and closed her eyes.

He lay down on his towel. Chin on hands he watched the trees on the far shore.

'Have you ever been invited to Mr. Runners' parties?' Deo asked.

Slim squinted at her. 'Why would he invite me?' He regarded the trees again, coolly green against the seared blue.

'He might have,' she retorted. 'He invited me.'

'That's different,' he said. 'You're a girl?'

She sat up. 'What's so different about being a girl?'

'Why ask me?' Slim said. He mumbled. 'I'm the last guy to ask.'

'Well, I'm trying to find someone who has been so I can find out how they dress,' Deo pouted.

'Ask that waitress, Jane,' Slim suggested. 'She hangs around with guests.'

'She's lucky,' Deo said resentfully.

'Maybe,' Slim closed his eyes. Approaching footsteps on the dock boards bounced his chin.

Johnnie O'Dreams spread his beach robe beside Deo. 'Hi chicken!'

'Hello,' she drawled.

He sat down and clasped her thighs in one hand. 'Turn over on your back.'

She rolled over. 'Oh, I wish you'd leave me alone.'

'That's better,' he said. 'I want to see who I'm talking to, you know!'

'Why does everything have to be the way you want it?'

'It isn't, is it?' Johnnie said. 'We had a date which you broke for the manager's sake. You're getting what you want both ways.'

'What do you mean?' She sat up, pouting angrily.

He pushed her back and leaned over her. 'I don't have to tell you, honey.'

'I don't see why you're mad,' she said. 'It's just a party. You go to lots of them.'

'Mad?' He turned in surprise to Slim. 'Hey, Buster, do I look mad?' He brushed his hair back from his face.

'A little worried,' Slim said, 'but not mad.'

Deo laughed.

'You smart little....' Johnnie shook his fist. 'You're a caddie aren't you? Wait till I get you carrying for me.'

'Oh Johnnie, you're cruel,' Deo complained. 'He was just fooling.'

'So am I, Deo dodo.' He jumped up, ran on the diving board and sprang, arching into the water. 'Come on,' he shouted brushing back strands of wet hair. 'It's great.' He swam out.

'Johnnie's crazy,' Deo giggled. 'He doesn't want me to go to the party.'

'Did he say so?' Slim asked.

'No, but I know him.' Her eyes brightened. 'Which is why I want to go. Look at him, the drip.'

Johnnie was duck-diving and wiggling just his hands above water. Deo went to the ladder and lowered herself into the lake.

Miriam walked onto the dock. 'Hello Slim,' she said smoothly. 'May I sit beside you?'

'Might as well grab a place before the dock is overflowing,' he said.

She sat on her towel beside him. Slim looked shyly at her. He casually adopted an off-hand manner with girls as provocatively attractive as Miriam.

'Heard you went mountain climbing!' he smiled.

'Who told you?' She puckered her lips in amusement.

'Don Clarking. The guys respect you for not quitting, you know.'

'That's flattering to hear.'

Slim didn't like her to talk down to him. 'Catch any grizzly bears?'

'Almost,' she said, 'but they all ran away.' She laughed. 'You see, you can't tease me.' She watched Johnnie crawl.

Slim was disturbed. He wanted her whole attention. 'Next time you go, will you take me along?'

'There won't be a next time,' she smiled. Their eyes met, inquisitively. She noticed him. 'Unless you take me.'

'I like going out on roasts better than mountain climbing,' Slim said.

'It's easier,' she grinned.

'More fun. I like watching a camp fire.'

'The girls are having a wiener roast tonight,' she said pensively.

'Oh yeah.' He sensed a quickening interest. 'What girls?'

'The cabin girls--my group,' she said. 'I haven't asked anyone yet.' She paused.

'I like wiener roasts,' Slim said.

'Do you want to come?' she asked, brightening.

'Sure,' Slim nodded.

Deo screamed as Johnnie pushed her under. She came to the surface, blubbering. Johnnie pursued her to the dock. Breathless, she climbed up and stood panting.

'Leave me alone,' she puffed as Johnnie put his towel about her shoulders. 'You're cruel.'

Johnnie laughed and sat down. He regarded Miriam.

Miriam was not aware of Johnnie's attention. She was reflecting on her boldness in asking Slim to the roast. She intended to ask D'Arcy but as he seemed to be avoiding her, she lacked the courage. Something she had done had turned D'Arcy away. Slim would probably behave in the same manner. But at least she wouldn't sit in the cabin while the other girls were having fun.

'Who's your friend?' Johnnie asked.

Slim introduced them.

'What lovely black braids you have?' Johnnie eyed her.

Miriam shrank from him. His forwardness put her on guard. 'I like my hair this way.'

'I'm going,' Deo said.

'Wait a minute, baby.' Johnnie moved closer to Miriam. 'Where do you work?'

'Here.' Miriam smiled. 'I'm part of the staff.'

'Good-bye, Johnnie,' Deo called stepping onto the path.

'Damn it,' Johnnie said slipping into his robe and running after Deo. 'I'll see you around, eh?'

Miriam tossed her head with a smile. She sensed Slim's alarm which pleased her. Slim seemed naive, the kind of boy she could trust.

'I don't like him,' she said. 'He's a wolf.'

'He knows his way around,' Slim said.

'You're more my type,' she smiled. 'I'm glad we met like this. It seemed funny to know you just to say hello.'

'That's the way it goes up here, if you don't come out on blanket parties.'

'I've never liked anyone enough,' she said. 'Anyway those parties seem like a waste of time.'

'Smell of wood in the fire is good.'

'But you sing the same old songs. I had enough of it when I was a camp counsellor,' she frowned.

'How old are you, Miriam?'

'Twenty-five.' She regarded him blankly.

'Gosh! you look younger.'

'That's not so old,' she smiled and stood up. 'Coming in?' She dived.

Slim was intrigued. He thought an older woman would teach him about love. If so, he could not have welcomed a more attractive teacher. Her dark presence was exciting. He dove after her.

Miriam splashed water on him when he came to the surface. He retaliated. She swam back to the dock. Slim splashed her again.

'Don't!' she cried laughing. 'Our towels will get wet.'

As Slim pulled his lean bronzed body onto the dock, a car slowed almost to a stop on the bend in the road at the far end of the lake. Allan Steel watched lasciviously as Slim stretched in the sun and lay down on the dock. He gripped the wheel and accelerated. He had been to his cabin, found Bett absent, had a drink, and was on his way to the lodge to seek convivial companionship. Tall and thin, he was distinguished by a close-clipped fair mustache and darting brown eyes. Heavy eye-pouches gave him the wistful mien of a bloodhound, when he was not in company.

16

Allan Steel stepped from the bright sun into the dark lobby. He blinked, regarding the bellhops preparing to meet the new arrivals. There were unfamiliar faces. He hesitated between continuing to the verandah or turning down the office corridor. On instinct he wheeled and plunged through the lobby to the snack bar. Stool after stool lined the counter which ended at Jack Flowers who leaned over it as he whispered to a white-jacketed waiter. Allan, trailing a finger along the stool seats, sauntered towards him.

Flowers glanced up. His face clouded in suspicion then broke into a smile. He smoothed his mustache and stuck out his hand. Allan touched it and asked the waiter for cigarettes.

'Looking well, Jack. Had a hunch you'd be back this summer.' He patted Flowers under the arms. 'Lost weight, I think.'

'You didn't gain,' Flowers said mildly.

The waiter handed Allan the cigarettes. Flowers prevented Allan from paying and nodded the waiter away.

'Where's the big boss?' Allan simpered. 'Does his wife let him out?'

'He spends the first part of the afternoon with the family,' Flowers said.

'On order, I bet.'

'He's holding a party tomorrow night. I'll get you an invitation,' Flowers said.

'Interesting,' Allan nodded. 'Have you seen my creature?'

Flowers frowned.

'Bett,' Allan said resignedly.

Flowers nodded. 'She left with a full-blooded hearty.' He grinned faintly.

'As long as she has fun,' Allan slurred his words. 'Wears down the rough edges. Keeps her out of my hair.' He saw Flowers glance at his thinning hairline. He turned away impatiently. 'Can we hit the town tonight, Jack? I need a little mixing.'

The snap of a metal lid distracted them. Alick Sandhurst appeared behind the counter. He held a ledger and a pen to the side as he peered at the ribbon of the cash register. Preoccupied, he had not seen them. Winking at Flowers, Allan leaned stealthily over the counter. He stretched his arm out and goosed Sandhurst. 'Bung-ho!'.

Alick started into the cash register with a sharp cry and dropped his ledger. Allan and Flowers roared. Alick, blushing, turned, shyly indignant.

'I should have known it was you,' Alick said petulantly. 'You are not out of your schoolboy stage.'

Allan roared louder. 'See yourself. Look in the mirror.'

Alick nervously backed away to bend down for the ledger and stood up before the wall mirror.

'Like someone's maiden aunt,' Allan chortled.

Alick grinned at himself.

'Too loud, boys!' Flowers warned. 'Alick and I planned to dine together.' He looked questioningly at Alick.

'He can come if he leaves his bag of tricks at home,' Alick said.

They laughed uproariously.

'That neutralizes me,' Allan said. 'Shall I pick you up at the lodge?'

'Better to meet in town,' Flowers spoke softly, shifting his eyes at some guests who had strolled into the bar.

Giving Flowers a pat on the knee, Allan left him abruptly. Alick busily copied figures into his ledger.

Allan decided to walk to the clubhouse for a drink. He followed the road by the garage and traversed the pebbled area where golfers parked their cars. He stood still. Kate was standing by her car. She was brooding, unaware of him. Tiptoeing on to the grass he approached and pinched her bottom.

Kate startled, jumped round. 'Allan Steel! You are the sneakiest character I know!'

'Just thought I'd give you a little thrill,' he said quietly.

'I'm just thrilled to pieces,' she said. 'Does Bett know you're here?'

'She never knows where I am, thank God. But let me look at you, Kate dear.' He cupped his hands in front of him as if clasping her face. 'Few more lines around the neck. Been crying a bit. Watch the squinting; it's beginning to show.'

'Stop it, you louse!' Kate turned her head away. 'I can say the same about you.' She surveyed him from the corners of her eyes and touched her cheeks. 'Looking sallow. Seedy about the mouth. Ever try a hair-preserving shampoo?'

'That's no longer amusing,' he barked.

'I'm sorry, but I didn't think you were funny either.'

'Are you going in for a drink?' He motioned to the clubhouse.

'I'm waiting for a friend.'

'Ah! When Mac's away, Kate has her day.'

'If you must know, I'm waiting for Bett.'

'I bet,' he said. 'By the way, I bumped into a mutual friend--Julien Kowalski. Remember him?'

'Julien!' she cried. 'Haven't seen him for ages.'

'He's coming up,' Allan observed D'Arcy striding towards them. 'Well!' he breathed. 'Enjoy your picnic, sweetie.'

'Oh!' Kate whirled round and cried out to D'Arcy. 'There you are!'

'I won't embarrass you further,' Allan moved away. 'Hello, Morgan, how are you this year?' he called.

D'Arcy tossed him a nod of recognition and climbed into the car with Kate. She stalled the motor and restarted it.

'Oh dear, I'm worried,' she said. 'I don't trust that man. He's liable to make up all sorts of stories.'

'Who cares?'

'I care! What if Mac hears about us?'

'Make up your mind,' D'Arcy said grimly. 'Do you want to go swimming with me or not?'

She sighed. 'Of course, but you have to understand, D'Arcy.'

'Let's get to Bear Lake. We'll talk about it there.'

She drove on to the road. A turmoil of doubt, coiling in her mind, worked its way to her stomach. She braked. 'You drive.'

D'Arcy went round the car and took the driver's seat.

She remarked upon his youth and handsomeness. Life was short, transient. He drove quickly, determination lining his face. Love gave her meaning, something to make life travel smoothly until she struck the bump at the end of the road. Did Mac expect her to stay home and knit?

'Do you love me, D'Arcy?'

'Maybe,' he said. 'How do I know what love is?'

'Do you cherish me?'

'I do when I don't have you,' he smiled.

'Oh! be serious,' Kate snapped peevishly.

'Isn't it enough that I'm with you?' D'Arcy asked. 'That ought to mean something.'

Kate pondered the significance. Certainly if she were not with D'Arcy, she would want to be with another man. But then, she had preferred D'Arcy. He meant adventure, realism. Take Bett. She was another sort. She found adventure in looking for another man. She believed in fantasy; the next will be greater than the last.

A mama bear hurried her pair of cubs into the woods.

She had an obligation to her children. She wanted to be morally pristine for their sake. But Mac made it so impossible!

Sylvester was on duty at the patrolman's shack and watched them shoot by. Kate was staring worriedly out the window. D'Arcy frowned over the steering wheel. Sylvester would not have taken them for lovers.

D'Arcy took a side road to its dead end. He drew the car up under a beech tree. Kate reached in the back for her bathing suit and they got out.

'I'm not enjoying this,' she said. 'Oh D'Arcy!' She ran to him and buried her head on his chest. 'I'm sorry. This isn't fun for you.'

'I'm enjoying it,' he said. 'For once I'm not the one who's worried.'

She caught his meaning and giggled. 'Jake Slade was nice, wasn't he?'

'A good guy.' D'Arcy directed them to the path.

'If Mac was like him, I wouldn't be doing this.'

D'Arcy halted. 'If you think it's wrong, don't do it.'

'I don't know what to think.'

'Then we're heading back.' He started for the car.

'Please,' Kate seized his arm. 'I want to go swimming.' She shook her head. 'I get these crazy ideas sometimes. I don't know what's wrong. D'Arcy, you make me feel wonderful. Kiss me.'

He kissed her.

'Presto!' she cried. 'The world changes. Come on.' She led the way along the path.

Smiling, D'Arcy followed.

'When I'm with you,' Kate said, 'I feel I'm living for the moment. Why do you have this influence over me?'

'I am an evil genius,' D'Arcy said.

'Seriously,' she looked back, 'do you live for the moment?'

'No, because I don't have to make hedonism an excuse for what I do. I have no obligations, hence I don't need excuses. Life is a stream of events for me. Sometimes I'm in control, sometimes I'm not, but whatever happens, I don't have to answer for it.'

'But what if you do something wrong?' she grinned.

'I'm not a fool. I don't appreciate myself at the detriment of others.'

The path grew narrower. Balsam and pine scented the way. Kate yearned for D'Arcy's naked arms about her body, but she was determined to hold out until they reached the lake. Mac's business-like aura still clung to her spirit, though it was gradually being loosened.

They came upon Bear Lake, a calm circle of a dark water with trees clustered thickly by its shore. Kate started towards the water but stopped in sudden fright. 'D'Arcy!'

A bear swirled about in the water immediately in front of them. D'Arcy took Kate's hand and led her in a dash back. The bear scampered from the water, crashed through the trees and disappeared.

'Oh! It gave me a fright.' Kate clasped her throat.

'He looked like Charlie,' D'Arcy said. 'Haven't you seen him around the lodge?'

'I couldn't tell one from another,' Kate sighed. 'Let's not swim there.'

Laughing, D'Arcy took the trail running alongside the lake. 'Animals make the best trails,' he said. 'Feel how easy this is to walk over. It's picturesque. No straight lines, no sign of a human having bulldozed his way through the bush.'

'It's wonderful,' Kate thrilled. 'D'Arcy, I wish I'd climbed Pyramid with you.'

'It was a wet climb,' he said.

'Did you wish I had come with you?'

'Don't ask foolish questions.'

She puzzled. D'Arcy's thoughts were a mystery. At moments she thought she knew him but she was mistaken. 'What's foolish about it?'

'Only a fool would want to be without you,' he joked.

'You just won't be serious with me,' she cried.

'This is the spot.' He stripped off his shirt and kicked off his shoes. Kate looked about for a place to change.

'You don't need a bathing suit,' he said.

'Haven't you one?' she raised her brows.

He stood naked. 'No one comes here.'

She watched him step down the bank and plunge. She set her clothes on top of his. She picked up the bathing suit, held it out, and impulsively threw it in the pile. She slipped into the water.

'It's lovely and cool,' she cried.

The ripples gleamed in the sun. D'Arcy tread water. She swam to him. He went under and seized her legs. She gripped his hair and went under with him. She slipped down against him and embraced his neck. He struggled, broke away, and burst the surface for air. She popped up beside him.

'Darn near drowned me,' he gasped.

'That was a bear hug for Bear Lake,' she smiled.

'I'll bear that in mind,' he said, crawling for shore.

He reclined on the bank. The sun warmed his skin. He watched Kate circle. She lay on her back with her breasts cresting the water and her legs pumping lazily.

'Come ashore!' he called.

'If you want me,' she said. 'You'll have to come and get me.'

He licked his lips. The distance between them was about fifteen long strokes. Kate instinctively lengthened it.

'Come out and rest,' he said persuasively. 'You'll be tired.'

'I'm resting perfectly well,' she said.

D'Arcy stood up, eyes gleaming. Kate gave a thrill of laughter and turned over in readiness to flee.

'Last chance,' D'Arcy warned.

She began to crawl away. D'Arcy dove and came up racing in long gliding strokes. Kate passed through cold currents as she swam. Afraid of cramps, she turned towards shore. D'Arcy had his head down. She dove under and swam for as long as she could hold her breath.

D'Arcy noticed her coming up and went under before she saw him. She looked about warily. D'Arcy surfaced ten yards away. Screaming, she thrashed out for shore with D'Arcy hot in pursuit. She gasped for breath. D'Arcy gained rapidly. She heard him splash behind her as she reached the bank. She pulled herself out and took several steps when D'Arcy brought her down with a low tackle. He crawled up beside her and put his lips on hers. She exploded with laughter. He frowned.

'It's not what you do, D'Arcy, it's the way you do it,' she giggled.

He smiled. He smoothed her wet hair and smelt the freshness of her skin. The forest was intensely still, the water soundless. He kissed her breasts and nibbled lightly at her shoulder and neck as they prepared to love. A fire burned under his skin just as the fire burned from the sky.

'You know Kate,' he sighed. 'I'm glad you're not frigid.'

She laughed. 'Why D'Arcy, what an extraordinary thing to say.' It reminded her how agreeably young he was. She fingered his profile with pleasure, then sighing threw her arms about his back.

A cicada began its long drowsy whistle. Others picked up the song. Later, the toot of the thrush punctuated the stillness of the afternoon. High firs stirred fretfully against the blue sky. D'Arcy stretched his neck and sat up. The sun sent longer shadows across the water. Like an Indian, the evening was creeping up behind the bushes.

'Kate, darling, wake up.'

She yawned and sat up beside him.

'Where do you think we left our clothes?' He searched the shore line.

'I didn't make much of a circle.' She pointed at a bushy spot on the bank that was indistinguishable from any other. 'It was there.'

D'Arcy took her hand. 'Let's swim for it.'

'Oh no,' she yawned. 'Let's not.'

He pulled her into the water. They swam slowly. D'Arcy climbed the bank to the path. 'I don't see them.'

Kate stepped beside him. Arms on hips, she looked up and down the path. 'I'm sure they were here.'

'You go that way,' D'Arcy pointed. 'I'll go this.'

They separated. After several minutes of naked walking, D'Arcy called out. 'Have you found them?' Kate's voice answered plaintively from the distance. 'No.'

'My God,' he mumbled. 'Start back,' he called.

They met at the original spot.

'Do you think someone is playing a trick?' he asked anxiously.

Kate reared back. 'No one ever comes here,' she said, 'quote, unquote.'

'Someone must have,' he mused.

Kate forced a grin. 'Perhaps Charlie took our clothes. His family has to endure a cold winter in these mountains.'

'Aren't you even worried?' he frowned.

'D'Arcy, I've come to depend on you so much that I'm leaving our situation completely at the mercy of your ingenuity. Anyway, nature seems to be your particular playground.'

'This is no time for sarcasm.' He scanned the bushes near them.

'Look!' Kate gasped.

Their clothes were arrayed on the spreading branches of a pine away back from the trail.

'Someone has been here!' She jumped behind a bush.

D'Arcy angrily peered around him. He marched up to the tree and pulled down their clothes.

'Everything seems to be here,' he said.

Kate ran up to claim her belongings. They dressed hurriedly.

'My bathing suit!' she cried. 'Where is it?'

D'Arcy nodded to the base of the tree. Her suit was fitted on a small log of silver birch. At one end of the log were their two pairs of shoes, at the other was D'Arcy's handkerchief pierced with twigs in such manner as to resemble a grinning face.

Kate blushed. 'I wonder who did it?'

'I'm willing to bet they were from Bampers,' D'Arcy laughed.

He helped her retrieve the bathing suit. They put on their shoes and headed back, silently.

Kate took his hand. 'Well, I hope this has taught you a lesson, nature boy.'

137

17

The culprits were Gregory and Dixie. They had planned to swim in Bear Lake that afternoon. If D'Arcy and Kate had not been concerned with Kate's moral equivocations, they might have seen Gregory at the roadside when they whizzed by. Gregory was patiently waiting for Dixie to finish his business in the woods. The two caddies arrived at the lake just as D'Arcy chased Kate into shore. Unwilling to trespass on lover's paradise, they decided to make for the next lake. But before pushing on, Gregory suggested the Christmas tree display, and devils that they were, they arranged it.

When they passed Bear Lake on the way home, the clothes were gone.

'I wonder if they realized it was meant to be a Nativity Scene,' Gregory said.

'They wouldn't,' Dixie rasped. 'They haven't got our imaginative sense.'

'The moneyed rich have no imagination,' Gregory said. 'I include Morgan in that class because he seems to want to include himself.'

'He's not after the money,' Dixie chuckled.

'Oh yes?' Gregory moved his bushy brows together. 'Can you name one person at Bampers besides us who is not after money?'

Dixie hummed in agreement. 'What are we doing there then?'

'We, my good man, are derelicts.'

'We get free board and lodging and work only when we have to,' Dixie sung. 'Man! Let's make a Dixieland number out of that.'

Gregory was not to be sidetracked. He allowed the pleasurable mood of rhetoric to rise from his lips. 'We are the innocent cast amongst packs of devouring wolves. We are the proud overruled by humble servants and buck-kissing puritans. We are the mighty in spirit stultified by crass mobbism. We are the untried, degraded by the foul superficialities of our society. Of what avail to work when by working we become that which we despise?'

'Hear! Hear!' Dixie picked up a stick and clubbed the tree trunks.

'Of what avail to soil our souls for the sake of weak applause from brain-washed idolaters? Of what avail,' Gregory's modulated voice soared, 'to think publicly when the public cannot understand?'

'Who wants to think?' Dixie cried. 'Get in the groove, man.' He charlestoned onto the road.

Gregory struck out with his finger. 'Do you know why we're in the groove? Because no square can fit in with us.'

'Yes sir, yes sir, three bags full,' Dixie sang.

'I very much doubt,' Gregory said, 'that any individual at Bampers is capable of doing anything which is not connected with material gain.'

'You have a warped view,' Dixie said.

'I am a realist,' Gregory intoned. 'Warping comes from sentiment.'

'You have a soft spot for yourself and your own genius,' Dixie said.

'I am a misanthrope,' Gregory whispered. 'I believe in genocide.'

'It is six-thirty,' Dixie reminded him. 'My tum-tum wants yum-yum. Hurry up.'

'Speed is a trait of the gods,' Gregory said. 'Hunger can make man immortal like them.'

'I take it,' Dixie smiled,' we have to die to become god-like.'

'Yes,' Gregory sighed. 'Speed is irrelevant. When we are dead, we will have no more hunger, hence, we won't need speed; therefore, it stands to reason, we shall have conquered speed.'

'Which makes us pretty fast boys. But you forgot one thing,' Dixie said. 'Hunger will have to conquer us first and I'm damned if I'll let it.'

'Cheers, Dix. You are the battling Canuck. Front trench and all that.'

'Pick up the pace, Gregory, or I'll report you to the caddie master.' Dixie trotted ahead.

He ran onto the main road, Gregory whooping behind. A lodge car rounded the bend, its looming hood rocketing at them. Dixie flailed the air and hummed to the screech of the tires. The driver was a lenient square.

'I'm only doing this because I had a big tip. Twenty bucks to drive a family to the Ice fields.'

Dixie and Gregory whistled appropriately. They opened the door.

'No!' The driver threw up his arm. 'In the back seat and get down. I'm taking no chances.'

They got in and crouched.

'Humiliating,' Gregory said over the roar of the motor.

They slowed down at the patrolman's gate. They were hailed to a stop.

Dixie closed his eyes. 'Are these buggers going to search the goddamn vehicle?'

'There's been a child lost on Lake Edith,' the patrolman said. His job was to inform all lodge personnel. 'We're arranging search parties at the lodge. They may need you to drive.'

'The hell,' the driver said. 'I have to eat and I'm tired.'

'I haven't eaten,' the patrolman said. 'I volunteered to stay while my relief went on the search.'

'What am I supposed to do? cry?' the driver squawked.

Dixie sat up. 'We'll bring some food out, man.'

The driver jerked the car forward and sped away. Dixie waved from the back.

'Do you want to get me fired?' the driver asked.

'He's on our side,' Dixie said.

'To hell with it!' The driver sped down the road and into the lodge grounds. 'Okay get out. There are your do-gooders for you.'

Buses were filling with staff members. Slim and Miriam were lining up to climb on board. Bundled up warmly, the searchers looked grim.

'Slim!' Dixie hailed. 'What happened?'

'A little girl,' Slim drawled. 'Her parents stopped their car at a stand for a minute. When they came back the girl was gone.'

'And all these people are going to look for her?' Gregory looked round in amazement.

'The response is wonderful,' Miriam cried, flushed with excitement. "We were going to a roast, but the girls decided to postpone it. The RCMP asked the staff to help.'

'Let's go,' Dixie cried. 'Hey, Slim, come and get a plate of food for the patrolman at the gate. He's faint with hunger.'

Slim blinked. 'Save me a seat, Miriam.' He went to the dining hall with them.

Miriam tried to imagine what the parents were feeling. Horror, fright, it was impossible to think. The spirit of the search displaced all sense of grief. The novelty of adventure inspired volunteers. Scores of young men and women bent to the purpose of assuring success. Moreover, the mounties were on the case.

Slim came back as the line boarded the last bus. He carried a basket which Davey had packed with left-over sandwiches and a large thermos of coffee. He left it with the driver to give to the patrolman at the gate. As the bus started, Dixie and Gregory ran up, halted it, and squeezed aboard. They had put on windbreakers and were munching buns which they pulled from their pockets.

Slim accidentally brushed his leg against Miriam's. He felt the shock of response. She smiled at him and held his hand. He wished suddenly that they had gone on the wiener roast.

'This animation is incredible,' Gregory said between mouthfuls.

'I feel like a Boy Scout,' Dixie said. 'Look! Here we are. We're giving the patrolman his dinner.'

The driver opened the door and handed out the basket. Dixie waved, and the patrolman took off his hat in reverence. The bus speeded on to Lake Edith.

In the meantime, Kate cut by it on one of the turns. She drove furiously. D'Arcy had to work, but she was determined to devote herself to finding the child. When she first heard the news, she was worried. She dashed to a telephone and although she knew she was being foolish, spoke long distance to a girl's camp in British Columbia. Only when she heard the sound of her daughter's voice was she able to relax.

When she arrived at the place of the search, the volunteers were strung out in long lines and all available flashlights were distributed among them. It would soon be dark. Two mounties held out a map before a group of forest rangers. Some rangers were deploying the searchers. A signal was given. From the roadside, the lines began to march slowly over bush, under branch, covering every foot of ground.

Kate saw a middle-aged man, face creased with worry, head bowed, standing silently with other men. A woman's voice carried in the sudden twilight. 'She was last seen going along the road.' Night fell. Bampers' buses arrived. Searchers were quickly arranged in lines. The soft murmur of respectful voices represented the hundreds of people. Flashlights digitally probed the ground. A quarter moon moved from behind a bank of cloud. Kate stepped into a line. She joined hands with the persons on either side. The tall male on her left made an impression. She looked closely at him. 'Slim!'

'Oh, hello, Mrs. Carr.'

'All right,' said a voice of command. 'Move slowly and look sharply. Don't leave a rock unturned.'

Slim held Miriam's hand on the other side. In spite of the seriousness of the occasion, he revelled in his sensational position.

'Do you think we'll find her?' he asked Kate.

'Oh God. I hope so!' she whispered.

They stumbled over clumps and stamped through long grass all the while peering by the aid of the moon and stars and the swinging beams of flashlights.

Miriam leaned close to Slim. 'They've been shouting through the woods for hours.'

Kate took a good long look at her.

'She may have fallen asleep,' Slim said. 'And didn't hear them.'

A helicopter whirred over the woods, its green and red lights marking its course through the dark.

'Is she your girlfriend?' Kate smiled.

'Well,' he blushed, 'for tonight.' He hoped Miriam had not heard. He glanced at her but could not tell her reaction in the darkness. 'How's it going?' he said to her.

'Fine,' Miriam said. 'I'm wondering if she could have been kidnapped.'

'How?' Slim asked.

'A car could have whisked her away from the roadside and be driving over the border right this very moment.'

Someone stumbled and the line halted for a moment.

'It's getting chilly,' Kate said cosily. 'I'm glad I have your hand to hold.'

Miriam regarded her sullenly. The line moved again. They had to drop hands because of the trees. They scoured the shrubbery around the trees. After an hour, some of the searchers became disillusioned. They voiced their doubts of finding the child.

'Please, let's go on,' Kate urged. 'You never know how far she may have wandered.'

Occasionally, men's voices called the girl's name. 'Eloise!' Searchers stopped walking. Silence in the dark forest. They moved onward.

Kate spoke to Slim. 'After a while it's as if the child were your very own.'

Slim nodded. 'I hope she wasn't kidnapped.'

'How?' Kate gasped.

'A car could have whisked her over the American border.'

Others overheard him. The rumour spread quietly. The air grew colder. Coughing along the line. Kate and Miriam held hands with Slim for an open space. He regretted having to let go to penetrate the woods.

D'Arcy arrived at the scene on the back of a truck. Most of the hops had been released from duty at eleven to help in the search. Men dragged the lake. Oarlocks squeaked. Lights crisscrossed over the water.

'Look on the shore,' said an official. 'Any piece of clothing, any clue.'

D'Arcy stumbled over roots and made his way onto the shore path. The search area felt activated by a hundred tramping feet and ghostly voices. Over all lay an air of despondency. Suddenly, the quarter moon blinked out. The stars disappeared. It began to rain softly. D'Arcy continued far along the shore. He heard voices in discussion on the road. A whistle blew. The search was to be abandoned. He climbed to the road. Shapes moved through the blackness. He moved with them and listened to the words of disappointment. 'Kidnappers!' people suggested. 'Must have been.' Groups moved from the woods and grass onto the road. D'Arcy heard Kate's voice distinctly.

'Yes, but I don't think we should be giving up at all.'

'We've covered the ground,' Slim said justifyingly. 'We've come almost in a complete circle, and the other lines have been directed over different places.'

'We can't continue all night,' Miriam snorted.

'If it were your child, you'd walk all night,' Kate retorted.

'And behave so emotionally that you'd be a perfect nuisance,' Miriam said sharply. She took Slim's arm.

They saw their way with one flashlight serving a large group. D'Arcy stepped up to Kate.

'It is senseless to go on,' he said.

She cried, 'D'Arcy!'

He hushed her. "Will you drive me back?'

'Of course, darling. I'm taking Slim and his girl.'

Miriam drew close to Slim's arm. She held his elbow against her breast. Her heart flipped at D'Arcy's appearance.

They came to the bright road lights and the lighted cabins from where the search was directed. D'Arcy saw Miriam with a shock. He smiled hesitantly. Miriam nodded coldly.

'D'Arcy!' Kate whispered. 'There's Runners.'

The thin figure of a beak-nosed man moved erectly in the shadows. Kate guided them silently by him. Slim and Miriam sat in the back seat. D'Arcy sat in front with Kate.

'We all need a stiff drink,' Kate said.

'Please take me straight back,' Miriam spoke up.

'Aren't you cold?' Slim asked, tenderly feeling her hands.

'But she doesn't drink,' Kate laughed. 'I meant to give you hot chocolate, dear.'

'I still have to rise early tomorrow,' Miriam said.

'Ah yes, a working girl,' Kate sighed.

'Well, I don't have to get up early,' Slim said, 'unless Mrs. Carr does.'

Kate laughed abruptly. 'That sounds incriminatory.'

D'Arcy laughed when he saw that Slim did not understand. 'Hey, Slim, watch out for that mountain climber, she's tough.'

Kate glanced back. 'Was she the lucky girl to go with you, D'Arcy?'

'I don't see why you call me lucky,' Miriam said.

'Well,' Kate explained archly, 'I was supposed to go, but couldn't at the last moment.'

D'Arcy stared angrily ahead.

'I'm glad D'Arcy brought you down safely, anyway,' Slim said.

'Thank you,' Miriam clasped his hand, 'for the kind words.'

'Slim is always ready with a kind word,' Kate said airily. 'I wouldn't go a round without him.'

'I guess the little girl is lost for good,' D'Arcy said. 'It all looks pretty hopeless.'

They drove in silence. As they came onto the highway from town, Kate jammed on the brakes in time to allow a car to hurtle by on its way to the lodge.

'Drunken driver,' she said, speeding after it.

The car swerved from one side of the road to the other.

'Don't get close to it,' Miriam said anxiously.

The car swung onto the shoulder of the road. The right back tire went flat. The car lurched to a stop. The driver immediately jumped out and leaned with both arms on the roof.

'It's Allan Steel!' Kate cried in amusement and pulled to a stop behind the car.

Allan Steel was chuckling. He squinted into Kate's headlights and stuck out his thumb. Alick Sandhurst crept out from the other door. He grinned shyly and ducked his head back in the car.

Kate got out and approached in a saunter,

'It's all right!' Alan called joyfully. 'Friends. We're saved.'

'Lucky we weren't provos,' Kate said.

'I can smell a policeman a mile away,' Allan leered.

'He could smell you too,' Kate said. 'I suppose you need our help.'

'No, no,' he waved peremptorily and opened the trunk.

Alick Sandhurst appeared beside them. He swayed with hands in pockets and watched complacently. Allan struggled to lift out the spare tire. D'Arcy moved beside him and picked up the jack.

Kate observed the black-haired scalp of a man in the back window. 'Who's that?'

'Sh!' Alick pressed a finger to his lips. 'Mr. Flowers is sleeping.' He fell back against the car and raised his head in silent laughter.

Kate looked significantly at D'Arcy.

'We are not in need of your help, bellhop,' Allan slurred, 'but as you are at our service, go ahead.'

D'Arcy fitted the jack under the rear bumper. 'Make sure it's in gear,' he said,

'Oh dear!' Alick grinned.

'It was in third when I stopped,' Alan chuckled. 'I don't know what it's in now.'

Kate looked in the windows as D'Arcy began to jack up the car. Jack Flowers sprawled hugely across the back seat, his chest heaving with sonorous breaths.

Slim stood idly behind the men. 'Can I help, D'Arcy?' he asked.

Allan eyed him sharply. He took his arm. 'Are you a strong enough boy to pull out the spare?'

'Sure.' Slim smiled. He pulled it out with one arm.

'Mr. Sandhurst!' Allan called loudly. 'Who is this boy? What's his name?'

Alick shuffled over to them. He looked sideways at Slim. 'I wish I knew,' he smiled bashfully.

'High enough, Slim?' D'Arcy asked.

Slim went to the side. 'Yeah.' He pulled off the hub cap.

'Slim,' Allan said with a nod of approval. He leaned on Alick's shoulder. 'Record that name in your big black book,' he snickered.

Kate moved into the light. 'You've been having a ball,' she said. 'Didn't you know about the search?'

'Search?' Allan squinted. 'We've been at it all night but there's nothing but women in that town.'

Alick stepped back apprehensively.

'Kate's my friend,' Allan told him. 'Aren't you, dear?'

'I'd sober up your other friend quickly,' Kate warned. 'He is supposed to know about the lost girl.'

'What girl?' Alick asked in alarm.

While Kate informed them, D'Arcy and Slim changed the tire. Alick rushed to kneel inside the car. Leaning over the back of the seat, he shook Jack Flowers by the lapels and called to him.

Smiling Jack peeped from eyeslits. 'What?'

The headlights of a slowing car flashed in the windows. The car stopped in front of them. Runners incisive voice pierced their ears.

'Too late,' Alick said.

Flowers sat up with a jerk. He stared wildly at the lean Runners stalking towards the car with his chauffeur striding behind him.

'Don't move,' Alick whispered.

Runners walked by them. His chauffeur stopped to peer in the windows. Flowers glared murderously and slid down in the

146

seat until his knees rested on the floor. The chauffeur gaped and straightened up.

'Kate!' Runners cried. 'Can I be of assistance?'

'It's all done, thanks, Tony,' she said warmly.

'Hello,' Allan nodded.

'Ah,' Runners twisted a smile of greeting. 'It was reported to me that you were in the area.'

'It was reported correctly,' Allan said.

D'Arcy lifted the flat tire into the trunk. Runners regarded him with astonishment.

'What are you doing here?' he shouted.

Slim clanked down the jack at that very moment and D'Arcy did not hear.

'What are you doing?' Runners screamed in fury.

Surprised, D'Arcy answered quickly. 'Coming back from Lake Edith, sir.'

'I'm driving them home,' Kate said.

Runners frowned. The corners of his mouth twitched. 'We have trucks for that purpose.' He turned to glare down the road.

D'Arcy and Slim retired to Kate's car out of earshot.

'Boy! I'm shaking,' Slim said. 'He scares me.'

'He's mad,' D'Arcy said. 'Completely insane.'

Runners spoke affably to Kate. 'You know, I don't like my staff to mix with the guests. It just won't work. I have to be severe and draw a strict line.'

Kate smiled understandingly. 'I know, Tony.'

'They're good boys,' Allan slurred. 'Changed my tire.'

Runners scrutinized him. 'You're not fit to drive.'

'Nonsense,' Allan said, edging towards the door of his car.

'You live on Lake Edith, but you are driving to the lodge,' Runners said. 'Explain yourself if you can.'

Allan stared dumbly.

'I think I'll have to drive you,' Runners stepped forward.

'No, you wont,' Allan cried. 'I'll knock you down.'

Runners smiled slyly. 'You act as if I were dangerous. It is a pity that your good friend, Flowers, is not here. You would believe him.'

Kate went to her car. 'If everything's fine, I'm going. Good-bye, Tony.'

'That bellhop,' Allan said, as if inspired. 'He'll drive me home.' He beckoned frantically. 'Mr. Morgan!'

Runners disdainfully watched D'Arcy approach. 'How is he going to get back from Lake Edith?'

'I'll lend him my car,' Allan said resolutely,

'I'm not sure that I approve,' Runners said.

'Get back in your machine,' Allan cried fiercely, signs of hysteria in his voice. 'I'm giving the orders.'

Runners eyed the windows of the car. 'You haven't seen Mr. Flowers have you?'

'No.' Allan held onto the car for support. 'Now, if you don't mind, I want to get home.'

'I've had a bad night also,' Runners snapped. 'I sent everywhere for our good Mr. Flowers.'

'Your job is not mine,' Allan said. 'Complain to your secretary.'

Runners stiffened. He stalked to his car and sat in with the chauffeur. His car drove off, followed by Kate.

'Whew!' Allan puffed. He jabbed at Alick crouched in the front seat. 'Get in the back.'

'Get me up,' Flowers groaned. 'I can't move.'

Alick pushed the seat forward and Allan helped him raise Flowers from his cramped position. They grunted and strained. Flowers flopped back with a huge sigh. Alick elbowed him over to make room for himself in the back.

'Okay, Morgan,' Allan said, sitting in. 'We're away.'

D'Arcy sat behind the wheel and slammed his door. 'Lake Edith?'

'I guess, then escort these gentlemen to the lodge,' Allan mumbled. He laid his head on the seat top and closed his eyes.

D'Arcy had not driven far on the lake road when Allan gripped his arm. D'Arcy froze. Allan Steel clasped his other hand to his mouth and was pushing with his elbow on the door handle. D'Arcy stopped the car. Allan stumbled out and vomited.

D'Arcy looked at the men in the back. Flowers was drowsing with an arm about Alick's shoulders. Alick was hunched in thought. Buses and cars coming from the search area whizzed by them. It began to rain again. Allan stumbled in and closed the door. He directed D'Arcy. There was one lamplight marking the scene of the search, otherwise utterly deserted. The Steel cottage was a half-mile farther. Allan insisted on being let off at the driveway and walking in.

'Get them back fast,' he ordered. 'I'll pick the car up in the lot.' He started away but wheeled back on D'Arcy. 'Wait! Here.' He handed him two dollars. 'For the trouble.'

D'Arcy stuffed the money in his pocket. He sped along the empty roads. His mind kept imagining a small girl appearing out of nowhere so that he half expected her to step from the roadside into the glare of his lights.

Alick was explaining their predicament to Flowers. His mumbling seemed to issue from the soul of the dark forest.

Flowers propped his arms on the back of D'Arcy's seat. 'Don't say a word about this.'

'No, sir, I won't.' D'Arcy urged more speed out of the car on the straightaway by the patrolman's shack.

Flowers sat back with a wheeze.

'He'll be in a better mood in the morning, I think,' Alick said to him. 'Please be careful going to your room.'

'Why should our slave-driver bother me?' Flowers demanded. 'I've worked harder than anyone else he could have got.'

'That's so true,' Alick murmured. 'He's allowed me only one day free since the beginning of the season.'

'Is that all?' Flowers demanded. 'That's atrocious!'

'I don't think it's fair,' Alick said.

'Even the bellhops have one day off a week, don't you?' Flowers demanded.

'Yes, sir.' D'Arcy slowed the car. 'Here's the lodge. Where shall I let you off?'

'The cabin beyond the patio,' Flowers groaned. 'This is too much trouble just for a drink.'

D'Arcy stopped the car and jumped out to hold the door. Flowers climbed out and stumbled forward. His heavy body wavered like a spineless fish. Sandhurst prepared to climb out.

'Jack!' resounded like a clap of thunder in the night.

D'Arcy pushed back the seat and jumped in. He gunned the motor as Runners moved from the side of the lodge. Sandhurst gaped through the back window in fright. The car jolted them away from a scene of certain disaster.

D'Arcy swerved into the parking lot and screeched to a halt. He scrambled out and held the door for Alick.

'Don't be afraid. I'll take the keys,' Alick smiled. 'Mr. Runners will have forgotten it all by morning. We are lucky he was not drunk.'

149

'You can say that again,' D'Arcy slammed the door.

Alick held out his hand. 'Thank you for looking after three fools."

D'Arcy, surprised, shook hands.

'I should see how Jack is,' Alick murmured. 'Good night.'

D'Arcy ran for his cabin.

Alick walked slowly back to the lodge. He feared Runners as much as anyone, perhaps more. Runners could make him work unnecessarily. He went to bed nights with columns of figures running through his brain and Runners' eyes burning in pursuit.

A sharp cry of command shot the night. Alick came into view of the lodge. Runners was stepping stiffly away from Flowers. His heels clicked over the stones of the patio. Flowers put his arm on the lamp post and leaned his head against it. Alick approached noiselessly. Flowers was crying.

Alick waited a few minutes. An anger boiled through him. If Runners had reappeared, he might have struck him. He looked up at the black sky. Rain spattered his cheeks, gradually cooling his temper. Flowers was quiet, his shoulders were still.

'Come, Jack,' Alick said. 'I'll see you home.'

Flowers turned sullen features to the light. 'I'll manage,' he said softly. He walked steadily to his cabin.

Alick turned to pursue his own way. The high cry of the wolf caught his attention. He thought of the little girl who had not been found.

18

Before dawn the search began again. Townspeople and cottagers marched until the afternoon. Guests and staff from Bampers joined them. The same ground was covered several times. No clue to the girl's disappearance was found. The search was called off.

Runners was at the scene for most of the day. He had left a chastened Flowers in charge of the hotel. It was important to the tourist industry that the child be found alive.

At supper time, word came that the rangers shot Charlie, the bear. They suspected him of eating the child. They cut him open but they found no trace.

'What did they expect to find?' Dixie smirked.

'Her red riding hood,' Gregory said, sipping his soup.

'But Charlie! He was tame,' Legourmand cried. 'He wouldn't kill a little child.'

D'Arcy, coming into the room, overheard him. He sat with them. 'Charlie wasn't anywhere near the scene,' D'Arcy said. 'I saw him on Bear Lake.'

'Yeah,' Dixie said excitedly. 'But the girl was lost at two o'clock.'

'What of it?' D'Arcy frowned.

'You weren't at Bear Lake that early.'

'How do you know?' D'Arcy leaned towards him.

Dixie paled. 'Too soon after eating to swim,' he smiled.

'As a matter of fact, you're right,' D'Arcy said. 'We weren't there till about three.'

'Still,' Legourmand looked doubtful, 'it's five miles between those lakes.'

'Bears can really travel when they want to,' Dixie intoned.

'Who cares?' Gregory sighed and pushed away his soup. 'She wasn't found which is the main thing.'

'He cares,' D'Arcy indicated Davey who was looking glumly from the kitchen at the eaters. 'It means two tragedies to him and the second is closer to his heart.'

'It was a heck of bungling,' Legourmand said. 'The bear should not have been killed unless they were sure.'

Gregory laughed dryly. 'They wouldn't tell us Charlie had eaten her. Print it in the American newspapers and the lodge goes bankrupt.'

'Sure,' Dixie said. 'They'd keep it secret.'

'Also, they wouldn't pick out one bear to shoot unless they were sure,' Gregory frowned superiorly. 'These men are trained to protect the animals. They don't kill unless it's for a good reason.'

'You think she was really eaten?' Legourmand asked in alarm.

'They don't know,' D'Arcy scoffed. 'Anymore than we do.'

'Yeah.' Legourmand stood up. 'Well, I'm not hungry.'

Gregory and Dixie sniggered when Legourmand was gone. D'Arcy forked beans into his mouth while he stared thoughtfully through the screen door. The shooting of the bear had a curious effect; its death was made to seem a just retribution for the child's disappearance; the episode was terminated; no one need think of the child again. The excitement had reached such an emotional pitch that a significant climax had had to be enacted.

Jane and Deo strolled by the door. D'Arcy watched them talking animatedly as they entered the Staff Hall.

'Jaimie wants to take me everywhere,' Jane was saying. 'But I've got this darn job.'

'Are you going to marry him?' Deo asked innocently.

'Good gracious, no!' Jane laughed. 'I haven't given it a thought.'

This was a sore point with Jane. She wanted to marry into money but she perceived indications that she was ineligible for the Rabbinowitz name.

'But it is a possibility,' Deo insisted.

'I have just gads of things to do before I think of marriage.' Jane set an elbow on the counter.

The record machine was playing softly. A few people lounged about in the great room or sauntered out through the entrances on either side.

'What does Jaimie like to do most?' Deo asked.

Jane looked at her askance. Deo giggled.

'Seriously, he golfs,' Jane smiled. 'He talks golf, wears golf pants and shoes. I tell him he is Mr. Golf Junior; he doesn't like it either.'

'I always thought he was nice,' Deo frowned with disappointment.

Jane cast her a sharp look. 'He is very nice. Otherwise, I wouldn't be going around with him.'

'I didn't mean that,' Deo's face fell, her blue eyes oval with misgiving. 'I just thought he was more mature.'

Jane swept the room with a look of nonchalance. 'He is rich and he is young. I can wait for maturity.'

'Not me,' Deo said. 'What is his father like?'

'He's mature,' Jane said laughingly. 'You're not getting ideas, are you?'

'I just want to meet some interesting people tonight, that's all.'

'There won't be many bachelors,' Jane smiled. 'I'm warning you.'

'Oh,' Deo pouted. 'I've just got to get out of this staff rut.'

'But Johnnie's nice enough, isn't he?' Jane said patronizingly.

'I'm tired,' Deo said. 'I want to be like you.'

'Like me?' Jane pointed to herself in surprise. She laughed. 'Don't take me for your model.' She smiled at the girl behind the counter. 'Two cokes, please.'

'But you know how to act,' Deo said. 'You know what these people expect of you.'

'I'll check your dress before you go,' Jane said. She set a straw in her coke. 'Who's coming for you?'

'Jack Flowers,' Deo grimaced.

Jane burst into laughter, spluttering coke. Deo sniggered.

'Well, he's a start,' Jane said. 'He'll get you there.'

'But what an impression we'll make coming in the door together!' Deo held hand to mouth.

'Never mind; he's very nice.'

'But he's staff.' Deo made a face.

Jane sighed. 'Don't be impatient. Honestly, I've never met anyone who detests the staff so much.'

'I don't detest anyone,' Deo said. 'It's just that since I'm here I might as well make the best of it.'

Jane regarded her briefly. She tossed her head. 'For tomorrow we die. When I'm with Jaimie I forget about the tomorrows. It would be tragic if I fell in love with him, wouldn't it?'

'Aren't you?' Deo smiled.

'Thank heavens, no. Fortunately, I was experienced in *l'amour* before I met him.' Jane pursed her lips.

Deo's eyes flashed. She finished her coke. 'Thanks. I'm going back to work.'

'I'll watch you tonight,' Jane smiled. 'Don't be nervous, sweetie.'

Blair St. Clair walked by them. Both girls tried to catch his eye but Blair was preoccupied with the dog leg on the fourth fairway.

Aurmand was standing alone at the far end of the counter. He was nursing a glass of milk. Blair stood near him.

Aurmand had been fired from his dishwashing job. He had quarreled with the chef. Although the afternoon was sunny, it looked black to Aurmand.

Blair noticed him and smiled in his casual way. Aurmand smiled shyly in return.

'Haven't seen you around lately,' Blair said.

'No?' Aurmand said. His eyes watered. He felt homesick, as if he were in a foreign land. 'I will not be around.'

Blair frowned quizzically.

'I want to go back,' Aurmand explained.

'Another month yet,' Blair said.

'I'm not happy. I make no money,' Aurmand said. 'I will hitch-hike.'

Blair grinned. 'Impossible through Canada. Go through the States.'

Aurmand nodded glumly.

'This is the time of low morale,' Blair said. 'Most people want money, a lot want sex. I want to win the tournament.'

Aurmand looked surprised.

'Do you want to caddie for me?' Blair smiled.

'Don't ask me.' Aurmand said in alarm. 'I am not good.'

'Then you won't be telling me what to do.' Blair's eyes twinkled.

Aurmand considered the offer. He felt pleased. 'Sure you want me?'

'Sure.'

'Okay,' Aurmand nodded seriously. 'I will try.'

Blair held out his hand. 'What's your name?'

They introduced themselves. Aurmand straightened up with pride. When Blair left him, he felt he had to tell someone. He scurried to the caddie cabin and burst into his room. Slim was sitting on his bed counting his money.

Aurmand was about to blurt out his happiness when he caught sight of Bruce Bannister reading a comic book on the top bunk. He checked himself. Bruce might laugh at him for being elated over such a small thing. He didn't want to give the enemy another excuse to make fun of him. Eyes twinkling, he decided to keep it a secret and surprise everyone.

'What's up?' Slim asked.

'Nothing.' Aurmand went to the sink and washed his hands. He looked out at the sunny afternoon. He would caddie for a round and begin reacquainting himself with the lay of the ground.

That night Jack Flowers called on the dot for Deo. She was ready and confident. Jane had inspected her dress, a bare-backed gray and pink pleated taffeta, and pronounced it gorgeous. Flowers escorted her into a lodge car.

'You remembered my high heels,' Deo said gratefully.

Flowers drove. 'But I forgot a chauffeur. We will have to park the car. But we will be walking on pavement for the sake of your heels,' he smiled charmingly, his black mustache giving him a roguish look.

'Oh, I'm so excited about this evening.' Deo clasped her hands.

'A word of warning,' Flowers cautioned. 'Don't be too friendly with the guests. Mr. Runners notices everything.'

'But can't I be natural?'

'Not if it takes you out of your staff category. Remember, we are secondary personalities. We didn't pay for our room and board.'

'We do more,' Deo exclaimed angrily. "We work for it.'

'I must also warn you that Mr. Runners asked me to report on your attitude.'

Deo stiffened with fright.

Flowers parked the car at the garage. They left it and crossed the road on the narrow sidewalk leading to Runners' cottage.

Deo was the daughter of the assistant-manager of a hotel in Kamloops, B.C. She was not allowed to mix with its guests who, in anyone's books, were far below the standard set by the prices of Bampers.

Flowers offered his arm and she slipped her thin wrist onto it. The lighted porch of Runners' cabin intrigued her as they approached. But when Flowers opened the screen door, she realized they were the first to arrive. Bright and bare of people, the waiting room awaited them.

Mrs. Runners rushed out from a side room. She saw Flowers. 'There you are. I have to dim this down.' She turned off the top lights. 'There, it's more suitable for the occasion, don't you think?' Her angular face revealed its lines of worry as she came to them.

Flowers introduced Deo.

'You're the girl my husband mentioned,' she said soberly. 'Reservations, isn't it?'

'Yes,' Deo paled. The austere features of Mrs. Runners intimidated Deo; she had often seen her but they had never spoken.

'Just be reserved and friendly and I'm sure you will get along well with the guests. Would you like to freshen up?'

She took Deo to a powder room adjoining the bathroom and returned to Flowers.

'Pretty, isn't she?' she said.

'Nice decore,' Flowers agreed.

'I don't blame Tony for choosing her. I hope she behaves.'

Flowers grunted pleasantly and shuffled to the table. He snapped up a chocolate from a small silver-plated basket. As he chewed it, Mrs. Runners took him away to the table with drinks.

'Pour us four whiskeys. Tony will be right out.'

A child wailed from the inner recesses. Mrs. Runners hurried away to quieten it. As Deo returned, Runners stepped out from another hallway. He went to her, a foxy smile playing across his features.

'Glad you were on time, Deo. I am glad I can depend on you.'

Flowers handed them drinks. He looked stolidly submissive-- a major-domo. There were voices from the lane and the screen door opened.

'This is so thrilling,' Deo gushed.

Runners gently touched her arm, handed his drink to Flowers, and went to greet his guests.

'He's in a good mood,' Flowers whispered. 'Watch that he remains in it.'

'He's so gentle and kind,' Deo sighed.

Flowers looked curiously at her. Mrs. Runners brushed by them. More guests arrived. Deo was introduced to them. She separated from Flowers and, in the course of the evening, noticed that he stood in the same spot either alone or in company with his back to the wall.

As she was finishing her second whisky she felt the eyes of a man strong upon her back. She turned a little and caught sight of Horace Rabbinowitz. He averted his gaze quickly.

'It was nevah understood if I or my husband first interested the pasha but it was at my door he was knocking the next morning,' concluded a robust lady to the amused group.

Deo went to the sideboard as if looking for more drink. Passing close to Horace she turned hesitantly with glass held out in front of her. A waiter moved swiftly, but Horace reached for the glass.

'You're drinking whisky, aren't you?' he said.

She watched him tip the bottle over her glass. His dark sophistication and his maturity were fascinating. A pearled ring flashed on the hand that held her glass. She took the drink mechanically and looked up full into his stare that seemed to burrow deep.

'How did you know?' she asked, too stricken to act coquettishly.

He raised a brow in surprise and smiled. 'Whisky you mean? I suppose because it's much the best drink for this climate.'

'How do you know I'm not from the Maritimes?' Deo teased, encouraged by his easy manner.

'I don't know it,' Horace said nicely, 'but I compliment you with knowing when to drink what.'

Deo tossed her blonde hair and grinned. 'As it happens I am from the west coast and I know loads of persons who won't see you eye to eye on that.'

'Then they are not like you and me,' Horace said quietly. 'They don't know.'

Deo laughed. 'I would rather listen to you than them anyway,' she said.

'Ah, now you make the compliments,' he joked. 'What is your name may I ask?'

Deo rounded her eyes. 'Deo.'

'It should be deess.' His eyes twinkled.

To Deo the joke was as old as high school but she sensed the attraction behind the words and revelled in it.

Mrs. Runners intruded. 'I haven't had the opportunity to talk with you since you've been here, Horace.' She looked sternly at Deo.

Horace cleared his throat and straightened his shoulders like a gallant. 'Unfortunately.'

Deo drifted away. Jane and Jaimie entered. Jane was popular. She saw Deo but pretended to be too occupied to greet her at the moment.

Deo watched complacently. This was Jane's day; let her enjoy it while she could. Runners stood by Deo's elbow. He smiled and was leaning to whisper into her ear when the porch door opened, catching his attention. Kate Carr stepped in. Deo was still wearing an expectant smile as Runners stepped across to Kate. She frowned with annoyance as Runners bent to whisper into Kate's ear.

'You're looking very lovely this evening,' he said.

Kate bit her lip to keep from laughing. Allan and Bett Steel had persuaded her to come with them, so she was present on sufferance. She intended to amuse herself regardless of her distaste for Runners.

'Tony, remember, you have other guests,' Bett said behind him. 'Stop blocking their way.'

Runners glided aside. 'Forgive me.'

'Forgiven.' Allan patted his shoulder. 'It is only us.'

'Jaimie dear,' Bett sang. 'You remember Allan.'

Jaimie welcomed them with a pleasant smile.

Runners looked about for Deo, who had disappeared, and saw Allan Steel talking animatedly with Mrs. Runners. Their rapport never failed to amaze him. Runners watched Horace Rabbinowitz sidle away to Kate's circle and stepped into the hall leading by the ladies' powder room. He paused, listening. The door opened. Deo confronted him.

'There you are,' he grinned. 'Are you enjoying yourself, my pet?'

'Oh yes,' Deo said.

'Meeting enough people?' He took her hands and moved close.

'Yes,' she sighed.

Mrs. Runners' voice seemed to disengage itself from the party. Runners dropped Deo's hand and went quickly down the hall into a room. Deo met Mrs. Runners.

'Have you seen my husband?'

'No.' Deo looked innocent.

Mrs. Runners grimly continued along the hall. Deo smiled. This was fun.

Bett Steel greeted her and introduced Allan. Cold hand, Deo thought. Mrs. Runners came to them. 'Have you seen, Tony?' She looked worried, almost frightened.

Just then Runners accompanied guests entering the front door.

'The invisible man,' Allan said. 'Didn't see him go out.'

'Nor did I,' Mrs. Runners frowned.

Bett took Deo's arm for several paces to the side. 'Who, my dear, have you set your sights on?'

'Why, no one!'

Bett put tongue in cheek. 'You can't hide that brilliance in your eye.'

Deo darted a look at Horace. Bett followed it. She raised her brows in congratulation.

'Where is Johnnie tonight?'

'Singing,' Deo said as if unconcerned.

'Swan Song?' Bett smiled.

'No comment,' Deo said.

'Be careful of Horace,' Bett said. 'He's happily married and what's worse, he's even more conservative than he looks.'

'I like mature men.'

'Hmm,' Bett nodded, 'you might have caught him in the right spot at that.'

'What do you mean?'

'His age,' Bett whispered. 'Stay there. I'll lure him to you.'

Deo stayed her. 'But where's his wife?'

'Sniffles,' Bett smiled. 'In bed with a book and a box of chocolates.' She sidled up to Horace. 'Am I intruding?'

Horace looked past her at Deo.

'Bett, darling,' Kate said. 'I want you to meet two interesting men.'

'Anytime,' Bett said eagerly.

Horace moved away to Deo. 'I believe I had just called you a goddess when you were chased away by a fierce-looking dragon,' he said.

Deo laughed merrily. 'That's not very polite.'

'It certainly wasn't. I should have chased the dragon off if I'd been any sort of gentleman,' he smiled.

Deo's laughter attracted Jane who looked at them with surprise.

'Are you a golfer like your son?' Deo raised her eyes to him.

'Do you know Jaimie?' he asked curiously.

Deo hesitated. 'I just know he golfs.'

'Ah! He catches the attention of the young ladies.'

'He takes after you,' she smiled.

'When I was his age, yes,' Horace said, 'but that was some time ago.'

'Modesty doesn't become you,' Deo pouted.

Horace regarded her keenly.

'Maybe you just use it as a defence,' Deo added.

'Maybe I need it when I meet young ladies like you.'

'Now you are treating me like the dragon,' Deo frowned.

'Oh no, I am not,' Horace said. 'I may be old but I am not blind.'

Deo eyed him flirtatiously. 'To tell the truth, I have always found modesty very attractive.'

Horace glanced about them. 'Are you staying at the hotel long?'

'I work at the Front Desk,' she said.

Horace allowed a flicker of surprise to cross his face. 'Then perhaps you know more about me than I thought.'

'I'm sure you are more interesting as a person,' she smiled.

'Hello,' Jane said. 'I see you have met our reservations clerk, Mr. Rabbinowitz.'

'Yes indeed,' Horace nodded. 'I now understand why the hotel is so easily booked up.'

Deo tittered. 'Oh, the waitresses do their bit.'

'Jane has made quite a hit with us,' Horace grinned.

'Your wife has been so good to me,' Jane said.

Horace narrowed his eyes humorously.

'You've been so good to Jaimie,' Deo said.

'Yes.' Jane's eyes hardened. She turned to Horace. 'Jaimie and I are going on.'

'You go along,' he said. 'Would you like to come with us, Deo?'

'I'm afraid not,' Deo said sadly. 'I have to stay, you see.'

Horace nodded. 'I'll finish my drink with you. Then I'll catch you up, Jane.'

'Have fun, Deo,' Jane smiled and went back to Jaimie.

'An enterprising girl,' Horace remarked.

'I would say so,' Deo said sharply.

'But not one of your best friends.'

'No!'

Horace laughed. He put a hand on her arm. 'I'm truly sorry you cannot come on with us. Perhaps we will arrange it another time.'

'I hope so,' Deo said expectantly.

The guests were leaving. Deo watched Horace go. Bett stopped beside her. 'I think you have made your mark. Now go home and pray that the sniffles continue, my dear.'

'I can't go until Mr. Runners says I can.'

'If you wait for his word you'll never get out of here,' Bett said.

Kate approached happily. 'The tides are out. We're off to the Van Clark's.'

'Deo can't come,' Bett said sadly.

'Oh, oh,'' Kate clucked. 'Never mind. Mrs. Runners will see you get back safely.'

The girls laughed.

Allan appeared. 'Been trying to persuade Jack to come with us.'

'I'm sure you have,' Bett said. 'Well, what is it? no dice?'

'He's here on business.' Allan looked bored.

'Too bad, darling. Why don't you stay?'

'Because you'd hate me for it,' he smiled.

Runners confronted them. 'You're not leaving?'

'Tony,' Kate patted his cheek. 'We simply have to. It was lovely.'

Deo, on impulse, gave him a jealous glance. She felt mischievous. Runners started and smiled shyly. He saw his wife watching him.

'Can't we take Deo with us?' Bett pleaded.

'I'm afraid not. I have to keep an eye on my staff.'

'Watch Jack Flowers,' Allan joked.

'I am,' Runners snapped, 'closely.'

The Runners bade their guests good-night at the door. Deo retreated to Flowers.

'How did you like it?' she asked.

Flowers mumbled indistinctly and brightened as Mrs. Runners approached.

'You've done very well,' she said. 'Tony and I think they enjoyed themselves.'

'It was a great success,' Deo said.

'Yes.' Mrs. Runners surveyed her. 'You'll see her to her cabin, Jack.'

'There's no need to bother Jack,' Runners intervened. 'I'll take her.'

'No, darling. I have something to say to you.'

'Can't it wait?' he frowned.

'No, dear.' She smiled severely. 'Good-bye. Thank you.'

Flowers opened the door for Deo. Runners held it for him and smiled affectionately at Deo.

'See you tomorrow. I shall not forget how you looked tonight,' he said.

Flowers chuckled with embarrassment.

'Oh, thank you,' Deo flirted slyly. 'I won't forget this whole wonderful evening.'

Flowers walked stolidly beside her, mumbling laconically when she spoke to him. As they came to the lodge car, Deo expected to get in. But Flowers declined. He walked her up the road and over the gravel lane.

Furious, Deo didn't say a word.

As if to break the discomforting silence, Flowers complained that his feet hurt.

Deo stopped and took off her high heeled shoes. She walked stoically over the stones.

Flowers looked abashed.

At her door she turned to glare at him. 'I must tell Tony how nice you have been,' she said and went in.

19

Entries to the staff tournament were limited to those who scored under eighty for the course in a preliminary round. The field of competition narrowed down quickly through many defaults and easy victories. It appeared, as was expected, that Blair and Johnnie would meet in the finals. From the returns on Thursday evening, it was certain. Friday morning, bright and clear, saw the two opponents striking the ball and striding confidently over the lush green. Blair smiled a good deal and joked with Aurmand who carried his bag. Johnnie struck at blades of grass and swung his club in happy abandon. Dixie, who was caddying for him, smiled sardonically at the small crowd of spectators.

Both players birdied and eagled on the early holes. They were in fine fettle and gave promise of a spectacular match. Johnnie had the longer drive which gave him an advantage on the straightaway of the sixth. At the start of the seventh, he was one hole up on Blair. However, Blair evened the score by a deft iron shot on the short seventh. They stayed pretty well even at par until the fifteenth when Johnnie overshot the green and got snagged in the rough. He was one hole down with three to go. He cursed quietly to Dixie. On the sixteenth Johnnie hooked his approach shot into the lake. He threw his iron down in disgust. Dixie grinned humorously and retrieved the iron. Blair went on to take the hole. The result seemed fairly certain. Blair, the golden-haired hero, was going to win the cup for the second straight year.

Dixie spoke to Johnnie on their way to the seventeenth tee. 'Hit it hard, man. Swing out. Knock this complacent bastard off his perch!'

Johnnie was frowning dispiritedly. 'The more I try, kid, the better he gets. I'm just pushing him uphill.'

'Forget about him,' Dixie snarled sarcastically. 'He'll loaf on the homestretch--sail over him, right on by.'

Blair hit a fine drive. Johnnie took his stance and stared down at his ball until it became a white globe filling up his vision. He swung hard in a clean straight drive that brought a gasp of admiration as the ball carried down the fairway, struck a knoll and bounced and rolled between the traps. Blair was still smiling as he reached his ball. He lofted it short of the green. Johnnie put his second shot beside the cup and Blair granted him the hole.

Johnnie swung free and easily on the eighteenth. He and Blair landed equidistant on the green with the same number of strokes. As Johnnie stepped on the green, he saw Deo with Horace Rabbinowitz. She had her arm through his. They were obviously enjoying each other's company. He gritted his teeth and sunk the ball. Blair putted just short of the cup. The score stood at nine holes even.

Blair suggested a rest before they started another round, but Johnnie wanted to continue right away.

'I'm just getting up steam, Blair kid.'

Blair brushed back his forelock. He bit his lip pensively. He felt that his game was slipping. He had to finish it right away by winning the first hole. A tie would give Johnnie the confidence to win on the second.

'Okay. Your honor.' He turned abruptly and ambled over to Aurmand. 'We're going on. I'm scared stiff.'

'You do fine,' Aurmand said seriously. 'Don't be afraid.'

Aurmand felt that he was responsible for Blair's game. His bad luck appeared to be overshadowing Blair.

'Maybe I don't go with you,' he suggested.

'What do you mean?' Blair asked in astonishment.

Aurmand looked down. 'I'm making you lose.'

Blair frowned. 'You're good for me. Quiet and steady. You're a tonic. I've never hit so good.'

Aurmand looked up. His thin delicate features were pale and concerned. 'If you don't win, it will be my fault.'

Blair swallowed. 'I'll win.'

Dixie set Johnnie's ball on the first tee and strolled up to him.

'Look at that blonde witch,' Johnnie said bitterly. 'She burns me up.'

'Forget about her,' Dixie rasped. 'Take this one and she'll be all over you.'

'I don't want her,' Johnnie snarled.

'Then put her out of your mind.'

Johnnie approached his ball in anger. He blasted a low drive down the centre of the fairway.

Blair took a drink of water. He looked concerned. His drive landed just behind Johnnie's ball.

The spectators followed them resolutely. Many guests had swelled the numbers. They wanted to be present for the kill.

Blair sliced the next stroke, setting the ball in the fringe of the woods. His friends murmured in concern. Blair shook his head. It was the most serious mistake he had made and at the crucial moment.

Johnnie hammered his ball. It fell short of the green.

'Should have used a wood,' he complained.

'You're in man,' Dixie grinned.

Aurmand found Blair's ball in the long grass. It was suspended an inch off the ground. Blair closed his eyes when he saw it. Aurmand fingered a three iron. Blair frowned. 'Like baseball,' he smiled. He took the iron. 'If I hit a homer, we've had it.' He took a stance half a step further away than usual. He swung wide and flat, socking the ball at the rise of the green. It bounced up and onto the green.

Aurmand let out a long sigh.

'You can only try that once,' Blair said.

Johnnie regarded Blair curiously. He was piqued. He tried to loft his ball lightly onto the green, but it rolled to the far side.

'The damn grass is dry,' he cursed. The early afternoon sun blazed down mockingly. 'It was wet this morning.'

'So was my throat,' Dixie said bitterly. 'Finish it and we'll have a beer.' He handed Johnnie the putter, his eyes burning with determination.

Johnnie seized it, took a deep breath, and strolled nonchalantly to the ball. He sighted the lay of the green and stroked. The ball rolled to a stop on the left of the cup.

Blair putted. His ball took a bad turn. Frowning, he putted again. The crowd held its breath. The ball stopped six inches short. Under a murmur of irritation sounded a note of jubilation.

Johnnie grinned broadly. Just one simple putt and victory was his--at last! Johnnie looked at Deo who was standing apart from Horace. She smiled at him. He smirked and then winked at Dixie. He addressed his ball and stroked softly. It went straight for the cup and nudged the grass on the rim. But it didn't fall.

Johnnie threw up his head and shouted at the sky. His anger thrashed at the spectators. His putter sailed high in a loop and came down beside Aurmand.

Nervously, Aurmand picked it up and walked across to Dixie who accepted it with a stoic expression. Already Blair was set to putt. He sank his ball. There was a smattering of applause. Even score.

'For Christ's sake!' Johnnie cried at Dixie. 'I can't do it. I just can't do it.'

'Take it easy,' Dixie grinned. 'You've got another chance. Smother him.'

'With what?' Johnnie glared over at Deo. 'Get that gold-digger out of my sight. She's undermining my game.'

On the stretch between the green and the second tee, Dixie intercepted Deo.

'Look, have a heart,' he said. 'Can't you see you're getting on his nerves?'

'What do you want me to do?' she frowned imperiously.

'Beat it.'

'I've got as much right to watch as anyone else,' she retorted.

'All right, but stay out of sight.'

'Why should I?'

'Because if you don't, I'll brain you.'

'What seems to be the trouble?' Horace asked. He glowered at Dixie.

'He wants me to go away for some crazy reason,' she pouted.

'She's upsetting Johnnie O'Dreams,' Dixie complained. 'If he sees her, he'll go off his game.'

'What nonsense!' Horace hissed. 'You pay attention to your job. You've made enough trouble in the past.'

'She's got to go,' Dixie clenched his teeth.

'You'll go. I'll see to that,' Horace barked.

People were looking at them.

'You don't understand,' Dixie said. 'She used to be Johnnie's girl friend.'

Horace, flushed with anger, shot his arm out at the tee. 'Go! Now!'

Dixie shrugged hopelessly and trudged after Johnnie.

'Goodness!' Deo sighed. 'Everyone I've ever dated thinks that I'm their personal property or something.'

Horace smiled affectionately. 'I can't say I blame them. A beautiful girl can invite any man's envy. Especially that O'Dreams. He seems particularly unstable.'

'Oh he is,' Deo agreed.

Blair spoke quietly to Aurmand. 'Do you know something strange about the second fairway? It's the same distance as the fourth but it has a dog leg to the right rather than to the left like the fourth.'

'Yes,' Aurmand said hopefully.

'I've been concentrating on the fourth.'

'Yes?' Aurmand looked puzzled.

'If I slice on the second at the same angle I hook on the fourth, maybe we'll get there.' Blair took his driver.

'Hey! Watch out for those gaping sand traps,' Johnnie warned, tossing his head in humour.

'I've been in them before,' Blair said.

Blair sliced his drive beautifully round the corner of the woods.

Johnnie squared off. He sent a long drive to the end of the stretch of fairway. 'Sets me up for a good approach,' he said to Dixie.

When they reached the bend, they saw that Blair's ball lay twenty yards in advance on the near side.

'Look where it is!' Deo's voice rang out exultantly.

Johnnie frowned. The spectators near him stirred uncomfortably.

'She doesn't care, eh?' Johnnie murmured.

'She called in the Rabbinowitz prestige,' Dixie said sarcastically.

'Let her ride,' Johnnie said. 'The dumb blonde.'

166

He looked despondently at the red pennant limp on its staff in the distance. The power seemed drained from his stroke as the ball bounced short.

Blair used his advantage to strike close upon the green. Aurmand nimbly handed him his iron. He strode excitedly beside Blair. With all his will, he restrained the exultation bubbling to his lips. He tried to think pessimistically and wore a sober expression to keep bad luck at bay. He knew that he must not distract Blair by deed or word. The calmness of the young man inspired his admiration. He pictured Blair moving steadfastly toward a dozen dangers.

Johnnie's next shot went into the bunker in front of the green. He groaned and took his sand blaster. As he stepped onto the sand, he called out in a laugh. 'If I don't come back, send out the Foreign Legion.'

His long muscled arms swung down hard in a mighty blast. A cloud of sand flew up and fell like spray on the grass. The ball had jumped ahead about six inches. Johnnie felt heat split the top of his head. Raising his blaster on high, he took a step forward to thrash wildly at the ball.

'Johnnie!' Dixie barked.

Johnnie paused, one arm holding up the blaster, his face contorted.

There was silence. A faint breeze lifted the flag tip. Johnnie scowled at the sand. 'What's the bloody use?' He dropped the blaster and walked from the bunker.

Dixie walked beside him. They stopped by a tree at the side of the fairway.

'You're crazy to give in now,' Dixie said. 'You can tie it.'

'And repeat the performance on the third.'

'Get this one,' Dixie said, 'and he'll break up. I know Blair.'

Johnnie held his jaw in the palm of his hand. He looked worriedly into a copse of slim trees. It seemed to represent the maze he had been worming through for many years. Blundering on in all phases of disillusion and desperation, he had not given up. He looked back at the crowd. Horace Rabbinowitz was keeping a group of people amused. Deo was listening to his comments and giggling. Johnnie set his jaw. He returned to the bunker, picked up his blaster and lofted the ball onto the green. Some of the men raised a polite cheer. Dixie regarded Blair sardonically.

All this while, Blair had been watching Johnnie's antics with a composed expression. He had selected his club and waited by his ball just in front of the green for play to resume. Now he quickly sighted the cup and chipped the ball. Aurmand, who was holding the pin, jerked it excitedly from the hole. His eyes seemed to magnify through his glasses as he watched the ball roll into the cup.

'Hey there!' Johnnie shouted. He threw back his long hair and strode with arms out to Blair. 'Great! Unbeatable!'

They shook hands, Blair glancing bashfully about him, his face breaking into smiles at each new congratulation. Aurmand retired with flag pin in hand to the side of the green. He unfolded a handkerchief and wiped his eyes and glasses. Dixie came up and clapped him on the back.

'It's only a game,' he said. 'Cheer up. Anyway, you won, you dolt.'

Aurmand cleared his throat. 'I did nothing.' He shook his head.

'You kept Blair smooth all the way around,' Dixie said. 'You can't tell me that he could do it by himself. Johnnie was forcing him to break.'

Blair approached.

'You lucky bastard,' Dixie smirked.

Blair pretended to cuff him. He picked up his bag, shouldered it, and threw an arm about Aurmand's shoulders.

'Hey!' Dixie cried, coming after them. 'You taking back a souvenir?' He swiped the flag pin away from Aurmand. 'Jeez!'

Aurmand gasped with surprise and began to protest his innocence. Dixie and Blair laughed together. Aurmand sensed their affection for him. He broke into a wide smile, too overcome to speak.

Dixie set the pin back. He snatched up Johnnie's bag and ran after the group surrounding Johnnie. The orchestra boys were with him. Kate was holding his hand. Johnnie was laughing. 'Never again. I'll never play tournament. So help me!'

'Blair won't be back next year,' Toots said.

'He won't be?' Johnnie considered. 'Maybe I'll try just one more year.'

Amidst the peals of laughter, Dixie turned round to see Deo and Horace walking alone. As if by instinct, everyone was giving them a wide berth. They looked subdued and intent on getting away as quickly as possible.

20

Kate left the group as it neared the garage. She was supposed to have met D'Arcy an hour ago. She took the path to the riding stables. The day was August at its best. The sun burnished the leaves and bronzed the dead pine needles underfoot. The underbrush luxuriated in the warmth that radiated from overhanging branches. The dry air stirred in the soft breeze.

Kate entered the clearing. A man was saddling a pair of horses in front of the red stable. She surveyed the dark brown yard and the old wagons and the bits of harnessing. D'Arcy was sitting against a tree at the clearing's edge.

She walked to him. 'This makes up for the times you've been late.'

'Okay, sit down,' he said.

'Aren't we going riding?' She gestured at the horses.

'They're not for us.'

Slim and Miriam came from the stable. Miriam mounted unsteadily with the help of the cowboy. Slim was more nimble.

'They're getting awfully friendly,' Kate said.

'Friendship. That's about what it is,' D'Arcy snorted.

Kate smiled. 'Maybe it's better that way.'

D'Arcy frowned. 'Is that a hint?'

'Well, we don't seem to be getting on well. This is only the third time I've seen you in a week.'

D'Arcy plucked a blade of grass and bit on it. 'Sit down, why don't you?'

Kate sat on the grass.

'Let's face it. You're bored, aren't you?' D'Arcy asked.

'Well,' Kate wound a blade about her finger, 'we don't do very much.'

'If I could go to those parties and get drunk with you, I guess you'd think we were doing something.'

'We'd be having fun anyway.'

'It'd be damned boring,' D'Arcy said. 'Here we've got an afternoon of riding and you come late. The trouble with you rich people is that you get too lazy.'

'What do I hear?' Kate mocked him. 'Grumblings of discontent from Comrade Morgan?'

'Grumblings of disillusion from your lover boy is closer to the truth.'

Slim rode close by them. 'Hi! Are you coming riding?'

'Hello Slim,' Kate smiled.

'We'll see you,' D'Arcy said. 'Have a good ride, Miriam.'

Miriam gave him a slow smile.

'I wonder,' D'Arcy looked after her, 'why she wears pigtails and tries to look as much like a little girl as possible.'

'Does she act like one?' Kate asked.

'That depends on whom she's with.'

Kate laughed. 'D'Arcy, the way you say that makes my heart bleed for you.'

D'Arcy smiled tiredly and stood up. 'I'll ask them to saddle a couple.'

While he was gone, Kate lay on her back and gazed at the deep blue. She felt D'Arcy's disinterest stronger than ever; perhaps it was because she was beginning to recognize her own. Their passion was still enjoyable but not as exciting. At first she expected he would rejuvenate her interest in life, but she could not sustain any strong feeling for him between their times of meeting. The sophistication of hotel life caught her in a web of drinking and uninspired babble, inveigling her with the promise of effortlessly enjoyable hours. And today Mac was returning. The sweet smell of the long grass lulled her thoughts.

'The very fact that you're wearing riding breeches shows that you must be fond of the sport,' D'Arcy said, reappearing to sit beside her.

'I used to like it,' she said. 'But I couldn't get anyone to ride with me.'

'Not even your husband?'

'Mac telephoned me last night. He'll be driving up in time for dinner, so I must be back by six.'

D'Arcy straightened with shock. 'This may be our last little get-together then.'

'It may be,' she smiled archly.

'Can't say we haven't had fun,' D'Arcy said, 'can you?'

'More than I've had in a long time, D'Arcy.' Kate sighed and leaned on her elbow to look at him. 'Even if there had been no Mac, we would've had just a few more weeks.'

D'Arcy felt a sudden desire for her languorous form. He reached out and settled his hand on her hip. 'Let's have those weeks anyway.'

Kate smiled whimsically. 'The horses are ready.'

D'Arcy grimaced and helped her up. He admired her stroll as he had when they first met. She looked exceptionally desirable.

They mounted. Kate's horse led the way, trotting along the bridle path.

'She knows where she's going,' Kate called back amused. 'Which is more than I can say for myself.'

D'Arcy caught up to her. They slowed their mounts to a walk.

'You're not in any doubt,' D'Arcy said. 'It'd take a pretty romantic guy to get you away from Mac.'

Kate looked at him questioningly.

D'Arcy explained. 'You wouldn't sacrifice years of intimacy to start from scratch with someone else. Too much effort,' he said. 'Too demanding at your stage in life.'

Kate frowned. 'Why are you trying to make me sound like a dissolute sod?'

'Because your life is that way.'

'Oh, is it?' She raised her brows. 'So the solution is to leave Mac for a nice healthy boy like you and I'll be all right.'

'You wouldn't want me,' D'Arcy said. 'I'm poor and unorthodox.'

'Then who?'

'Some solid type who hasn't too much money.'

'D'Arcy you're mad.' She spurred her horse. 'You just don't understand women.'

He kept up. 'I like you, Kate, and I know you pretty well.'

She reined in and glared. 'D'Arcy! Don't ever speak to me about this again. If I left Mac, it would be the end of me. You don't know how much I depend on him.'

'It will be the end of you if you stay with him,' he said.

'You don't know! I have two children and a home.'

'You'll have them anyway.' D'Arcy rode on. 'But you know best.'

171

'You really want me to leave Mac, don't you? What do you have against him?'

'Skip it!' D'Arcy galloped his horse.

Kate watched him go with misgiving. She had spoken rashly, perversely. D'Arcy had irritated a wound made years ago when she discovered that Mac valued her no more than other women. Of course, D'Arcy meant her to take measures to heal the wound. Yet could it ever be healed? she thought. Wasn't D'Arcy being idealistically impractical? Her own psychological make-up was as much at fault as Mac. Years of medicating her wound had taught her that.

She took a side path leading up hill at an angle off the main trail. She wanted to ride alone until she threw off this difficult mood. Then D'Arcy could find her.

She observed the bright green foliage of the ravine. Above on a ridge rode Miriam and Slim. How coy she looked! A great healthy hunk of beef with cow eyes. Slim deserved better than her.

She turned back onto the trail and climbed to a level. D'Arcy was waiting with an amused look, his forearms resting cowboy-fashion on the saddle horn.

'You!' she winced. 'I was just beginning to enjoy my ride.'

'I have to keep an eye on you to make sure the bears keep their mitts off.'

She scoffed. 'What could you do?'

'Ride for help.'

She smothered a laugh. 'I've got an idea. Let's scout Slim and Miriam. Pretend we're Indians.'

'I'm game.' D'Arcy watched her expression curiously. He sensed that she was envious of Miriam, that she wanted to spoil a romantic tryst.

'This way.' She led him up a path.

They circled to a stony trail cutting along the ravine lip and rode swiftly. They reached the point where the shelf veered in, becoming flat with the mountainside. They halted and listened.

Slim's voice rose plaintively. 'Why not? For heaven's sake!'

Kate giggled. Miriam's reply was inaudible.

'But I can't wait forever. I'm not made of steel,' Slim whined.

172

Kate dismounted and lying flat looked over the edge. Miriam was lying in Slim's arms on the shelf below. She was reaching up and stroking Slim's face while their horses grazed.

'Calm down, that's it, be calm. Be a man, Slim,' she was saying.

Kate came away with a wry expression.

'Is she beating him with pigtails?' D'Arcy asked.

'I understand why she plays little girl with you.' Kate mounted. 'But she's Big Mama with Slim, the poor guy.'

D'Arcy laughed.

'Sh!' Kate warned. 'They'll hear you.'

'Leave them to their frustrations,' D'Arcy started away. 'It's not our business.'

'Somehow, ' Kate sighed, 'I feel responsible for poor Slim.'

D'Arcy felt a jealous quiver. 'He's a puritan. He has to find his own salvation.'

'He should be helped,' Kate said. 'Why don't you help him?'

'That's ridiculous.' Their horses stepped carefully along the mountainside. 'He knows about the birds and the bees. There's nothing I can tell him.'

'I suppose he'll meet someone,' she said.

D'Arcy remarked a tinge of regret in her tone. He suddenly saw Kate as a victim of her whims--a modern Madame Bovary. Perhaps he was just one of her distractions, meant to help her pass the time until she found a new one He felt peculiarly estranged.

'D'Arcy,' she looked alarmed. 'What's wrong?'

He regarded her pretty face screwed up with concern. His distaste quickly faded into an arousal of erotic yearning. 'Are we going to make love after your husband is back?'

She glanced down and fingered the reins. 'I don't know how to answer you.'

'Just say one way or the other.' He frowned impatiently.

'How do I know what I'll feel about Mac? How do I know what freedom I'll have? I thought you understood,' she glared.

He pressed his hand to his head. 'I did understand. I think I still do. I wonder what came over me.'

She smiled naughtily. 'You think I like Slim, don't you?'

D'Arcy's heart skipped a beat. 'Maybe.'

'Don't worry, darling. I don't rob cradles.'

'Who's worrying?'

Kate laughed teasingly. 'It would be a blow to your pride wouldn't it?'

He started. 'It would mean that you have none.'

She blushed and regarded him with hurt eyes. A retort leaped to her lips, stumbled, and died with a toss of her head.

D'Arcy grimaced. 'I'm sorry. It sounded worse than I intended.'

'Because it's what you really think of me,' she cried. Tears stood in her eyes. 'You think I sleep around just for something to do. You think I'm cheap, don't you?' She glared. 'Don't you!'

'No, I don't. I wouldn't be with you if I thought you were cheap.'

'Like hell you wouldn't!' She heeled her horse and spurted ahead.

D'Arcy watched her disappear. He wanted her and yet he didn't. A mixture of sorrow and relief tempered his desire. Their affair was blighted when her husband first returned; after which their relationship had sickened. There was no point in trying to resuscitate it. Perhaps she realized this which caused the tears. They would both be looking for someone new--not looking exactly, but preparing.

D'Arcy arrived on a promontory overlooking the valley. Kate was just riding on to the flat. A horseman hailed out, tried to ride with her, and turned aside. He looked up and saw D'Arcy. He wheeled his mount and started up the hill. D'Arcy rode down to meet him. They drew close before he recognized Allan Steel.

'Chasing the girls, Morgan?'

'They go too fast,' D'Arcy smiled.

'They're not worth it.' Allan turned to ride down with him. 'Take it from a man who knows.'

'They're certainly not worth it,' D'Arcy said humourously.

Allan regarded him with a half-smile. 'You're the kind whom the girls would chase.'

'They don't do that,' D'Arcy said. He felt uncomfortable with Allan Steel.

'By the way I picked up my car keys at the Front Desk all right. Thanks for looking after us that night.'

'That's okay.'

They rode on to the flat.

'Tell me, what do you bellhops really think of the guests? I bet you get fed up with the goings-on.'

'We're here to make money.'

'You don't make much, do you?' Allan smiled. 'The rich are careful, aren't they?'

'The tips mount up.'

'But their morals are not the best. They're loose and sometimes disgusting, I bet.'

'Bellhops are like the three monkeys who don't know evil.'

Allan laughed. 'You can put up with anything as long as you're paid, eh?'

'Don't confuse us with the guests,' D'Arcy said wryly.

Allan sat back in the saddle. He was uncertain of D'Arcy. He wondered whether he was being too friendly, whether D'Arcy disliked him.

'I think I'll go after Kate,' D'Arcy said.

'You'll never find her,' Allan smiled. 'Ride with me. I'm alone.'

'Sorry,' D'Arcy moved ahead. 'I feel I should find her.'

Allan waved him on with a look of disgust.

D'Arcy crossed a stretch of white earth and went into a grove of firs. He followed the winding path to the riverbank where he rode over the stones. Within a few minutes he came upon Kate's horse standing by a spruce. He dismounted. A great flat rock jutted from the bank. He discovered that one could climb down beside it. He came onto a small pebbled beach. Kate was sitting on a stone and dangling her bare feet in the river. She did not hear him approach. He squatted beside her. She turned and gave him a look of annoyance.

D'Arcy nodded at the aquamarine water. 'It looks cold.'

'Just right for cooling down angry people,' Kate said.

'I bet you're hissing right up to your ears,' D'Arcy smiled.

She grinned. 'We're so silly for fighting. I'm sorry, D'Arcy.'

'It's a bad way to part,' he said.

'But this is so completely crazy,' she frowned. 'It happened suddenly without warning.'

'It had to,' D'Arcy said. 'Your husband means more to you.'

'No,' she shook her head strongly so that blonde strands fell over her cheeks, 'he doesn't. It's something else, something about myself.' She took his hand. 'We've had fun, D'Arcy.' She winced. 'I hope I haven't hurt you.'

He laughed. 'Don't get sentimental.'

She looked fondly at him. 'I wonder if we could see each other just once more.'

D'Arcy looked into her eyes. He sensed the easy attraction, the familiarity of skin, hair, and breath. 'Tonight?'

'No.' She shook her head. 'I shouldn't. But will you be working?'

He nodded.

She considered. 'We'll be playing bridge in the lobby. I'll try to let you know.' She glanced at her wristwatch. 'Oh, I've got to be back.'

They stood up, a sense of business formality springing between them. He helped her scale the bank.

Above on a distant ridge where the river bank curved sharply, Allan Steel sat motionless astride his horse and watched them. The road from Bampers Town touched the high bank at this spot. An open convertible sped along it. Allan, at the sound of its motor, peered round and squinted through its windshield. He threw up his arm in spontaneous greeting and waved frantically for the car to stop.

Julien Kowalski drew off to the side. Mac, red-cheeked, leaned on the seat to shout back. 'Steel! You old bugger! How are you?'

Allan galloped up to them. He leaned down and shook Mac's hand. 'I heard we'll be seeing you for cards tonight. Hello Julien. Finally made it.'

'I'm not playing with you?' Mac barked, feigning anger. 'You're too damned tricky. I don't trust him, Julien, you know that?'

Julien smiled and nodded sympathetically.

'Just been watching Kate,' Allan said plaintively. 'You trust her all right.'

'Where?' Mac sprang out.

Allan pointed to the two figures riding over the bleached sand.

'Christ!' Mac choked, blood rushing to his head. 'Out of my sight for five minutes and she's letting her pants down to any jerk.'

Julien stood beside him. 'There's no proof, no sign, no reason for thinking such a thing.'

Mac cursed. 'You don't know my wife!'

'Yes, I do. I have known her as long as you,' Julien said severely. 'She doesn't deserve to be calumniated by your foul mouth.'

Mac gawked at him, frowned and set his hand uneasily into his pocket. 'Who was with her, Allan?'

'I'm not quite sure,' Allan sat mounted, peering at the riders disappearing into a copse of firs. 'I think it was a bellhop.'

Mac tensed. 'D'Arcy Morgan?'

Allan, white-faced, bowed his head. 'It resembled him.'

Julien felt the name D'Arcy enter his heart like a knife. He gazed up at the stone mountainside. The sun was nipping behind the topmost peaks. Long shadows covered vast areas of forest and rock.

'I have a goddamn good reason for calling her every name under the sun,' Mac barked.

'Not for taking company with her when she rides, not for talking to a bellhop, not for anything,' Julien said.

Mac looked quizzical. 'Julien, why don't you make it your profession to defend the fair sex? They say there's money in it.'

Julien walked away. 'I don't because I would constantly be doing battle with jealous men like you.' He slid into the driver's seat.

'Do you think I'm imagining things?' Mac asked, willing to be persuaded.

'Aren't you?' Julien flared. 'Get in and we won't mention it again.'

Subdued, Mac sat in.

'I agree with Julien,' Allan said. 'They were just talking. There's no harm in that.'

'You may be right,' Mac admitted. 'I guess I'm acting like a fool.'

'We should be grateful,' Julien murmured, starting the motor, 'for our keenly observant bystander.'

Mac gave him a puzzled frown as they drove off.

Allan overheard Julien. He watched guiltily until the car took the bend out of sight.

21

That evening, Allan waited by the lamppost at the front of the patio while Bett parked the car. He looked up through the glass squares of the lantern frosty gold as of ye olden times and tapped the post in time with Toots Ainsworth's orchestra resounding from the ballroom. Bett's heels clicked over the road.

'We wouldn't be late if you had come home when you were supposed to,' she grumbled.

'Beautiful day, beautiful horse,' Allan explained. 'Don't tell me you weren't enjoying the afternoon just as much, if not more.'

'How did you know?' Bett smiled. 'Did you see us?'

'A little bird saw you with your man Harry.'

'A little faery bird?'

Allan chuckled and pinched her elbow. They entered the lobby. Myriad table lamps sparkled like pearls throughout the interior. At first glance, every table appeared occupied. Guests moved about in evening clothes or conservative suits, passed into the ballroom and back again, and mingled round the Front Desk meeting one another on pretense of waiting to speak to the clerk for information or mail. Logs piled up on either side of the fireplace in anticipation of a chilly evening. The dark-stained wood, which vaulted this grand concourse, gleamed by the light of crystal chandeliers.

'Over there,' Bett nodded. 'Horace is with them.'

She hustled past tables, looking straight ahead, shawl held loosely to reveal the shoulder-line. Her eyes deviated from her goal to flicker upon a handsome man who looked up as she approached. Allan strode behind.

'We thought you'd never get here,' Kate said.

'My dear. I had odds we wouldn't.' Bett slid into the seat beside her. 'Hello Mac, Horace darling.'

'What's the damn hurry for, anyway?' Mac said. 'Just to take their money.'

'We won't play you for money,' Allan said, taking a vacant chair from the adjoining table and sitting down. 'You're too poor a loser.'

Mac opened his mouth to retort, paused, and smiled sardonically. 'It has been a good year since I have had the pleasure to skin you.'

'You know, you sound formidable,' Horace said. 'Really, no sportsman would challenge you.'

'Card games are our personal battle-ground,' Allan said. 'Mac and I get rid of our grudges against the world this way.'

'And we girls are just the catalysts,' Bett said

'Shall we get started?' Kate glanced nervously at Mac. He had been strangely subdued and was tending to regard her critically. 'Let's hope we're not too late for a table.'

Horace started up. 'Here are my family. Excuse me.'

Mrs. Rabbinowitz guided Jaimie to a more select circle. She avoided having to look at the Carr table by turning to Jaimie as they walked.

'I'll arrange it,' Allan said quickly. He went to the bell captain.

Nick was next on the Front Sheet. He set up a card table in his usual concerned manner: wondering which spot suited them, over which shoulder they preferred the light, did they smoke? If so, he'd bring over some ash-stands. Would they prefer arm or folding chairs? Was it too noisy? Perhaps that corner....

'The cards,' Allan said, 'where are the cards?'

'Oh, I have them, sir, I have them,' Nick brought a pack from his pocket. 'Would you like two packs, sir? I'll get you another.'

All the while Nick was wishing that Mac had ordered the table because he tipped liberally. Allan was the type who had to be nudged up from a quarter to fifty cents.

Allan brought change out of his pocket and regarded it in the palm of his hand. He picked out a quarter.

'Are the ladies comfortable?' Nick blurted. 'Would you like a pillow, Mrs. Steel? Awfully hard chairs for a whole evening.'

'All right,' Bett said, flattered, 'it sounds like a good idea. How about you, dear?'

'No, I'm all right, thanks,' Kate said.

Nick dashed away for a pillow and came back breathing heavily. 'Where would you, uh, like it, Mrs. Steel?'

She leaned forward. 'Just at my back.'

Allan smiling grimly handed Nick fifty cents. Nick went triumphantly to the desk and checked the Front Sheet.

'The skinflints are beginning to creep in,' he said to D'Arcy as he sank on to the bench. 'You can see their faces from last year floating around in this crowd like evil genies.'

Flowers passed, limping slightly, his heavy body tilted forward from the ankles resembling a lake trout rising for bait.

'Who for instance?' D'Arcy demanded.

Nick narrowed his eyes and leaned to whisper. 'Kowalski.'

D'Arcy hunched his shoulders. 'Did he come in?'

'Right when our shift walked on at six. If he'd come five minutes earlier, the other guys would have got him.'

'Did he stiff you?' D'Arcy smiled.

'Ha, ha,' Nick said. 'He sure did. "I'll see you in the lodge," he said. "I haven't any change with me."'

D'Arcy laughed. 'Still, you're better off than me. O'Flaherty fined me fifty cents for being late.'

'Why were you?' Nick sucked in his lips to keep from smiling.

'Never mind.'

'Out prancin' and romancin', eh, D'Arce?'

'Never mind,' he said sharply.

'Getting testy, tut. tut, D'Arce. You'll lose your touch.'

Julien Kowalski appeared in front of them. 'I would like a card table over there, please.' He pointed vaguely.

Nick elbowed D'Arcy. 'You're Front.'

D'Arcy stood up and gazed dumbly in the direction Julien indicated.

'By those gentlemen standing, do you see?'

The gentlemen turned to regard them as if they had heard through the chatter and swirl by telepathy. Julien continued round the Front Desk.

Nick sniggered into his hand.

D'Arcy looked appealingly at O'Flaherty. 'Shouldn't this be last boy?'

'Well!' O'Flaherty thought.

'I roomed him today,' Nick reminded him. 'D'Arcy has to take him.'

'Why make it "last boy?"' complained the last boy from the end of the bench.

'It's a Front,' O'Flaherty decided.

D'Arcy gestured feebly with open hands.

'Get going,' O'Flaherty smiled.

180

D'Arcy took a card table from the hops' cloakroom. Nick signalled him that Julien was lurking by the corner of the Front Desk. D'Arcy went round and confronted Julien.

'Now, sir, where do you want it exactly?' he asked.

Julien frowned. 'I said, where those gentlemen were standing.'

'They seem to have gone, sir.'

"What?' Julien stepped out quickly and peered at the spot. 'No. There they are.'

'Where, sir?'

'Don't you see them?' Julien demanded in annoyance.

'There are so many gentlemen,' D'Arcy scrutinized the distance in vain.

'Well,' Julien sighed, 'come with me.'

D'Arcy followed, smiling to himself. The only way to make Julien tip was to shame him in front of the other men. Unfortunately, Julien knew this maneuver and would be looking for a pretext to avoid it. Julien pointed at the floor. 'Here.' The gentlemen stepped back still engaged in conversing. Julien sidled to the Carr's table. He looked over Kate's shoulder and whispered. 'Is that bellhop named D'Arcy?'

She started and glanced at D'Arcy setting up the table. 'It's finito!' she said.

'What's finito?' Mac barked. 'You're not letting our side down?'

'No, there's a good card,' Julien said. 'She's all right, Mac.'

D'Arcy overheard Mac's question. He regarded Kate steadily as he slowly unfolded the last leg. Kate looked up apologetically. D'Arcy smiled and shook his head as if in pity. He set the table on its legs. The gentlemen pulled up chairs and sat. D'Arcy waited for Julien who seemed engrossed in the Carrs' game.

'Do we have the cards?' asked one gentleman politely.

D'Arcy reflected that if he went, Julien would return to the table. He dashed away and waited behind the pillars by the bell captain's desk. Julien looked round warily. He seemed to sniff the air. Then setting his hand on Kate's shoulder in farewell, he rejoined his companions. D'Arcy stepped up and presented a pack of cards.

181

'No, thank you,' Julien said curtly, drawing a pack designed with a clipper ship from his pocket. 'I have my own. Thank you very much.' He shuffled and dealt.

D'Arcy looked at the other men but they shunned him. He returned mouthing bitter words to the bench. Nick, who had been watching, was clutching his stomach in silent laughter. D'Arcy sat down glumly.

Runners sidestepped from the milling throng. 'Captain!' he cried.

O'Flaherty jumped as if hit. He ran up to Runners. 'Yes, sir.'

'Is there anything the matter with that boy?'

O'Flaherty looked disdainfully at Nick who was now sitting soberly straight. 'No, sir.'

Runners frowned, drilled Nick with his beady eyes, and stepped to the corner of the Front Desk. He paused to look back over his trail for suspicious signs, then, satisfied, he backed up to Deo's partition.

'Hello, Mr. Runners,' Deo's eyes glittered appreciatively. 'Nice of you to pay me a visit.'

'Evening, Deo.' The lines of his face softened, his eyes grew lustrous. 'Busy?'

'Just everyone wants mail and sometimes they ask two or three times.'

'Sorry you have to work late,' he said gently.

'That's all right' she beamed. She met plenty of guests in the evening and strong admirers like Horace Rabbinowitz who was now regarding her over Runner's shoulders from out of the throng in the lobby. 'Besides, I'm off at nine.'

'I'll take you to your cabin at nine,' Runners said abruptly.

'Will you?' she sparkled. 'That'll be very nice.'

Wearing a foxy grin, he moved down the far hallway where there was a room and a bottle which Mrs. Runners didn't know about.

A guest asked for mail. Deo scanned the pigeon holes and plucked out a letter. The sound of the orchestra starting a number caught her attention. Johnnie sang, his velvety voice reminiscent of romance in the golfer's cabin.

'We'll build a bungalow... big enough for two...oo.'

Horace curled his lips with a look of kind superiority as he stood in front of her.

'Mail, sir?' Deo asked brightly.

'No.' He shook his handsome head. 'Female.' His lips flicked up at both corners.

Deo trilled. 'You and your corny jokes.'

'That is all the humour remaining to me this evening. My wife insists on sitting with the dullest lot in the lodge.'

'You unlucky man. But you don't have to sit with her.'

'I do ninety percent of the time to keep eyebrows from being raised,' Horace said. 'May you never know the penalty of dull society.'

'It can't be anything like yours,' Deo flirted. 'I loved that evening we spent.'

Horace smoothed his dark hair behind his ear and carefully looked at the lobby. 'We'll spend another when I have the opportunity.'

'But why do we have to wait?' Deo complained.

'My wife has made many engagements with these dullards whom she considers important. But I'll escape soon for your sake,' he smiled charmingly.

'Is that a promise?' Deo coaxed.

Horace dropped his eyes over her agreeably. Jaimie stopped near-by to regard them. Deo directed Horace's attention to him by a subtle shifting of the head. Horace thanked her politely and stepped up to Jaimie.

'There's no mail, my son.'

'I asked a few minutes ago,' Jaimie said suspiciously. 'I thought you knew.'

'You inform your mother of everything and entirely forget about me,' Horace admonished him. 'Where are you going?'

'To see the Carrs,' Jaimie said.

'That is where I am going. You go back to your mother.'

'Oh dad, I can't stand it.'

'We both can't go to the Carrs' table. There isn't room.'

Jaimie pondered. 'Maybe Jane's free.'

'Be careful. Not too much of her,' Horace warned.

'I might as well get it out of my system while I'm young,' Jaimie said sharply, 'otherwise it might plague me when I'm old.'

'What do you mean by "it"?' Horace frowned.

'Romance, of course,' Jaimie nodded at the reservations partition.

Horace regarded him askance. 'You will have to improve your vocabulary. I think "plague" is the wrong word.'

Jaimie grinned. He whirled about and set off for the outdoors.

Horace mused after him, then seeing his wife in the company of rather ugly ladies, he retreated to Deo. 'What time are you off work?' he asked.

'I'm tired,' she said apologetically. 'I want to go right to bed.'

'My wife wouldn't notice if I went home early,' he suggested.

Deo reached out and tightened her fingers about his hand. 'Not tonight, please.'

'Telegram,' announced a clerk at her back.

Deo looked at the name. "Bett Steel". She rounded her eyes and entered the name in a column. 'Excuse me, Horace, just for a minute.' She went to the Front partition and left the telegram. The Front Clerk called 'boy' and D'Arcy, whose turn had come up again, took the telegram.

He disliked having to accept a tip from the Steels. But he couldn't afford to lose another Front; small earnings demoralized him. In order not to feel the slightest degree of humiliation, he assumed an official posture and paged Mrs. Steel.

Allan hailed him. D'Arcy handed the telegram to Bett and nonchalantly pocketed a quarter from Allan. Kate smiled broadly up at him in spite of Mac's cold stare.

'Thank you, D'Arcy dear,' Bett said, splitting open the envelope with her fingernail. 'Do excuse me, gentlemen.'

D'Arcy retired, sidestepping to avoid Horace approaching.

Bett read: 'Love and Kisses - Jake.'

'What on earth! Ah, sweet! Isn't it a good omen, Kate?' Bett gave the telegram to Kate.

'You have a bright future,' Kate said, folding it and handing it back.

'What's it say?' Mac queried.

'It's private, dear,' Kate said.

'Woman's secret?' Allan suggested.

'I'm afraid so, Allan dear. I mean, it's going to be a big surprise,' Bett sighed. 'I can hardly wait.'

Allan winked at Mac who didn't respond. 'I think we men should have our own secrets, don't you, Mac?'

'Not until we finish this card game,' Mac growled. 'Let's get serious.'

'Is Mac making it unpleasant for you, Allan?' Horace asked. 'May I kibitz?'

'Certainly,' Allan said. 'Mac is unpleasant because the score's against him.' He saw Flowers move through the crowd and flickered his eyelashes at him.

'Mac is unpleasant,' Mac said angrily, 'because Kate's mind is not on her game.'

'Horace,' Kate grimaced, 'will you take over my hand?'

Horace looked non-plussed.

'Katie dear,' Bett cried, 'I mean, are you sure?'

Kate stood up.

'Let her go,' Mac barked. 'Horace is the man I need. Bail me out.'

'Well,' Horace looked sympathetically at Kate, took her hand of cards, and sat in her place. 'I can't stay long.' He made a face at the cards. 'I suppose this means my money is at stake. Whose move?'

Kate snatched up her purse and went directly to the ballroom. She watched Johnnie singing and then accepted an invitation to dance.

D'Arcy was watching from the bellhop's desk. Kate's swaying figure rekindled his interest. He glimpsed Runners near him, stooped to empty an ash stand, and glanced at the clock to see how soon the evening's work would be done. Only nine.

Runners moved stiffly around the Front Desk.

'Ready, Deo?' Runners hiked an eyebrow.

She nodded. He went down the corridor. She waited a moment, then swiftly followed. When she stepped outside, he glided from the shadows and took her hand.

She smelt alcohol.

He put an arm about her waist. 'We'll take the long way.'

Deo cuddled close against him. 'Where's your wife?'

Runners avoided the glare of the street lamp. He chose the dark shore path. 'Watching the children.'

'Hmm!' She nudged her head against his chin. 'This is comfy.'

Runners' nose twitched with the exhilarating smell of her perfume. 'You are beautiful, Deo.' He knew he was tight, acting foolishly, but what the hell! he was living.

'Where are you taking me?' she purred.

'There is a bench along this way,' he said.

Deo looked up. The stars were out in full. Runners brought his face against hers. She closed her eyes and puckered. Runners kissed nicely, rather excitingly in fact. She provoked another to be sure of it.

'Deo,' he sighed. 'I wish we'd been able to get together sooner.'

'We could have if you tried.'

He reared back in surprise. 'I didn't know you felt that way.'

'To tell the truth,' she smiled, 'I didn't know, either.'

'That's strange, isn't it?' Runners caressed her back. He pointed to the bench.

'I knew I liked you when I saw you at your party,' Deo said.

They sat down together.

'Was that when?' Runners said. He caressed her arms and shoulders.

'Funny how dark and peaceful the lake is,' Deo said.

'It is sleeping,' Runners whispered. 'Like all happy people, it sleeps peacefully.'

Deo hummed. 'Yes, I can believe that.'

'Are you warm enough?' Runners murmured.

'I like your hands. They keep me warm.' She turned her face and he kissed her lips and neck and ears and her lips again.

"There is a small cabin in back of us,' he said. 'We'll be warmer there.' He stood.

'All right,' Deo smiled, and, standing, brushed her cheek against his shoulder.

Trembling with expectation, Runners led her by the hand across the grass.

A large broad figure moved from behind a tree. Twigs cracked as it moved toward them. Runners stopped, petrified. He swayed back against Deo who was ready to scream.

'Stand still,' he croaked. 'It may not attack.'

A blinding light struck them in the eyes. Runners blinked into the beam from a flash lamp.

'Oh, it's you, is it, sir?' said Archie.

'What in damnation!' Runners cried. 'Turn off that light!'

The light went out.

'What are you doing here?' Runners thundered.

'Just making my rounds, sir,' Archie's amazed voice emanated from the blackness.

Runners felt Deo squeeze his hand. There was no time to stand and talk.

'Then get on with it,' he snapped.

Deo thrilled to this energetic voice of authority which she found especially exciting because she expected to be controlling a few of the vibrant tones before long.

Archie stalked away.

'A good watchman,' Runners muttered, 'but stupid.' He led her up the steps to the one-roomed cabin. Instead of turning on the light, he lit a candle by the door. He flicked out the match flame, held out his arms, and grappled Deo to him.

Archie tramped between the trees and nodded wisely. It wasn't the first time he had caught Runners in a compromising situation. If he wanted to hurt Runners, he told himself, he could do so very easily. He didn't like being shouted at. There was movement ahead. He stepped behind a tree.

D'Arcy paced behind the bushes. He stopped to watch Kate's white and red dress in the lamplight. She ran up the steps to him. They embraced, then moved behind the bushes.

'I tried to sneak out,' she whispered, 'but I think Mac saw me.'

'I just want to hold you again,' D'Arcy said, keeping his arms tight about her. 'Giving you up is not as easy as I wanted it to be.'

She smiled and rubbed her head against his neck. 'I'm sorry, D'Arcy. It's hard to be seeing you in the lobby and not be loving you. I don't even know if I'm doing the right thing. Do you think it's right?'

'Don't ask me,' he said. 'I guess it's right. Anyway, it's more convenient for you.'

She pulled away. 'But not for you.'

'Keeps me out of danger,' he smiled. 'There's no jealous husband or snooping hotel manager or envious co-workers to trouble me.'

'Then it is convenient for you,' she said.

'It isn't when I dream of you. It's damned inconvenient.'

She laughed softly. 'You'll find someone else.'

'Probably,' he said. 'But I don't feel like having anyone else. I don't feel like having anything. This whole atmosphere depresses me. The only times I can forget us are when I'm alone with nature or with you.'

'I know what you mean, darling. You helped me get through the better part of this summer. But when Mac's here, there doesn't seem to be enough of you to counterbalance the effect. If anything, I think I'd feel worse.'

'So we compromise for the sake of convenience. Both words are ugly,' D'Arcy said. 'The whole place reeks with them.'

They heard steps on the stones. Kate seized him tightly. The steps paused then continued past the bushes. They saw Julien and waited until he passed out of hearing.

'I wonder where he's going?' Kate said, staring into the dark.

'Probably dating a waitress,' D'Arcy smiled.

'Let's see,' Kate said. 'I'm curious.'

D'Arcy frowned. 'Why?'

'I just am,' she smiled. 'Come with me.' She pulled him.

Archie crept after them. As he reached the bushes, he peeked over them and saw Mac Carr come from the lodge, look up and down the road, then mount the steps two at a time. Mac stopped within two yards of Archie, glared down the pathway, and pushed on.

Archie watched the lodge for another minute in case someone else appeared. His caution gratified him. Mrs. Steel rushed over the patio, her heels striking the stones. She ran up the steps and down the pathway. Archie whistled softly to himself.

Meanwhile, Julien, the head of this peculiar chase, had penetrated to the centre of the Staff area. He ducked into the Staff Hall where couples danced to Toots Ainsworth's music piped in from the lodge ballroom. Satisfied that Kate was not there, he walked to the next cabin. A brief whistle shrilled from the side. He went round the corner to find Jaimie standing by the windows.

'Oh! hello, Mr. Kowalski,' Jaimie said, startled.

'Evening,' Julien nodded. He looked along the cabin as if he were inspecting it.

'I guess Jane isn't back yet,' Jaimie said, strolling to him. 'Are you waiting for someone?'

Julien rocked back on his heels. 'Maybe.'

Jaimie smiled. 'Why the big secret? I won't tell anybody.'

'There's nothing to tell, young man. I am taking in the fresh air.'

Jaimie grinned. 'You sound like dad.'

Kate and D'Arcy watched Jaimie walk away. They were in the shadow of the mess hall.

'Julien must be meeting a girl,' Kate said. 'He's loitering about the waitresses' cabin.'

'What does it matter?' D'Arcy complained. 'You'd think he was your husband.'

'I want to see what he does,' she insisted.

'I've got to go back on duty.' D'Arcy said. 'Will you see me after twelve or won't you?'

Kate shook her head irritatedly. 'No!'

Jaimie passed by without seeing them.

'Then I'm going,' D'Arcy said. 'Good hunting.' He started in Jaimie's direction.

'Hello Mac,' Jaimie's voice bounded in front of him. 'Are you here too?'

'What do you mean, "too"?' Mac growled.

Jaimie laughed. 'I think father must be setting an example.'

D'Arcy showed Kate a look of terror and escaped in the opposite direction.

'I don't know what you're talking about,' Mac said gruffly, pushing by him.

Kate pressed against the logs as Mac walked by and continued into the Staff Hall. She gathered that he was looking for her, but to be sure, she waited for him to reappear.

Julien was wandering back to the Staff Hall. He thought he saw a bellhop enter a cabin beyond the Mess hall. He changed directions to cross the lawn between the cabins to reach what he presumed was the hops' quarters. As he entered the shadows close to Kate, he turned to regard the brightly lit Staff Hall once more. Mac was coming from the entrance. Julien stepped back with surprise and stood unwittingly just in front of Kate. Mac looked about, put his hands in his pockets, and perched on the right parapet. He dangled his legs and lit a cigarette.

Julien moved backwards slowly. He had to find Kate and prevent her from acting foolishly, he thought. His hand touched flesh. He whirled, looking straight into Kate's grin.

She clasped her hand to his mouth and leaned against the wall with him.

Julien took away her hand. 'What are you doing?' he whispered.

'What are you doing?' she asked naughtily.

'I was looking for you.'

'Ssh!' Kate hissed. 'Don't move.'

Mac jumped off the parapet and paced restlessly. He seemed to be waiting for some sign to give him direction.

Meanwhile Bett, seeing Jaimie approaching, had veered off the path and taken shelter by some trees. She observed D'Arcy hurrying over the grass. Running out, she seized his arm and brought him to the trees.

'Where's Kate?'

'She's back there,' D'Arcy nodded.

'Her husband's looking for her.'

'He's welcome to her.'

Bett regarded him curiously. 'Are things really over between you?'

'Yes,' D'Arcy said, faintly amused. 'Why?'

'Then why put her in trouble with Mac? I saw you signal to her in the lobby,' she said accusingly.

'You're observant, Mrs. Steel.'

'All right, it's none of my business,' she smiled. 'It just so happens that Kate is my friend.'

'Is that why you are holding my arm so tightly?'

She released him. 'I'll deal with you later, D'Arcy Morgan.'

'After midnight?'

'Don't be fresh.'

'I'm free as a bird,' he challenged.

'I'm not,' she said, 'at least, this evening. Are you going back to the lodge?'

He took her arm. 'I see friend Archie on the prowl. Be quiet till he passes.' He leaned over her and they embraced.

'Are you sure you're not free?' he smiled.

'I didn't say that, sweetie. I said not tonight. Come on, he's gone.'

They continued over the grass. D'Arcy wiped the lipstick from his mouth.

Archie nodded blankly at Jaimie as they met. He wondered at the extent of the guests' invasion of Staff quarters.

The immoral carryings-on seemed to be out of all proportion to the extent of his duties. His authority was even deprived of managerial backbone for the evening. He hurried into the lights from the Staff Hall and confronted Mac.

'Good evening, Mr. Carr. Can I be of assistance, sir.'

'Good evening. No, no, I don't think so.' Mac peered about them.

Archie stared at the sky. 'Bad night. Might storm.'

'Where is the bellhops' cabin?' Mac barked.

Archie gaped. 'I don't think it's your business to be knowing it, sir.'

Mac regarded him quizzically. 'I don't follow your meaning, policeman.'

'It's perfectly clear that you shouldn't be in staff quarters at this time of night, sir.'

Mac clenched his teeth. 'I am looking for my wife. I am on the point of tearing these bloody shacks to pieces unless I find her right away. Is that perfectly clear?'

Archie looked aghast. 'You're in no mood to meet your wife, Mr. Carr. Go back to the lodge. I'll find her and send her to you.'

Kate and Julien, attempting to steal away while Mac's attention was distracted, overturned a garbage can. The hollow clang of the empty can announced their presence like the low note of a ceremonial gong. Kate broke into a run. Julien followed swiftly.

'There they are!' Mac cried. 'You go that way.' He pointed at the far side of the cabin and dashed in pursuit.

Archie lumbered away in the direction he was told.

Kate and Julien crossed the lawn by the bellhops' cabin and cut toward the garage. As Julien was gasping for breath, Kate flopped behind the first hedges they reached and Julien knelt beside her.

'If he comes this way, I'll run, you stay,' she whispered.

'But he'll accuse me,' Julien said between breaths.

'He'll need both of us to prove anything,' she said.

'This is silly,' Julien choked. 'I'm not even guilty.'

She seized his hand to silence him. Hiking her shoulders, she smiled kittenishly. 'It's fun.'

Mac had observed two figures run under the porch light on the bellhop's cabin. He was certain they hadn't taken refuge in the cabin. Pausing just beyond the porch, he listened for running footsteps and looked about him at the hedges and tennis courts for a clue to Kate's whereabouts.

Archie, slowing to a walk, continued along the path towards the lodge. Experience had taught him to let the criminal do the running. He would catch him at a convenient point near his goal, which, he figured, was the lodge. As he neared the steps he glimpsed the red lapels of a bellhop by the bushes. He stole quietly over the grass.

D'Arcy and Bett, having been overcome by the passionate impulse, had retreated out of the light to embrace until such time as they could continue to the lodge. They were unaware of anything outside of themselves and the ground under their feet.

With a great bound, Archie fell on D'Arcy's back and grappled long arms about both romantics.

'Mr. Carr,' he cried. 'Come quick, come quick.'

At first Bett and D'Arcy were paralyzed with surprise. When D'Arcy tried to free his arms, he found Archie's grip Titanic and his own position unadvantageous.

Mac spurted between the tennis courts and reached them within seconds. 'Okay, let them go,' he commanded in the tone of a wrathful conqueror.

Archie, having dragged them on to the path, took away his arms. D'Arcy smoothed back his hair in the light. Bett stepped up to Mac and with lightning speed slapped his face.

Mac was amazed, speechless. D'Arcy, seeing his horrified expression, laughed loudly.

'I thought you were Kate,' Mac stammered apologetically.

Bett, somewhat amused by D'Arcy's enjoyment, smiled wryly. 'That's the first compliment you have ever paid me, dear. But really, you don't need a policeman to do it.'

'But where's Kate?' Mac insisted.

'Come along, D'Arcy,' Bett said. 'Let the poor demented man find his own way home.'

They sped down the steps, D'Arcy, wiping his mouth and Bett inspecting her person.

'You go in first,' she said, 'I'll go in the front way.'

'See you,' D'Arcy smiled, happy in his new conquest.

Mac regarded Archie murderously.

'I'm sorry, sir,' Archie said. 'I thought that was your wife.'

'I wouldn't be married to her for all the money in the world.'

'Yes, sir. Will we go on looking?' Archie suggested respectfully.

Mac waved him away in disgust. 'I'm going to bed.' He descended the steps slowly, thoughtfully.

Kate and Julien hearing the commotion, although unaware of its form, made good their escape to the border of the lake. They smoked Julien's cigarettes and strolled and talked for an hour before she returned to her cabin. She was careful not to awaken Mac from a sound sleep.

About the same time, Jaimie was making another call on Jane. While waiting patiently at the side of the waitresses' cabin, he was surprised to see Mr. Runners escorting Deo through the shadows to within a short distance of the cabin door. When she kissed him goodnight, he was amused. He could hardly wait for the apposite moment to inform his father.

22

Horace was not amused at being left alone with Allan Steel for the evening. After a few hands of poker and small talk, Horace escorted his wife to their cabin. Allan drifted about the lobby to chat with old acquaintances.

Bett came for Allan. She gave no excuse for her prolonged absence. They drove home.

'Rabbinowitz didn't think you were polite. Poor fellow sat down expecting to play bridge, ended with the prospect of solitaire.'

'Someone had to warn Kate,' she said. 'Her friend D'Arcy is a devil.'

'Yes,' Allan agreed. 'Something ought to be done about him.'

'You don't like him, I see.'

'I don't trust him,' Allan said. 'He'll ruin Kate's marriage and break Mac's heart.'

Bett smiled secretively. 'You've become quite the sentimentalist all of a sudden. I mean, I thought you despised attachments of the heart.'

'As far as others are concerned, I can tolerate them.'

'I know,' Bett accelerated. 'I know.'

She telephoned Kate first thing in the morning. Mac answered gruffly and passed the receiver to a sleepy Kate.

'Darling, has Mac told you what happened last night?'

'Not yet,' Kate yawned. 'I just woke up.'

'Well, he won't unless you do, so don't say a word.'

'I don't understand,' Kate said. 'Anyway, I wouldn't say a thing, lest it incriminates me.'

Bett laughed. 'Listen, dear, he found me with D'Arcy and he thinks we're lovers.'

Kate gasped. 'He must have a reason.'

'Never mind,' Bett said. 'The main thing is you're off the hook.'

'What's this about you and D'Arcy?' Kate asked suspiciously.

'He told me that your affair was over just as you did.'

'Yes, go on,' Kate urged.

'Mac saw us together.'

'Yes.'

'That's all there is to tell.'

'I see,' Kate said. 'I guess you'll be looking forward to Jake's arrival.'

'Oh, he's not coming for another week or so,' Bett sang. 'I don't think of my chickens until they hatch.'

'Thanks for ringing, dear. I'm very relieved.' Kate hung up.

Bett hesitated to see D'Arcy. If she did meet him, it would have to be kept secret from Kate. Yet once the match was struck, she had to nourish the flame until it could burn on its own. She drove to Bampers about ten. On the pretense of taking a short cut to the parking lot, she went through the staff section. D'Arcy was not in sight. The area looked dead. She set off on foot. The little flame had to stay alive, because it would keep her going until Jake came. She went into the Staff Hall-- empty except for the girl behind the counter. She asked for an ice cream soda and sat with it in the far corner.

Customers came and went. Few noticed her so eager were they to escape from the morning barrenness of the place. The counter girl played records of popular songs continuously, varying the volume according to her whim.

About ten-thirty, D'Arcy entered wearing the trousers to his uniform and a sports shirt. He didn't notice her at first. She sat very still. Gradually, as if by instinct, he looked round, his eyes focusing upon her.

He carried his ice cream dish to her table.

'Why didn't you call out to me?' he smiled.

'I wanted to see if you would find me,' Bett said. 'I believe in chance.'

'It was a lucky chance to see you in this dark corner.'

'This way my net can't be seen,' she said seductively.

D'Arcy nodded to the door. 'Come on outside where your net can't get me.'

She held his little finger as they walked over the floor and released it when they stepped into the sunlight.

'How long do you have?' she looked up teasingly.

'Only an hour.'

'I'll take you for a spin. My car's over here.'

They got into Bett's sports car and rolled over the trail leading through the staff grounds to the road. D'Arcy saw Slim watching him with surprise and he winked.

Slim envied D'Arcy. Two of the sexiest women he had laid eyes upon were D'Arcy's companions one after the other. Sex had come to mean a great deal to Slim. He strove to satisfy his desire for Miriam but met a stone wall of reproach. His lust increased in ratio with his frustration. There was another wiener roast tonight. He would sit with his arm about Miriam, looking into the fire. His other arm would be holding a long pointed stick poking a wiener in the flames. For Miriam, this was the climax of the evening, followed by a few good-night kisses which were insignificant by themselves. Slim wondered how D'Arcy would handle Miriam; he felt inferior, a failure as a lover.

He entered the caddies' cabin and strolled to his room. Dick Andrews was expounding on the magnificence of the forthcoming tournament. His straight handsome features faced the light from the window. Bruce Bannister sprawled on his upper bunk. Don Clarking sat with chin in hands on Slim's bed below. Aurmand perched on a chair beside the sink; his popularity was established since Blair befriended him and together they had won the Staff Cup for the caddies.

'King Gillespie will be given to Blair, of course. He's worth a hundred buck tip.'

'That much!' Don Clarking gasped.

'Chickenfeed to him,' Dick assured them. 'King Gillespie makes five million a year on his records alone. He's got so many houses and swimming pools he forgets where they are.'

'How do you know?' Bruce challenged him.

'I read it in *Time Magazine*. You know Swing Along Lee who's in the end cabin? Nelles got ten bucks for rooming her and each of the hops he told to carry the bags got five. She's a sort of poor cousin to this guy Gillespie.'

Slim listened attentively. Rumours that King was coming had circulated but no one really believed them. It seemed incredible that the fabulous crooner known in the four corners of the earth would appear in their midst, although he had come for the tournament two years ago and glamorized the Rockies with his song.

'Boo, boo, boo, bop, bop, bow,' Slim crooned. 'Boy, is Blair ever lucky.'

'We didn't know you had secret ambitions,' Bruce said.

'King Gillespie's been my hero since I could open my mouth,' Slim said.

Bruce blew him a large smoke ring.

'Sing for him,' Aurmand said. 'He can help you, Slim.'

'Not unless he can make money out of him,' Don sneered. 'Let's hear you, Slim.'

Slim caught his breath. 'Way down upon the Swannee River.'

'Cut it out,' Don said. 'You want to start us croaking?'

'All I want to tell you guys,' Dick Andrews continued,' is that you got to line up the big money spenders now. Get them before the other guys.'

'How?' Don squealed.

'Use your head,' Bruce said.

'Be a brown nose,' Don sneered, 'like lots of guys I know.'

'I've never asked for any favours,' Bruce said, piqued.

'I don't mean you. I mean Legourmand. He bootlicks around that clubhouse.'

'He won't get any of the big shots,' Dick said confidentially. 'He isn't a good caddie.'

An air of superiority prevailed suddenly.

'Can we be lucky?' Aurmand asked.

'That's what I'm telling you guys. Right in this room we have the nucleus of the good caddying staff,' Dick said. 'But we have to be on our toes, see?'

'Okay,' Don jumped up. 'I'm going for a round right now. Are you guys coming?'

Bruce leaped down, slapping the floor with his heavy soles. 'I need money for tonight anyway.'

Aurmand sighed and went with them.

'My steady doesn't go for an hour,' Dick called after them. He regarded Slim curiously. 'Aren't you going?'

'There's a women's tournament also, isn't there?' Slim asked.

'Yeah, but no stars,' Dick said. 'The women play in the afternoons.'

'I'll be caddying for Mrs. Carr then. She's pretty good.'

'But there's no big money there. You've got to get these company presidents who'll last up to the final rounds. I'm telling you.'

'Who have you got?' Slim asked suddenly.

Dick lowered his voice. 'Don't tell anybody but I've got a pretty good player lined up. He was runner-up last year. He gave his caddie a trip to New York City.'

'Yeah, but any money?'

'Are you crazy?' he sneered disdainfully. 'Who wants a trip to New York without money?'

'How'd you get him, Dick?'

'Eddy picked him for me. He wants to see you by the way.'

'Really!'

'Yeah, really. Gosh, Slim don't be such a naive little boy. You make me feel sorry for you. Do you know why he's giving me this guy? Because I said I'd talk up the tournament and get the guys eager to work. You've got to have a spirited corps of caddies if you want a good tournament he told me. So I'm talking it up.'

Slim frowned. 'Does that mean that King Gillespie isn't really coming?'

'Oh, for crying out loud! Of course he's coming! I may be advertising, but I'm not telling lies. Blair's going to get him. Eddie told me. Go down and see him. He likes you.'

Slim spun round and ran down the corridor. He cut across the lawns and rushed into the clubroom.

'Eddie!'

Eddie was swinging a new club, testing its balance. 'Oh, hi.' He lifted the club. 'Do you want a set of clubs like this?'

'Sure do.'

'I've got a player for you. When I caddied for him a couple of years ago, he gave me a new set of clubs and about a hundred bucks.'

'Holy Moses!'

'I said I'd get him a caddie as a favour. You're the best one I know.'

'Come off it,' Slim blushed.

'Will you do it?'

'Sure I will.'

Eddie swung. 'Okay, I'll let you know.'

Slim went out humming. With all that money he would have his university fees paid. He looked over at the putting green. Kate was practicing. She smiled at him and beckoned.

'Hello, Mrs. Carr. Getting in shape for the tournament?'

'You'll keep me in shape, won't you?' she teased. 'Maybe you'll have to take me riding some day.'

'I'd like to,' he blushed.

She laughed. 'Did you have a good time with Miriam?'

'Sort of,' he smiled. 'She's a nice girl.'

Kate nodded knowingly. 'Just the kind you should marry.'

'I'm too young to get married. I have my whole life to live yet.'

'That's the end it?' she laughed. 'I don't blame you but don't take Mac and me for examples.'

Slim glanced away shyly. He didn't like discussing private affairs, especially concerning her. He felt also that she was alluding to some latent meaning that he was supposed to see but couldn't.

'Did you know that King Gillespie is coming?' he asked.

'Yes, I knew him when he was here the last time,' she said with amusement. 'Is he your hero?'

'One of them. I can hardly wait to see him.'

'He's just like he is in the movies,' she smiled. 'An easy-going guy with a pipe.'

'I started smoking a pipe.' He produced the pipe. An eagle face was carved on the front of the bowl. 'I bought it in town.'

'Well!' Kate looked impressed. 'Haven't you smoked before?'

'No. I turned green when I first tried it but I'm used to it now.' He stuck it in his mouth.

'It looks fine. I like you with a pipe--very handsome.'

'Oh, thanks.' He shyly returned the pipe to his pocket.

'You'll have to smoke it for me sometime.'

Slim felt embarrassed. She was treating him like a child. He had no manly way with women. He nodded with a faint smile and walked away.

Kate putted and missed the hole.

Julien strolled over. 'Too stiff,' he said. 'Relax before hitting the ball.'

She dropped another ball, breathed out easily, allowed her arms to hang limply and stroked. The ball stopped short of the cup.

'It's useless,' she sighed. 'I'm just not feeling relaxed.'

'Have a drink then.'

They strolled to a lawn table that had just been vacated. Empty glasses and slices of lemon had yet to be cleared away. Julien moved them to the far side of the table.

'Sit back and relax,' Julien advised. 'A long gin and Collins?'

Kate nodded. Julien ordered. The boy cleared the table.

'Did Mac say anything,' Julien asked, 'about last night?'

Kate told him what Bett had said over the telephone. 'Mac hasn't ventured on the subject so I guess she's right,' she added.

Julien giggled. 'Mac must be feeling foolish.'

Kate smiled. 'I wouldn't be surprised if D'Arcy had planned to make it look as if Bett was his girlfriend. I'll have to congratulate him.'

'Don't,' Julien shook his head. 'Once you are away from him, stay away.'

'I have a stronger will than you think, Julien dear.'

'I know you better than you know yourself,' Julien admonished her. 'Don't get entangled with him again.'

'Oh, Julien,' she laughed, 'you don't know me.'

'Spend the rest of your holidays happily with Mac.' He signed a chit for the drinks. 'Mac deserves it.'

'You know, dear, it strikes me that the foundation of all your lectures to me has been a plea for the preservation of the family. Rather strange coming from a graying bachelor, isn't it?'

'A battle-scarred bachelor,' Julien corrected. 'One who sees the value in faithfulness to an ideal.'

'I never knew bachelors could be wounded,' Kate smiled. 'They can flee a dangerous situation. Married people aren't so lucky.'

'I have been suffering from a wound for a long time,' Julien said. 'If I had been able to marry, it might have been healed.'

'But you can marry whenever you want,' Kate cried.

'Not the girl I want,' he smiled grimly.

Kate's cheeks reddened. She looked away. Julien's eyes spoke his love for her again. Through the years she had become accustomed to his hints and expected to accept the next one with blasé unconcern. Yet his sincerity struck through to the heart and made her blush.

'Oh Julien, I've never asked you; are you entering the tournament?'

He sat up as if he were jolted from a dream. 'No.' He blinked and smiled. 'I'm here to cheer you on.'

'I'll need it, every little encouragement.' She stood up. 'Watch me putt a bit.'

Julien watched her studiously stroke the ball around the putting green. She seemed to have forgotten him. He left the table, told the waiter he was coming back, and strolled over the thick green lawn to settle his emotions. Johnnie O'Dreams, emerging from the garage, hailed him. Julien went to meet him.

'Hey! You're out of luck,' Johnnie laughed. 'I've already combed the place for lost balls.'

'I hear you're out of a job' Julien said.

'Eh?' Johnnie looked alarmed. 'Oh yeah, for about a week. This Gillespie,' he snorted, 'he's a crowd pleaser. He can sing all my songs if he wants. I don't care. But I bet he won't sing more than two or three. Toots will be working me, don't you worry.' The sombreness in Johnnie's eyes showed that he was prepared to be hurt by his eclipse. Gillespie's arrival would teach him his place: just one band singer amongst tens of thousands while Gillespie would nonchalantly fill his role as the Voice personified.

'I liked your blonde,' Julien said. 'What was her name?'

'Deo,' Johnnie said sadly. 'She's not mine. She belongs to Runners. Isn't it ridiculous? The madder I get at that guy, the more reason I have to be mad at him.'

'She looked like an opportunist,' Julien said sagely. 'I'm sorry to hear she is.'

'I'm sorrier,' Johnnie spat. 'Horace Rabbinowitz is going to be burnt if he doesn't watch out.'

Julien raised his brows. 'This girl sounds interesting. I'll have to meet her again.'

'Yeah,' Johnnie frowned. 'Well, I have a rehearsal.'

'Say, John,' Julien stopped him from going. 'Do you know D'Arcy Morgan?'

'He's all right,' Johnnie said. 'Kate went after him. She really did. He's a good kid.'

'I'd like to see him.'

'The hops are having their liquor roast tonight. Better see him before because he'll be stoned afterwards.' Johnnie hiked away.

Julien remembered the hops from the last year reeling in the lobby on the morning after their drinking session. He smiled. He thought of Deo. He wondered if he dare leave Kate any longer. He needed postage stamps. Walking quickly he reached the lodge in two minutes and strode to the mail and reservations section of the Front Desk. Deo stared at him with big blue eyes.

'Hello,' he smiled fetchingly. 'Do you remember me?'

Deo put a finger to her mouth. Her eyes brightened. 'At Bett Steel's party! I could never forget you.'

'I haven't forgotten you,' he said. 'And I hope you won't let me forget you.'

'Oh!" she tittered, 'since you put it that way, how could I?'

Julien leaned on his elbows closer to her. 'Then let me take you away from all this heavy work some evening.'

'You would? I'd love to be taken away.' She clasped her hands. 'But I'm busy tonight,' she pouted regretfully. 'And the next two.'

Julien pulled in his chin. Obviously Horace had the richer reputation.

Runners sidled up beside him, cleared his throat, and stuck out his hand. 'Mr. Kowalski, back again. Nice to see you.' Runners' rubber grin stretched uneasily.

Julien shook hands. 'I was wondering if I had any mail but I'm just not lucky today, I guess.' He noticed that Deo was regarding him officially. There was to be no fraternization when the management was about unless it was with the management. 'I'd like a dollar's worth of five cent stamps though.' He put down a dollar.

'We're expecting good weather for the tournament.' Runners swayed back on the counter. A bellhop came up and handed him a message. He read it frowning.

Julien winked as Deo gave him the stamps. She stepped back out of Runners' view and grinned cutely. Runners flinched as if he had felt her grin singe his cheek.

'I'll be back again,' Julien said to her meaningfully.

Runners smiled and dipped his knees in a small bow. His eyes wavered mournfully to the radiant Deo, but he had no time to speak with her as a very corpulent guest, leaning on a cane, confronted him.

Julien returned at a fast clip to the golf club house. As he crossed the lawn, he observed Bett stop her car a short distance up the road. D'Arcy jumped out and waved. Bett drove off. The scene seemed to verify Kate's suspicions. Julien knew that if Kate learned of it, her pride would force her back to D'Arcy; and Bett knew it, the thoughtless girl. This flirtation had to be stopped!

Kate was sipping gin at their table. She looked up at Julien piteously. 'I thought you were teaching me to putt.'

'I had to see a man about a dog,' he said.

'Um hm,' Kate nodded. 'And was the cat pretty?'

Julien winced. 'Couldn't have matched you,' he said, 'or I wouldn't have come back, would I?'

She laid her hand on his arm. 'That's what I love about you, Julien dear. You are always reliable.'

23

Julien felt that he was more than reliable with Kate: he was devoted. No other man would take the trouble of meeting with a bellhop for the sake of her peace of mind. It was getting dark as he reached the bellhops' cabin. There was an ambiance of excitement. A hop ran up with a box full of jingling glasses.

'D'Arcy Morgan?' Julien asked.

'He's inside. Wait a minute.'

A shout of applause issued from the room into which the hop disappeared. D'Arcy came out a minute later. He knew Julien only as a non-tipper.

'Mr. Morgan, I'd like to talk with you for a moment.' Julien looked along the path. The porch light came on.

D'Arcy wondered what he had done wrong. He walked with Julien.

'I'll come to the point,' Julien said. 'It's about Mrs. Carr. She is in love with her husband. You have a hold over her that is, from anyone's viewpoint, evil. If you carry on you will separate her from her husband.'

'But I don't see her anymore,' D'Arcy said. 'I don't have any hold over her, as you describe it.'

'On the contrary,' Julien said sternly. 'By carrying on with her best friend, you are going to make her jealous. Now jealousy is irrational and destructive, but it is also unavoidable in the human make-up.'

D'Arcy laughed. 'This is preposterous. Kate doesn't want anything to do with me. How could she be jealous?'

Julien directed them away from the garage. 'You don't understand women.'

'Yes, I do,' D'Arcy said. 'If Kate is jealous, it means she loves me in spite of herself.'

Julien turned on him furiously. 'She doesn't love you! Get that out of your silly bellhop head.'

D'Arcy smouldered. 'You disdain anyone who waits upon you, Mr. Kowalski. Your stinginess says more than words.'

Julien blinked with surprise. 'I don't believe in tipping.'

'Neither do I,' D'Arcy said. 'But if the rules of a society are set up a certain way, we have to follow them. Bampers' staff works for tips, not for a salary.'

'I didn't see you to talk about money,' Julien said. 'I consider you impudent.'

'You are not being exactly gracious by expecting me to talk over my private affairs with you and take abuse at the same time.'

'Then let me put it this way: I'm warning you to stay away from Mrs. Steel and Kate. There're plenty of nice girls on the staff.'

'You are warning me? I don't understand you.'

'The management won't tolerate such goings-on,' Julien said. 'It would be a shame for you to miss the climax of the season, I would imagine.'

'I understand you very well now.' D'Arcy turned abruptly and left him.

Nick ran under the porch light. He balanced a huge cauldron on his hip. The shiny metal clanged against the wood as he plunged through the doorway. D'Arcy smiled at the sight. His problems seemed to stay behind with Kowalski.

The cauldron was the final step in the preparation of the roast; its theft from the kitchen was the definitive act which separated the hops from the hotel. Just catching a glimpse of it made D'Arcy glow with expectation as if he had already purged the money-grubbing and the servitude from his guts. He heard the jubilation. Nick had come through again.

It made him glad to have Nick on his shift which had the responsibility of getting the food and drink while the other shift was on duty. He was also proud of O'Flaherty and the boys who took the hop money collected in fines for the season, seventy-eight dollars and twenty-five cents. 'A hell of a lot of liquor,' O'Flaherty had said before setting off for town. He proved as good as his word. The hops had just transported cases of gin and Collins mix to the far side of the staff lake on their wooden baggage cart. As D'Arcy entered the hall a hop shoved a carton of wieners and marshmallows into his arms.

'Let's go, Morgan. You might as well do some work around here.'

At the lake shore, Nick was mixing gin and Collins in the huge cauldron. Gleefully, he emptied one bottle after another. The fire blazed beside him. A hop, with blocks of ice in a hamper, stumbled into the clearing. He put the ice into the drink mixture. Gradually the hops from the other shift invaded the fireside as the hotel business succumbed to the night. By eleven, all, except the night hop, were present and roasting wieners and marshmallows. The night hop would sneak off duty soon. The hops gripped the stems of grapefruit glasses. The great bowls mushroomed over their fingers. The fire blazed up consuming pine boughs. Nelles led them to the cauldron. One by one they dipped their glasses and held up the faint green liquid before their faces. When all glasses were poised in toast to the invincibility of bellhops, the party officially began. They drank their glasses to the dry bottom and scooped up more liquor again and again. Elated, they felt happy together. The harsh crackling of the fire against the soft background of the forest made them conscious of their human companionship, which seemed almost to declare them separate from the elements.

As their cheeks reddened from the heat of the flames and the gin, they turned their backs on the forest and forgot it. The fire formed the heart of their universe. The life force emanated from it and along the sticks upon which they held their marshmallows and wieners. Their hungry stomachs, awakened by the succulent smell of roasted wieners, ravenously received one after another as quickly as they could be warmed. When the life force weakened in intensity, they returned to the cauldron. They raised their glasses in competition, and, at Nelles' command, drank to see who could finish his drink first. The winner was challenged in like manner. They tired of the game.

Reeling and exhausted, they slapped their arms about one another's shoulders and sang at the tops of their voices. This was Valhalla; the resting ground of the valiant bellhop. Nick took out his joke book, flipped the pages, glanced at a first line and carried on from there, bringing everyone to tears of laughter long before the punch line. They sought out those amongst them who appeared the most sober and gathered around singing, 'Chug-a-1ug' until the hop finished his glass. They chug-a-lugged him for another glass if he seemed to need it. When the night hop arrived, the whole company joined arms and chug-a-lugged him faster and faster through nine glasses until he collapsed to the ground. They filled empty bottles with lake water and doused him back to consciousness. Nelles proposed they eat more so they could drink more. Half the vat was still to be emptied. 'Very good stuff,' he said dryly. 'Can't waste it.' He fell over a log and sat down heavily, spilling his drink. He held up his glass. 'Fill her up, but pay no attention. Your head bell man set a bad example.' He grinned rakishly and accepted the help of the hops near him.

D'Arcy saw the ground rise and fall as he walked. He stumbled into O'Flaherty and hung on. O'Flaherty clinked their glasses and sang 'Toor-a-loora'. Others joined him. D'Arcy stepped back to a tree and stuck out his hand to the trunk as if straight-arming it. Nick loomed before him. Nick's face was contorted with hate.

'I dreamt I'd scratch your eyes out,' Nick said. 'I'm going to do it!'

D'Arcy was shoved back through a bush crackling under him. Nick was grappling his throat. D'Arcy brought up his arm and slung it out with all his force. Nick slid off him. Hands seized D'Arcy's arms and shoulders and lifted him. He swayed on his feet.

'Look at his face!' someone cried. 'All scratched up.'

'Bring him over here,' Nelles said.

Nick was slumped asleep against a tree. D'Arcy flew and landed in cold lake water. He opened his eyes as if for the first time since the party began. Nelles peered down at him, a firebrand held aloft.

'Are you all right, D'Arce?' a voice asked.

'Sure,' he jumped to his feet. 'Have we finished the gin?'

'Fill his glass,' O'Flaherty ordered. 'Oh, fill his glass, fill his glass,' he sang.

D'Arcy reached for the bowl of the glass twinkling in the firelight and swallowed the cool liquid. 'More,' he said.

'More, more!' the shout went up, and they laughed and sang and left him to fill his own glass.

Gradually their spirits flagged. They squatted and sprawled about the fire. They felt the cold slightly. It was time to stage the final act of the night: a call on the Sabine Women, a noisy dash through the waitresses' cabin.

Some of the hops couldn't get up. Nick was still asleep. A hop set the emptied cauldron beside Nick so that he would not forget to take it back.

D'Arcy found himself pushing a large wooden baggage cart with another hop. Inside the cart, sat Nelles, smiling benevolently. The wheels bumped over roots, got caught in brambles, and broke onto the macadamized road with a rumbling din. Nelles was magnificently composed amongst the boisterous hops as they rallied the cart uphill towards the cabin. D'Arcy felt the handle slip from his grasp and the cart roll back against him. Other hops pushed against it; the cart hovered, then shot forward and reached the top.

The door of the waitresses' cabin was open. The hops charged down the hallway. They banged on doors and rattled tin cans. The girls, forewarned, had locked their doors and lay soundlessly in their beds. D'Arcy pushed the cart through the entrance and down the hall. The hard wood of wall boards cuffed his shoulders and hips. Hops were shooting off fire extinguishers. The clamour filled his head. He couldn't see Nelles. The cart struck a radiator, driving the handle into his stomach. He flattened out, tried to straighten up and push the cart, but it was wedged to a halt between the wall on one side and the radiator on the other. A strong beam flashed from the end of the hallway. A cry, "Archie!", rang out shrill as a fire alarm. D'Arcy panicked. He stumbled over the feet of the hop pushing the other handle, raced him down the corridor and out the door. The ground dropped down a hillside and rose to meet his chin as he ran to the cover of the trees. Clasping a tree, he turned round to see Nelles calmly pulling the cart out of the cabin. He closed his eyes as the night swirled in upon him.

'Then let me put it this way: I am warning you to stay away from Mrs. Steel and Kate.' Julien's voice spoke from a corner of his brain.

Kate's pretty features formed from a white mist. She longed to be with him. She cried out to him just before she vanished. He had no feeling of lust, no thoughts of love. Only the pain of betrayal ached in his chest. He ran recklessly through the trees, stumbling, striking branches, over the lighted areas and across the lawns to the guest cabins.

Signs of dawn shot the dark in ghostly streamlets. He fell breathlessly on the steps to Kate's cabin and laid his head against the fibrous carpeting. The world stopped heaving and became distinctly realistic. A sense of sacrilege spun from his incongruous position on the porch of a guest cabin. He slowly regained an upright stance and walked uncertainly across the front sitting room to Kate's door.

His insignificance frightened him. A penniless servant of the rich was about to demand an explanation from a millionaire. Runners' long angry face could be conjured up at the snap of Mac's fingers. D'Arcy regarded the dirty smudges on his clothing. His face was smarting faintly from the scratches, although he felt numbed, as if under local anesthesia. His appearance would alarm them. His suffering would strike Kate's heart or her conscience. She would see that he was not just an indifferent playmate. He leaned against the bell and waited. No sound from within. He rang again. Something fell to the floor. A key turned in the lock. The door opened a crack. D'Arcy glared.

'Kate,' he said.

'What do you want?' It was Mac's voice.

'I want Kate.'

There was a long pause, then whispering behind the door. An angry retort. A sharp protest. D'Arcy smiled.

'She doesn't want to be disturbed. You will hear from me in the morning,' Mac said and closed the door.

D'Arcy stared dumbly at the panelling. He heard Kate scream. He threw himself against the door and beat upon the wood thundering his anger. One hand sought the knob and the door sprang open. He stumbled head-first into Mac, striking into his chest and driving him back against the wall.

Mac thrust him away spasmodically. D'Arcy reeled, tripped over a stool and fell on his back. He lay still. Kate knelt beside him.

'Are you all right?' she asked shrilly.

D'Arcy looked at her with Mac frowning over her shoulder. They represented a force that made him shy. He struggled to sit up and leaned on one elbow. He tried to think why he had come: to destroy? to wreak vengeance?

'D'Arcy, are you hurt?' Kate was alarmed.

'I just came to see you,' he said.

'He's not hurt,' Mac said. 'I'm phoning the lodge.'

'Don't you dare,' Kate glared at him.

Mac hesitated, his face wrenched in angry query.

'Did he hurt you?' D'Arcy asked.

'No.' Kate stood up. 'What did you want to tell me?'

'I don't know. I think I wanted to know why you don't love me.'

Kate smiled. 'I can't love everybody. I have Mac to look after.'

D'Arcy looked away in disgust. 'Love is where the money is.'

Kate coloured.

'Now,' Mac said grimly, 'will you let me phone?'

'Go ahead,' D'Arcy said. He got to his feet. 'I don't care. I came to find out about something that doesn't exist. So, it's my fault completely.'

'What do you mean?' Kate frowned.

'I can't explain,' D'Arcy sighed. 'It has something to do with reciprocation.'

'He's so drunk he doesn't know what he's saying,' Mac sneered.

D'Arcy shrugged and walked out. Shoulders straight, he marched from the cabin. Half the sky was seared white. The bulbs on the cabin porches burned yellow in the early light. He felt defeated, mistaken, forlorn. Kate's body had disintegrated; her boredom, her laughter, and her husband remained. An insipidity emanated from her life to invade the marrow of his bones, even to the timber of the cabins and the great lodge, which stretched lantern-lit like some eastern temple of worship in the dawn. The lodge seemed to swarm with human roaches weakening its natural resilience. Its magnificence was ruined sickeningly with sumptuousness. Built as a home from which one could enjoy nature, it became a bazaar trafficking in sordid tinsel and so-called sophistication. Its spirit had succumbed, like Kate's, to the brilliance of the superficial. Yet, as D'Arcy pushed through the screen door, he sensed the presence of divinity. The eerie light filtering through the window curtains and the clacking machine encaged behind wooden bars transformed the lobby into a nave almost supernaturally alive in the morning solitude. Lou, the high priestess, left off tapping messages to Osiris and surveyed the ghastly, mud-caked apparition, waddling to the altar side.

'Enjoy the party, piggy?' she asked.

'I'm a little messy,' D'Arcy said. 'Did anybody call up complaining?'

Lou's hard mouth broke into an indulgent smile. 'If they did, I didn't answer. I've been much too busy to watch the switchboard.'

'Oh.' D'Arcy walked round the desk and, entering, went to the switchboard. Lou had turned off the buzzer. D'Arcy was beginning to feel elated, almost slap-happy. He had overridden the experience with the Carrs buoyantly.

A light blinked on the switchboard. It was Runners' home. Fastening on the ear piece, D'Arcy shoved in the plug.

'Yes, sir,' he said smartly.

'On duty,' Runners said. 'Just checking. How was your party?'

'Great, just great!' D'Arcy laughed.

Runners sounded friendly. 'Glad someone is on the job. I admire a sense of responsibility.' He hung up.

D'Arcy dialed Bett's number. He counted four rings before she answered.

'Are you asleep?' he asked.

'Darling, who isn't at this hour?'
'Are you alone?'
'Who is this?'
'D'Arcy.'
'Yes,' she said. 'I am alone.'
'Well, I'm in a pretty poor condition. I need your help. I'm starting to walk down the roadway and hope to meet your car. Okay?'

She paused, thinking. 'Okay. Don't let me miss you. By the way, are you drunk?'

'Yep.'

'Then don't let me hit you either.'

D'Arcy made his way down the shadowless road. He was feeling very tired, but the cold air pricked him awake. As Bett's car hummed in the distance, coming closer and closer, so did her warm body. He threw up his arms at the machine. It stopped.

'Brother! Do you look dead!' Bett said. She helped him into the car.

D'Arcy put back his head and rejoiced in the wind coming through the window. He paused, then stepped upon cement while needles pricked his legs and cramps seized upon his back. He took off his shoes, pulled off his clothes, rubbed against white sheets and felt Bett's lips upon his ear.

24

The bête in Bett revealed herself to D'Arcy in their love-making late in the morning. She was a slithering mermaid, a veritable naiad, radiating joy and rejuvenation through the pores of his body. His skin tingled long afterward in a flow of passion.

D'Arcy went back to sleep while Bett made them breakfast. She returned with a tray of coffee, ham and eggs, toast and marmalade. Setting the tray on the bedside table, she rolled D'Arcy over and kissed him awake.

The firmness and compactness of her body entranced D'Arcy throughout breakfast. She was amused and flirtatious by turns which held his fascination. When they finished eating, she padded back to the kitchen with the dishes.

D'Arcy remarked that it was noon by the bed-clock. He should have been working, of course. This sort of behaviour was another example of his irresponsibility. He watched Bett's comely form move towards him. When denuded, she appeared sensuously exciting; when clothed there was the barest hint of her powerful attraction. Certainly, the cult of the body had reached its culmination in Bett.

'Let's have fun again,' she smiled impishly.

D'Arcy took her in his arms. They made love. D'Arcy sat up to find it was one-thirty.

'I'd better phone in. They'll be out with a search party.'

'A posse of men,' Bett suggested. 'Let me handle them, darling.'

'You could too,' he joked.

He spoke with the captain of the other shift who informed him that he hadn't been missed. 'Ranks are just beginning to close up,' the captain said very officially as if he were tight.

'No drinking on duty,' D'Arcy said.

The captain cackled, 'Have to keep the colours flying.'

'Yeah, well, remember what they did to Danny Deever.'

'He was a mere private, like you, Morgan.'

D'Arcy hung up before he received an order. Bett was dressing. The long mirror on the boudoir door showed him a tousle-headed lover, stubbled, nonchalant, and culpable. He brushed off his clothes and dressed.

Bett peeked from behind the door. 'You can't wear that shirt. I'll give you one of Allan's.'

'This shirt is just perfect,' he enunciated, buttoning it. 'It's clean enough to get me home.'

Bett laughed. 'You don't have to be offended. I mean, he isn't Mac Carr.'

There were sounds of men entering in the front door.

'There he is now.' Bett slipped an orange strap under her hair and snapped it closed on top.

'Will he come in here?' D'Arcy asked, dressing quickly.

Bett tucked her tongue in her cheek. 'You should have thought of that last night.'

D'Arcy went to the window. 'I can leap the bushes.' He put on his windbreaker and began unhooking the screen.

'Don't be silly!' Bett laughed, stopping him. 'I thought you knew Allan better than that.'

211

'He can still be jealous.'

'No fear. Our relationship is strictly spiritual with a strong dose of economics.'

D'Arcy was amused. He wished he had known Bett earlier. This sort of arrangement seemed marvellous. Besides, she was more entertaining than Kate though he missed Kate's softness which Bett lacked, and her tenderness which Bett showed only in flashes of sincerity. Though why should he try judging on short notice? Bett made him happier than Kate had. Bett's epicurianism was more fundamental; it sprang spontaneously, truthfully from her nature, whereas Kate used it as a means of escape and really detested it at bottom. Though who was to say which attitude led to the avenue of happiness in the long run? He followed Bett into the living room.

'Hell!' Allan stood up in delighted surprise. 'Mr. Morgan in person.' He shook D'Arcy's hand. 'You've met Mr. Sandhurst.'

Alick smiled shyly and referred to the accident of the flat tire. 'In stranger circumstances.'

They laughed lightly. D'Arcy listened for any innuendo in Allan's friendliness which, however, seemed sincere. They sat chatting while Bett fixed them lunch.

'Heard about your party last night,' Allan chuckled. 'Quite a stag.'

'We all got enough to drink,' D'Arcy smiled.

'I should say,' Alick giggled. 'The chef caught Nick with the huge cauldron used in the kitchen. He complained that the vegetables would smell of gin.'

'Did he report it to Mr. Runners?' D'Arcy asked, alarmed.

'Oh no! He just likes to complain. We all get a bit of a kick out of it.'

'Don't worry about Runners,' Allan said breezily. 'He's a frustrated old woman with a nervous bark.'

'That description could apply to Runners' missus,' Alick smiled. 'If you are on good terms with her, you needn't fear him.'

'And Alick is on very good terms with her,' Allan winked.

'Oh ho,' Alick flapped his hands in protest, 'Don't over-rate my courage. Mr. Morgan will be forming the wrong opinion of me.'

'I will be of Mrs. Runners at any rate,' D'Arcy said.

They laughed.

'Alick's sense of purpose has never met a stiffer test than with Mrs. R,' Allan Steel smiled. 'Something like you and Mrs. Carr.' He looked full upon D'Arcy to catch his reaction. 'It must have been awfully hard to escape from her.'

'I didn't try,' D'Arcy said. 'In the end she avoided me.'

Allan seemed disappointed. 'Well, of course, Mac means something to her.'

'Mac pretends to be angry,' Alick said, 'but I wonder if he really is at heart.'

'You're right. He isn't.' Allan sat forward. 'He likes to see men run after Kate. It elates him, makes her seem valuable. Above all, a thing must have value for Mac.'

'It costs him nothing to call a halt because he is the law and order of the family,' Alick added.

'You mean, he enjoys having men make love to his wife?' D'Arcy asked pensively. 'Yes, he probably gets a thrill out of the whole thing.' He stopped short as he realized that the same observation might be applied to Allan and that Allan was regarding him with slight alarm.

'Triangles are the complications that give his life some pace,' Allan said, getting up to meet Bett with the tray. 'Not so with me. I'm a unilateral man.'

'It's all right, darling,' Bett sidestepped him. 'You can fetch the other in the kitchen.' She put the tray on the table. 'I hope you don't mind buffet, my dears. It's disgracefully lazy, but that's how I feel today.'

D'Arcy eyed the tomato sandwich. 'It looks good.'

'Are you hungry?' Bett smiled impishly. 'I wonder what gave you such an appetite.'

'Gin has that effect on one,' Alick said, watching the two lovers grin like cats at each other.

Allan returned with the tea tray. He was sobered by D'Arcy's remark. It made him think about himself and his married life. He had to admit that Bett's extramarital affairs gave him pleasure, although he suffered the disdain with which some of her lovers treated him. What horrified him was that other people could suspect him of having such pleasure. He said little during the meal, yet his reticence was not noticed. Bett was doing most of the talking.

'Good-bye, dears,' Bett patted D'Arcy's cheek as he left with Alick. 'We'll be out to see you very soon.'

213

'I'm going on night duty,' D'Arcy said, 'but I'll be free in the day.'

'Oh, what a pity,' Bett said disappointedly.

'Alick,' Allan said. 'Leave the car at the garage will you. We'll pick it up there.'

Alick smiled sheepishly and, shaking his head, walked back to Allan. 'The keys,' he said.

'Ah, yes,' Allan produced them. 'Keep your eyes on the road. Don't let Mr. Morgan distract you.'

'Can't you call him D'Arcy?' Bett complained.

'That's up to him,' Allan's eyes twinkled.

'Sure,' D'Arcy grinned. 'I'll call you Allan.' He felt rather fey.

On leaving the driveway, D'Arcy glanced back through the window to see Bett standing on the walk alone, watching them go. D'Arcy couldn't help wondering how the two got along. They appeared strangely well-adjusted, but again that was a point of view which might change on closer association.

'Bett is very understanding, isn't she?' Alick said, eyes on the road.

'I think Allan is,' D'Arcy countered.

'He can be,' Alick smiled, 'when he has no other alternative. I've known Allan for a long time. Though I just met his wife this summer, I would side with her in any argument. She is able to judge more objectively than any other woman I have met. Allan is like me. He's impetuous.'

'Bett must have to put up with a lot then,' D'Arcy fished.

'I shouldn't talk about them, I suppose,' Alick said, 'but I should warn you that she is fanatically attached to Allan. I wouldn't become involved if I were you.' He added quickly, 'I'm saying too much, aren't I? I'm sorry, I speak out of turn often--a bad habit.'

D'Arcy tossed back his head in a snort of laughter. 'Bett's great but I could never get crazy about her or any woman.'

Alick lowered his chin. 'Men have said it before.'

'Why is she fanatically attached to him?' D'Arcy frowned.

Alick looked at him sadly. 'I don't know the secret. I wish I did.'

D'Arcy watched the road. 'Have you spent all your life in hotels?'

'Yes, doing accounts. Not what one could call exciting, except when the manager hounds you for figures. Then, you work day and night.'

'It must be a lonely life.'

'Not really, when I have friends like the Steels.'

They fell silent. The road snaked into Bampers Lodge. After letting D'Arcy off in the staff area, Alick parked the car at the garage and went to his cabin. His papers were fixed in lots upon his desk. He took up the lots he wanted, put them in a briefcase, and glanced at his watch. Time. He strutted along happily. This was one of his better days--work finished, no deadlines to meet, the lodge was making money. He felt sympathetic for the staff, boys like D'Arcy. He knew how little they were paid and how great was the lodge income. Scrambling for tips did not foster an independent or noble character in the young, although it taught them about life-- that unfortunate part of life which he avoided as best he could. Yes, they should know about the nasty side of scrambling for a livelihood. He was grateful that his work was straightforward, honest.

As he neared Runners' cabin, he heard the scolding voice of Mrs. Runners. He waited outside the porch. She was in a temper, storming in a rain of abusive words. Worriedly, he returned to his cabin to await a call from Runners. His heart quaked as he thought of the fury which Runners would wreak upon him. His beloved figures began to mean nothing--they might all have to be done again. At such trying times, he envied Allan whose wife encouraged him to tell the world to "go to hell".

25

Mrs. Runners had discovered her husband's affair with Deo, although he had been painstakingly cautious. Either Archie or Alick Sandhurst, who knew he had boosted Deo's salary, could have informed her. But Runners doubted that they had the temerity. His suspicion was demonic, creating an atmosphere of tyranny. Staff morale sank low.

Mrs. Runners did not insist that Deo be dismissed. She added to her husband's agony by allowing temptation to parade out of his reach. Moreover, she knew that Deo was liked by many of the guests and some would know whom to blame for her dismissal. Making enemies unnecessarily could lead to the dismissal of her husband.

The bellhops were reprimanded by note for their excessive partying. The three bottom boys on each shift had to scrub the white extinguisher spray off the walls of the waitresses' cabin, and Nelles stood an hour before Runners to hear his responsibilities recited. D'Arcy escaped the fearful perambulations of Runners and Flowers by going on night duty at the switchboard. He had chosen this week because the last half of it included the early stages of the tournament when he could market plenty of liquor to the gregarious guests. The laws of the province forbade the buying of strong drink except from government retail stores which were open only during the day; therefore, bootleggers made large sums from the tourists. Buying from a hop was considerably easier and cheaper than searching out a bootlegger in town. So the more daring hops stocked drinks in the cloakroom and sold them to those guests willing to pay well. D'Arcy had stocked his corner of the cloakroom with twelve ounce bottles of Scotch whiskey. The smaller the bottle, the faster it is drunk; the more trips from lodge to cabins, the more the lucre is gained.

D'Arcy set the buzzer on the switchboard and went to sleep on a sofa in the lobby. The odd call that might sound during the night was answered by Lou. If the light beneath Runners' number was lit, Lou shouted for D'Arcy who woke up and came to do his duty. But it was unlikely that Runners would call, especially as his days had become rigorous with inspections and reprimands. D'Arcy slept well the first night. Just before leaving in the morning when the girl operators took over, he telephoned Bett for a rendezvous that afternoon. Their tryst, lasting through dinner at the Steels until Bett drove him to work before midnight, was so pleasant that they repeated it every day until the weekend. Meanwhile, Kate partied contentedly with Mac in the heart of the hotel life. She golfed with Julien and flirted at a distance with Runners. Horace Rabbinowitz dated Deo twice, his wife seemingly indifferent or perhaps ignorant of the fact. Jaimie and Jane sped to the Columbian Ice fields for a romantic holiday, she being given free time before the exacting visits of Conventions in early September. Johnnie O'Dreams carried on desultorily with cabin

216

girls, with one sharp eye upon Deo. Slim and his friends worked constantly because some caddies had left either for home in the east or for hitch-hiking adventures to the States in the south. The caddies remaining saved money and waited impatiently for the big-paying tournament players to arrive. Life at Bampers was running smoothly for all concerned when Jake Slade appeared on Sunday upsetting the status quo.

D'Arcy had an indication that something was wrong while finishing dinner at Bett's. Bett came back from the telephone with a wistful expression and said that she had to drive him to the lodge right away. He hung about the Staff Hall until he went on duty. At twelve-thirty, he answered a call from Mr. Slade for whiskey. The familiar drawl had a disquieting effect. On his way to the cabin he began associating the call with Bett's abrupt behaviour. Jake opened the door but didn't appear to recognize him in the dark. As Jake went for his wallet, D'Arcy peeked through the crack and saw Bett, legs tucked under her, on Jake's bed. She was smoking with an expression of delicious abandonment. D'Arcy fiercely hiked the price two dollars over the usual. Although Jake screwed up one eye, he paid. Disheartened, D'Arcy returned to the switchboard. His spicy affair with Bett was finished. Most of all, he regretted having to return to the Staff dining hall for his dinner. He received several more calls for liquor from newly arrived golfers who had not foreseen their thirst in this green desert of sociableness. The money he made was a consolation. He resolved to charge as much as the traffic would bear.

The same greed kindled in Slim's mind when Eddie introduced him to Jake the following day. Jake laid a hand on Slim's shoulder.

'You look like a smart fellow,' Jake said. 'I think you are.'

'Thanks.' Slim glanced embarrassedly at Eddie.

'If you're as good as our friend here says you are, this tournament is going to be a cinch for us.' Jake squinted at him. 'How's your eye? Can you help me line up putts.'

'I can try,' Slim said.

'That's the spirit,' Jake winked at Eddie. 'Let's get a bag. I'll try driving a few at you.'

Excited, Slim grabbed up a sack of golf balls, spilled them onto the practice tee and ran up the fairway to chase Jake's drives. He liked Jake's easy manner and tanned good looks which gave him an air of sportiveness and wealthy sophistication. He ran like a hare for the first half-hour and still felt energetic when Jake signalled a rest.

Dick Andrews, standing near him while waiting for his man to begin driving, suddenly pointed to the road beyond the clubhouse. A light blue convertible winged by.

'Gillespie?' Dick said jubilantly.

'How do you know?' Slim cried, eyes glued to the spot where the car had disappeared behind the trees.

'A hop told me it was his. He checked in this afternoon.'

The ground swayed under Slim. He sat down. Orpheus, the musical god, had descended from his ethereal universe to these mundane shores. His enchantment touched the green hills, the rock of the mountains, the lakes, the whole of the valley. His personality, spun from reams of celluloid and countless discs, centered upon the lodge in a spirit of grand frivolity. Slim awoke to Jake waving his driver. He jumped to his feet, watched the slow back swing, and chased the ball as if in a dream. Soon Jake called him in.

'That's good for today,' Jake smiled affectionately. 'We'll take a practice round in the morning. I don't want to go stale before we begin this tournament.'

Slim laughed appreciatively. 'About what time, sir?'

'Say ten, ten-thirty. That is, if you can make it.'

'Oh, I'll be here.' Slim ran to join other caddies heading for the cabin. He marvelled at Jake Slade; a formidable will was faintly revealed behind his lackadaisical mannerisms: he gave promise of lasting well into the tournament; his long solid drives testified to that.

Jake was pleased with Slim. 'That boy gives me a sense of mission. By God, I feel I'm going to take this tournament,' he told Eddie. He strode over the lawns to the main lodge where he saw Gillespie's convertible parked by the patio. Gillespie himself was standing one foot up on the step of the portico and talking to a lean man in a golfer's cap. Rather short and sharp-featured, Gillespie wore a gray fedora and a cherry red sports shirt, loosely hanging over his trousers. His voice flowed melodiously in the mountain air just as it had through years of Sunday radio programs. Jake sensed the general elation and could not help admiring the man who caused it. Yet he was skeptical and somewhat envious, for he had been the promotion manager for his company and knew how greatly King Gillespie was dependent on million dollar advertising schemes. Yet, again, Gillespie was made of true metal. He had ridden the tides of popularity and endured when others faded. His nonchalance and apparent modesty figured in the dreams of every man. Jake had to admit grudgingly that Gillespie was a sort of hero for him also. He might disclaim the hero-worship of the crowd, but he had to bow to the talent and resilience of a man who had given pleasure wherever his voice was heard. He stopped to look more closely, pretending to scrutinize one of the plants on the patio. Mac Carr approached him.

'I didn't know you were a plant lover,' Mac said sarcastically.

'Just investigating,' Jake smiled. 'See if it's been watered.'

'It's being blessed with a presence,' Mac said, smoothing his bald crown. 'At such a time it only drinks champagne.'

'Who's the guy with him?' Jake asked.

'The champion of Nevada, so I heard. Gillespie brought him up. I don't know what his game is, but it looks like the local competition isn't good enough. You know Gillespie won the tournament the last time he was up.'

'So the newspapers told me,' Jake smiled. 'But I think Gillespie just wants company. It must be lonely being a demi-god.'

'Hell!' Mac said. 'His voice is his best friend. What more does he want?'

'How is your lovely wife, by the way?' Jake said.

'Looking great,' Mac eyed him. 'Bett is bringing you over to us tonight, so you'll see for yourself.'

'That's good,' Jake nodded. 'It'll be great to relax before I plunge into the days ahead.'

'Just hope you don't meet Gillespie in the first round. The crowds get on your nerves.'

Deo walked by and smiled slightly.

'Watch this,' Mac said. 'That girl's after a movie contract.'

They saw her approach Gillespie in a slow measured walk so that the singer could not avoid looking at her. She smiled broadly and Gillespie nodded with an amused expression. She sidled by him but he didn't turn to look after her.

'They're a dime a dozen where he comes from,' Mac said. 'Lucky guy.'

'He's aware that we're watching,' Jake said. 'I'm moving along.'

'Don't be shy,' Mac chided. 'We've got as much right to this place as he has.'

'That's not the point,' Jake said sharply. 'See you tonight.' He walked towards the patio.

Gillespie glanced at him as Jake passed. They exchanged amicable looks.

Mac stared perplexedly after Jake. Why be afraid of Hollywood glamour? he wondered. As he turned to continue to the golf club, he saw Jaimie Rabbinowitz drive up with his girl friend, Jane, who made him screech to a stop. Jane jumped out with a cry. At first, Mac thought she was greeting him, and, surprised, he prepared for an ostentatious meeting. But she ran past him up to Gillespie, who carefully put his arms about her shoulders. Jaimie looked on with bewildered anguish. Jane gestured animatedly and didn't glance back. Gillespie laughed and together with his champion friend escorted Jane into the lobby. Jaimie frowned bitterly at Mac and drove off. These women, Mac thought, you can't trust them.

'Never mind,' Horace advised his son. 'You had your fun with her.'

'But she left me,' he snapped his fingers, 'like that.'

'Isn't it how you would have had to leave her. With more decorum, yes, but essentially in the same way?'

'But I treated her pretty well,' he moaned. 'We went through about five hundred bucks at the Ice-fields.'

'A lot of ice,' Horace cracked.

'If you think it is amusing,' Jaimie barked, 'I don't.'

'Come now. You may be imagining that she's left you. She probably knew Gillespie when he was here before.'

'She was a guest then,' Jaimie said. 'The little two-face.'

Horace dropped his chin. 'Never speak of a woman like that. Learn that women can be fickle and never expect them to be faithful. Once you know that lesson by heart you can treat them lightly.'

'Is that how you're treating the reservations clerk?' Jaimie asked suddenly,

Horace glared. 'I didn't volunteer to discuss my affairs.'

'It just so happens,' Jaimie said, 'that I can test your detachment. Do you know Mr. Runners has been having an affair with that blonde?'

Horace threw back his head and laughed. 'My dear Jaimie, I know that poor Runners tried to have an affair. But he is like you. He is much too serious to play the game well. Perhaps he is cleverer than you. He has real obstacles whereas you create your own.'

Jaimie blinked. 'I don't care about her anyway!' He grimaced, trying to recover from his surprise at his vehemence. 'We're leaving soon. I don't have to see her again.'

'Except at table,' Horace smiled.

'I'll have room service bring me food here.'

'You don't take my advice seriously. By all means forget her, but show her that you have.'

Jaimie sat up. 'Okay, I will.'

'But kindly,' Horace warned.

Mrs. Rabbinowitz entered the room. She regarded Jaimie quizzically, then went to him, hands out placatingly, 'Oh, Jaimie, what's happened?'

'Nothing,' Jaimie turned away and went out.

'His little affair has just ended,' Horace chuckled.

'They all do, don't they?' she said meaningfully.

Horace picked up a magazine and scanned its pages.

'I've been thinking that our holiday has lasted long enough,' Mrs. Rabbinowitz said. 'The hotel is beginning to bore me.'

'Me too,' Horace murmured.

Mrs. Rabbinowitz nodded knowingly and retired to another room.

Horace had not known that Runners was having an affair with Deo. He turned the possibility over in his mind. The idea seemed disgusting, though not unnatural. If he had not trusted Jaimie's word, he would not have believed such a rumour. He jumped up, snapped his fingers, and marched angrily about the room. The logical move would be to take his own advice and forget her, but he picked up the telephone and asked for reservations. Deo answered sweetly.

'Horace speaking. Excuse my abruptness but I'm rather rushed. Are you busy tonight?'

'No,' she said.

'Tomorrow night?'

'Why, no.'

'The next night?'

She giggled, 'No, I'm not. Why?'

He relaxed and said charmingly, 'I would like to see you tonight.'

'Certainly,' she said. 'Same time?'

'Same place,' he smiled. 'All right?'

'All right.'

He resolved to make this the last time, for his wife's sake as well as his own.

Mrs. Rabbinowitz entered. 'Business?' she asked.

'Just finding out the time.' He moved away from the telephone.

'What is it?' she smiled.

'They didn't know,' he said irritatedly.

Mrs. Rabbinowitz raised her brows and, picking up a magazine, began to scan its pages. Horace went out for a walk. Miriam, the cabin girl, crossed the lawn and passed in front of him. She swung her keys at her belt and rolled her brown eyes in friendly greeting. He smiled, conscious of his attraction for women. How on earth had he become involved with a dumb blonde? He came to the main lodge and entered the lobby. The tournament draw was posted. He regarded it over the heads of others, then sidestepped to a spot where he could observe Deo behind the counter. Runners passed by her and she grinned girlishly. He felt his heart leap in protest and fall back. How on earth had he allowed himself to fall victim to such a predicament? He determined to end his vacation right away. The hotel was no longer agreeable; all the important guests had left the place to tournament players. King Gillespie walked by. Every head in the lobby turned to watch him. How utterly plebeian! He simply had to take his family away.

26

D'Arcy was as disgusted with the hotel as Horace and for the same reason--because it was making him disgusted with himself. He bootlegged all night, slept in the mornings, and swam in the late afternoons. In spite of his noble aim of earning a university education, he felt crooked. Each night it was more difficult to demand a high price for his liquor. He couldn't look the buyers in the eye, though in most cases they were happily inebriated.

His isolation from the rest of the staff and his solitary hours of contemplation at the switchboard deepened his thought and intensified his memories of the summer. The maturation of his affair with Kate seemed like an unconscious sinking into dissolution, and his intimacy with the kind of life led by Kate and her friends introduced him to the slothful behaviour of hotel lotus-eaters. The effort of studying and the keen concentration needed for learning the foundations of his future career, whatever it might be, loomed before him like an unscalable mountain. If it were not for the shock of the termination of his affair with Bett, he might never have been made to look up at the summit.

At the start of his last night, he answered a call. He was in two minds about delivering liquor.

'Bring a bottle of Scotch to this number,' the caller demanded sternly.

D'Arcy hesitated. The voice reminded him of Runners.

'I don't have any,' he said.

'You've sold it to my friends,' the man argued. 'Now, bring it along quickly.'

'We're not allowed to handle it,' D'Arcy said, certain that he was speaking with Runners. 'It's against hotel rules.'

The man hesitated, as if to add something, then hung up. D'Arcy felt cold sweat run down his chest. Obviously, someone had complained to Runners about the price.

'Lou,' he called. 'Who's at this number?' He quoted it to her.

She found it on the room sheet. 'It's empty,' she said.

D'Arcy let out a deep sigh. The game was up. He would have to inform Nick who was next on duty to lay off for the first night.

He answered another call. The mild voice reminded him of Julien Kowalski.

'Is Lou there? I'd like to speak to her.'

D'Arcy called Lou who went to the booth. Curious, he pushed back the key to listen.

'But if I'm caught, I'll be fired,' Lou pleaded.

'Just for half an hour,' Julien said. 'Is that too much to ask? I'm lonely, I want to see you.'

'Well,' Lou's husky voice relented.

'Not for long,' Julien wheedled.

'Just half an hour,' Lou said.

D'Arcy released the key. Lou stopped by the switchboard.

'I'm stepping out for a minute. Be a sweetie and watch the desk for me?' She snapped her purse shut.

'Sure,' D'Arcy smiled. 'Don't worry.'

He was alone--the only moving thing in this monstrous temple of Mammon. He went to the Front Desk and gazed over the oriental carpeting. To leap from this atmosphere into a history course seemed an incredible feat. He had done it at the end of previous summers, but this time he had become more involved. He was burdened with loot and the scent of sophisticated women.

Runners sidled up to the desk. His nose appeared to twitch with suspicion. His thin face was blotched from drink. 'Why aren't you at the switchboard?'

'Just stretching my legs, sir,' D'Arcy replied.

'Where's Lou?'

'In the washroom. I don't think she's feeling well.'

Runners regarded him sharply. His eyes burned with deeper suspicion. 'Get her for me.'

'But I shouldn't leave the switchboard,' D'Arcy said meekly.

Runners' face suddenly sank into a state of sadness. The fire in his eyes flickered out. 'Never mind,' he muttered. He looked about at the darkened lobby. His long fingers tapped a rhythm on the desk. When he turned back to D'Arcy, he had not quite mastered the disappointment in his voice. 'Give me a wake-up call at seven. Tell Lou that I hope she will be feeling better.' He walked away.

D'Arcy answered several calls for liquor in the negative. Suddenly Jane's face beamed through the wooden bars at him.

'So it's you!' she cried. 'King, we're in luck. There's an old friend on duty.'

'What ho!' Gillespie said, looking over her shoulder. 'Luck, is it?'

'That depends,' D'Arcy said, concealing his surprise, yet wondering more at the presence of a movie star than at what they wanted from him.

Gillespie puckered and eyed Jane. 'Moolah?' he suggested.

'Probably,' Jane sighed.

'Money nothing!' D'Arcy said furiously. 'That depends on what you want.'

'Don't frighten our little girl,' Gillespie put his arm comfortingly about her shoulders. 'That's no way to behave, young fellow.'

D'Arcy blushed at the soft-spoken reprimand. 'I'm sorry, but I don't know what she's talking about.'

'She wondered if you could give us some strong drink,' Gillespie said succinctly.

'You don't have to if you don't want to,' Jane said.

'Mighty nice if you would,' said the lanky champion behind King. 'We're as dry as old bones.'

'Okay,' D'Arcy said. 'I think I've got some left.' He took two twelve ounce bottles from the cloakroom.

'How much?' Gillespie asked pulling out his wallet.

D'Arcy quoted the retail price.

Gillespie nodded with a moue of satisfaction. 'Very reasonable,' he said to Jane. 'We have a friend in need.'

'Darn nice of you,' said the champion taking the bottles. 'Jane, mebbe he knows your friend.'

Jane grinned at D'Arcy. 'Do me a favour?'

'I already have,' he said.

'But a big one, for old times sake? You know Deo. She's in the room I had last year. Ask her if she'll have a drink with us.'

D'Arcy scrutinized her.

'Here,' Gillespie handed him the payment with five dollars extra. 'Don't spend it all on the same friend.'

D'Arcy accepted it as if it came from a machine, an industry. 'Thanks.' He looked again at Jane. 'No hop can dare go near the waitresses' cabin since we had our party-- especially at this hour of the morning.'

'Oh,' Jane pooh-poohed. 'You can do it quietly.'

'But I'm the only one on duty,' he said angrily.

'We'll keep an eye on the place for ya,' said the champion, inspecting the labels on the bottles. 'In fact, I'll come up with ya just to persuade her.'

'Come now, my children,' Gillespie said admonishingly. 'We are inveigling a good man away from his duty.'

D'Arcy responded to the singer's understanding. 'Okay, I'll do it. But promise to watch the place. Come on,' he said to the champion who handed the bottles to Gillespie, 'let's hurry.'

'If anyone asks where you are,' Gillespie called after them, 'I'll say you're on an errand for me.'

The words rang superciliously in D'Arcy's ear, yet they carried great potential power. With Gillespie to vouch for him, a bellhop could do no wrong.

The champion showed that he had been drinking. His gait grew unsteady as they approached the girl's cabin.

'Wait on the stoop,' D'Arcy said and went along the side of the cabin.

He tapped on the screen and whispered for Deo. After a moment she came to look out.

'King Gillespie's friend wants to see you,' he said.

'Why?' she gasped.

'Jane is with Gillespie. They want a fourth. But I don't think it's for bridge,' D'Arcy smiled.

Deo blew her nose. Her eyes were red with crying. She had waited half an hour under a tree by the roadside for Horace to pick her up. When she returned to her room, she found a telephone message from Horace that one of the girls had forgotten to give her. It simply said that he couldn't keep their appointment. There was a fatalistic ring to it. She hadn't been able to sleep for worry that she had lost her charm and her luck. Now this proposal to jump out of bed for the sake of Gillespie's friend, who wasn't much without Gillespie, and play second fiddle to Jane, sounded insulting. She sniffed peremptorily.

'Tell them, "some other time",' she said.

'Aw, come on, honey,' the champion drawled, having snuck up behind D'Arcy. 'I've been wanting to hold your hand since I first laid my eyes on you.'

'Ssh!' Deo hissed. 'You'll wake up everyone.'

'Come on out and talk then,' said the champ.

'Just for a minute, but I'm not going anywhere.' She disappeared.

'Boy!' the champ whistled, following D'Arcy back to the stoop. 'You boys sure know your way around.' He peeled off three dollars and held them out.

D'Arcy hesitated and then accepted the bills. He had an impulse to turn down the money, but he thought it would be a lost gesture misunderstood in this way of life, and meaningless in his role of a Bampers' bellhop.

Deo came in her dressing gown onto the stoop and sat down with the champion. 'I'm staying for only a minute,' she said, 'then I'm going back. How did you think you could find me at this hour?' she asked, lowering her long eyelashes.

'I guess money bribes a way to everything,' the champ nodded after D'Arcy.

The insinuation stung D'Arcy. Had he played the pimp by bringing this man to Deo? How fantastic yet how possible! He glanced back at the two chatting on the steps. Could the champ have meant what D'Arcy understood? Or was D'Arcy becoming hypersensitive? He hurried back to the lodge. No one was in the lobby. Jane and Gillespie had taken the bottles with them. D'Arcy was not concerned over their neglect to keep their promise. He was wholly occupied with the mercenary character that was being revealed in him.

A few minutes later Lou returned smiling. She had been gone over an hour. D'Arcy decided not to tell her that Runners had chanced by. Her happiness was too rare, too lovely to spoil with an unconscionable threat.

In the early days of the tournament, Slim accompanied Jake Slade like a shadow. Since the first practice round, he had lined up Jake's putts, advised him on the club to use, and treated Jake's opponents as his own. First they defeated a paunchy, middle-aged man whose roughly dressed aspect discountenanced him amidst the smoothly-tailored rich. He fussed at Slim kneeling and lying on the green to find the lie of the ground. Intimating that Slim made him nervous, he lost out on the fourteenth. The following opponents put up a stiffer fight, but, by luck and resourcefulness, Jake made his way into the semi-finals. Jake had two bad shots; sometimes he shanked into the woods on the fourteenth fairway and he tended to hit short of the sixteenth green. As for his putting, he had come to rely on Slim's sharp eye.

Slim observed King Gillespie only at rare moments. Gillespie and the pro had breezed through their party on the practice round. Dressed brightly, Gillespie made a joke about his drive that caused general laughter, and, tipping his hat, hiked quickly away. Sometimes Gillespie sat on the clubhouse lawn with a handful of young people on the grass at his feet. These lucky few were friends of Jane, whom Slim did not know. Jane and her friends never took notice of him. Jane waited for Gillespie at the finish of the course. The crooner put his arm about her shoulders and walked her from the green to the clubhouse bar. Slim was fascinated by her achievement, and he noticed from the light in her eyes how heavenly was the mantle of glory upon her shoulders.

Gillespie's presence had quickened the pulse of the competitors. On practice rounds his voice echoed in song over the fairways. His wisecracks were repeated and enlarged upon. His golf game was steady and sure, like his singing, like his personality. His opponents were aghast at the great crowds following them over the course. Men were employed to balance long poles like tight-rope walkers and space themselves so as to keep the fans at a distance.

Gillespie was considerate and respectfully silent during tournament play. He took all the adulation in his stride and kept on relentlessly chalking up the under-pars which netted him the match surprisingly early in the course. One of his opponents employed his wife and oldest child to run ahead and take movies of him striding with Gillespie. Sweating profusely, grinning quickly at everyone and everything, trembling in an extreme attack of nervousness so that he scarcely hit a straight ball, this opponent offered himself for slaughter to the great god. They shook hands on the twelfth green, the vanquished beaming triumphantly, the family movie cameras churning, the more sensitive spectators blushing, and Gillespie cheerfully accepting the offering as serenely as if he were his father, Apollo, watching the proceedings from a clear blue sky. Gillespie then retired to wipe the man's sweat off his hand and whisper a few words of wisdom to Blair St. Clair. 'I'll use a three iron on the approach here. Won't have to smack it like the devil.'

King Gillespie reached the semi-finals to confront Jake Slade.

Slim with pipe in mouth was regarding the tournament sheet posted on the clubhouse lawn. He was alone and concentrating on the lines that issued from Gillespie and Slade to meet in a space for one name. From the side of his eye, he observed another pipe and, turning, recognized Gillespie who was studying the sheet.

'Going to be a big day tomorrow,' Gillespie said.

Overjoyed that Gillespie spoke personally to him, Slim controlled his emotion with stern resolution. 'Yes, it will be,' he said.

Immediately a crowd sprang from the ground behind them. When Slim looked back at Gillespie, only the top of his fedora was visible amongst all these people who appeared intensely interested in the tournament sheet. Disgusted, Slim walked away. Kate Carr waved to him. She was sitting alone at a table, the rosy rays of the dying sun reflecting off streaks of cloud on to her broad-brimmed hat. He had caddied two afternoons for her until she sprained her wrist and defaulted from the women's tournament.

'Come and sit with me,' she smiled invitingly. 'Don't be shy. It's the end of the season and fraternization will be overlooked.'

'Well thanks, Mrs. Carr,' Slim sat at her table.

'Will you have a drink with me?'

'Oh, I don't drink much.' He was afraid of liquor but unwilling to disappoint her for she seemed to want company.

'Let me order you a bit of cognac,' she raised her arm and the boy obediently took her order. 'It's a mellow drink and goes well with a sunset,' she smiled. 'Mr. Slade was trying to tell me that you were a good caddie. I had to tell him that you were the best, that you were mine, and I was only loaning you to him for the tournament.'

'He's a good player,' Slim said.

'Oh,' she pouted. 'Better than me?'

'I meant in a different way,' Slim blushed.

Kate stroked his cheek. 'I know what you mean.' She took her hand away and glanced round uneasily.

The boy arrived with the drinks and Kate signed for them.

'I'd hate to have to keep track of what everyone owes in this place. The head accountant must have a terrible headache from it all,' she said. 'And just look at all the expenses to be paid out. The man who can figure it all is worth his weight in gold.'

'The hardest thing to do is to please the guests,' Slim said wisely.

'If they all had good-looking caddies, they'd have no reason to complain,' she smiled wickedly.

Slim smiled back, feeling bolder by the minute and certain of their attraction. 'Well, if all the caddies had beautiful golfers, there'd be no reason for them to complain either.'

Kate laughed, thrilled. 'You are awfully sweet, Slim. I'm going to get this wrist better right away so that we can do the links again before the lodge closes. Would you like that?'

Slim sensed the power drawing him towards her and struggled for seconds to find an answer. 'I'd like it more than anything else.' He blushed at his frankness. The cognac burnt his throat bringing water to his eyes.

Kate regarded him with studied intimacy. Bett and Jake strolled arm in arm to the table.

'Hey there!' Jake frowned. 'You're trying to sabotage me. Leave my caddie alone.'

Slim sprang to his feet. 'Oh, hello, Mr. Slade.'

'"I'm not doing nothing" unquote,' Bett laughed, 'except maybe falling under the spell of Mrs. Carr.'

Slim turned beet-red. Kate, noticing his embarrassment, snapped, 'Mrs. Steel is jealous, Slim. Give her a smile and keep her happy.'

Bett winced. 'Kate! I mean, really!'

'Do you think that only you can be rude?' Kate smarted.

'Girls, girls,' Jake drawled, 'you are quarreling over my caddie and so let me have the last word.' He looked at Slim. 'Leave the cognac, put away your pipe, and get plenty of rest for tomorrow morning. I'm depending on you to get me through this. We've been working together, Slim, building up power, steaming ahead with increasing impetus, and we don't want to get thrown off-stride by crazy women.'

'No sir, I won't be,' Slim said earnestly. He smiled at Kate, 'Good-bye.'

'I'll be watching tomorrow,' Kate smiled fetchingly.

'He's a good boy,' Jake said when Slim had gone. 'It'd be a pity to corrupt him.'

'What are you implying?' Kate glared.

'Men shouldn't talk,' Bett snorted, coming to Kate's rescue. 'I mean, Adam more or less had Eve trapped in that garden of theirs.'

'It has never occurred to me to treat Slim as a man,' Kate said.

'Besides, he's old enough to know the facts of life,' Bett said. 'He's going to look ridiculous if he doesn't.'

'All right, all right,' Jake put his hands over his ears. 'So he's becoming a puritan and needs to be rescued from a state worse than hell. But, you know, there's something nice about

230

his innocence right now. Maybe that's because it's in full bloom just before it's ready to drop.' He stared thoughtfully at the ground and folded his arms across his chest. 'I hope he isn't hurt when he loses it. Some females can be real bitches.'

'Bitter, bitter,' Bett teased and linked her arm through his. 'Darling, you don't really mean what you're saying.'

'None of it applies to you or Kate,' he grinned at them, 'but I'll tell you something that does. I'm going to bed early and I'm going to sleep alone so I'll get plenty of rest to face this yodelling baritone.'

'I agree,' Bett said impishly, 'and I'll make you a big breakfast.'

'It would be best to let him rest,' Kate said, standing and giving her hand to Jake. She smiled into his eyes. 'Best of luck.'

Jake pressed her hand gently. 'I'll need every charm you can spare.'

Bett frowned. She was furious with Kate and managed to show it with a dart of the eyes as Kate turned to stroll away.

'She's quite a girl, that Kate,' she said. 'I feel like keeping you awake on beer and crackers all night and send you reeling up to Gillespie just to spite her. But I won't. She's not worth it.'

'Thanks,' Jake said. 'I think I see your husband over there.'

Allan was talking with a group of golfers.

'Okay!' Bett grinned shyly. 'I'll take the hint.' She stood on tip-toe and bussed Jake on the cheek. 'Till tomorrow, darling.'

He nodded abstractly. He went to the tournament sheet and followed through the wins and the scores that had bearing on Gillespie. There was no doubt in his mind that tomorrow would be the climax of his golfing career. He felt that if he lost, he would never again be in the running. There were such things as age and fading spirit.

27

The match between Slade and Gillespie was a big attraction for the Bampers' folk. Spectators formed a gigantic following the width of the fairways and several rows deep.

By the fourth fairway Jake conquered his stage fright. The smooth, straight-shooting Gillespie had an advantage of one hole. Jake eyed his short putt. Gillespie's ball was farther away. The singer waited.

'What do you think, Slim? Straight?' Jake asked.

'No sir,' Slim said decidedly. 'To the right about three inches.' He stepped away with the flag pin. He saw a glimmer of surprise light up Gillespie's face.

Jake stroked. The ball passed the cup about three inches to the right. Slim hung his head. Jake said nothing. Gillespie sank his ball to move him two holes in the lead. On the way to the fifth tee Jake coldly asked for his club. Slim felt nauseous with shame. He could not look at the crowd. Jake lost the fifth -- three down. Slim thought that he had inadvertently sabotaged Jake's game.

On the approach to the sixth green Jake asked Slim his advice on the club to use. As the ball sailed high to the right Slim stood straining to see it. The crowd closed in around him. He felt a pair of hands shove him roughly from behind. He turned to see the sharp eyes of Gillespie glaring at him as the crooner made his way to his ball. Shocked that the reincarnation of Orpheus could be angry and underhandedly show it, Slim backed away in confusion. His spirit sank lower. His hurt hardened to resentment. By the time the play reached the green, his will for Jake to win fired his spirit and governed his every impulse. Jake took that hole on a long putt.

The crowd must have expected Jake to crumble like Gillespie's other opponents because on coming from the eleventh hole, Jake, being only one hole down, there was a surge of enthusiasm. Jake's friends strode rapidly alongside him and smiled encouragement. Kate Carr made a thumbs-up sign to Slim, but he could only respond with a grim look. The one hole down was his mistake. It dogged him like a curse. Jake was asking him to line up putts again. His confidence in Slim had been restored. Yet Slim suffered in agony after giving his advice until Jake made the shot.

Gillespie's somber look was no longer for show. He really was concerned. His game depended upon his approach to the green, which was as constant and exact as he could wish. He discussed his approach shot to the hidden green on the long thirteenth with Blair. Until then, Blair had carried Gillespie's bag and handed him his clubs only. Blair managed to look knowledgeable, though, compared with Slim's involvement, he was like a pack horse following its master.

When the party came to the brow of the slope concealing the green, Gillespie's ball was seen to be next to the pin. Gillespie winked at Blair, which indicated a substantial addition to his tip.

Jake wasted an extra stroke getting on the green and lost the hole. There was no indication that the strain was affecting him. Gillespie's safe manner of play exasperated other opponents, but Jake showed no irritation. His American drawl had sharpened to his old Canadian accent. His languorous mannerisms were replaced by a tense alertness. His eyes were watching, measuring, judging, and asking Slim.

He was in the spot on the fourteenth where he had a habit of shanking. Slim had a presentiment of disaster as Jake started the back swing. Helpless, he watched the ball veer off into the woods.

Jake fought his way out but he lost the hole. He was three down with four holes to play. Gillespie looked sure of himself again. The spectators were waiting for the end. Jake's friends wore sorry expressions.

Jake tied the short fifteenth. He was three holes down with three to play. The audience seemed disappointed because for a while Jake was playing sharp, determined golf which could have routed Gillespie. Now on the treacherous sixteenth, which was made for the approach artist because of an inlet before the green, Gillespie was sure to tie the hole if not win it, thus ending the match.

Maybe it was the hopelessness of his situation that caused Jake to open up his game. He slammed the ball, reaching the green in two strokes.

Gillespie landed near the cup in three strokes. He stood back satisfied to watch Jake try to putt from far on the uphill side of a steeply slanted green. He folded his hands over his putter with an air of finality.

'Well Slim,' Jake said quietly, 'how do I hit?'

Slim kneeled and studied the roll of the hill. He pointed to a spot above the cup and waved his finger along over the path the ball should follow.

'This way, sir.'

Slim retired to the fringe of the crowd pressing thick around the green and kneeled. He was downhill from the cup. Jake studied the course that Slim indicated and got set. Slim bowed his head. He began to pray frantically. All his will flowed out in silent words asking God to make Jake win. His nerves poised toward that end. His throat choked with emotion. He looked up to see the ball roll into the cup. A cry of exaltation went up from the spectators. The huge crowd broke spontaneously into applause. Slim was amazed at the surge of sympathy behind Jake Slade. He could sense it almost crystallizing in the air.

Gillespie looked shaken.

The seventeenth fairway was uphill, but, again, Jake swung out and landed on the green a stroke ahead of Gillespie. Jake had a thirty-five foot putt whereas Gillespie's ball was eight inches from the cup. Jake kneeled behind his ball and called Slim to sight over his shoulder.

'What do you make it?' Jake asked.

'I'd say about an inch and a half to the right,' Slim said.

'I make it an inch,' Jake said grimly.

Slim went to the edge of the green and kneeled again. This time the crowd maintained a respectful distance. He was in clear view in front. He clenched his fists and hoped. The ball rolled beautifully, struck the lip of the cup, bounced up, and stayed on the rim. Slim threw himself backwards landing on his neck. Gillespie gave him a quizzical glance and hurriedly stepped up to his ball to finish off the match. Slim, slightly embarrassed by his antic, watched Gillespie confidently strike the ball and turn white with alarm as it rolled up and away from the cup. Jake tipped his ball in, winning the hole.

On their way to the eighteenth tee, the spectators rumbled with excitement. The players and their caddies just managed to hold themselves in control, though sounds of confusion and turmoil echoed in their ears as a warning of what would happen if they lost their nerve.

Gillespie was obviously furious with himself. He was also surprised at the reaction of the spectators. It was not often that he found an audience against him. He was at pains to understand why. He was not prepared to admire Jake Slade just because he gave battle.

Strangely Jake, who teed off first, tightened his swing as if shy of coming to the fore. He hooked the drive a shade so that it struck the downgrade left of centre and bounced to the edge of the fairway. Gillespie placed his drive dead in the centre.

Slim reached Jake's ball and looked at the way to the green. His heart sank. A sand trap gaped in front of him. A tall fir spired on its sandy lip and obscured half the green, set like an oasis in the distance between bunkers.

An excited spectator mumbled to Slim. 'He should hit onto the fairway. Play it safe.'

Slim thought Jake had to keep the pressure on Gillespie and take risks. If he played safe, Gillespie would beat him.

'What do you make of it, Slim?' Jake said tersely.

There was a hint of humility in his voice. The handsome, broad-shouldered Jake seemingly built with granite, began to question his luck, unconsciously, destructively. His looks, the hair graying over his temples, made him seem more distinguished than Gillespie. But there was an underlying bravado in the singer that implied superiority. Gillespie still held the upper hand: the middle of the course, the reputation for his approach shots, and the certainty that one hundred percent of his blood was American. It was a combination that demanded respect at this crucial moment.

Slim looked hesitantly at the tree; its branches were splayed up from the spiry trunk.

'Do you think I can miss it?' Jake asked.

'It'll be close,' Slim said. 'But you've got to do it.'

Gillespie was patiently waiting by the side of his ball in mid-fairway. Jake selected his club, addressed the ball, and stroked it cleanly. The ball rose, seemed to pause like a white orb in space, smacked the trunk and fell onto the sandy lip behind a sweep of branch, the solid noise of its collision resounding knell-like in Slim's heart.

Without a word Slim gave Jake his blaster. They didn't watch Gillespie's shot. Jake worked to find a position in which he could get free of the trap. His first attempt was fouled by the branch which deflected the ball onto a clearer section of the lip. From there, Jake reached the fairway. He had no thought of winning. He merely wished to finish the match as honourably as possible.

Gillespie landed in the bunker on the right. He overshot the green and entered the bunker on the left. He frowned with irritation and disgust. The fatal interception by the tree had unnerved him. He was too anxious to use his advantage and finish the match. His fans were being treated to the spectacle of bad golf and his angry humiliation.

When Jake saw what was happening to Gillespie, he took courage. Unfortunately, his approach came to rest short of the green. Gillespie fluffed his first try from the bunker, but reached the green on the next stroke. Jake chipped close to the cup. He was six strokes; Gillespie five. They studied their positions gaining time to settle their nerves.

Jake's position appeared hopeless because he had to win the hole to keep the game going. But the crowd was still fascinated, expecting a repetition of the miracle of the last two holes.

Gillespie addressed his ball. His putt snaked shakily over the slight rises to come to a stop between Jake's ball and the hole--stymied. Jake grinned and shook Gillespie's hand. The crowd breathed audibly in relief and broke rank.

Slim, crestfallen, tried to smile as he shook Jake's hand. Jake, though, appeared happy. He met his friends with his old air of gay nonchalance.

'Listen, listen,' Mac insisted. 'Gillespie picked up a pine cone in front of his ball when he was in the bunker. That's against regulations.'

'He can be disqualified,' Julien said, striding beside them. 'When he did that, he lost the hole.'

'It's probably not the same in American rule books,' Jake smiled.

'But why don't you raise hell?' Mac frowned. 'I would.'

'Oh no,' Jake said casually. 'I don't want to do that.'

'But why?' Mac blazed. 'You'll win the match.'

Julien pulled Mac aside and spoke mildly to Jake. 'We just want to say that we're ready to testify that we saw him do it.'

'No,' Jake shook his head. 'Thanks.'

Slim's admiration for Jake soared. For Slim, Jake was the true victor. He did more than refuse to debase the spirit of the sport by consorting to the rules; he seemed to deny the importance of winning.

A hand grasped Slim's arm. Kate regarded him sympathetically.

'Are you very disappointed?'

'Not so much now,' Slim said. 'I guess he can be proud of his showing.'

'That's better,' she smiled sweetly. 'You were an enormous help to him.'

Slim blushed. 'Thanks.'

'I was so proud of you, I wanted to have you to myself again. So what about it?' She tossed her head laughingly.

'Sure.'

'Shall we say in the morning after the final gets underway? Oh look!' She pointed to a group on the eighteenth. 'The other match is walking in. I guess it's the champ versus Gillespie for tomorrow.'

As Slim looked, he felt her hand gently clasp his own, sending a thrill through him. He stood stock still until she stepped away.

'I'll be waiting for you, Slim,' she said.

His mind swirled with the series of excitements and the milling people. He put away the clubs. The steward told him to return late to clean them because of the confusion.

Gillespie was sitting alone by the porch rail in the midst of hundreds. He was waiting for Jake to make his way through the crowd to him. Slim could no longer picture him as the god of happy music; he looked forlornly unheroic.

28

Since it was O'Flaherty's day-off, and Nick was on night duty, D'Arcy was senior boy on the shift that evening. There was no fear of the head bell man because Nelles appeared only in the afternoons for the roomings; he disdained the chicken-feed picked up at other times. D'Arcy paced before the bell boys' bench with hands clasped behind his back and assumed his role as guardian of the lobby. He kept the boys busy emptying ash-trays and darting away on fronts--paging, delivering telegrams, and setting up the odd card table. Few guests were playing cards; most were in the ballroom listening to King Gillespie who was singing as a special concession since this was staff night at the lodge. The event had called forth even those gentlemen who derided dances, notably Dixie and Gregory. Sitting in a corner of the bandstand was Johnnie O'Dreams, a false smile badly concealing his gloom.

Gillespie lifted his foot on a chair and leaning on his knee spoke into the microphone. 'Do you have any favourites that I might just happen to know? Hmm? What do you say there?'

He cocked a hand by his ear and listened to the shouted names. Slim and Miriam could not make themselves heard.

'Hey now!' Gillespie signalled for silence. 'We've gotta choose some number that old Toots here can play. I don't want the boys to leave me on my own--might mean the end of my career.'

As the audience laughed and the guests remaining in the lobby drifted into the ballroom entrance and strained to see, Gillespie conferred with Toots, turned smiling back to the microphone, and announced "Stardust".

Amidst the elated applause, D'Arcy surveyed the lobby with cool professionalism. He went to the reservations partition. Deo glanced at him and returned to sorting the mail.

'Mad at me?' D'Arcy asked.

'No,' she said. 'But you hops stop at nothing for money.'

'I thought you wanted to know Gillespie.'

'Yea, but not his side-kick. After five minutes on the stoop with that man, I found out he didn't respect me, or women for that matter. I don't go for that kind of guy.'

'He's a champion golfer.'

'Phoo! He's only an amateur.' She glanced at the clock. 'He said he'd introduce me to King, though.'

'Our friend Jane seems to have cornered the market,' D'Arcy smiled.

Deo's face grew hard. 'In five minutes I'm going in there. Then you'll see where Jane stands.'

D'Arcy drew down his mouth as if impressed. He went into the cloakroom, opened a packet of American cigarettes and smoked. Gillespie's clear melodic voice penetrated his sanctuary while the skipping beat that was the trade mark of Toots Ainsworth's orchestra resounded at the door. The song ended to applause. He stepped on his cigarette and returned to the lobby. Gillespie had left the stand. Guests were moving into the lobby. The hops on the bench were playing at crossing their legs in unison and kicking them out. The orchestra played dance music and Johnnie O'Dreams was singing a plaintive ditty. D'Arcy perched on the stool at the bell captain's desk, glanced over a news despatch, and noticed that Deo was preparing to leave her post. A whoosh of air and flame shook the wall behind the Front Desk. The clerks turned, petrified. D'Arcy gasped at the tonguing flames

'Open the doors,' D'Arcy shouted at the hops who dashed for the patio and front verandah doors.

The clerks scrambled over the counter. D'Arcy shouted at the amazed guests to get out. The crowds poured from the ballroom to both exits. A din of shouting and tumbling chairs and tables drowned out the music. Smoke enveloped the Front Desk. Wood crackled. D'Arcy dashed down the corridor and seized an extinguisher which he had continuously passed and never thought he would use. An alarum sounded, beating at his temples. Flames cut off his return to the lobby. He sprayed at flames with the extinguisher, but the heat and smoke forced him to retreat down the corridor.

Many of the dancers escaped via the snack bar to the back of the lodge. Archie and one of the chefs were alone in the kitchen. Archie was forking a potato into his mouth when he heard the clamour. He jumped up and ran into the dining room. Fire blazed through the lobby towards him. He ran back into the kitchen where the chef was snatching up the Room Service receipts and together they dashed for the open air.

Toots Ainsworth gallantly led his men through the sweet tune they had begun while he waited for the terrified guests to clear out. Johnnie jumped from the stage, ran to the fringe of the pushing crowd, leaped from table to table along one side of the ballroom and sprang into the lobby. He darted for the Front Desk, closed his smarting eyes and held his breath as he penetrated the smoke. He glimpsed the sign 'Mail' and leaped over the counter. A beam crashed to the floor near him and in the blaze of light he saw Deo lying at his feet. He gathered her in his arms, made his way to the entrance and tripped on the rug, bringing them both to the floor. His coat was alight. He rolled for several turns and rolled back. He struggled to pick up Deo, succeeded, and stumbled through the cloud of smoke onto the verandah and finally onto the cool green grass. When someone took her from him, he passed out.

Guests and staff, attracted by the alarm, hurried from their cabins to the main lodge which was flaring to the sky.

The rattle-trap fire engine chugged forth from the garage. The chief engineer gave up the lodge for lost at first sight. He directed the engine's hose onto the neighbouring cabins to soak them. Some of the staff seized lawn hoses and pointed them at the inferno.

Runners and his wife dashed from their cabin and stood stricken behind the patio. Alick Sandhurst ran up.

'The records!' Runners shouted. 'We can't lose the records.'

'I've got the keys,' Alick cried. 'I'll get them.'

He darted into the corridor.

'No!' Runners bellowed. 'Come back.'

Flowers had seen Alick go. With a glance at Runners he ran after Alick.

'Tony,' Mrs. Runners gasped, 'I hope he'll be all right.'

'He knows what he's doing,' Runners said, watching the windows of his office.

The fire hose sprayed the far side of the lodge, causing billows of smoke. The wind shifted bringing the smoke onto the Runners and the guests around them so that they ran choking and gasping for air onto the hill by the tennis courts.

Runners grew white. Allan Steel stood beside him.

'Sandhurst is in there,' Runners said. 'God help him.'

'What!' Allan screamed.

'The records,' Runners explained. 'He was worried about the records.'

Allan looked at him in terror. 'The idiot!'

Bett and the Carrs reached him. Allan ran forward, then stopped in dismay at the blaze before him.

Bett seized his arm. 'Allan! What are you doing?'

'Alick's in there,' he said. He gave her a long look, twisted his arm from her grasp, and disappeared into the smoke.

Bett stood shouting his name. Kate and Mac went to her and coaxed her back to the lawn.

Runners found his way to the fire vehicle and directed the hosing. Mrs. Runners went amongst the guests. She tried to find out whether everyone had reached safety. The orchestra boys, grasping their instruments to their chests, ran from the snack bar exit.

Allan reached the corridor but could not enter because of the flames. He circled round to the patio. He heard the breaking of glass and saw smoke pour from the office windows.

A hand smashed at the fragments. In a spasm of joy, Allan sprang to the window. A head and shoulder pushed into the space. He recognized Jack Flowers and pulled him out onto the patio stones. Flowers was bleeding and seemed semi-conscious. Allan supported him with his shoulder and, unable to see, helped him toward what he thought was safety.

Slim caught sight of them and nudging Dixie, he ran to help. Both men had fallen on the patio when Slim and Dixie reached them. They dragged them onto the lawn and, ignorant of what else to do, applied artificial respiration. Allan came to immediately. Dixie helped him to sit up. Mac Carr tore his shirt and bound Flowers' wounds. The lodge nurse happened by, directing the men to take him to the infirmary. Bett and Kate knelt beside Allan.

'Alick,' he said. 'Is he all right?'

'We don't know,' Kate said.

Allan groaned and gazed at the holocaust of falling timbers and roaring sheets of flame. The crowds were thick and silent, watching the destruction with as much fascination as if they were witnessing the furnaces of hell.

D'Arcy dashed by them. He had sent the hops to the cabins for fire extinguishers. Together with those guests who had thoughtfully grabbed extinguishers on their way to the fire, they formed a front on one wing. But the intolerable heat prevented them from drawing near enough to be effective. They were content to spray the trees and keep the blaze at bay.

'D'Arcy!' Kate shouted.

D'Arcy stopped and spun to stare at them. His uniform was soaked with perspiration and his face and front smudged with pitch. He frowned impatiently.

'Have you seen Alick Sandhurst?' Bett asked.

D'Arcy came up to them. He shook his head. 'God!'

'You look ghastly,' Bett said.

'Horrible,' Kate added.

D'Arcy looked penitently at them, women of whom he had been a part, his best friends really. He had an impulse to blurt out his worry. 'I think I'm responsible,' he said.

'For what?' Bett frowned incredulously. 'For Alick?'

'I was in charge of the lobby,' he said.

'Oh, D'Arcy,' Kate said sympathetically. 'Do you think the fire is your fault? It isn't! Tony Runners is the manager. He's responsible.'

'Don't run about anymore,' Bett said. 'You're not doing yourself any good.'

D'Arcy wanted to confess to smoking in the cloakroom, but fear stopped him. He glanced at Allan who was sitting and meditating on the burning lodge. If once D'Arcy let his secret escape, it would spread like wildfire about him, and he would stand accused.

He smiled guiltily at Bett and Kate, who both wished to console him but held back in deference to each other. His secret must remain with him until the proper time came to confess it. He could not be absolutely certain that his cigarette had kindled the lodge.

'I've got to help,' he said. 'What did you ask me?'

'About Alick Sandhurst,' Bett said. 'Have you seen him?'

D'Arcy threw up his hands and shook his head as he started away.

'We shouldn't just stand here,' Kate said.

'You're right,' Allan stood up. 'Going to see if I can help.'

'They might need us at the infirmary,' Kate said and hurried towards it.

Bett was on the point of following when she saw Jake. She went to him.

'Isn't it awful?' she said.

He drew her against him. 'It's too bad, honey. All that workmanship dissolved in a few hours. Ought to teach us a lesson about ourselves.'

'The horrible thing is that some people may have been trapped,' she said.

'No,' he drawled. 'Everyone got out okay.'

'Did they?' Her eyes sparkled hopefully.

'Sure. Don't worry about it.' He grinned down at her. 'It's easy to imagine a situation worse than it is.'

The breeze had died. Men with hoses and pails encircling the lodge kept the fire from spreading. They watched the flames feed upon and gradually consume themselves.

Davey opened the staff dining room to anyone who wanted hot coffee and biscuits. Word had got round that no lives had been lost, and, of course, the lodge was insured. Guests began to regard the tragedy as an adventure. Some spoke of their narrow escape to those who had not been in the lodge. Gillespie was handing out coffee; his fame seemed to have been eclipsed for the moment and he was regarded as just another survivor. Many spectators did not go to bed until early morning when the lodge was a heap of burning coals and foul smoke. A transience was felt to hover over the valley when dawn came.

Firemen from town rushed their modern equipment through the night but found the hydro-pressure too weak to make it function. Their frustration was merely a shadow of the desperation that Runners experienced. Runners listened to Flowers recount Alick Sandhurst's death from an infirmary bed.

'When I got to the corridor, he was opening the office door. I got into the outer office and yelled at him. There was so much smoke I couldn't see into the inner room, but I knew he was in there. So I went in. He was on his knees piling up his ledgers and shoving paper into his case. The wall started to break through. I told him to come on and grabbed his case. I guess I left the hall door open because the whole bloody office was in flames. I don't know what happened then.'

'He didn't have time,' Runners said.

'I don't know what I did with his case,' Flowers said worriedly.

Runners emitted a derisory blast of air between his teeth. 'What good are records without a hotel?' He went to the door and spoke without turning round. 'Thanks, Jack. I'll let the right people know what you did.' He muttered, 'And what I didn't.'

Mrs. Runners was waiting for him in their cabin. She took him compassionately to her bosom. He closed his eyes tightly and kept back the tears of remorse. His future lay in ashes like his hotel. He stepped away from his wife and regarded the cold hearth. There was a bottle of whiskey on the side table. He thought of smashing it against the stone. He poured himself a drink.

'Would you like one?' he asked. 'Have to meet the guests, put on a brave front, you know.' He smiled sadly and poured her a glass.

She didn't take it at once. She went to the window and looked out over Lake Beautiful. A gossamery white sheened over the water. Incongruously, she was filled with a sense of airy release.

At the same moment, on the path from the staff kitchen, Nick was complaining to D'Arcy. He had stored a case of liquor in the cloakroom.

'Do you know how much money that is? One whole case?'

'Yes, no,' D'Arcy muttered. 'I'm dead tired. I want to go to sleep.'

'Listen,' Nick insisted. 'I want to know how it started. You were there.'

'I don't know,' D'Arcy closed his eyes. He felt sleep attack him.

'The desk clerks say it must have started in our cloakroom,' Nick eyed him darkly. 'If that liquor caught on fire, no wonder the place burned so fast.'

D'Arcy had been in high tension all night so that his nerves accepted any surprise as a matter of course. He did not react to Nick's insinuation but walked on with his eyes half-closed.

'Was anyone in the cloakroom before the fire broke out?' Nick inquired off-handedly.

D'Arcy hesitated. 'I was but I didn't see anything strange.'

'Yeah,' Nick nodded significantly. 'Some of the guys said you were.'

'Look!' D'Arcy cried, stopping him. 'Do you think I purposely lit that fire? Do you?'

Nick smiled at him mockingly. 'How am I supposed to know, D'Arce? You were there.'

D'Arcy's head seemed to swell with heat. D'Arcy brought his fist flat into Nick's face. He rocketed both hands into Nick and punched furiously. Nick grappled one of his arms. He knocked Nick against a tree and, freeing himself, hammered at Nick's stomach. He saw Nick lying on the ground. Men were shouting at him. They seemed to float over the lawn. He darted into the bellhops' cabin and took refuge in his room. There were steps running along the hallway. He took off his uniform, blood from his nose soaking the coat. Opening his door quietly, he tip-toed naked along the hall and into the shower. The water was hot. Feeling lethargic, he sat in a corner of the shower, leaned his head against the wall, and fell asleep in clouds of warm vapour.

29

The finals were postponed a day. The news of Alick Sandhurst's self-sacrifice shocked the Bampers populace. A state of sombre introspection settled upon the guests. Some of those golfers who went to the practice tees were unable to escape a feeling of incomprehension, as if something was lacking in their view of life. Their activity only increased that awareness. But in the staff section there was a spirit of animation. The kitchen workers and chefs from the main lodge began working with Davey and his group in the staff kitchen. Room service boys delivered meals to the cabins. The waitresses served their guests in the cabin sitting rooms. Gradually, the guests admired the staff's efficiency and willingness to surmount the inconveniences. They began to see the situation as a novelty. The book-keeper's death lost its air of tragedy. Instead, it gave significance to the smouldering ashes, as if symbolizing man's heroic gesture against nature's destructiveness.

Morning mist hovered in the mountain ranges and the night's frost left its bite in the air. King Gillespie started the final match with his lanky companion, the champion of Nevada, who had not encountered difficulty so far in the tournament. A small crowd of spectators followed, perhaps because the skies were cloudy and threatened rain, or because interest in the tournament had been eclipsed by the fire.

Slim was cleaning Jake's clubs with steel wool and water. The grass stain had had a night to dry, which made it hard to remove.

The club steward called him. 'Mr. Slade is looking for you. I didn't know you were here. He's still on the porch.'

Slim walked along the porch. By the middle steps, he saw Jake hand a twenty dollar bill to Eddie. He remembered the promise of new clubs and a big cash tip. Obviously it was coming to pass because Eddie was receiving a large tip for nothing. Eddie smiled broadly. Then Jake hurried towards Slim. Smiling with a shade of embarrassment, he shook Slim's hand. Slim felt a small hard bundle press into his palm.

'You've been swell, boy,' Jake said. 'Thanks a lot.'

'Thank you, Mr. Slade,' he said gratefully. 'I hope you win next year.'

'Oh,' Jake stuck out his bottom lip and shrugged, 'may never be a next time.' He backed away. 'Take care of yourself, Slim.'

Slim descended to the walk and opened the bundle of notes. It amounted to thirty-five dollars, the same that other caddies received. For an instant he felt cheated. Then he remembered how emotionally he had been caught up in the play, how Jake included him in the tournament as no other caddie had been. The vision of golf clubs and big money soured beside the thought. He was glad. He felt that Jake truly appreciated him. Somehow excessive payment would have falsified the bond that had sprung between them, just as winning by the rules would have defiled the clean feeling of sportsmanship that Jake had helped him to experience.

As he passed the fee window, he saw Eddie who was pretending not to notice him. The hard straight lines of Eddie's face belonged to the predator. A big tip was all that Eddie could understand and was all that he deserved, Slim thought. He was inclined to pity him--a middleman, a procurer.

He sat on the steps of the caddie shack with a handful of caddies.

'Won't I be glad to get the hell out of this place,' Dixie rasped. His man was put out in the first round so that he only netted five dollars from the tournament.

'You sound too eager,' Gregory said. 'If they hear you, they'll keep you longer. Runners has spies.'

'I'll kick them in the ass and tell them to report it in kind,' Dixie said.

'There's nothing for us here,' Gilles griped. 'They ought to let us go.'

'They're going to make us rot like they did in June,' Don Clarking suggested loudly. 'We're going to have to strike to get home.'

'Nothing doing,' Bruce Bannister snarled. 'They're trying to make us strike so they can fire us and don't have to pay our fares home. It's the easy way out.'

'You are all wrong,' Gregory announced. 'The truth is that Runners suspects a caddie of arson. He is waiting until he can prove his suspicion before giving the word for our departure.'

'Crap!' Dixie grinned.

'I suggest that we appoint a man to confess until our fares are all paid.' Gregory pulled in his upper lip. 'At which time he will retract his confession and earn our undying gratitude. In other words we need a martyr--rather, a pseudo-martyr.'

'Who?' Don Clarking asked.

'Slim is the perfect selection,' Gregory nodded benignly.

'Hear, hear,' Dixie said solemnly,

They saw Kate drive up behind the clubhouse and step from her car.

'I have other things to do besides being a martyr,' Slim said, starting toward her.

'Hey! Hey!' Don Clarking called mischievously. 'Remember what happened to Jane.'

'Shut up!' Gilles kicked him. 'Slim just caddies for her.'

'I know it,' Don complained.

'If Slim had guts,' Bruce said, 'he'd be driving that car like D'Arcy used to.'

'What did happen to Jane?' Gregory inquired.

'Got a note from Runners,' Don giggled, 'saying to lay off Gillespie.'

'I wonder,' Dixie said softly, 'if Gillespie got a note from Runners asking him to lay off her.'

The caddies chortled.

'Well, Slim,' Kate's eyes sparkled as he came up to her, 'a bad day. It's going to rain.'

'Looks like it,' he said.

'No golf,' she smiled. 'Mrs. Steel wouldn't come.'

'Okay.' Slim took a step away. 'Maybe tomorrow.'

'Wait, Slim,' Kate put out her hand. 'You're not caddying for anyone else?'

'No.' He sensed a decisive moment rise between them.

'Come for a ride. I'm at a loose end too.' She turned towards the car.

He swallowed hard. 'Okay.'

She sat in and leaned across to open the other door for him,

When the caddies saw Slim get into the car, they took a deep breath of wonder.

'How long has this boy been holding out on us?' Dixie rasped.

'Jeez!' Bruce Bannister said, goggle-eyed.

Kate drove away quickly as if she sensed they were being commented upon. Once on the road snaking out of Bampers, she relaxed and glanced at Slim as she drove.

'You see, we are leaving tomorrow. Mac is worried about the work that's been piling up. Anyway, the convention will be here and all those coloured hats and tin horns are a dreadful bore.'

Slim was disturbed by the news.

'You mean, you won't be playing golf anymore?'

She laughed lightly. 'Not here, Slim. Maybe next year. Are you coming back?'

'I don't know. Right now I don't want to think about it. I won't come back as a caddie.'

'No, of course, you'll be a bellhop or a driver.'

They shot along by the river and across the bridge. Kate took the highway leading away from town. The sheer cliff rose out of sight at their side.

'It's a pretty drive this way,' she said. 'You're in wild country in a matter of minutes.'

Slim nodded agreeably. He remarked a purposefulness in Kate's driving. She seemed to know where she was taking him.

'Mac and Allan are away on an overland trip,' she said. 'Allan, the poor boy, was quite broken-up about Alick Sandhurst. '

Slim liked the fact that she used first names with him.

'They took horses and went to an outpost back in the mountains. Mac said the food is terrific and the lake simply teems with rainbow trout.'

'Just the two of them?' Slim asked, thinking of the grizzlies.

'Oh, they'll be all right. An old friend of ours, Julien Kowalski, went with them. Anyway, Mac's done it before and they'll be back tomorrow.'

She turned onto a side road and shifted into second for the climb. 'In fact, this friend of ours has a fishing shack up this way. It's a pretty spot. Do you want to see it?'

'Sure,' Slim said enthusiastically.

'He doesn't use it much. Sometimes he comes up in the winter for ice-fishing.'

Slim nodded. They fell silent. Kate felt younger and fresher than for some time. Clusters of high brush reached out for the car in a final surge of summer greenery before the Fall. They reminded her of a woman clutching her youth--like herself, she mused sadly.

The road wound into the back country, mounted to clearings, and dove into the foliage.

'How far is it?' Slim asked.

'You're not worried?' Kate smiled. 'Think I'm kidnapping you?'

Slim laughed.

'In fact, we are here,' Kate said as they rounded a bend and came to the shore of a small lake. 'We'll park under these tall pines and walk to the shack, shall we?'

They left the car and took a path by the shore.

'The road goes on to another lake where there used to be a logging camp, but no one is there now.'

Slim sensed their aloneness.

'How does your friend get here in the winter?' he wondered.

'He flies in and lands on the ice. It's simple.'

A modest cabin sat propped on stones at the water's edge. Kate paused to look over the lake. Slim knew he need only put his arms about her. Trembling, he stepped up behind her. She turned a little and raised her face. He sank his lips onto hers and pulled her against his chest. The excitement stormed through him. His emotions rushed beyond his control. He kissed her frantically. ⸲

'Slim, not here,' Kate coaxed. 'In the cabin, please.'

She led him to the door, took a key from her purse, and unlocked the padlock while Slim feasted his eyes on her in a rapture of promise and sensuality. They stepped inside. Slim swept her to him and fumbled at her clothes.

'I can do it,' she said naughtily. 'You look after yourself.'

They undressed rapidly. Slim rushed her to a bed covered with a blanket, his heart, mind and organs swirling as one. He tried to remember the lessons in the medical book but couldn't think of a word. He felt Kate guiding him, and, seemingly without effort, he was working a miracle. He had no idea how long his achievement lasted. He lay in Kate's arms for a long time afterwards, delighting in the sight and feel of her body.

Kate was the first to speak. 'I knew you'd be wonderful, Slim. Do you know I have been waiting for you since the beginning of the summer?'

'I wish you'd told me,' he said.

Kate laughed and trailed her finger about his features. 'That's so much like you. It's a misfortune in a way. You will never take, you will always wait and receive. Poor Slim. You'll always need someone like me.'

He didn't understand. 'No, I just want you,' he said and kissed her.

She fixed her arms comfortably about him. 'Let's sleep for a while and then we'll go back.'

Slim closed his eyes. The long song of summer ended on a rosy note of achievement. As a soft drizzle fell on the cabin roof in the mountains, back at Bampers the champion of Nevada sank the putt that won him the tournament on the twenty-first hole. The club professional stepped up with an open umbrella, and cameramen took photos of the new Bampers' champion laughing with King Gillespie. Snug at a table in a dark corner of the cavern in Bampers Town, Deo held hands with Johnnie O'Dreams. She was thinking of the note that Horace Rabbinowitz sent her before he left with his family; it congratulated her on her escape from the fire and named Johnnie as a worthy successor. She turned aside and put her other hand to her mouth to stifle a giggle, heard perhaps by Horace's inner ear as he prepared for a trip to Europe.

The Staff Hall had been converted into the main lobby leaving no room for an orchestra. Toots Ainsworth and his boys were being shipped east. As the day wore on, Deo and Johnnie grew sadder. They were not only parting; she was destined to return to Kamloops.

Most of the guests departed on the day following the tournament final, the day that Mac, Allan and Julien returned in good spirits from their outing. Whereas Allan planned to stay north with Bett for several more weeks, Mac and Julien drove with Kate in the afternoon for Edmonton. Kate drew their attention to Gillespie's light blue convertible parked at a look-out point near the Ice-fields. It reminded her of golf. She took a key from her purse and handed it to Julien.

'Did you go fishing?' Julien asked in surprise. 'Up at the cabin?'

She nodded, eyes twinkling into his. 'It's one of the greatest sports I know.'

'Hey,' Mac cried, slowing the car as they passed by King Gillespie and the golf champion gazing over the valley from the roadside. 'Julien. Shall we go back and get you an autograph?' He laughed.

'You are a silly fool,' Julien said testily. 'You can't look after....' He bit his lips and looked guiltily at Kate.

Mac frowned. 'I was just joking, you nut. Take it easy.'

'So was I,' Julien said. He took Kate's hand and held it while Mac turned the curve in descent.

Jake Slade was sitting in an observation car as his train took a similar curve along the river bed. The young lady opposite him was trying to catch his eye. But he was intent on reading a magazine and taking the occasional sip from a long Scotch at his side.

Back at Bampers, a group of experts attributed the cause of the fire to faulty wiring, which meant the insurance money would be paid. Bampers' shareholders were not as greatly relieved as D'Arcy Morgan.

30

Runners noticed that Alick Sandhurst's conscientiousness had set an inspiring example. The staff thought of him as a symbol ennobling the task of working at a hotel. His self-sacrifice demonstrated the responsibility of a hotel job so that the students began to respect their work, an attitude which was in sharp contrast with their summer-long forbearance of menial servitude.

Runners decided to "save" the hotel money, and, thereby, win some favour to lighten his blackened future by refusing to cancel a September convention scheduled for the long weekend. When he timorously sounded the staff for its support, he received a generous response, which, considering this was his last season, touched him deeply.

The conventioneers spent their time shouting "Aloha", throwing orange garlands around their necks, holding long conferences, and drinking until late in the night. Since there was no need for caddies or greens men, Runners gave the order for their release. Much of the staff came to the station to wish them bon voyage as was the custom. Attachments formed during the summer were revealed in many shades of humour and romance at the side of the train. Waitresses and cabin girls kissed their friends first, and, as departure time grew closer, they began kissing acquaintances, making the rounds, finding themselves in the arms of boys they had admired and never had the chance to meet. The good-bye was a rash impulse to savour to its full extent the fleeting moment of their youth, which was why it seemed so sadly inadequate.

As the tall boys grinned down at the girls who maneuvered to wish them a warm adieu, they reverted into undergraduates. The collegiate cut of their clothes suddenly claimed them. The shouts, the laughter, the embracing, and the tears brought a nostalgic reminder of the campus they would soon be inhabiting, which all the staff dances with their medley of tramping and chorusing college songs could not do.

The train jolted, the boys scrambled aboard, waved from windows, grasped hands with those below, glided forward and lost their grip with the comradeship and the disappearing reality of a summertime.

Slim Johnson watched Miriam waving with the others until the groups became a blur beside the track. The world had changed for him; it had expanded and it had a fundamental order and its contents were responsive to the touch. He strode down the aisle. Aurmand had his feet up and sticking out. He was playing poker with Dixie and Gregory. Slim stopped at the end of the car beside Blair who offered him a cigarette. The golden boy no longer resembled a hero. Slim was ready to identify Blair with himself--as just another man.

The drivers, half the waitresses, and most of the hops left after the weekend on the train with the departing conventioneers--which must have been a ball. D'Arcy, having learnt that Nick was leaving on that train wisely volunteered to stay over for the next trip. Nick apologized for insinuating arson and D'Arcy apologized for knocking him down. They shook hands at the station, an offhanded joviality spread thinly over their mutual dislike.

'Nelles, O'Flaherty and those guys aren't coming back next year,' Nick said clapping him on the shoulder. 'If the new lodge is built, maybe we'll be captains.'

'Maybe,' D'Arcy agreed, 'on rival shifts.'

'Yeah,' Nick sang, stepping aboard, 'wouldn't that be great? So long, D'Arce.'

'So long, Nick.'

As D'Arcy walked away, he was glad that he and Nick went to universities in separate parts of the country, that neither of them played intercollegiate sports which might bring them together, and that he was never returning to Bampers so that he would not see Nick again.

The patrolmen, the least and the last, were allowed to go with the porters, the cabin girls and the remaining hops on the following day. Since the cabin girls were numerous, this arrangement gave two and a half girls to each man which was not bad for a four day trip. Sylvester was sitting beside D'Arcy as the train pulled out. The frosty nights had a dazzling effect on the trees as seen in the day, imparting an intrinsic splendour to their greenery which they watched from the window.

'There's something about the Rockies that gets you,' D'Arcy said sadly. 'But, you know, once you leave them, you never have to come back. They stay with you.'

'Do you feel the same about Bampers?' Sylvester asked.

D'Arcy looked at him strangely. 'I guess I do, though I shouldn't. There's always some part of a guy that likes to deal with the devil.' He saw Sylvester frown and he smiled engagingly. 'Don't mind me. We'll be studying Faust this year. You know, the guy who bartered his soul.'

'I didn't have the chance to know,' Sylvester said grimly. 'I was just a patrolman.'

D'Arcy's green eyes twinkled. 'Never mind. Next year you'll be a driver. Then you'll know. And you'll never forget it.'

finis

(Trout Lake, North Bay, Ont.)

FOR OTHER BOOKS BY DR. BEASLEY REPRODUCE AND SEND THIS PAGE TO DAVUS PUBLISHING, 150 NORFOLK ST. S., SIMCOE, ON. N3Y2W2 CANADA or P O BOX 1101, BUFFALO, N.Y. 14213-7101 UNITED STATES (tel: 519-426-2077, fax 519-426-0105, Email: davus@kwic.com) or ASK YOUR BOOKSTORE.

PLEASE INCLUDE $3 FOR POSTAGE AND HANDLING FOR ORDERS FROM 1-3; $4 FOR 4-7; $6 FOR 8-10. Distributed by University of Toronto Press tel: 800-565-9523 (toll free in U.S. and Can.)

PLEASE SEND ME (1)   COPIES OF PAGAN SUMMER, $14.95 Cdn, $10.95 U.S. Staff and guests in sexual combustion at a summer resort in the Canadian Rockies. A roman a clef.

(2)............COPIES OF WHO REALLY INVENTED THE AUTOMOBILE for $17.95 (Cdn) $13.95 (U. S.) "Only automobile enthusiasts whose interests begin after World War II will not find this an engrossing book. It is excellent." Charles W. Bishop.

(3)............COPIES OF THE GRAND CONSPIRACY; A NEW YORK LIBRARY MYSTERY FOR $10.95 (U.S.). & 14.95 (Cdn.) Rudyard Mack on the trail of political kidnapping and international crime syndicates.

(4)........ COPIES OF THE JENNY; A NEW YORK LIBRARY DETECTIVE NOVEL AT $7.95(U.S.).& $9.95 (Cdn) Library detective Mack solves case of biggest stamp theft in U.S. history. "Held me rivetted"--*ROTARY ON STAMPS;* "a fascinating tale,"--*STONEY CREEK NEWS.* "fun reading,"--*GLOBAL STAMP NEWS.* "The solution is as surprising as it is ingenious."--*THE SIMCOE REFORMER.* "It gets Gold for the "whodunnit" plot and the exciting, don't-put-me-down read that it is."--*CANADIAN STAMP NEWS.* "The writing is fast paced, ... a pleasant diversion on a hot summer afternoon."--*THE CANADIAN PHILATELIST.*

(5)........ COPIES OF HAMILTON ROMANCE; a Hamilton-Toronto Nexus $19.95 Cdn., $14.95 U.S. (Romance and society after World War II. A sesquicentennial edition.) "A good read... funny and sad, just like life itself, as it traces the tale of young love... when everything seemed so different, yet things weren't really so different."--STONEY CREEK NEWS.: "thoughtful and often humorous... an enjoyable, rebellious, anti-establishment rant,...deserves a wide audience" *VIEW*

(6)..........COPIES OF CHOCOLATE FOR THE POOR; a story of rape in 1805 $13.95 Cdn. $11.95 U.S.. (Berkshires in 1805; a father accused of raping his daughter) "Held me spellbound," Angela Ariss, Children's Rights Advocate. "Gripping story...interesting cast of colourful characters...well written novel...Beasley paints pictures with short phrases."VIEW. "The political intrigues are brought to life vividly....Beasley allows us to see, and more importantly to feel, some of the forces that enmesh a man only too easily and drive him to acts otherwise incomprehensible." HAMILTON SPECTATOR.

(7)............ COPIES OF THAT OTHER GOD, A NOVEL $18.95 (U.S. and Cdn) American mystic brings people through telepathic communion into the universal subconscious to a realization of the God of humanity. "Compelling, really interesting, exciting...a cry for peace at a time of anarchy," *BRANTFORD EXPOSITOR;* "Absorbing....Gripping style, detailed observation; poetic images. Vital, entertaining, apocalyptic," Peter Rankin, NYC. "Compelling story [of] the saving values deep within the human spirit," *HUMAN QUEST.*

(8).............COPIES OF THROUGH PAPHLAGONIA WITH A DONKEY; A JOURNEY THROUGH THE TURKISH ISFENDYARS [illus.] $9.95 U.S. $11.95 Cdn. "Charmingly written,"--*EXPLORERS JOURNAL;* "Now that I have concluded my fourth re-reading, I have become...a thorough-going dweller in Paphlagonia and an ardent partisan of Bobby, the donkey"--*LOCAL 1930 NEWSLETTER;* "Insightful for students of cross-cultural communication."--*INTERNATIONAL JOURNAL OF INTERNATIONAL RELATIONS.*

(9)............ .COPIES OF THE CANADIAN DON QUIXOTE; THE LIFE AND WORKS OF MAJOR JOHN RICHARDSON, CANADA'S FIRST NOVELIST $6.95 Cdn.; $5.50 U.S. "Definitive "; "Not only a good read but the fulfillment of 'an aching void'." *BRICK;* "Very useful... mass of new information," *TORONTO GLOBE & MAIL.* "A roaring good adventure yarn about a highly eccentric dreamer," *LIBRARY JOURNAL.* "Brings to life the early history of this country," *KINGSTON WHIG STANDARD;*

Forthcoming: *Douglas MacAgy and the Foundations of Modern Art Curatorship.*

NAME:

ADDRESS:

ENCLOSED PLEASE FIND A CHEQUE TO DAVUS PUBLISHING FOR $.....................